GHOST TRAIN

GHOST TRAIN

A NOVEL

Stephen Laws

BEAUFORT BOOKS
Publishers · New York

No character in this book is intended to represent any actual person; all the incidents of the story are entirely fictional in nature.

Library of Congress Cataloging-in-Publication Data

Laws, Stephen
Ghost train.

I. Title
PR6062.A933G4   1985   823'.914   85-9057
ISBN 0-8253-0315-X

Published in the United States by Beaufort Books Publishers, New York.

Printed in the U.S.A.   First American Edition

10 9 8 7 6 5 4 3 2 1

For the Portland Club (1977–1981)

Acknowledgements

Lyrics of 'Locomotive Breath' from *Aqualung* (Jethro Tull) by Ian Anderson. Copyright 1971. Ian Anderson Music Ltd/Chrysalis Music Ltd. Reproduced by kind permission.

Lyric from *Showdown* (Electric Light Orchestra). Words and music by Jeff Lynne. © 1979 CBS Songs. Reproduced by permission.

Contents

Part One
Mark

In the shuffling madness
of the locomotive breath
runs the all time loser
headlong to his death.
He feels the piston scraping
Steam breaking on his brow
Old Charlie stole the handle and
the train won't stop going
No way to slow down.

He sees his children jumping off
at stations one by one
His woman and his best friend
in bed and having fun.
Crawling down the corridor
on his hands and knees
Old Charlie stole the handle and
the train won't stop going
No way to slow down.

He hears the silence howling
catches angels as they fall
and the all time winner
has got him by the balls.
He picks up Gideon's Bible —
Open at page one
Old Charlie stole the handle and
the train won't stop going
No way to slow down.

Locomotive Breath by Ian Anderson

all-night boozing sessions at the students' flats. Even worse when, like last night, they 'had partaken of a little shit', as Alan liked to call it. It always seemed to leave him particularly irritable after the effect wore off, making him at times a real pain in the arse. Paul sometimes wondered why he knocked around with him at all.

They were both twenty years old, both taking the same degree course at university, and both looking forward to the weekend to come: an open-air rock festival down south. It had been Paul's idea originally; they were nearing the end of term and the pressure was building up. They had both been working bloody hard and a couple of days doing their own thing would loosen them up before they had to slot their brains into top gear again for the exams. They had the cash, so why not? Alan had needed little convincing, especially after his most recent downer about Diane; a circumstance for which Paul felt partly responsible.

Alan groaned, rubbed his beard with one hand, and stood up. 'Too bloody heavy!' he growled, pulling himself out of the cramped seat and nearly colliding with a trampish old woman as she hurried back to her seat with a crumpled newspaper clutched in her hand. He made for the juke-box, fishing in his jeans pocket for change.

Paul grunted in semi-amusement, watching as Alan hunched over the juke-box and began to look for another, presumably less-heavy record. Nearby was a bloke of about thirty, wearing a reefer jacket and just sitting, staring into his coffee. His face seemed unnaturally white, almost bloodless, and with a strangely haunted quality. It was a faraway, lost look, which affected Paul in a strange way he could not quite understand. There was a loneliness, a hidden distress there, which made him feel as if it might somehow be contagious. He shook off the feeling, attributing it to the after-effects of last night's booze and grass. His thoughts returned to the events of the party. The usual crowd had turned up; all packed into Graeme Grantz's flat. Poor acne-ridden Grantzy, who revelled in the fact that people always seemed to use his place for parties; believing it to be his own popularity and nothing to do with the free booze which was often provided, or the fact that he had the best stereo deck in the entire student block. Paul had reckoned that a good 'bender' would be the best way to start their weekend and was feeling really high when the party got under way. But he had reckoned without Alan's sudden lapses into melancholy whenever Diane was present. She and Alan had been knocking around together for about six months, on what Diane liked to call a 'non-heavy basis'. But it was pretty obvious to anyone with eyes that, while outwardly accepting Diane's stance, Alan had really gone ga-ga on the fiercely gregarious and outgoing girl with the tight jeans, close-cropped hair and, Paul had to admit, not unscrewable body. At parties, she would always be right there in the middle of everything, while Alan, beer can in hand, followed her around trying to keep pace; eventually ending up sprawled on a chair, pissed, morose and silent. Curiously, at the end of the evening, Alan and Diane would invariably leave together. When Paul saw him the following morning with his face beaming and his joke-a-minute patter, he would know that Diane had found a way to keep her lap dog happy. Sometimes it made him sick to see what she had done to him.

Last night's party had been the last straw. It had followed the same pattern: Diane laughing and putting herself centre stage; Alan sulking in the kitchen, opening another can and pretending to listen to Grantzy waxing lyrical about how great the party was going. Paul had been chatting up one of the girls from the Arts course but was getting nowhere, when Diane asked him to dance. His first reaction had been to say: *What about Alan, you bitch? Or do you just want to see him squirm?* But tonight was different. Alan's behavior was getting on his nerves and, besides, he felt horny. When Alan emerged from the kitchen, they were both locked together in the middle of the floor, bumping and grinding to the music. It was obvious that Diane had been waiting for him to emerge; Paul felt, rather than heard, her laughing as she pressed closer to him. By some curious stroke of fate, Dr Hook was singing from the turntable: 'When you're in love with a beautiful woman, watch your friends.' Alan stiffened, turned and marched back into the kitchen, head lowered. Paul watched him go, thinking: *You stupid bastard! Can't you see she enjoys getting you worked up like this?* His irritation with Alan was suddenly redirected towards Diane. He pushed her roughly away. She was smiling at him in a sarcastic, self-satisfied way.

'Diane, you're a cow.'

14

'Screw you, pal.'

That night, Diane left with a swarthy Greek from Engineering while Paul, by now feeling guilty, had spent the rest of the evening trying to pull Alan out of his depression by explaining that he hadn't been after Diane. Attempting to save the coming weekend, he had bought some expensive shit from Grantzy which they both smoked, until Alan seemed to have recovered. Paul had given him a few home truths about his non-heavy relationship with Diane and had taken Alan's silence to mean acknowledgement and acceptance of the facts.

Now, in Newcastle Central Station cafe, they sat waiting for their train and trying to fight off the effects of the night before. Alan returned to his seat, muttering about the crappy selection of records on offer. Trying to ignore him, Paul looked up as the tall man in the reefer jacket stood up stiffly with the aid of a walking stick and made his way to the serving counter. As he passed their seat, Paul felt a curious chill. He shrugged it off.

'What's the matter with you?' asked Alan.

'Someone stood on my grave,' said Paul.

'So now it's grave talk. Bloody heavy.'

'Look . . . Alan . . .' began Paul earnestly, 'about last night. There was nothing going on . . .'

'Forget it, pal.' Alan was smiling. 'I know what she's like. She's a cock teaser. Just not worth it.'

Paul had never heard him speak like that about Diane before. He seemed to have finally made the breakthrough.

'Let's just have a real bender of a weekend,' said Alan, still smiling. 'Where's that damned train, anyway?'

* * *

Mark returned to his place and sat down heavily. He drew in a sharp breath at the pain in his knee and then huddled forward over his third cup of coffee, trying to keep those bad memories at bay. But they were always there, stalking around the edges of his mind. And the memories seemed to feed the Impulse which now began to creep over him: that same, terribly familiar Impulse which he fought to contain. He cradled the cup, felt the heat sting his fingers and then gripped

15

tightly, hoping that the pain would take his mind away from these horrible feelings. God, would he never be warm again?

He had been lying in bed the previous night, forcing himself to stay awake, listening to the sound of the wind outside his bedroom window. Low and crooning. Saying something. Trying to tell him something.

Mark . . .

Oh, God.

His wife lay next to him, warm and soft. He could hear her quiet, rhythmical breathing. The sound of the wind and the sound of his sleeping wife were beginning to have a hypnotic effect on him. He knew that sleep was not far away.

Oh, God!

He bit deeply into his clenched fist to restrain the sobbing which threatened to convulse him as he remembered. Slabs of cold, granite-coloured light shone sporadically through the dilapidated criss-cross framework of girders across the skylight of the station roof, making strange alternating waves of light and dark as steel-wool clouds passed overhead.

The sound of the wind. And the shadows of branches on the bedroom wall. The rustling, restless silhouettes from the tree outside his bedroom window. Spiny, skeletal fingers tapping at the glass. And somewhere out there, somewhere in the night, the faint, mournful sound of a train's siren.

*   *   *

Eric Morpeth had been a railwayman all his working life, rising to his present position of ticket collector. In his job, he reckoned, you got to be a good judge of character. He had seen some weird types hanging around stations in his time, especially late at night. But there was something about this particular bloke that disturbed him. Okay, he looked fairly ordinary. Some trendy in his late twenties or early thirties with a gimpy leg and a walking stick. You probably wouldn't look twice at him in the street. Nothing fruity looking about him, nothing weird. But this bloke came into the station almost every day and just hung around. At first, when Eric came on his shift, he would be sitting under the big clock. By mid-morning, the guy would probably be sitting in the cafe. And then out under the big clock again. And then he would walk around a little, maybe

16

buy a newspaper. But he would never *read* the newspaper. That's what bothered Eric. Obviously, he was waiting for somebody. But he was also obviously very scared. And for some strange reason, that made Eric a little scared too, although he was buggered if he could understand why.

Eric was standing in his booth at the ticket barrier and now the frightened man was heading towards him. Shit, why did he make him feel so uneasy?

'Ticket, please?' said Eric, holding his hand out. The man stopped, his breath condensing like steam in the cold air, looking past Eric towards the tracks. Close to, Eric could see how disturbed he was and wished that he would just piss off. The man began to shuffle his feet, his breath rising in clouds.

Again: 'Ticket, please?' But the man didn't seem to hear him. 'Listen, mate. I haven't got all day. Either you've got a ticket or you haven't. If you haven't, the ticket office is just over there to your right.'

Two student-types with knapsacks pushed past the man, one of them with some kind of smirk on his face. But the frightened man's gaze remained directed across the tracks.

'If you're waiting for somebody, you'll need a platform ticket to get on . . .'

But Eric was talking to thin air. The man had turned abruptly and was now heading back in the direction of the newstand.

'Bloody loonies, eh?' said Eric to the two students, punching their tickets. They said nothing, moving past him up the ramp. One of them turned round briefly to look at the strange man before hurrying on. The sight seemed to disturb him. Eric watched as the man with the walking stick reached the benches underneath the big clock. The man sat down and began to stare back at the ticket barrier again.

Christ, there was something funny about that fella.

Two

Mark was trembling, but not with the cold. He couldn't do it. He had tried to pass through but he just couldn't do it. He tore his eyes away from the barrier and the memories of the previous night flooded over him once more.

It always began with the same swirling, purple fog. It enveloped Mark and gave him the feeling that he was suspended in mid-air. There was no up or down. Nothing. Only fog. He clawed at it, kicked out but could feel nothing. Not even the ground beneath his feet. And then, as always, those strange images swimming in the fog: a roughly hewn stone about two feet square, suddenly obscured by curious ornamental bars and then lost in the fog. In its place now, a crude miniature coffin containing a wooden doll. The purple shrouds of mist enveloped the coffin, leaving Mark once more floating in limbo.

When the mist cleared, he could see that he was standing on a familiar hilltop overlooking a valley. He had been here before. It was sunrise and the first rays of early morning light stabbed across the horizon, bathing the nearby trees in a ruddy glow. He knew what would happen next and turned his attention to the circle of prehistoric standing stones which jutted from the clearing below him in the cradle of the valley. These stones were different from the others he had seen. They formed a rough circle in the shape of tilted arches; a curious grouping which seemed somehow significant but whose purpose eluded him. In the middle of the circle was a single, horizontal and rectangular slab of stone around which the grass appeared to have been scorched by fire.

Looking beyond the circle of standing stones, Mark saw a slowly moving column of cowled and cloaked figures dressed in drab grey robes, approaching along a rough, sloping track. He wondered if they were druids. They were moving in double file, marking time with their footsteps, arms clasped within the folds of their robes, heads bowed and hidden. There appeared to be some kind of commotion at the back of the procession and, as the fingers passed slowly through the stone arches and began to form a circle around the single slab in the center, Mark

18

could see that two of the men were dragging a young girl along between them. She was struggling furiously in a desperate, silent attempt to get free, but the faceless druidic figures were too strong for her.

The purple mist appeared from nowhere again and Mark found himself swathed in the rolling clouds as the scene was completely swept away. When the mist parted once more, he found himself standing down in the clearing beneath one of the stone arches. The cloaked figures were now all in the center of the circle. There were about fifty of them and some had lit torches, even though sunrise was imminent. The nearest were only feet away from Mark, but he knew that they could not see him. From somewhere in the closely crowded group, he could hear a curious sing-song voice intoning in a language he had never heard before. As he watched, a section of the crowd moved to one side and, in the next instant, the struggling girl was dragged forward to the slab. Mark was advancing through the crowd now, drawn by a force which he was powerless to resist. It was a floating sensation and, in a curiously detached way, he realised that he was passing through the figures which clustered around the slab as if he had no more substance than a ghost.

Now he was standing beside the slab and could see the curious stains on the roughly hewn rock as the two cowled figures hauled their captive over and held her firmly across it. Mark understood at last why the terrified girl could make no sounds. Her lips had been sewn together.

The chanting of a single voice had been joined by others and the curious, lilting intonation seemed to hang heavily in the air. The sun was rising over the rim of the valley and rays of sunlight were stabbing across the sky. Mark found his attention drawn to one of the standing stones forming the circle. Atop the stone, on a kind of mounted pedestal, he could see an intricate carving. Even as he watched, a single ray of sunlight struck the carving, making it light up in a chiaroscuro of color. In seconds, the stone pattern seemed to glow red hot. As the angle of the beam changed, another shaft of reflected sunlight burst from the carving. Mark swung round to see that it was shining directly onto the girl's face as she lay spread-eagled over the slab, furiously twisting her head from side to side to avoid the glare. A cowled figure on the other side of the

19

slab moved forward and seized her head in his hands as another moved to her side. The chanting was faster now, more urgent, and Mark could only watch in paralysed horror as the second man drew a long-bladed knife from the sleeve of his robe. The girl thrashed wildly at the sight of the knife but was held fast to the stone by the two men on either side who were holding her arms. The figure with the knife suddenly bent over the girl, doing something to her face, but Mark's view was obscured. There was a loud and echoing scream of sheer horror and pain as the man stood upright again, and Mark could see that he had cut away the stitching from the girl's lips. Now she was giving vent to her terror and the man seemed to be well satisfied with this. He nodded sagely as the screaming reverberated through the crowd, up to the uncaring sky, and the blinding light continued to shine on her upturned face and blood-flecked lips. Mark tried to look away but was frozen. The entire spectacle was cruel and hideous and he was powerless to do anything about it. The crowd of onlookers seemed to acknowledge each scream with a responding surge in their own song. The leader was gripping the knife in both hands and holding it over the girl. Her screams reached a new crescendo of terror as the leader slowly began to raise the knife above his head and the blade glinted sharply in the ray of light. The chanting had become a frenzied babble of sound and Mark wished that he could clasp his hands over his ears. He could not understand the language of these barbarians but he knew that the chanting was a vile blasphemy; an affirmation of evil; an anathema to mankind. When it seemed that the sound must burst his eardrums, at an unseen, unheard command, it ceased. And in that instant of silence, the girl's expectant screams were agonising and dreadful. The knife plunged downwards and Mark could do nothing as it sheared into her breast up to the hilt. The girl convulsed as a wave of crimson pumped from around the knife, soaking into the virginal white of her gown, making it cling tightly to her body before splashing in rivulets onto the slab. One of the druidic figures had moved quickly forward from the crowd and Mark could see that he held a small, wooden miniature of a coffin reverently in one hand. He knelt quickly by the slab, dipping his fingers into the girl's blood and anointing the small wooden figure in the coffin – the same miniature wooden coffin that Mark had seen earlier.

The girl's mouth was working soundlessly now in shock as the purple mist flowed in through the stone arches, obscuring the dreadful scene from sight.

And then Mark had woken up screaming.

*   *   *

Now, here in the station, watching the passengers bustling through onto the platforms, he relived the horror of that hideously vivid nightmare, one of a succession that increased in frequency and intensity every night and made sleep a thing to be dreaded. The dreams had started after he had recovered from his terrible accident fourteen months ago. But they were more than just dreams. They were real. They terrorised and haunted him. And he, in turn, driven by some terrible, almost irresistible Impulse, haunted the station day after day.

Something was compelling him to cross the ticket barrier as he had done on that horrific day fourteen months ago. And an unreasoning fear of something unknown which lay beyond the barrier prevented him from doing so.

When the warring impulses and emotions converged on him again he was not surprised. It always happened that way. First the fear would dissipate, although its clutching tendrils remained encircled around his soul, forming an unbreakable umbilical cord stretching back to the unfathomable depths of the station platform. And, as the fear receded, as it settled into his bones and waited for his next attempt to cross the forbidden barrier, the Impulse would course through his mind. This was the worst of all. Because Mark could not ignore it, could not force it out of his mind. It was a feeling which he could not describe as easily as the fear. It seemed to emanate from outside . . . not inside, like the fear. It enveloped him, seeped through and into him. It whispered in a voice without words which his brain could not interpret but which his soul could understand. It drew him. It implored, begged and insisted that he do its bidding. With a strange velvet persuasion, it tried to tell him to turn round and walk back to the entrance. It told him that everything would be all right if he would only show his ticket to the inspector and pass through the barrier. It promised him that his problems would end; the fear would disappear; his mind as well as his body would heal, if only . . .

And it was this emotion which, more than anything else, Mark felt was the indicating factor of his emerging schizophrenia. It seemed external, independent, a force completely outside himself. Something which seemed to have a will of its own; something completely divorced from his own psyche. Dual impulse. Two minds. Schizophrenia. It was all one and the same. And he didn't need Dr Aynsley to tell him otherwise.

He headed for the cafe, his usual refuge. The Impulse seemd to sense that it might lose the battle again. It was turning inwards on him, remonstrating and cajoling. Mark mentally flung it down knowing, at the same time, that it would re-emerge just as persistent as ever. If only it would leave him alone.

Why the hell am I thinking about it as if it were a person or something? he raged silently as he entered the cafe and stalked to the counter. *Because, my dear Mark, you're schizophrenic. That's why.*

'Coffee . . .'

The middle-aged woman standing behind the counter in her neatly pressed British Rail uniform shot him a glance meant to kill at his abrupt manner, at the same time pouring coffee which slopped over the rim of the cup into the saucer. Mark pulled out his wallet to extract a pound note and a small newspaper clipping fell from one of the pockets onto the counter. Hastily, he snatched it up and handed the money to the woman. She banged the change unceremoniously down onto the counter. Mark moved to his usual seat at the cafe window. *My seat,* he laughed. *I might as well ask British Rail to put a bloody reserved ticket on it.*

He cradled the cup in both hands and stared into it. The rush hour would be over very soon. The Metro on which he had travelled had been the last of the peak-hour trains. The crowds on the platform would soon give way to a steadily dwindling stream of late-comers and over-sleepers, hurriedly concocting excuses for their late arrival at work.

Mark sat back, thrusting both hands into his jacket pockets, and found the newspaper cutting again. He extracted it, leaned forward and smoothed it out on the table before him. He practically knew the wording by heart:

22

Mystery still surrounds events leading up to the fall from a high speed train of Newcastle father and senior civil servant, Mark Davies, in September last year.

Mr Davies was found lying beside railway tracks in Doncaster after plunging from the 125 Edinburgh-to-King's Cross train. The alarm was raised when passengers noticed that a door was open and a subsequent search revealed Mr Davies at the foot of the embankment in a critical condition.

Police investigations have so far resulted in no explanation for the incident, despite an intensive six-month enquiry. Since that time, Mr Davies has been in a coma, under close examination in Newcastle General Hospital's Intensive Care Unit, unable to assist police enquiries.

Last night, in a statement to the press, Detective Inspector Les Chadderton, officer in charge of investigations, said: 'All we know for certain is that Mr Davies left Newcastle alone on the King's Cross train to attend a meeting in Doncaster. During the journey, Mr Davies fell from the train. Despite interviews with all passengers on that particular train, no light has been thrown on the matter. We can only hope that Mr Davies will make a full recovery. Until such time, the circumstances leading up to the fall, whether by foul play or otherwise, must remain inconclusive.'

Doctors at Newcastle General Hospital have indicated that Mr Davies' physical recovery has been remarkable, but can give no indication when, or if, he is likely to emerge from coma.

Mark read the clipping three times before he finally folded it and put it back into his wallet. It was as if he were reading about someone else. Some other Mark Davies who had broken nearly every bone in his body and spent eight months in a coma. His entire memory of the incident was gone. The police had waited eight months for him to recover, only to find his mind an absolute blank. He couldn't even remember boarding the train. And then the nightmares had begun.

The police file on Mark Davies lay on a shelf somewhere gathering dust while Mark Davies himself sat in a railway station cafe, sipping coffee and going slowly insane.

Mark took another sip. He could feel his internal conflict beginning again. The Impulse to get up, walk to the ticket barrier and cross over onto the platform warred with the unknown terror of something that lay beyond and of what would happen to him if he did pass over. Mark's hands were trembling, he was spilling coffee. Slamming the cup down into the saucer, he ran his hand through his hair and glared hopelessly towards the cafe door.

Three

'Come on, I've told you before. You can't sleep here . . .'

Martha felt a rough hand on her shoulder, shaking her from deep sleep. And as the luxurious comfort of sleep left her, she became aware again of the aching rheumatics in her bones. The euphoria, the sense of well-being engendered by the bottle of cheap red wine which she had scrounged earlier from a couple of drunken students in the waiting room, and which had led to her impromptu slumber on the station bench, was a distant memory. Only the icy cold of the empty station, the unyielding solidity of the bench and the rough hand on her shoulder were real. Reluctant at first to leave her pleasant dreamland, Martha whimpered and groped blindly at the intruder. But the grip on her shoulder was unrelenting.

'Come on, you old bag. Before I get the police.'

Martha rose creakily to a sitting position and, as her vision adjusted, saw the ticket collector standing over her. She had seen him before. He was called Eric Morecambe or something. He was a pig. Muttering under her breath, she groped for the two plastic carrier bags on which she had been lying and which contained all her wordly goods. As she staggered to her feet, the empty wine bottle, wrapped in the newspaper she had cadged from the man with the gimpy leg earlier in the day, rolled from the bench and shattered at her feet, eliciting a groan of impatience from the ticket collector.

'Out!'

'All right, all right! Bloody stations. Can't get a bit of peace. Always some bloody little Hitler interfering. Public servants, you're supposed to be . . .'

'Get out of it, before I kick your arse all over the station.'

24

'Twenty years ago . . .'

'Yeah? Well, that was twenty years ago.'

Martha shambled towards the main entrance, mumbling curses under her breath. Within seconds of leaving the station, she had forgotten her encounter with the ticket collector. Such occurrences were much too frequent to remain in her memory. They had all merged into one, amorphous argument that seemed to have lasted for years. It might as well have been the same man, the same station, the same argument.

She trudged slowly down the silent, empty street. A forgotten derelict. In her mind's eye now, she was fifteen years old and reliving an argument she'd had with her stepfather, the old bastard! She'd really told him where to get off that day, she had. That was the day she had finally left home. She would show him, show everyone, that she would make it on her own; be bigger than any of them would ever be. And, in her own mind, she had. Martha had relived that argument over and over again; each shouted phrase, the same words repeated in a random order, improving on it each time. Suddenly, the memory was gone. Locked away in cold storage in another part of her brain.

She suddenly became aware that she was standing beneath the harsh blue light of a street lamp, her breath rising in steaming clouds. She had long since left the town center, lost in her thoughts, and now stood by a railway embankment wall on the riverside. She knew where she was now. She'd got her bearings. A hundred yards ahead, a section of wall had collapsed, giving a clear view across the River Tyne to Gateshead. And then she remembered where she had left something very important.

She shambled forward until she reached the opening and stopped for an instant to look out across the dark, industrial skyline. The silent river moving sluggishly to the sea: the giant specters of cranes, keeping a lonely, silent vigil over the waters. She couldn't be sure, but she was vaguely aware that she'd lived over the river somewhere once upon a time; with a husband and kids. Yes . . . there had been kids. But the memory faded, too elusive to grasp.

A lonely foghorn echoed mutely as she clambered over the fallen stones and started down the steep, grass slope of the embankment towards the railway lines. Reaching the shallow, gravelled gully which ran alongside the main track, she strained to see across to the other side. The dark blue night was still and silent and, even with her poor eyesight, she had no difficulty in making out the scrapyard sign almost directly opposite. Good! Martha turned to her left and began a slow waddling march, counting out her steps aloud as she moved and cursing when her unsteady feet stumbled on the shifting gravel. Two hundred steps later, she had found the treasure trove. Rummaging through the weeds beside an abandoned bedstead, her numb fingers found what they were looking for: a can of diluted methylated spirit. She looked around suspiciously, sat down painfully in the weeds, unscrewed the rusted can and lifted it awkwardly to her mouth. A dent in the can suddenly straightened out with a hollow, reverberating clank, spilling a liberal amount of the mixture over her chin and down the front of her overcoat. She cast an anxious glance around her, half expecting to see the shambling form of the ragged tramp from whom she had stolen the can. Lifting it to her trembling lips once again, she took a deep swallow. It made her vomit. But that didn't matter. She always vomited after the first swallow.

And as Martha drank, she became aware of the magic again. She smiled as it became clearer with each swallow, knowing that the magic was her magic and no one else could ever know about it. No one else could hear the sounds that the railway lines made.

Thrum . . . thrum . . . thrum . . .

It was a warm, comforting sound.

After half an hour had passed, Martha was in the same frame of mind that she had been in before falling asleep in the station. But even through her haze, she knew that she must not fall asleep in case *they* came out of their hiding places and came looking for her. She had seen one when she had first hidden the can. It had been hiding in the long grass watching her. She had thrown half a brick at it and it had scampered away into the darkness. Bloody things! She hated them . . . and feared them. But she knew that as long as she stayed awake they would keep their distance. In the past, she had never seen more than one or two of them at a time. These were the spies, sent to watch for her; waiting for the moment when she fell asleep so that they could summon the others to swarm all over her. She had dreamt once that they had crept up on her while she had been

26

sleeping in the bandstand in the park. They were in her hair, crawling and squirming; in her clothes, trying to bite out her eyes. She woke screaming. But she should have known better. She was safe in the park. They lived down by the railway, by the riverside, and would never venture from there. She was safe on the embankment as long as she stayed awake.

Slowly and painfully, Martha dragged herself to her feet, cradling the can in both arms like a sleeping child. Perhaps she had better leave, just in case she did fall asleep . . .

She began to stumble back down the track in the direction she had come from, crooning a tuneless, wordless song in time to the sloshing of the methylated spirit inside the can. Dimly, she became aware that a wind seemed to have blown up. The grass at the top of the embankment was hissing angrily, but she paid no heed to it. The fact that she could feel no wind on her face and that she did not have to strain forward against its force, did not register with her. Only when she had reached the spot where she had originally descended to the railway line and was moving up the embankment towards the gap in the wall did she notice the ominous, almost stealthy, rustling of the grass. A thrill of warning was trying to fight through her subconscious into her conscious mind, struggling to shake off the effects of the drink. Something at the back of her mind was trying to tell her to get away from this place as quickly as possible. Martha stopped, clutching the can of methylated spirit tightly to her chest and watching the strange, rippling effect of the grass above and beyond. Something was moving along the top of the embankment. Something which had been keeping pace with her as she walked and was now lurking in the deep grass ahead. And with horror mounting steadily in her befuddled brain, Martha realised that there was more than one thing in the grass. There were lots of little things. Hundreds of them. Hundreds of things that squirmed, rustled . . . and squeaked. A high-pitched babble of sound, increasing in intensity and emanating from the shadowed, weaving grass above her. Martha took a faltering step back, watching as the grass thrashed in an ever increasing frenzy. Another step, and another. And then she was back in the gully at the side of the railway track.

'No, you can't . . .' she said in a terrified protest. 'You can't. Not while I'm awake.'

At the sound of her voice, the shrill piping and squeaking

27

seemed to intensify, rising and swelling to a fever pitch. An angry, hysterical, *hungry* shrieking. She could see them now. They were pouring over the rim of the embankment and through the grass towards her in a writhing, twisting mass of fur and teeth.

Martha stumbled on the rough gravel, dropping the can and looking frantically back along the embankment on either side. *Oh, Jesus* . . . The entire bank was swarming. There were millions of them. And she knew what they wanted.

Martha turned and staggered across the railway tracks, arms flapping at her sides to maintain balance as she stepped over the steel rails. It wasn't right! It couldn't be right! But her fear was too real. She could not trick herself into believing that it was all just a bad dream. Her lungs were aching with the strain of her effort, the cold air biting deep into her chest.

Oh my God, my God, my God . . .

Behind her, she could hear the scuttling, rustling sound of thousands of small, clawed feet on the gravel beside the track. They had reached the line and Martha did not have to turn round to know that even now they were swarming over the railway track towards her. Sobbing in exhaustion and terror, she cleared the second railway line and saw the embankment and scrapyard on the other side. Her cry for help choked thickly in her throat as she stumbled against one of the railway lines and nearly fell.

She was almost on the other side now. Only one more track to cross and she would be on the other embankment. Her eyes were streaming with tears, blurring her vision so that the shadows cast by the scrapyard sign on the grass verge seemed to be quivering and weaving before her. A jumble of movement; squirming, writhing and . . .

No, no, no, no . . .

They were on the other side, too. Wriggling and scampering in a dark, formless mass in the gully between the track and the embankment, as far as she could see. They made no attempt to pursue her but, in the darkness, she could see a multitude of small, restless, piercing pinpoints of light. All watching her with a keen and hungry intensity.

Martha whirled around to see that the horde on the other side had swept over the first and second railway tracks towards her like a pulsating, black carpet. But they had stopped fifteen

28

feet from where she stood in the centre of the third track and made no movement towards her.

'You can't . . .' Martha began imploringly, her whispered voice swept away amidst the rustling and squealing. For an instant, she thought of grabbing a handful of gravel and throwing it at the undulating mass. But the frenzied pitch of their cries struck a chord of terror in her soul. She knew that she could not afford to anger them any further. She had killed too many of their number. And now, after all these years, they wanted revenge.

There was only one thing left to do. Martha began to stagger back along the track towards the town center, gasping a prayer that they would keep their distance.

Please God . . . Please God . . .

They were running along the track on both sides now, keeping pace with her as she ran. When she stopped momentarily to gasp for air, she could see that they had also stopped, squirming and climbing over each other in a frenzy. She started to move again, wondering in spite of her terror why they were keeping their distance. And then she heard the old, familiar noise again. Faintly at first, but growing stronger as she ran. The magic noise which pulsed in the rails. It was pulsing now through the railway lines on either side of her as she ran. Throbbing with invisible power like a heartbeat that only she could hear. And Martha knew that it was the power in the lines which kept her pursuers at bay. They could not . . . *would* not . . . cross over the lines. It was the old magic. It had returned to protect her.

Sobbing with relief, she realised that if she followed the line it would bring her directly into the Central Station. Perhaps the ticket collector who had thrown her out of the station was still there. He would help her. From somewhere ahead in the darkness, a long way away, she could hear the long, mournful wailing of a train siren. It couldn't be far now . . .

But now the dark, wriggling hordes on either side of the tracks had split their ranks and were swarming furiously over the lines in front of her. Martha stumbled around as a multitude of sleek, furry bodies repeated the maneuver behind her. Trapped on the railway line and surrounded by the dark, squirming mass, she saw that her old magic had betrayed her. It

29

had lied. It was their magic . . . not hers. And they had been *herding* her.

The lonely drone which she had heard in the distance became a savage, ululating scream of malice when the train finally hit her . . .

Four

By the time the train pulled into King's Cross Station, Paul's irritation with Alan had turned to anger. When they boarded the train at Newcastle, Alan had sprawled on one of the double seats in the second-class compartment, leg hooked over the armrest, and had fallen asleep. He had stayed that way for most of the journey. When the train pulled into York, Paul had shaken him awake to ask if he wanted any coffee. Alan emerged sharply from his sleep, growling and telling him to piss off. Paul had tried to start a conversation but was faced with clipped, one-word answers. After a while, he stopped trying. Alan returned to his sleep, and Paul began to wonder why the hell he had suggested going down for the festival in the first place.

Since Doncaster, when he had finally awoken again, Alan had sat and stared out of the window, his face set in an angry scowl. Paul found him too pathetic for words and had gone for a long walk down the corridor to the cafe car for a smoke and a can of beer. When he returned to his seat, Alan did not appear to have moved. He was in the same position, with the same look of thunder on his face, his eyes apparently fixed on a spot about three inches past the window. Paul began to read his newspaper from cover to cover for the second time.

After what seemed to Paul the longest journey he had ever undertaken, the King's Cross train began its rumbling entrance into the station. As the train slid past the first of the platforms, Paul stood up to retrieve the knapsacks from the overhead racks. The echoing din of the human traffic in the station

30

drowned out an announcement on the speaker. Then suddenly
Alan lashed out at him.

'I can get my own knapsack!

Paul was amazed. 'What the bloody hell's the matter with
you?'

'Just leave it, that's all!' Alan tugged his knapsack from the
rack and bundled out of his seat towards the door. Paul stood
for a second watching the departing figure. Alan was certainly
moody, but this was completely out of character! Shaking his
head wearily, he retrieved his own knapsack and followed
Alan, jumping through the door and down onto the platform.
Alan had joined the milling throng heading for the ticket
barrier without a backward glance. Paul hurried to catch him,
almost colliding with a young woman and her child, cursing
Diane for the stupid bloody effect she had on Alan.

'Alan! For crying out loud! Hold on!'

A rough line had formed at the ticket barrier and Paul
found himself separated from Alan by half a dozen people.

'Alan!'

Paul watched as, without any acknowledgement, Alan proffered his ticket to the Indian ticket collector, waited for it
to be clipped and then hurried on towards the exit. This was
becoming ridiculous! Impatiently, Paul shoved his ticket into
the Indian's hand. For an instant, he lost sight of Alan in the
crowd, then spotted him beside the station cafe.

You stupid bastard! he thought angrily, and began to run
after the hastily retreating figure.

'Alan!'

He grabbed for Alan's shoulder and pulled him to a halt.
Alan spun round and levelled the same look of hostility at him.
Paul could see that he was trembling with rage, his lower lip
quivering and beads of sweat standing out on his forehead.

'Look, I don't know if I said anything wrong last night about
Diane. But I thought you'd got over it. You said she wasn't
worth it . . .'

For a moment, Paul thought that Alan was about to launch
himself at him. The knapsack dropped to the ground from his
shaking fingers. Alan took a step towards him.

'Hell, man!' Paul stood back, believing him now to be on the
verge of some kind of fit. And then Alan whirled round and
stalked into the cafe itself, leaving his knapsack where it lay

31

on the ground. Dumbfounded, Paul watched as he marched quickly past the clustered tables to the serving counter, braced both hands on it and lowered his head. Paul followed him into the cafe; he could see that Alan's shoulders were heaving, his body racked by sobs of frustrated rage. The clatter of cutlery and hubbub of conversation had suddenly died away as the cafe customers stopped to stare at the strange spectacle.

Paul was directly behind Alan now. The poor sod was obviously having some kind of nervous breakdown. He reached out a comforting hand and placed it on Alan's shoulder, at the same time moving round to one side, trying to look at his face.

'Alan . . .'

At first, in the flurry of movement, Paul thought that Alan had simply turned and struck him heavily on the side of the face. In outrage, he tried to yell abuse at him. But he could not speak. His voice was somehow choked off; thick with a warm and cloying substance which, instead of speech, resulted in a curious gargling sound. It was only when Paul moved his hands to his throat, felt the protruding handle of the table knife, and saw the jetting of scarlet over his hands that he realised what had happened.

The cafe seemed filled with a high and distant screaming and Paul noticed in a curiously detached way that he was now kneeling before Alan. And then, as he looked up, it seemed that Alan was swinging like a pendulum before him. Crazily tilting from side to side, looming over him with huge white, trembling hands held stiffly at his sides like claws. There was blood on those hands. Just before the momentum of the pendulum tilted to the left, Paul could see that Alan had picked up another knife from the tray on the serving counter.

'You can't have her, you bastard! No one can have her!'

As Alan drew the knife sharply across his own throat in a savage, parallel motion, a crimson wave dissolved everything from sight and Paul knew no more.

Five

Again, the swirling purple fog. Again, Mark felt as if he were floating in some unfathomable limbo. The rough block of stone swam into view as it always did, only to be obscured in turn by the strange ornamental bars. It vanished. And the crude miniature coffin containing its small, ragged doll glided through the purple fog, to be swallowed again by the billowing clouds. Then came the familiar feeling of a great pressure on his chest which began gradually to increase. Instantly, he knew what terrible form this dream was going to take. He could not breathe. His nostrils and mouth were clogged with mud and soil. Living things squirmed in his mouth and eye sockets. He tried to scream, knowing that he was buried alive; that there were tons of earth lying on top of him. But no sound would come. He was suffocating . . . he must be dead . . . dead and buried . . . and then the pressure was gone, the purple fog shrivelling wispily away. Of the two types of nightmare which Mark endured, he did not know which was worse: the dreams of forlorn countryside and lonely moorland with its standing stones and its strangely carved rock formations; or the other type of nightmare characterised by foul, suffocating blackness and the stench of the grave. In these dreams, he knew that he was underground.

Now, the dream would take one of two directions. Mark might feel himself floating upwards, the pressure on his chest rapidly disappearing. The purple fog would dissipate and Mark would see that he was rising wraith-like through a station platform. Passengers bustled along, hurrying for trains and walking straight through him as if he were the dream, not they. He could hear the speaker, the din of station activity, the rumbling of trains. Mark had been to this station before. It was King's Cross.

But the other underground dreams were worse. Much worse. And Mark knew now that this was to be one such dream.

At first, as he gasped for breath and fought desperately to awaken, there was only blackness. Then, he became aware of two blurs of light on either side of him. His vision focused, the scene shifted and he could see that the light came from two primitive torches fastened to either side of a chamber which had been hewn roughly out of the earth, soil banked high on either side and supported by crude wooden beams.

He was in a burial chamber.

And he knew that he would not remain alone for long.

There was an aperture above him. The chamber was open to the sky, it was night and after a while he could see the pinpoints of stars. He could feel the rough ground beneath him but he was unable to move. Once again, something had taken command of his body and for hours he seemed to lie in the same position, the guttering light of the torches throwing rearing, looming shadows. He prayed that he would awaken before the dream got worse.

Suddenly, Mark felt his head turned roughly to the left by the unseen force. He was lying on one of several beds of chalk and, beyond him, he could see a ragged aperture leading into blackness. Now, he could hear the sounds of shambling footsteps and a strange, guttural, brutal chanting. He tried again to will himself awake but could only watch as a procession of hunched, fur-clad figures advanced into the burial chamber. They seemed unaware of his presence as they shambled around the chalk beds, their chanting not unlike that of the druids in Mark's other dreams. Their hair was unkempt and straggling, broad and slanting foreheads protruding over wild and deepset eyes; their paint-streaked faces framed by wide, prominent jawbones. Mark knew that his dream was taking place many thousands of years before the druids.

No! I don't want to see! Let me wake up!

The singing continued as the primitive men filled the chamber, forming a circle around the chalk beds.

God, let me wake up!

The chanting ceased as the last of their number entered the chamber. From somewhere in their midst came a guttural command and the crowd sat down quickly on the chamber floor. A cloud of chalk dust swirled over Mark, momentarily blinding him. When it had settled, he could see that a horribly familiar figure had entered. The man was naked but his entire body had been painted with blue woad, and dark, lank hair straggled over his shoulders down to his waist. With great reverence, he carried in both hands a roughly hewn limestone

34

block. Mark recognised it immediately as the same block of stone which prefaced every one of his dreams. A low rumbling issued from the rough-hewn entrance behind the Blue Man; the opening had been sealed by a large stone. The Blue Man moved to the chalk bed beside Mark, lifting the limestone block up towards the aperture and the glittering stars above. Silently, the other wild men watched as he sat, placing the stone reverently before him. The Blue Man began to stare intently at the stone.

The purple mists swept over Mark again. He could still feel the ground beneath him and now became aware of a strange vibration, distant at first, which seemed to issue from the depths of the earth itself. It was a booming, thundering noise gradually intensifying into a surging, horrifying impulse of unknown power. The mists cleared and, with a feeling of sinking despair, he saw that he was still lying in the burial chamber. The scene remained the same: the silent sitting figures, the Blue Man, the guttering torchlight, the stars and the block of stone. The surging sound beneath him had gone. But Mark knew what was to happen next and found himself empowered to stare at the limestone block. Even now, it was beginning to glow with an ever-increasing pulse of blue light which seemed to emanate from within. The Blue Man was smiling now as he raised his hands in the air.

No! I . . . must . . . wake . . . up!

The pulsing blue light suffused the chamber, highlighting brutal, terrified faces. The Blue Man reached forward to touch the stone with both hands, and Mark could see that it appeared to have no effect on him; the stone was not hot. For a long while, he remained in that position, and then, slowly and stiffly, he stood up. Mark did not want to look at his face but the invisible force which controlled him forced him to do so. Underlit by the pulsing blue stone, the features were scarcely human, demonic and grimacing. A wild blue light reflected from eyes that were somehow too wide, and saliva dripped from lips that were drawn back from jagged teeth. The Blue Man stepped forward.

The men sitting nearest to him flinched away, but still held themselves in terror-stricken obedience. The Blue Man chuckled; a hideous, echoing sound in the sepulchral chamber. The man directly before him began to babble desperately in an unknown tongue, eyes tightly shut. The Blue Man leaned down and touched him on the head.

The man ceased to babble. His eyes, now glazed, stared vacantly ahead.

The Blue Man picked his way among the other men, slowly and deliberately, as if searching. Suddenly, he wheeled and touched a thick-set man on the shoulder. The man's head slumped forwards.

The Blue Man threw back his head exultantly and grimaced at the aperture above him. He shrieked, a long, ululating, animal howl. Again, Mark heard the sounds of the great stone being moved from the entrance. Quickly, and with obvious relief, the men in the chamber scrambled to their feet and began to file out silently. The Blue Man remained frozen, his gaze directed upwards to the sky. The two men who had been selected by their High Priest stayed seated, eyes glazed.

For a while, there was silence. Then came the sounds of struggling as someone was dragged into the burial chamber.

God in heaven, I don't want to see this again! Please let me wake up!

The two seated men raised their heads in unison and Mark could see that their features had taken on the hideously grimacing cast of the Blue Man. Two of those who had gone out returned, dragging a struggling figure into the pulsing blue light of the chamber. It was a young naked man, his face striped with blue woad. He was lashing and twisting as he struggled to free himself, giving vent to a strange muffled grunting and bracing his feet against the ground; but the men who held him were too strong and in a matter of seconds he had been forced to his knees in front of the Blue Man who now turned to face his prisoner.

Mark did not have to look at the young man's face to know that his lips had been crudely sewn together.

The two seated men rose stiffly and moved forward, each taking one of the prisoner's arms as the original captors shrank fearfully away and disappeared into the blackness.

Stop this! Wake up!

A broad, flint knife seemed to have appeared from nowhere in the Blue Man's hand. He moved forward and seized the young man's hair.

Stop this! For God's sake, stop!

36

The knife moved quickly and brutally. The young man began to scream. Mark remained frozen, head turned to watch as the two chosen men pulled their captive down, still struggling frantically, onto the chalk bed next to his. The pulsing of the limestone block had grown stronger now. It seemed to glow hungrily. Greedily.

The Blue Man knelt down beside the screaming man. He began his work with the flint knife.

The dream went on and on, with Mark an unwilling observer of the three nightmare faces revelling in their abominable act of torture. The screaming seemed to last forever.

Stop . . . stop . . . stop . . .

After an eternity, the purple fog began to seep up through the burial chamber floor and swirl around the terrible figures. The young man was barely alive and Mark prayed for his death as the scene of horror was swept away. But when the mists cleared yet again he was still in the burial chamber.

When will this ever end?

Much time, he knew, had passed. The night sky above was beginning to soften into the grey of morning.

He was lying among a pile of tortured, mutilated bodies. The Blue Man and his two servants sat cross-legged amidst the carnage. The blue stone's pulsing was slow and measured. Content. With revulsion sweeping over him, Mark could see that various internal organs had been laid reverently across the stone.

The Blue Man raised a hand. The two servants raised their heads and smiled ghoulish, cracked smiles. The Blue Man held out the bloodied knife and the nearest man took it gratefully, turning to his fellow, who now leaned forward eagerly, eyes glinting. The flint knife was jerked up swiftly to the hilt under the man's chin. He juddered violently, smiled, and rolled backwards in a welter of his own blood.

The Blue Man nodded, placed his hands on his knees and stared up at the aperture. The remaining servant slumped forward once more and remained for a short while with head bowed. Then, suddenly, he looked up and Mark could see that the demonic cast which had disfigured his face had now gone. He blinked, swayed unsteadily where he sat and surveyed his surroundings as if for the first time. Behind him, the limestone block suddenly ceased pulsing. The Blue Man remained seated, staring at the sky. Quickly, the man stood up, swayed again before regaining full control and turned to the limestone block. Carefully, he lifted it from the ground, turned once to look at the Blue Man and then hurried out, leaving only the Blue Man, the rows of corpses and Mark, himself as immobile as one of the butchered bodies beside him.

Mark's senses began to reel. The purple mists were rolling over the rim of the aperture. Once again, there was blue light in the burial chamber; a blue light which crackled and spread. Mark did not have to look to know what was happening.

Somehow, the Blue Man was burning. His body was engulfed in a living blue flame, consuming his entire body. Greasy black smoke swirled and eddied, mingling with the purple mist which now engulfed the chamber. The stench of burning flesh made Mark gag. Time lost its meaning as the fire burned to its peak, crumbled and collapsed into ash. Vaguely, Mark was aware that the fire had gone out; that disembodied hands were scooping up handfuls of the Blue Man's remains and putting the ashes into a large, crude earthenware container. He could hear the familiar chanting and see that the hands were making small doll-like effigies, smearing them with blood. The invisible force turned his head to look upwards and he could see that there was activity on the rim of the chamber aperture.

Oh, God . . . no . . . no . . .

Suddenly, there was soil on his face. Soil was being thrown into the chamber, covering it over. The sky had vanished, the purple mists floated against a backdrop of blackness. Everything vanished from sight and Mark was once again in suffocating darkness. He knew that he was being buried in this ritual chamber along with all the other corpses. That terrible weight was on his chest again, soil caked his face, cloyed in his mouth. He tried to scream and something slimy wriggled into his throat. The pressure was too great. His heart must burst. Mark knew that he must die in his sleep. He could almost hear the post-mortem verdict: heart failure.

Then the pressure had gone and he was floating. Drifting away from that horrible place. For an instant, the purple curtain parted so that he could see he was rising through the burial chamber and flying like a bird above it. He could see the humped mound of the ancient barrow below. The countryside was wilder than anything he had ever seen in Britain. There was

38

no sign of any habitation. Curiously, the landscape began to change. It was undulating, shifting and changing like the sea. Hills were levelled, new hills arose. The coloring of the long, earthen barrow began to change to a darker, denser and over-grown hue. As he whirled, Mark thought that he could make out pylons. And then the purple mist had closed in again. He knew that he had seen the burial chamber as it was many thousands of years ago and then as it was today. Drained, sickened and with his heart pounding, he felt the invisible force release him. He was falling.

Shouting hoarsely, he found himself sitting bolt upright in bed, covered in sweat, with Joanne shaking him desperately by the shoulders.

Six

'How are you feeling this morning?'

Mark finished his coffee and smiled up at his wife. The smile was weak and he knew it; but there was little he could do about that.

'Leg's a bit stiff, as usual,' he replied.

'Do you want to talk?' Joanne took Mark's coffee cup from the breakfast table, moved to the kitchen bench and began to refill it. Mark could see early morning light creeping in through the slats of the kitchen window blind behind her. He watched for a long time as she poured. She was wearing her red dressing gown, knotted in the middle. Her blonde hair was tied tightly up in a bun behind her head and the sleep still hadn't quite left her eyes. Even after all their time together, she still looked great.

'The dream?' he said at last.

'Yes.'

'It was just a dream, Jo.'

'*Just* a dream? You nearly brought the house down. Was it the same as the others?'

'Yes . . .'

Joanne waited for him to continue. When he did not, she did not press him. He was having a bad time and it wasn't fair to put any pressure on him. She brought his coffee back to the table, put it down in front of him and sat, staring at him with both fists clenched underneath her chin. He looked worn out this morning.

A strand of hair had fallen across Joanne's brow and Mark leaned across, stroking it back into position. 'Is Helen all right?' he asked.

'She seems all right now.'

'Poor kid.' Mark rubbed his face roughly with his hand, as if trying to wipe away a memory. 'What a hell of a way to be woken up. Her father screaming like a maniac . . .'

'What time is your appointment with Dr Aynsley?'

'Two o'clock.'

'Will you tell him about the dream . . . whatever it was?'

Mark smiled, cupped her face in his hand. 'Yes, Mrs Davies. I shall be the model patient. I'll lie on that black leather couch and give a full and lucid description of just how I'm turning into a stark, staring, grade-one loonie.'

Joanne returned his smile, taking his hand in both of hers and pressing it tightly to her cheek. Mark hoped that his bitterness wasn't showing through his words. He was putting on a brave face for Joanne's benefit and could not allow himself to tell her everything: how desperately worried he really was about the dreams he had been having every night since the accident; how increasingly vivid and realistic they were. The best thing he could do about it at the moment was to persuade Joanne that he was treating the whole business lightly. She had been through too much in the past fourteen months for him to expect her to endure more.

'And when's your physio?'

'Four o'clock.'

'Sounds like you've got a full afternoon. Want me to pick up anything in town for you today?'

'How about a new pair of legs, a right arm and a backbone?'

For an instant, there was a flicker of doubt in Joanne's blue eyes and Mark realised that his voice sounded humorless and strained. He drank more coffee as she stood up and began clearing the breakfast things from the table.

'Mark,' she began, with her back to him, her voice tensed. 'Eddie Roberts was on the telephone last night. He wanted to know if you fancied Thursday night out on the town. Like the old days. There'll be a few others from the Ministry, as well.'

Mark sighed in resignation. 'I can't, Jo. I just can't. I know what you're getting at. I shouldn't isolate myself like this. But honestly, love, it's like . . . well, I know it sounds self-pitying . . . but it reminds me of how I was before the accident. It reminds me of the things I can't do, the places I can't go . . .'

'You're right. It does sound self-pitying. It's negative thinking, Mark.'

'I know it. You know it. Dr Aynsley knows it. But I can't do anything about it. Not yet. Believe me, I've tried. I just can't help the way I feel. That last night out with Harry Johnson . . . and Ted . . . it was a disaster. They kept trying to say the right things and I ended up making them feel uncomfortable. They were bloody glad to get away at closing time. And I can't say I blame them . . .'

Helen's small voice drifted downstairs, finishing any further conversation on the subject. Joanne turned to go but Mark was already rising stiffly from his seat, reaching for the walking stick which was hanging by its crook from the kitchen table. Joanne could read two kinds of pain on Mark's face and didn't know which was worse: the emotional pain or the physical pain. When the walking stick clattered to the floor, she moved forward quickly to retrieve it.

'Leave it!' Mark's tone was savagely sharp and Joanne flinched back at his words. When he spoke again, his voice was quiet, regretful and thick with emotion. ' . . . Leave it, Jo.'

Slowly and stiffly, Mark knelt down on one knee, groping forward for the walking stick until his fingers closed around it. Bracing it in front of him, he rose slowly to his feet, too ashamed to look into Joanne's eyes.

'I'll go to her.'

As Mark left the kitchen, Joanne gave in to the tears which had been welling up inside her. She turned her back on the doorway and buried her face in her hands. Her tears were the silent tears which she had learnt to weep so well these past fourteen months.

Seven

Joanne had been gone for half an hour when Mark left the house. She was dropping Helen off at school when he descended into the Metro and, by the time she had reached the university, Mark was boarding an underground train bound for the Central Station.

It was a cold, grey morning and Mark was still feeling a little shaky after the vivid horror of his dream. He tried to take some comfort from the crowded bustling of early morning commuters on the platform and the crush of people on the Metro, but as the train pulled into the Central Station underground, he could feel the old fear returning again. It was eating at his insides as he allowed himself to be carried with the crowd moving from the train, onto the platform and up the escalators towards the station above. He gripped the moving rail and could see that his hands looked deathly white, crooked and almost skeletal; they were hands that had once been badly smashed. He looked up at the line of people standing above him as the escalator continued its inexorable ascent. It made him feel, not for the first time, that the same terrible destiny, the same strange urge which drew him to the station, was somehow omnipresent in the very fabric of the station itself. The escalator was alive. It was taking him upwards to his rendezvous. Rendezvous with . . . with what? With what, for Christ's sake? If only he knew, if only he could find out why the hell he kept coming here, then perhaps the dreams would go.

The escalator arrived at the check-point and as Mark walked with the hundreds of other commuters towards the main line station itself, he felt the loneliest man on the face of the earth.

The station was the same as always. Cold, echoing, grey and lofty. Mark followed the flow of people and fear was gnawing at his stomach as he joined the line at the ticket office. He was glad that it was a long line; it would give him time to think and rationalise. But the old Impulse refused to be rationalised and he suddenly found that he had bought a ticket for Doncaster again.

I'll try, he thought. *Today, I'll give in to it. I'll follow those people onto the platform and smash this thing for good.*

There was no queue at the platform entrance, just a continuous flow of people handing over their tickets for clipping
before moving on. It was easy.

Now, you cowardly bastard. Now!

Mark had given full rein to the Impulse and found himself
following closely behind a middle-aged man carrying a briefcase. He concentrated hard on the man's back as he moved;
concentrated everything on a small spot between the shoulder
blades in front of him, to counteract the fear which always
seemed to lurk in wait for him in the last few yards leading to
the ticket barrier.

He could see only the criss-cross weave of the man's tweed
overcoat. The small squares; the inter-connecting lines of the
material, the criss-cross lines, just like . . . railway lines.

Mark was standing at the platform entrance. The middle-
aged man had shown his ticket and moved on. The ticket
inspector was holding out his hand for Mark's ticket. But the
fear had found him again. He had blocked it out from his mind,
but his thoughts had betrayed him at the last moment and it
had scented him again. Its jaws had clamped shut around his
heart; his vital organs; his vocal cords. He had to get away.
Something inside his brain, something which was somehow
prevented from speaking directly to his conscious mind, was
screaming a wordless warning. But the shock waves were
enough to tell him what he had to do . . . what he *must* do:

Get away, get away, get away . . .

Mark knew that he was stumbling like a drunken man, that
the inspector was staring at him as he floundered away from
the platform entrance. He wanted to scream at the man: *All
right, yes . . . I'm a bloody madman!* But the words would not
come to his lips. His breathing came in short, sporadic gasps
between clenched teeth as he staggered out of the danger area
towards the cafe.

God in heaven, what's happening to me?

Eight

Monica bought a newspaper and a paperback romance from the stand in King's Cross Station before crossing through the ticket barrier. As she walked up the platform past the first carriages of the Edinburgh train, she could still hear her mother's words: *Always the romantic, that's my Monica.*

Jack was always telling her that, too.

She smiled as she walked down towards the second-class carriages. They had been married for thirty-five years and enjoyed the kind of simple, loving relationship which many people did not believe possible outside the realms of the romantic fiction on which Monica doted. Oh, she knew that life wasn't all sweetness and light. They had seen their fair share of rough patches in thirty-five years. The worst had been finding out that they couldn't have children. But they had weathered their own storms and come through smiling.

Jack was a long-distance truck driver; a job which he had held for over twenty years. Very soon now, he could look forward to retirement. Monica often wondered if the brief spells apart due to his job actually served to fuel their relationship and keep it strong. Maybe that was why they enjoyed their time together so much? She had once read in a woman's magazine that seeing too much of your spouse could actually spoil a relationship.

They had met at a dance in Barnes when Jack was on a bus trip with friends from the factory where he worked in Edinburgh and she had fancied him from the very beginning. He was a good looking man and could have picked any of the women there, she was sure. But he had picked Monica and so had begun a long-distance love affair as Monica commuted between Edinburgh and Barnes, and Jack did the same. Monica came from a large family; she had three brothers and four sisters and her widowed mother lived with the youngest daughter and her family. So she had no worries about leaving to live in Edinburgh when Jack asked her to marry him. She respected his own family ties in Scotland and was glad that she had made the move. She loved Edinburgh. She loved Scotland in general and had even acquired a Scottish 'twang' in her accent which amused her mother considerably.

Monica had promised her mother that she and Jack would stay in Barnes over the weekend for her eightieth birthday. But, at the last moment, Jack had been forced to undertake a long haul and Monica had had to make the trip alone. Jack had insisted that she go. The 'old lady' was looking forward to seeing her eldest daughter. It wasn't fair to disappoint her.

And Monica was glad that she had come, after all. Now, she was looking forward to going back home to her husband who, if she had timed everything right, would probably be asleep in bed after his all-night driving. She would cook him something really special when she got home.

She found a relatively empty second-class carriage, boarded the train and chose a seat facing away from the engine. She placed the paperback and newspaper neatly in front of her and looked at her watch. She must remember to get a new one. This one was always stopping. Even without the watch, she knew that she had made it with ten minutes to spare.

When the train moved off, Monica read the blurb on the cover of the paperback. She hadn't had a chance to see what the book was about when she bought it. But she didn't recognise the title or the cover, so it couldn't be one she'd read before.

She nearly laughed out loud when she discovered the subject matter. The story was about a young Northern girl who had married a long-distance truck driver who treated her abominably. She had married beneath her, and her swine of a husband took advantage of his nights away from home to indulge in extra-marital activities. In despair, she had found solace in the arms of Dr Solomon Cord, a man who could show her the world . . .

Stifling a giggle, Monica turned to look out of the window. Wait until she showed Jack the paperback! She settled back in her seat, suddenly finding herself remembering a Christmas party they had given five years ago. It had been her idea and they had invited the neighbours round for a few drinks and something to eat. Taking an empty tray into the kitchen, she had caught Jack giving Bertha Hitching a Christmas kiss. Jack's face had turned crimson and the three of them had stood in a frozen tableau for a long five seconds. Then, together, they had all burst out laughing.

Monica smiled. For a second . . . just a second . . . she had wondered . . . But, no! That was preposterous. The thought of Jack as a Romeo-on-wheels was really hilarious. She pulled herself together, straightened her dress and began to read the newspaper. She could savour the paperback later.

Her mind began to wander from the article she was reading. Her feeling of doubt on that day, five years ago, seemed startlingly vivid. She tried to shake it off and returned to the newspaper.

*   *   *

The King's Cross train pulled into the station at Edinburgh twenty minutes late. There had been a points failure just outside York. A fierce snow squall had begun in Durham and was still falling heavily when Monica passed through the ticket barrier. A bus was parked at the stop just outside the station and Monica hurried aboard as snow whipped heavily down from the black velvet sky. The snow reminded her of Christmas.

*   *   *

Jack was exhausted when he finally got home. He had made his delivery in good time despite the lousy weather. He had tried to ring Monica at her mother's house as planned, just to tell her that he was okay and to wish the old lady 'Happy Eightieth'. But their telephone was out of order. He had reported it and headed for home.

Yawning, he hung his donkey jacket over the banister and tried to ring Barnes again, even though he knew that Monica was already on her way home by now. The telephone was still out of order. Never mind. Pulling off his boots he headed upstairs for bed. Minutes later, as he rolled under the bedcovers, snow was whipping up against the window. He fell into an instant sleep.

*   *   *

46

The sound of movement wakened Jack from his deep slumber.
'Monica? Is that you?'

If there was a reply, he did not hear it. Snow was still blowing heavily against the window. 'Put the chip pan on, love. I could eat a scabby horse.' The statement did not bring the usual howls of laughter from Monica. 'How's your Mam, then?' Still no reply. Jack struggled to wake up fully, finding it extremely difficult. He must be getting old or something.

After a while, the smell of cooking wafted up the stairs and into the bedroom. Jack stretched and gave vent to a long, loud yawn. *Good old girl*, he thought. *She knows how to spoil me. A meal in bed.* He remembered the gift-wrapped package in his jacket pocket. A really classy watch which he knew she would like. He had used most of his bonus money to buy it for her. After he'd eaten, he'd pop downstairs and fetch it.

He had unknowingly dozed off again when he heard foot-steps on the staircase. The smell of cooking was stronger now and he smiled at the prospect of a meal in bed. *The best wife a man ever had.* The door was opening as he turned to face it. Through sleep-blurred eyes he saw Monica enter and walk slowly towards him. The smell of cooking made his mouth water as he struggled from sleep. He pulled himself into a sitting position and felt the bed sheets being whipped away from his body.

'Come on, Monica! It's cold, you know.'

Jack looked up at her, his vision finally coming into focus. 'What the bloody . . . ?'

Monica was holding the chip pan in both hands, glaring down at Jack as if she had suddenly gone insane. He could see that she was trembling with rage. The boiling fat in the pan sizzled and spluttered, the pungent smell now thick and cloy-ing in the confines of the small bedroom.

'What's the matter, love?'

Monica replied in a deep, sulky voice as if her rage would choke her at any moment. 'Don't think I don't know what you've been up to while I was away!' And then she upturned the contents of the pan onto Jack's naked body.

47

Nine

The real nightmare had happened one morning in October nearly twenty years ago. Mark was eleven. He was on his way to school, trying to invent a plausible excuse for not finishing his mathematics homework, when Robbie finally caught up with him. Mark heard the running feet behind him, recognised them and instinctively ducked in time to miss the swinging haversack aimed at his head – Robbie's usual form of greeting. The boy's momentum carried him well past Mark, and he spun around to face him, laughing wildly. Even though he was much shorter than Mark, he looked older and could bluff his way into cinemas to see 'X' certificate films with no bother at all.

'Have you done it, then?' asked Robbie, swinging the haversack back onto his shoulder and getting into step beside Mark.

'What do *you* think?'

'I think you've done it. You're scared shitless of Hopkinson.'

'Course I haven't done it. He doesn't frighten me.'

It was drizzling and the sky overhead was a dull grey dome as the two boys made their way down the disused tram track which bordered the school playing fields. Robbie flashed a knowing smile at Mark and, not for the first time, the latter felt that he could see right through him. He could see that Mark *was* scared shitless of the towering, fiery-tempered maths teacher, despite the show of careless bravado. Mark envied him more than any of his other friends. Robbie had been strapped twice by Hopkinson for talking in class; but he hadn't flinched on either occasion. And he had earned the class's admiration by proffering his hand contemptuously for an unnecessary third blow of the leather: a gesture of contempt which Hopkinson was quick to reward. Mark could never have done that. He'd only been strapped once in his entire school career and then he had been forced to fight back the tears. Robbie had been belted more times than anyone else in the class and his silent pride was respected and unchallenged by all.

'What are you going to say when he asks for it?' asked Robbie.

'I don't know. What are *you* going to say?'

'I'm going to tell him he's a wanker and he can stuff his maths homework.' Robbie burst out laughing and jumped over the pool of muddy water in front of him. 'And then I'll kick him in the balls, wrap that belt around his neck and chuck him out of the window.'

Robbie's wild mood of unconcern was infectious.

'I'd like to see that,' laughed Mark as he jumped across the pool to Robbie and they both continued walking.

'Got your gym kit in, then?' asked Robbie suddenly, and then, without waiting for an answer: 'I haven't. Don't fancy cross-country running in this weather. What about you? We could hop on a train to the coast if you like. I've got some money . . .'

The idea was instantly appealing to Mark. They could take a day off sick, forge a note and get out of having to hand in their homework. Mark could finish it off tonight when he got home – it didn't matter what Robbie said – and hand it in tomorrow. The grey, drizzling morning had taken on a new aspect as they turned and headed in the opposite direction.

*   *   *

The funfair was deserted. As they passed through the decorative iron gates Mark recognised the theme from 'Carousel' blaring from the speakers on the dodgem stand. He had never liked that music – it was too spooky. The canvas tents housing fruit and gaming machines dripped and flapped emptily. Cheap, garish debris from the previous night still fluttered on the grass which was steadily disintegrating into a quagmire in the continual, drizzling rain. To Mark, it seemed that everyone in the world had suddenly stopped what they were doing, had walked away and vanished. Just like the 'end-of-the-world' film he had seen last week, with its vast, bleak shots of empty streets and cities. Deserted roundabouts stood silently in the rain; rank after rank of gaming machines brooded under their canvas covers.

Robbie headed straight for a tent, fumbling in his pocket for loose change. Mark followed close behind. As Robbie entered the tent, Mark's attention was drawn to one of the sideshows bordering the small lot on which the fairground stood. *See*

49

the Tarantula Man! shrieked the placard above the weather-stained hoarding. A ghoulish monstrosity, fangs dripping with crudely painted gore, leered over a helpless and screaming woman. *See the Two Headed Pig! The Deadly Embrace of the Four Armed Woman!* Mark took two steps towards the garish sideshow in queasy curiosity before stopping and turning back to Robbie. The shabbiness of the hoardings, the outrageous, sick ghastliness of the painted freaks, made him feel a little uneasy. It was like the time Albert Florio had pinned a live rat to the schoolyard and started to cut it open with his penknife, pulling at the entrails and holding them up for closer examination by the circle of small, white faces. Faces that peered forward for a closer look, retreated in disgust . . . and then hesitantly looked back again. In his mind's eye, Mark could imagine Florio lurking in the shadowy recesses of that sideshow, unveiling the horrors depicted on the placard with a kind of insane glee and relish.

It occurred to him that if there was a Hell, its streets would be bordered by sideshows just like that one. And its citizens would be forced to watch and participate for all eternity.

Robbie had tired of his fruit machine: 'It's a swiz, that machine. I've put three bob in there and haven't won once.' There was no one to reprimand him, so he aimed a kick at the machine and moved away sulkily with his hands thrust deeply into his pockets, kicking at a paper bag which fluttered on the ground. Mark ran to catch him up and together they began to trudge through the mud past the various tents, billboards and sideshows.

'Let's go in here,' Robbie said suddenly.

Mark looked up at the ghoulish billboards which had been nailed together to form the rough approximation of a station platform. Painted across the backdrop, a green steam train was roaring past in a billowing cloud of smoke. The train itself appeared to be a hybrid monstrosity: the engine at the front looked mechanical but seemed to be in the process of mutating into a hideous, leering demon with pointed fangs. A skeletal driver leaned from the cab, one ragged arm on the train whistle. The passengers of each coach were devils, imps, ghouls and vampires.

'How much is it?' Mark asked Robbie, swinging up onto a balustrade which fronted the station platform.

'Sixpence each,' came a thick voice from the booth set back on the platform. Startled, Mark jumped down as Robbie moved to the booth, a hardboard approximation of a ticket office, with a small grille window and cobwebbed rubber spiders dangling from it. As Robbie fished a handful of change from his pocket and began to push it under the grille, Mark could just make out the man in the booth. He was in his mid-twenties perhaps, with Brylcreem-smothered hair glinting like jet under the harsh light of a single electric light bulb. He had been reading a copy of *Playboy* magazine and he made no attempt to put it to one side as the boys approached. It occupied half of the small counter and was open at the centerfold. Mark moved to Robbie's shoulder and peered over, trying to get a better look at the magazine as the Ghost Train Man handed over two tickets. For the first time, Mark became aware of the peculiar odor. A kind of . . . *machine* smell that seemed to emanate from the booth; a strong, cloying scent that he had smelt before but could not remember where. When he looked up into the man's face, he could see that he was grinning at him. A strangely unsettling, fixed smile which made Mark turn away. A smile with not the merest hint of good humour in it. He had never seen so many teeth before; row upon row of perfectly even, white teeth. But it was the man's eyes that disturbed him more than anything else. They reminded him of the eyes of his younger sister's doll: unmoving, black glass beads that shone like the lustre of his slicked hair. Mark did not like that smile. It was too much like the smile of Albert Florio in the freak sideshow.

'You'll go blind,' said Robbie to the man, pointing off-handedly to the magazine and grabbing his tickets from the counter. Mark found himself being bustled into the first carriage of the Ghost Train which stood at the platform. Robbie jumped in beside him and flung both haversacks into the back seat. Ahead was the tunnel entrance which led into the land of horrors. It took the form of an ogre's mouth, a gaping maw that yawned wide to receive them. Two metal doors had been painted to look like teeth. To Mark, they seemed curiously like the teeth of the man in the booth. The likeness was too unsettling to allow him to turn round as he heard the man emerge from the booth and come up behind them. He was pushing at the carriage, moving it into position for its journey.

There was a pause. Robbie was watching the man attentively and, when he caught Mark's eyes, winked and made a jerking motion with his hand. A whine of machinery. And then with a bone-shaking judder the train was on its way, Mark and Robbie the sole passengers on the 'Ghoul's Express'. As the carriage crashed through the double doors, the Ghost Train was swallowed by darkness. An echoing shriek thrilled sharply in their ears. The doors banged close behind them and a luminous skeleton loomed suddenly out of the murk ahead. The banshee's shriek reverberated again and Robbie struck out laughingly at the sensation of cobwebs on his face, at the same time digging Mark in the ribs. Frankenstein's monster had appeared from an alcove on their right, arms raised and grasping. But it didn't bother Robbie. He had its number. It was a wanker.

And, as the train crashed on its way, Mark could smell the same overpowring odor that he had noticed in the ticket booth. It was much more concentrated in here, acrid and sickly. Now he knew what it was. Ozone.

'Look at him!' yelled Robbie over the booming noise as a waxen figure in black cape and widow's peak began to sit up in its coffin. 'It's Hopkinson . . .'

Mark laughed loudly as a deep groan issued from the vampire and the Ghost Train rattled around a bend on the next stretch of its journey.

'And he knows he's not getting his stinking homework!'

Luminous bats dangled from the ceiling overhead; they hurtled down a catacombed corridor, each recess revealing a new waxen horror. As they passed, a mummified arm reached out over the carriage. Quickly, Mark stretched up and grasped it in a dignified handshake. This was too much for Robbie who doubled up in his seat with laughter, clutching at his stomach.

And then, with a sudden lurch, the Ghost Train stopped.

Mark found himself suddenly in complete darkness, the abrupt halt hurling him forwards so that he was forced to grab at the rail to prevent himself being flung over the rim. Even above the squealing of the metal wheels on the track, Mark heard the muffled thud of Robbie falling from his seat onto the floor of the carriage. The banshee's shriek was fading away from a high pitched falsetto to a low and droning bass as the tape slowly ran down. Groping in the utter darkness like a blind man, Mark found Robbie and helped him back into his seat.

'What's happened?' Robbie mumbled in the darkness. He groaned. 'I think I've cut my head . . .'

For a brief, unreasoning instant, Mark thought that his interference with the ghoul's arm might somehow have resulted in the breakdown. But logic quickly returned: 'I think there's been a power cut or something . . .' He could feel that Robbie's forehead was warm and wet.

'What are we going to do?' Robbie's voice sounded lost and miserable in the dark. Mark had never heard him like that before. He always so self-assured and in command that it made Mark begin to feel very much more afraid.

'Don't worry,' he said with as much conviction as he could muster, 'someone will come in a minute.'

'My head hurts, Mark. I think I've split it on the rail.'

'You're okay. It's nothing. The lights will come on any second.'

But the lights did not come on and the silence lay heavily upon the Ghost Train stranded in the middle of its papier-mâché nightmare. The smell of ozone seemed somehow more pronounced. Mark's eyes were becoming accustomed to the gloom. He could dimly see, at the side of the track up ahead, the rock outcropping which was supposed to be a cave entrance. With the lights on, the tatty moth-eaten gorilla within would have been laughable. But here in the dark, Mark could find nothing to laugh at. Dark, silent figures seemed to cluster and loom all around them. The silence was smothering and oppressive. Not even the distant sounds and music of the fairground were able to seep through from outside and Mark suddenly had a terrifying premonition that someone would lock the doors and leave them there forever.

'Come on,' he said at length to Robbie, 'we're not staying here. Let's get out!'

Just behind them, he could make out the luminous bats spinning slowly from the roof.

'We'll go back the way we came . . .'

Robbie was moaning slightly as Mark stepped down from the carriage onto the rough, wooden floor. Leaning back inside, he began to help Robbie out.

'Someone should have come by now,' groaned Robbie.

'That daft bastard back there must still be reading his dirty book.'

'Help!' Mark's cry seemed to be swallowed alive by the blackness and left him with a peculiar hollow feeling which made him reluctant to shout again. 'This way, Robbie. We'll follow the track back.'

With their arms on each other's shoulders, they started back along the track. The tattered, mummified arms of the ghoul protruded from the recess just beyond and Mark could feel a rising dread that it wasn't a wax dummy at all. That it was really alive and was just waiting for them to draw closer so that it could lunge forward and take them in its ragged embrace. He tried to avoid looking at its face as they drew level. And that was when they heard the noise behind them.

Something was moving back there in the dark. Just around the nearest bend behind them, something was coming their way, following the carriage lines. Something that was un-impeded by the blackness and which walked with a deliberate, exaggerated tread, one foot flopping heavily after the other like something wet . . . and dead. And it was chuckling as it came in a low, throaty way.

Mark felt his skin tighten; a spontaneous pulse of sheer terror swept through his entire body. Robbie's grip on his shoulder was hurting as he hissed into his ear: 'Oh Christ, Mark. They're coming alive.'

Alive . . . *alive* . . . there was something alive back there. It had crawled out of one of those horrible recesses. It had been waiting for the day the lights went out. Just waiting for two kids like them to be on their own. And maybe it wasn't alone. Perhaps they were *all coming alive.*

Even now, something was shambling round the corner towards them, arms hanging limply at its sides. And Mark heard its low chuckling again when it saw them, just before Robbie shrieked and they began to run. They ran as they never had before. They ran as if in a bad dream, with the terror trying to dull their limbs and slow them down so that the shuffling horror could catch up with them.

Mark could hear a low moan of horror issuing from his own lips as he blundered round the first corner. Robbie clattered ahead of him, flailing at the dark like a blind man in a panic. The luminous bats tangled and flapped around Mark's head as he hurtled after Robbie. Something ripped from the roof over-head, a rail perhaps, and the bats wrapped themselves round Mark's arm before he shook them off to the floor. Behind him, he thought he heard a man's shouted curse as he plunged on into the darkness; unaware that Robbie, faced with a blank wall and unsure of which direction to take, had stopped and was looking frantically around. But that couldn't be right. It wasn't a man back there. It wasn't human. Further speculation was wiped from Mark's mind as he crashed heavily into Robbie and went sprawling awkwardly across the railway line. Robbie catapulted into one of the recesses, colliding with Bela Lugosi's coffin and shattering it like balsa wood under the impact. In the murk, Mark could dazedly see Robbie's wildly kicking legs and hear his cries of fright and disgust as he thrashed to get up, dislodging the wax dummy in the coffin which keeled slowly over to the ground. Mark had an upside-down glimpse of a white, waxen face leering at him before he recoiled in alarm. But there was something much worse behind them.

'Robbie! Robbie! Come on! We've got to get out!'

Mark was clambering to his feet when the rough hand seized him by the collar and swung him up the rest of the way.

'You little bastards! You're wrecking the place!'

Mark felt a sharp cuff on the back of his head and was flung up the track as the dark shape moved quickly to the ruined coffin, leaned into the recess and roughly pushed aside a shattered spar of wood. In the next instant, the shape was dragging out a wriggling Robbie by one arm and a handful of his blond hair. Even in the dark, Mark could see that the thing which had followed them was not a ghoul or a zombie . . . it was the Man from the booth.

Robbie was suddenly flung towards Mark and the Man had bustled from sight. Mark rushed to his side as Robbie struggled to his feet, brushing dirt and sawdust from his face. When he spoke, a little of the fire in his voice had returned.

'Did you see? It was him. That bloke from the ticket office. He was trying to scare us.'

The whine of a generator filled the tunnel and as suddenly as they had gone out, the lights were on again. Blinking like moles in the light, they surveyed their surroundings and could see that the interior of the Ghost Train was only a mess of wires, tubing and decrepit props. The House of Horror was a mouldering dump of ancient, twopenny-arcade fright masks and crumbling shop dummies.

The Man had suddenly reappeared from the side entrance and was moving purposefully towards them, his slicked hair falling across his face in a long, straight wedge. Mark flinched back as he drew level with them.

'You leave us alone,' said Robbie defiantly.

'What's the matter, kid? Can't you take a joke, then? You gotta start smashing my place up like that just 'cause I put the lights out?'

'It wasn't funny . . .' began Mark as they slowly backed away from the Man down the track.

'You paid to come in, didn't you? You wanted to be scared?'

'Run for it!' Robbie's shout cut short any further argument and Mark turned to make a dash. But, in an instant, the Man had closed the gap between them. Robbie went down again in the confusion, and Mark felt a grip on his arm which flung him round and pinned him to the wall. The Man held him there with his forearm across his throat and Mark watched helplessly while he delivered a savage kick to the seat of Robbie's pants. The boy struggled to his feet and clattered from sight around the next corner.

'Get off me. Leave me alone . . .'

The Man turned back to Mark. He had the same horrible, toothy grin on his face and Mark could smell whisky on his breath as he tightened the pressure of his forearm.

'Skiving off from school. Is that what you're doing, eh? I bet nobody knows where you are today, do they? Just pissed off for the day. Came down here and thought you'd start smashing my place up.'

'We didn't . . .'

The Man's bony forearm squeezed his windpipe shut. Groaning, Mark felt himself sliding down the wall. A purple mist was spangling across his vision; just like the mist that closed in when the dentist was holding that horrible, rubbery mask over your face.

'This stuff's expensive. Got to be replaced. Costs money, you know. I should take you to the cop shop and report you. What would your Ma and Da say about that, eh?'

Mark squirmed to one side and felt the pressure ease slightly. But the Man quickly compensated, shifted his position and now took Mark by the throat with one hand, grabbing his hair with the other and slamming his head against the wall. The purple mist was beginning to creep in again.

'Anybody ever tell you that you've got a face like a girl, kid?' the Man continued. 'You look just like a sweet little girl. Bet they all call you a poof at school, eh? Bet they do. What would your Ma and Da say if I took you to the cops, eh? They wouldn't like that, would they? Their little poof put in prison for smashing my place up.'

Mark was now in a sitting position, his senses swimming. The lights in the Ghost Train seemed to have dimmed, the purple mist swirled heavily about him and, through the haze, he could see the Man's legs.

'So the best thing you can do is just take your punishment, son. I mean, you've got to be made to pay. And then we won't have to say anything to the police or your folks. So, you just take what's coming to you, say nowt to anybody, and we'll forget all about it . . .'

The Man was taking off his belt as Mark went over onto one elbow, the unrelenting pressure now gone from his throat. Weakly, he held up his other arm through the mist, expecting the sting of leather at any moment. In a curiously objective way, he realised that he was going to get the belt anyway. Not from Hopkinson, but from . . .

But the Man had dropped his belt to the floor and Mark could hear the rustle of clothing as he began to unbutton his trousers.

'You . . . leave me alone.' Mark began to crawl away and felt a foot slam hard against his shoulder.

'Don't touch me, you queer bastard!'

The foot slammed down again and Mark heard another stealthy rustle of clothing.

'Don't . . .'

Mark heard a heavy thud and looked up in time to see the Man suddenly freeze in mid-stance, his trousers hanging loose and open around his waist. And then he pitched forward against the wall, his face slamming hard into the plaster before he slid to his knees beside Mark. The Man remained kneeling for a moment, face still pressed to the wall, and then he slumped to one side over the metal line, just as the Bela Lugosi model had done earlier. And now Mark could see that Robbie

57

was standing behind him, breathing heavily, and clutched in his hand was a length of wood torn from the railings at the front of the Ghost Train's station platform. As the purple mist finally rolled in and Mark found himself enveloped in its satin clouds, his last conscious vision was of Robbie moving towards him, leaning down and calling his name softly . . .

❖   ❖   ❖

Mark was clawing his way to the surface of a boiling, purple sea. He was drowning and something told him that he would lose more than his life if he did not surface soon. When the purple cauldron suddenly dissipated, he found himself in total darkness. And then he realised that he was awake, lying on his back, and that his arms were raised upwards, hands still clutching at the air. For a horrifying instant, he believed that he was still inside the Ghost Train. That Robbie had left him lying there on the floor and the place had been locked up. He was still locked in the dark with the Ghost Train Man. Mark sat bolt upright in panic and in the next instant had reorientated himself. He was in bed with his wife, Joanne. Their seven-year-old daughter, Helen, was lying asleep next door. He was thirty years old and the Ghost Train incident had happened long ago, when he was eleven. He had been dreaming. Only dreaming . . .

But why, then, was the Ghost Train Man standing in the bedroom doorway? Why was his Brylcreemed hair glinting darkly in the moonlight, his doll-like eyes fixed on Mark? Why was he leering with that same horrible, fixed smile?

Oh, my God, thought Mark. *Oh, God . . . Go away. Go away.*

The Ghost Train Man sniggered and moved to one side; beckoning with a long, bony white finger to something which stood out of sight in the hallway and which, at first, seemed reluctant to enter. The Man leaned out of sight and when he returned, he had a length of rope in his hand which was attached to something Mark could not see. The Man had turned his knowing smile back to Mark as he pulled gently on the leash and his unseen companion moved into the doorway.

Mark was screaming as he clutched his hands over his eyes to block out the sight. Joanne was awake now, her arms around his shoulders; shaking him, pleading with him, begging him to stop. The Ghost Train Man and his companion were gone. But Mark had seen them. He had seen them and he knew that he would see them again.

He had seen the small ragged figure with the rope around its neck. The small figure that had been dead for all these years; eye sockets bulging and writhing with maggots; wisps of hair clinging to the decomposed skull. It had come from its recess on the Ghost Train track at the Man's behest; a skeletal jaw sagging loosely as it moved and the tattered remnants of a school uniform still visible on its frame.

It was Robbie. He had joined the Ghost Train Man and his friends on the sixpenny ride.

Ten

'I was there again this morning.'

Aynsley turned from the window of his consulting room which overlooked the city center. Mark was sitting slumped in the rather opulent upholstered armchair which the psychiatrist kept especially for patients, looking up at the ceiling. The tone of his voice seemed to carry with it an expectation that the doctor would remonstrate with him for giving in to his obsession again.

'I couldn't fight it.'

'Why do you feel that you have to fight it? Is it because of the fear you feel when you get there?'

'No . . .' There was a long pause as Mark continued to stare at the ceiling. 'It's not the fear itself. The fear is more like a warning. A warning to turn back.'

'We've discussed this before, Mark. You must realise that it is your subconscious mind that is affecting you in this way. You suffered an appalling accident; you fell from a train and received serious injuries from which you nearly died. It was an unparalleled physical and emotional shock. Not unnaturally, when you attempt to cross over onto the platform, your sub-conscious mind is terrified that it will all happen again. It therefore tries everything to stop you.'

'All right, but that still doesn't explain what it is that makes me want to go back to the station time after time. What it is that *makes* me want to cross the ticket barrier . . .'

'Have you tried to analyse the Impulse again, Mark? Can you tell me *exactly* what you feel?'

'It's . . . I . . . just can't put it into words. I just feel *compel-led* to go. I tried to resist it again today, but it kept nagging at me all morning. It wouldn't leave me alone.' Mark sighed deeply and looked across at Aynsley. 'This sounds so bloody ludicrous. I'm saying these things, trying to express how I feel, and it sounds so bloody ludicrous – even to me. No matter which way you look at it, I'm becoming schizoid, aren't I?'

'There you go again! I've told you before that you must rid yourself of that train of thought . . .' Aynsley raised his hands in the air and smiled wearily at Mark. 'Oh, my God, what an unintentional pun. Mark . . . you are *not* schizo-phrenic. You show none of the symptoms associated with schizophrenia.'

Mark shook his head and looked back up at the ceiling as Aynsley continued: 'As long as you keep that thought in mind, you're never going to make any progress. It's negative. You're a rational man, Mark. When we have our talks, you strike me as being particularly rational about these impulses and emotions. And it's exactly because you're a rational man that you find it so distressing not to be able to grasp the nature of the condition which your subconscious mind has imposed on you. You have no personality or identity problems. Look . . . schizophrenia sufferers may begin to hear voices in their heads, or develop a paranoid phobia that people are talking about them behind their backs. They could be beset by the know-ledge that a rat is lodged in their throat; or they may see that the living bodies of their friends and relatives are riddled with writhing maggots . . .'

Aynsley had not noticed the sudden rigidity in Mark's posture, the sudden flashing glance and intense expression on his face as the psychiatrist continued: '. . . All of these delusions can be experienced by a schizophrenic – not as

60

confusions inside the mind, but as objective facts of the exterior world.'

'I had a dream last night.'

Aynsley paused and took a cigarette from the golden box on his desk. Mark seemed to have cut him off deliberately. 'Another dream of standing stones and pagan sacrifices?'

'No. It was a different dream.'

'Tell me about it.' Aynsley sat back in his chair, lit the cigarette and drew deeply on it. There was a tension in Mark's voice which interested him.

'It was a dream that I haven't had since I was a kid. It used to plague me a lot. But it was more than just a dream. It was practically a blow by blow account of something that actually happened to me . . .'

As Mark recounted the nightmare of the Ghost Train, Aynsley could see the steadily mounting horror in his eyes. His hands were clasped tightly around the walking stick which lay across his lap. Aynsley noted how vividly Mark told the tale and how clearly the memory was burnt into his mind. He wondered just what on earth he could do to help him. Mark seemed so logical, so analytical of his own plight that he presented a fascinating puzzle to the doctor. Aynsley had been in practice for fifteen years and could not remember anyone like Mark Davies. Without doubt, his accident and subsequent recovery were sensational to say the least. And the psychological problems which remained were fascinating. Aynsley had rarely, in the six months or so that Mark had been receiving treatment, been able to converse so deeply and thoroughly with a patient on his own condition. At times, he had found that they were both discussing the problem in a manner and to an extent which excited and stimulated his own thought processes more keenly than since his college days. At other times, during the course of analysis, Mark could lead him into an abstract philosophical debate which was at the same time wholly relevant to Mark's own psychological problems. Aynsley had more than once forced himself to re-establish the doctor/patient relationship which had somehow drifted with the conversation. Despite this, he could still not isolate and explain the Impulse which forced Mark to make his constant visits to the station.

Mark's tale of the Ghost Train Man was far from abstract.

61

He told it with a graphic conviction which made Aynsley feel uneasy for reasons he could not explain. There was no dream-like quality about it in the way that Mark's dreams of ritual sacrifices were so obviously fantasies. Aynsley realised that Mark's subconscious had reproduced the event in a full and perfectly detailed flashback. Mark finished his story at the point when Robbie had arrived to rescue him, but the doctor sensed immediately that there was more to come.

'That's when I woke up. And that's when I saw . . .'

'Go on.'

'I was awake, Dr Aynsley. I was wide awake and I *saw* the Ghost Train Man standing in the bedroom doorway. He hadn't changed after all these years. He was just the way I remembered him. Just standing there, grinning at me. And there was something else . . . he had Robbie with him. He showed Robbie to me. There was a rope around his neck and he was dead. But the Ghost Train Man had brought him back. Oh, God, it was like one of those schlock-horror zombie films. There were maggots . . .'

Mark was clearly distressed. His voice tapered off. He found it impossible to believe that he had still been asleep, still dreaming, when Robbie and the Man appeared in the bedroom doorway. But if he had not been asleep, if he *had* really seen them . . . then all of Dr Aynsley's rationalising about his dreams and their birth in the trauma of his terrible accident failed to be comforting any more. It would mean that Mark's own diagnosis had been correct from the very first time he had spoken to him: that he was becoming schizophrenic and that the dreams had begun to impinge on reality. He was beginning to see things . . . horrible things . . . and slowly, but surely, he was going mad.

'The image persisted after you awoke?'

'I saw them both. I was awake.'

'What happened next?'

'I covered my eyes with my hands. It was the most horrible thing I've ever seen. When I looked back, they were gone.'

'Tell me more about the Ghost Train Man. What happened after Robbie hit him?'

Mark cleared his throat, leaned across and drank deeply from a glass of water on the table at his side. 'Robbie brought me round and dragged me away from the place. We just left

62

him lying there on the track. He was still alive, but Robbie had split his head open with that piece of railing. Robbie took me home and we just told our parents that I'd been taken ill at school.'

'You didn't tell your parents what really happened? You never went to the police?'

'No, we were too frightened.'

'So you never found out what happened to the Man?'

'Well, we never heard any more or saw anything about it in the newspapers. It was a pretty hairy few months, I'll tell you.'

'What about Robbie? How did he react to it all?'

'We never talked about it. I think we were both probably too shocked to think about the implications. I think we just tried to block it out of our minds as if it never happened. I never saw a great deal of Robbie after that. Six months later he was killed.'

'What happened?'

'I wasn't with him. He and some other kids had rigged up a rope swing from a tree in the park. Robbie must have got tangled up in it while he was swinging. It hanged him. By the time the others managed to get him down, he was dead.'

Mark cleared his throat, which Aynsley could hear had grown thick with emotion. 'But there's a postscript to the story. Eight years later, when I'd left school and got a job in an insurance office, I was invited down to the coast for a party at one of the guys' houses. Up until that time, I'd had an aversion to that particular area . . .'

'Understandably.'

'. . . But I made my mind up that it was time to go and see if the Ghost Train was still there . . .'

*   *   *

It was. Just as Mark remembered it. Except that now it seemed smaller, less imposing than it had done to an eleven-year-old boy. Mark saw the same billboard; the same lurid painting; even the carriages parked at the station platform looked the same. Business seemed bad. None of the carriages were being used.

'Come on, Mark,' said one of his workmates, 'let's see how good you are on the rifle range.'

'I'll catch you up,' said Mark, his gaze still fixed on the Ghost Train. His colleagues were suddenly swallowed up into the milling fairground throng and as he stood alone, staring at the Ghost Train, he wondered if he had the guts to do what he had intended to do.

A young girl squealed with laughter right into Mark's ear as she passed, burying her face in candy floss. Mark's heart lurched. *Just as long as they don't start playing 'Carousel'*, he thought as he began pushing his way through the crowd to the Ghost Train platform.

You paid to come in, didn't you? Mark remembered the Ghost Train Man's words. *You wanted to be scared.*

Now he was standing at the foot of the station platform. The ticket office had been given a new coat of paint. The rubber spiders dangling from the grille had been replaced by a row of rubber skulls. Someone was sitting inside the booth . . .

Mark climbed up onto the platform, not really knowing what he was going to say or do. Just facing the Ghost Train after all these years had been the really important thing. He steeled himself and moved to the ticket office, heart hammering, throat dry.

An old woman sat in the booth.

'That's thirty pence,' she said without looking up from her knitting. She was about seventy years old, Mark guessed, dressed in a hideous floral dress and, although her hair had been dyed blonde, it was still grey at the roots. 'Thirty pence, I said,' she repeated, looking up at last, her eyelashes thick with mascara. Mark saw that her left eye had a cast.

'Where is he?' Mark heard himself say.

'Where's who? Look, if you want to ride, it costs thirty new pence. Understand? We've gone decimal, you know.'

'The man who used to work here. He'll be about thirty-two, thirty-three years old now. Black hair.'

'You're drunk! Clear off before I call the police.'

'That's just what I should have done all those years ago. He isn't fit to walk the streets when there are kids about.'

'Clear off, before I . . .'

'This fella givin' you trouble, Ma?' said a voice from behind. It was eight years later, and Mark had grown in that comparatively short space of time from a boy into a young man, but he could never forget that voice for as long as he lived. He turned round slowly, already seeing in his mind's eye that towering, thin figure in dark trousers and white shirt. The shining, marble eyes and the glinting teeth. The oiled hair and the look of madness.

But this overalled figure could not possibly be the Ghost Train Man. He was much smaller, smaller even than Mark. His hair was receding at the front.

'Push off, pal. We don't want no trouble.'

But the voice was unmistakable. Mark's childhood demon was only flesh and blood after all.

'You remember me?'

'No. Piss off and find somebody else to bother.'

'Are you sure? Eight years ago. October. On a Wednesday afternoon. Two schoolkids skiving off from school.'

'Throw him out!' snapped the old woman from the ticket office. 'Drunken idiots coming up here and making a nuisance when we're trying to run a decent business. Always the bloody same.'

The Man moved forward, hand held out to take Mark by the arm and move him in the direction of the platform steps. Mark slapped out at the hand, knocking it away, rage building inside him.

'Bet you haven't forgotten that split head.'

The Man's eyes seemed to have acquired an unhealthy glaze. He stepped back, looking away from Mark, rubbing both hands on his greasy overalled hips. Behind him, Mark could hear the old woman saying: 'Oh, God . . . oh, God . . .'

'So you haven't forgotten, then?'

The old woman's voice was suddenly nervous and quivering. 'My boy's never done no one no harm. No one, do you hear? Now you leave us alone or we'll have you fixed good and proper.'

The Man seemed to be grinning, although there was no humour there, his lips drawn back from pearly teeth. 'Look, kid . . .' he began, moving forward with head held down.

And then he had swung his fist up into Mark's stomach. Mark doubled over at the crippling pain, the breath knocked from his lungs, the force of the blow slamming him against the platform rail. Through misted vision, he noticed with an almost objective curiosity that there was still a rail missing. There was another savage blow on the side of his head.

65

'Not here!' screamed the old woman. 'Not where everyone can see!'

Mark felt a boot hit him under the ribs. He struggled to rise. There was another blow in the small of his back and he heard the bustle and clatter of the woman clambering out of the booth, shouting at the Man to stop. Still winded, Mark felt a hand tangle in his hair, jerking his head up for a punch that would undoubtedly smash his nose. He saw the braced legs in front of him, just as he had done eight years ago. He lunged forward, fuelled by rage and knowing that the punch was already on its way. He jabbed his knee sharply upwards between the legs.

There was a high-pitched squeal and the Man crumpled backwards against the wooden border frame of the Ghost Train, his hands clutching his genitals. He began to gag as Mark bent forward, hands on knees, fighting to get his breath.

'You ... bloody ... you ...' Mark could not find his voice.

The old woman was screaming as she rushed to her son. After a few seconds, Mark moved forward to face the Man. He lay crumpled on the ground, moaning.

'You've squashed them, you bastard! I know you've squashed them!'

One punch, thought Mark. *Just one punch to alter his face and never let him forget. And then ... No ... that's not the way ... that's never the way.* He moved back to the railings, gasping for breath. A crowd had gathered to watch.

The woman began to cry.

'What have you done to my boy?'

'Nothing at all compared to what he was going to do to me.' Mark looked at the crowded faces. 'Take some advice, missus. Get a good solicitor. Because I'm going to do him for assault.'

Mark stepped down from the platform while the old woman cursed him and tended her son. His ribs hurt badly, perhaps one of them was broken.

'I saw that,' said a middle-aged man. His wife was holding a large toy panda and shaking her head in outrage. 'That man punched you for no reason at all. And I'll say so if you're going to take him to court. You want my name and address ... ?'

'Disgusting,' said the woman with the panda, her sentiments echoed by the watching crowd.

Mark smiled. He had never foreseen that things would turn out like this. But it seemed that everything was working out just fine, after all.

*   *   *

'What happened after that?' asked Aynsley.

'He was prosecuted for assault. There were dozens of witnesses. It turned out that he had a string of convictions. He was put away for eighteen months, but in the end his sentence was a lot longer than that . . .'

'How do you mean?'

'There was an incident in prison. He tangled with someone even more dangerous than himself and was knifed to death in the showers. It made all the headlines. Prison security, and all that. The funny thing is that I used to have a lot of nightmares about the Man, but after that second incident, I never dreamed about him again. Until last night.' Mark rubbed his hands over his eyes. Aynsley could see that the tale had taken a lot out of him. For a while there was silence.

'Just one more question, Mark. When you thought you saw the Ghost Train Man in your bedroom doorway, did he appear to you as you remembered him when you were a child? Or did he look as he did on that day you've described eight years later?'

'Just as I remembered him from the first time. Hideous.'

'I'm glad that you told me about this, Mark. It's very significant.'

'Significant? How?'

'It's so simple that you're overlooking it. Haven't you ever thought that your subconscious may have drawn parallels between the incident on the Ghost Train and the incident on the King's Cross train?' Aynsley stubbed out his cigarette emphatically in an ornate ash tray. 'It would seem to me that you've fused the two occurrences together. You can't cross the ticket barrier, not only because of your fear of another accident but also because, to your subconscious mind, it's the entrance to the Ghost Train.'

Mark could feel that Aynsley was correct to some extent. But there was more to it than that and he struggled to dig into his mind to catch the kernel of truth before it submerged into

67

the murk. He was too late. It had gone. But the theory sounded good. It really sounded good.

'And it's very interesting that you say your childhood dreams vanished when you went back to the fairground and attempted to face the lion in its den, as it were. I've got a feeling that if you were able to pass through the ticket barrier, you could do the same thing again.'

'I think you could be right. But God knows, I've tried to get onto that platform.'

'Mark . . . what about the accident? Have there been any images, connected memories or impressions in your mind since our last meeting?'

'Not a damned thing. Just a total blank.'

Aynsley lit another cigarette.

'They can kill you,' said Mark.

'So can falling from trains,' replied Aynsley.

Mark laughed aloud. He felt good. The tension which had begun to knot his shoulders and the back of his neck seemed suddenly gone. And he could tell that Aynsley felt good, too.

'Mark, do you remember we attempted hypnosis in the early months to try and find out what happened to you on that train?'

Mark nodded. He remembered how bad the dreams had become after that.

'I stopped the treatment because you were becoming too distressed when it came to answering questions about that day. As you know, I was also unable to get past the ticket barrier with you.' Aynsley blew a smoke ring which hovered lazily above his head like a halo. 'I think you may be ready now. We should try again.'

Mark thought that he could see light at the end of the tunnel. He smiled at the pun.

'I think so too,' he said.

Eleven

The ice-cold chill in the air was making Mark's bones ache again as he entered the Central Station from the underground connection. Snow lay heavily on the ground and a Metro tram had broken down earlier that morning, with resultant chaos for early morning commuters. After his talk with Dr Aynsley, Mark had felt better than he had done for months. But the compulsion and fear remained and obstinately refused to be rationalised. The ticket barrier still remained the focus of the strange inner drive which he could not placate.

He bought a newspaper from the stand, scrutinising the barrier as people pushed through. It was like a psychological mine field with an invisible no-man's-land around it. He fought the compulsion to move towards it. *Yes, I'll try again*, he told it. *But not now. I'm not ready for it.* He headed for the cafe, remembering the look on Joanne's face when he admitted that he had spent most of yesterday morning at the station. She had said nothing, but Mark could see it all written on her face: *Oh God, Mark. Not again.*

The cafe was fairly empty, as it normally was at this time of the morning, and Mark ignored the look of unabashed curiosity that the woman behind the counter gave him when he bought a cup of coffee and took it to his usual seat. She should be used to him by now. After all, the schizo was a regular customer. He had been coming here now for almost six months. *Christ, six months!* thought Mark. At first, after his recovery, he had only come once a week, but in the last couple of months it had been every weekday. And even then, the compulsion nagged him at weekends when he was with Joanne and Helen. He reminded himself of a hopeless junkie, deprived of his daily fix and suffering withdrawal symptoms because of it. But there was hope now. If Aynsley could unravel his mental block under hypnosis, if he could find out what had happened to Mark on that damned train, then perhaps the fear and the Impulse would be gone. He could brave the ticket barrier, pass through onto the platform, perhaps even board the train again and kill this phobia, this obsession, once and for all.

Further thought was vanquished as the Impulse to get up and head for the barrier seized him again. And, at the back of his mind, the cold unreasoning fear warned him not to attempt it.

Mark finished his coffee and walked stiffly back to the cafe entrance, aware that the woman behind the counter was watching him. He ignored her and moved outside into the cold, standing just by the entrance. He looked out across the station, watching the milling passengers, trying to divert his thoughts from the inner battle within him. He tried to guess the occupation of a young executive type; a tall, good-looking woman; a man and a woman with suitcases . . .

Come back.

A teenager with a duffle coat and college scarf; a young couple pushing a luggage trolley, looking bemused; a pensioner with a poodle . . .

Pass through. Enter.

No . . .

Two men in business suits engaged in animated conversation; three children dashing noisily into the newsagent to buy comics . . .

And then Mark saw the man in the black raincoat standing in the newsagent's shop, watching him. Mark looked away instinctively, but when he glanced back again, the man was still watching. Only now, he had seen that Mark had noticed him and was moving away, pretending to be engrossed in the newspaper he was holding. Mark was taken aback by the intense look of somber scrutiny on the man's face. He was middle-aged, stocky and with hair greying at the temples. But there was no mistaking the fact that he had been watching Mark with a keen and intense interest.

The stranger moved out of vision as Mark turned back into the cafe, bought another cup of coffee and returned to his seat, puzzled. Perhaps he was imagining it, after all. God knew, he was all to hell since the accident. Perhaps he was imagining now that people were watching him, another symptom of his emerging schizophrenia. What was it Dr Aynsley had said? . . . *a paranoid obsession that people are talking about you behind your back.* Perhaps that would be the next step . . .

Get up. Walk to the ticket barrier. Show your ticket to the inspector. Pass through.

Mark finished his coffee, rose creakily to his feet and saw

that the woman behind the counter was drying cups on a ragged towel, watching curiously for his next move. He gave a small, rueful laugh as he left the cafe again. His new suspicions seemed to be proved right. The woman continued drying cups, shaking her head sadly.

Mark's stomach was beginning to knot as he headed directly for the barrier, hoping that a line of passengers would not form at the last moment. If that happened, and he had to wait he knew his nerve would break again. The walk from the cafe to the barrier seemed interminable; the methodical click-click-click of his walking stick as he moved seemed somehow amplified over the crowd noise. There were no passengers at the Platform Nine gate. This time he would do it, this time he would . . .

Turn back. For God's sake, turn back.

Go on. Pass through.

Turn back. Turn back.

Oh, my God, my God, my God . . .

Come back . . .

I can do it. It's easy. If I do it, then I'll break this damned thing. It won't have a hold over me any more.

And then Mark saw the stranger again.

He was standing underneath one of the arches, just off to Mark's right, and scrutinising him as intently as before. The sight sheared through Mark's resolve with devastating effect. He was four yards from the gate, in no-man's-land, and the terror which stalked there had found him again.

Get away. Get away.

His nerve gone, Mark turned sharply and headed for the exit, feeling the stranger's eyes boring into his back. The hope which Dr Aynsley had instilled in him seemed a distant and bitter memory. Mark had been wrong. Things were not as black as they had been before. They were worse.

Twelve

Mark knew that he was dreaming again but was powerless to do anything about it. He remembered that, as a child, he had acquired the ability to wake himself if a dream suddenly developed into a nightmare. But then had come the dreams of the Ghost Train Man, and they refused to be ignored or terminated before they had run their full course. It had been many years since his regular nightmares. Now they had returned. Worse, the Ghost Train Man had returned and threatened to haunt not only Mark's dream world but his reality, too.

First, the block of stone, the ornamental bars, the coffins. And then, as the familiar purple mist receded, Mark could see that he was flying like a bird over a glittering expanse of water. It was dusk and the sinking sun was casting a ruddy glow on the waves. He was caught in the grip of an invisible bird and could feel the wind ruffling his hair as he moved swiftly onwards. As his eyes became accustomed to the darkness, he realised that he was travelling inwards from the sea down a long inlet; he could see the shore on either side, but no habitation. It looked like wild country. He was swooping lower now, skimming over the water towards a low promontory of land and could see, for the first time, what appeared to be a strange, irregular forest thrusting upwards towards the sky. As Mark drew nearer, he could see that they were not trees. They were standing stones.

From this angle, they appeared as an irregular jumble of jutting monoliths; but now he was moving over and around them, and to the right he could make out a large outcrop of natural boulders. The stones stretched from the boulders in a rough line before curving into a grouping of stones about forty feet across. From the centre of these, a taller, single pillar thrust upwards like an accusing finger. To Mark's left, he could see a long avenue of stones stretching away into the darkness. His vision misted and, at first, he thought that the dream was over. When he could see again, he was standing in the centre of the configuration with a line of stones stretching out on either side of him. All around him stood the strange monoliths, black in the fading light. There was something different about this dream. He could feel it.

The strange force which held him immobile, and which usually forced him to watch the horrors perpetrated in the prehistoric circles, burial chambers and alignments of his other dreams, was not present. The invisible something which had borne him here on its wings had gone. Mark found that he could move of his own free will and surveyed his surroundings before moving forward to inspect the clustering stones more closely. Darkness was falling rapidly as he tried to orientate himself. Where was he this time? It was hopeless. He could be anywhere in the world; past, present or future. And as he stood and looked, he could feel a strange uneasiness at the back of his mind. In all his other dreams, something terrible always happened. What possible horror could this new development hold in store for him? With a growing premonition, he began to move quickly out of the circle to his right. He felt too vulnerable standing there. He would feel the wind on his body, although he was not cold. He was wearing his black jacket and grey trousers. Mark congratulated his subconscious for providing him with warm clothing. *This is crazy*, he thought. *I can feel the grass under my feet.*

He passed between two angular stones, hesitated for a moment and then moved quickly to one of them, rubbing his hand over its rough surface. He could *feel* the ice-cold stone. He continued on. He was out of the circle now and moving down a long avenue of irregularly spaced stones stretching ahead of him into the night. The wind was building and it buffeted him as he walked.

It was after he had passed twelve of the stones and could still see more ahead of him that he first felt something was wrong.

He had been waiting for something bad to happen. It always did. But as he turned back to look the way he had come, he could see nothing. Only the wind hissing through the unkempt grass surrounding the silent, unyielding stones. Strangely, he heard the lonely, plaintiff call of a cuckoo from somewhere in the darkening gloom. But there were no processions of strangely clad figures; no rejects from a Boris Karloff movie; no struggling and mutely silent sacrificial victims. *There's nothing there*, Mark told himself. He repeated it aloud and wished that he hadn't. His words sounded hollow . . . and somehow challenging. *No*, said a whispered dread in Mark's

73

brain. *There is something back there. You can't see it. But it's there. And it's coming.*

Mark moved closer to the nearest monolith and placed his hand against it. God, he *knew* there was something back there. He screwed his eyes shut and willed himself awake. It would not work. When he opened his eyes, he was still standing by the pillar looking back along the line of stones towards the circle and . . .

Something had moved back there. He could swear to it. Something darker than night had passed between two pillars in the circle. Mark strained to see and suddenly felt an unnatural pulse in his fingertips where they touched the stone. It was a cold pulsing, like the single beat of an inhuman heart that had been dead for centuries. He pulled his hand away as if the monolith itself were alive and for an instant seemed to see a faint glow from the stone. A glow which revealed a bizarre network of living veins and arteries. The impression quickly faded and he looked back towards the circle and saw the movement again. Something was moving around the stones back there; weaving in and out. It was indistinguishable from the stones, perhaps dressed in a black, flowing garment of some kind which floated around it as it moved. It seemed to be following a strange pattern, perhaps tracing an unfathomable route marked out by the stones themselves. But it was the height of the tall, angular figure which struck a note of fear and dread into Mark's heart. Nothing so tall could be human. And now it had broken from the circle and was moving in Mark's direction, still weaving in and out between the stones. Mark seemed to know that the thing, whatever it was, was bound to the stones in some curious way. It was moving faster now, because it had seen him. And, whatever it was – it seemed to have horns.

This nightmare was worse than the others. There was something dreadful and unhealthy about the shape which advanced towards him. Mark turned and fled as the unspeakable figure swept nearer and, as he ran, he could hear the voice of Helen and her friends singing in the schoolyard: a childish singing that was somehow the most dreadful thing he had ever heard.

Eeny meeny miny mo,
Eeny meeny miny mo,
Eeny meeny miny mo.

Mark could not bring himself to turn as he ran blindly ahead. He knew that it was behind him. He knew that it was horrible. And that it was somehow bound to the stones. He was within its lair, within its domain, and he knew that if he could reach the last monolith in the avenue and run beyond it, the thing could not follow after him. It was a prisoner of the stones and could not follow. Another stone reared up ahead of him and he could hear his pursuer right behind him now. He could hear the *flap, flap, flap* of whatever it was that came.

Mark could see the last stone ahead of him.

Something sharp and covered in coarse fur scraped the back of his neck.

*   *   *

Mark found himself sitting up in bed, bolt upright and awake. The dream had ended. There was sweat on his brow even though snow was beating against the windows in the night. Spiny, skeletal shadows were dancing on the bedroom wall, cast by the tree outside. Joanne was sleeping silently beside him. He wasn't out in the godforsaken wild somewhere, wandering out in the dark among prehistoric tourist attractions. He was at home, in bed, and he had been having one of those terrible dreams again. It had been bad tonight. But not as bad as the Ghost Train Man. Mark prayed that he would never dream that dream again. Even so, the dark and confused image of the thing which had pursued him tonight must surely be the stuff of fantasy. This was something that H.P. Lovecraft would have written about. It wasn't, it *couldn't* be real. And the horrific fantasy of the image was in a curious way comforting, despite the terror of the experience. All Mark's previous dreams had seemed so real that he could not have sworn that they did not actually happen. Even tonight's dream had been incredibly realistic, but surely this one had all the ingredients of a true nightmare. It could not have been real.

Mark got out of bed quietly. He did not want to disturb Joanne. She had worried too much, put up with too much. He looked down at her silently sleeping form as he pulled back the quilt to cover her. *I love you, Joanne*, he thought. *And I don't know how you've been able to stay with me since the accident.*

If you'd wanted to leave me and taken Helen with you, I couldn't have blamed you.

He moved quietly out of the bedroom onto the landing and into the bathroom, turning on the taps and splashing his face with cold water to wash away the sweat. The horror had gone. And tomorrow he would be seeing Dr Aynsley again after physiotherapy. Mark caught sight of himself in the bathroom mirror. He looked thin, pale and dishevelled. There was a scar across his forehead which was yet another legacy of the accident. It seemed strange, looking at the thin, white line across his hairline. He had no memory of receiving that scar. He did not know why it had happened or how it had happened. It seemed somehow strange that he had not felt the pain of the wound. It was as if something had come, gone and left its mark and he had no say in the matter. Mark sighed and moved back out onto the landing. The sound of sighing and mumbled words drew his attention to Helen's bedroom. He opened the door and looked in. She was asleep and, as he watched her, he realised that she was dreaming. He stood in the doorway for a moment watching her. Yes, she was obviously having some kind of nightmare as she tossed and turned in bed, clutching at the quilt. Mark went into the bedroom and crossed quickly to the bed.

'It's all right, darling. It's all right. You're just having a bad dream, that's all.' *So speaketh the purveyor of bad dreams,* thought Mark ruefully as he took Helen gently around the waist. She woke sleepily, with the image of the dream still strong in her mind. She began to weep drowsily and Mark cradled her in his arms, whispering words of comfort and hoping that, as long as she lived, she would never have dreams like his over the last six months. 'What's wrong, darling? Don't cry. It was only a dream.'

'It's the little boy, Daddy. He's so sad. He comes to my room every night and talks to me. He doesn't like being dead.'

Fear and horror seemed to have sprung from the dark, from his own daughter, and seized his soul. It was like an electric shock. *No, she couldn't be talking about . . . she couldn't . . . no, this can't be right. I'm dreaming again. The last dream hasn't finished . . .*

'Which little boy?' Mark found himself asking.

'He comes here to talk about you, Daddy. He's your friend.

76

But he's so sad and frightened, and he won't let me look at him properly because he says he's been dead for a long time and his face is all yucky and stuff.'

Mark was stroking his daughter's hair. When he spoke again, he was surprised to hear his own voice; wondered why the words had not choked away and he had not plunged into screaming madness.

'What does he say?'

'Well, he can't speak very well because his mouth has gone all funny. But sometimes I can understand him. He just talks about Mummy and you and me. He asks me what we've been doing. And I tell him about my friends. He says that you were his friend once, a long time ago. He can never stay with me for very long because he's frightened that the Man will find out he's here.'

Oh my God, thought Mark. *What am I going to do?*

'He said for me to tell you that you mustn't go back. I don't know what he means, but he says that you'll know. And then he keeps saying a funny word. A word that I don't understand. But that's all he can say when I ask him to explain, Daddy. Because if he says any more the Man will hear him.'

'What word, darling?'

'It sounds like . . . like . . . "Has-he-mouth". Something like that. Oh, he's so sad, Daddy. He's been dead for so long and he's so lonely. I wish we could do something for him.'

'Don't worry, love. I'm here now. It was just a dream, that's all. Just a dream.'

Mark sat with his daughter until she had returned to her deep, innocent sleep. He tucked her in and walked back to the bathroom. He shut the door, bolted it and sat down on the lavatory seat. For a while, he fingered the small silver crucifix around his neck that Helen had insisted Joanne should buy him for a present on her behalf. The tile floor was cold on the soles of his feet. Outside, he could hear the wind blowing wildly against the house. He could not control his trembling as he buried his face in his hands. He looked down at the tiles between his feet. A large black spider crouched there, as big as a fifty pence piece; thick black legs splayed out at its sides. Suddenly horrified, he swept it aside with his foot, a wave of unexpected nausea coming over him. The feeling of sickness cramped his stomach and began to bubble upwards. He lifted the toilet seat and retched into the bowl.

What in hell is happening? he screamed silently in his mind.

Thirteen

'We've got to do it now.'

'Mark, do you have any idea what time it is? It's three o'clock in the morning. Now listen, I want you to . . .'

'You gave me your private number. You said I could ring you any time. We've got to do it *now*, Dr Aynsley! I can't take any more of this.'

'I'm not sufficiently prepared, Mark. For the kind of hypnosis I have in mind we need special supervision, special equipment.'

'Screw all that and screw what time in the morning it is! We've got to do it now or I'm going to lose my mind.'

'All right, all right. Calm down, Mark . . .'

'I'm coming over to your place. *Now!*'

'Not here, Mark. Listen, can you get to the clinic or do you want me to pick you up?'

'I can get there.'

'All right . . . take it easy . . . I'll meet you at the main entrance. I have my own central key but, to be honest, I can't see how this is going . . .'

'Now, Dr Aynsley.'

Click.

          *   *   *

Aynsley turned from the couch where Mark lay to check on the tape recorder he had taken from the top drawer of his bureau and placed on a small table beside them. It was less than two minutes since he had turned on the machine and Mark now lay in a deep hypnotic state. He had obviously been deeply distressed when he had telephoned earlier this morning. So distressed that the doctor had feared that Mark's anxiety about schizophrenia might have been realised after all. Incredibly, Mark had succumbed easily to hypnosis. It was almost as if he had willed himself into this state. Aynsley had met with varying degrees of success when it came to hypnotherapy sessions and some of his subjects were extremely receptive; but Mark had been induced into a hypnotic state almost immediately. There had been none of the violent reactions which had accompanied Aynsley's attempts to hypnotise him in the past.

The tape was still running. 'The subject is now in a receptive state,' said Aynsley quietly, resolving to end the trance the moment that Mark showed any signs of distress. 'Mark? Can you hear me?'

'Yes.' Mark's voice sounded slurred and far away, his breathing heavy and regular.

'Do you know who I am?'

'Yes. Dr Aynsley.'

'Do you trust me?'

'Yes.'

'I want you to listen to my voice very carefully. You are very relaxed. You feel very peaceful and there is nothing at all to be worried about. We are going to have a little talk . . .'

'Azimuth.'

'What? What did you say, Mark?' Mark had mumbled something under his breath and Aynsley could not quite make it out. He decided to disregard it and continued: 'We are going to have a talk, Mark. And I am going to ask you questions about the accident on the train.' Mark was frowning now, shifting uneasily on the couch. 'And when I ask you these questions, Mark, you will take the role of an outside observer. Watching yourself. And whatever you see, whatever you remember, it cannot harm you and you will not be afraid of it. Do you understand me, Mark?'

'Yes . . .'

'I want you to say that you will not be afraid.'

'I will not be afraid.'

'Good. Now, we're going back to the day of the accident. It's Wednesday morning, September 25th. You've just had breakfast. Can you remember what you had to eat?'

'Coffee. Toast. Can't take too long. I don't want to miss my train.'

'You're moving forward quickly now, Mark. You're at the station. You've just walked in through the main entrance.'

'Yes. It's cold today. Much colder than usual. Must have been the shortest summer we've ever had.'

'Where are you going, Mark?'

'I've got a meeting in Doncaster at 11.30 am. Can't complain. At least it's a day out of the office. If the car wasn't in dock I'd drive down.'

'What are you doing now?'

'I'm walking towards the newsagent. I'll need a newspaper or a magazine for the train. Yes, a newspaper will do, I think. They've put the price up again, the sly bastards . . . what time is it? Good, I've got half an hour. May as well buy a coffee. No point in standing here freezing.'

'I want you to tell me everything that happens now, Mark. In as much detail as you remember. And I also want you to remember that, no matter what happens, you will feel no fear. Absolutely no fear.'

'I'm in the station cafe, drinking coffee and watching people walk by. There's hardly anybody in here. Just an old woman and a young man. God, this coffee tastes horrible. I should have brought a flask with me . . . I'm getting up now. I'm walking out of the cafe. Hope I'm not too long in Doncaster. I'm walking towards the ticket barrier now. Platform Nine for me, I think . . . Yes, that's right. The King's Cross train. Now, where did I put my ticket? . . . There's a small line up ahead. It's still early so there's no problem. I expect the train won't even be in the station yet. I'm giving my ticket to the inspector . . .'

Mark paused and Aynsley sat forward intently, ready to bring him out of his trance. This was the point beyond which Mark had no memory and Aynsley expected him to react in the same way he had done all those months ago. He remembered how he had been forced physically to subdue Mark as he screamed and lashed at the empty air.

'He's punching it and handing it back. I'm passing through . . .' Mark's face looked calm and unconcerned as he continued. Aynsley checked the tape again. It was amazing. Mark had made the transition, remembered crossing the ticket

80

barrier and there had been no adverse reaction whatsoever. '. . . I'm walking up the ramp. God, it's freezing cold. I can see my breath. I'm walking over the bridge and can see a train drawing alongside the platform below me. Didn't hear an announcement but it must be mine. People pushing past me and hurrying down the next ramp. Yes, it's my train. Plenty of time . . . no hurry. Oh, damn. I've left my paper in the cafe . . .' Mark paused again and Aynsley realised that he had become quite excited as his patient talked. The palms of his hands were sweating. It had been so incredibly easy. Mark had not reacted adversely in any way and Aynsley's reservations about conducting the session without proper preparation had gone.

'I'm on the train now,' Mark continued. 'A first-class carriage not too far from the cafe car. If I've got my checkbook with me I might be able to afford a down payment on a cup of tea and a sandwich. There's no one else in the carriage with me. I'm on my own. Good, someone's left a newspaper on the seat . . . We're moving now . . . we're on our way . . . and we're on time, too. I wonder if I'll have time to pay a visit to that shop in Doncaster. I could buy Joanne another of those vases that she liked so much. I'll wait and see . . . We're crossing the river now. I wonder how many times I've crossed the Tyne. Must be thousands . . . thousands . . .'

Mark paused again. Aynsley checked the tape. It was still running. A minute passed by and still Mark said nothing. He lay in the same position, breathing deeply. Only now, a look of uneasiness was creeping across his face.

'Mark?'

'Yes . . .' Mark's voice sounded querulous and uncertain.

'Tell me more. Where is the train now?'

Mark began to shift uncomfortably. 'We'll be in Doncaster soon.'

'What has happened to you? What have you been doing between Newcastle and Doncaster?'

'I've just been reading my papers for the meeting, that's all.' Aynsley could detect a tone of reluctance in Mark's voice. As if he did not want to answer any more questions.

'Mark, I want you to tell me everything that happens from now on. The train is nearly in Doncaster and you've been sitting reading. Okay, now. Is there anyone in the carriage with you?'

'No . . . there's no one in the carriage with me. I'm on my own.'

'Tell me what happens now, Mark.'

'I don't want to remember. I'm afraid.'

'Listen to me. Remember what I said. You will take the role of an outside observer. You are watching yourself on a television set inside your mind. Whatever happens, it can't hurt you now. It will not harm you and you will not be afraid. I want you to tell me that you will not be afraid, Mark.'

'I . . . will not . . . be afraid.'

'Now tell me what happened.'

Mark opened his mind to Aynsley.

✻   ✻   ✻

Mark was suddenly awake. One moment he had been in a deep and thankfully dreamless sleep. Now he was awake and alert, as if someone had pressed a switch to wake him up. For a second, he had no idea where he was. He was not at home in bed. He knew that. And he was cold, too. Then he remembered: he was in Dr Aynsley's clinic. He had telephoned him early this morning and insisted that he meet him here to carry out the hypnosis session immediately. Something had happened at home which Mark refused to acknowledge and, in desperation, he had hoped that the hypnosis would solve everything and resolve all his worst fears.

Mark sat up stiffly on the couch and looked around. Aynsley was nowhere to be seen. Where had he gone?

And then Mark saw the tape recorder. It had been knocked from the small table and lay shattered on the floor, its innards littering the carpet. There were no spools of tape to be seen. Mark swung his feet over the edge of the couch.

'Dr Aynsley?'

He reached out for his walking stick and rose unsteadily to his feet, realising that he must have been lying like this for some considerable time. His body always stiffened up when he lay somewhere for more than a couple of hours. He crossed to the surgery door, opened it and looked out. It was morning, and a cold, bloodless grey suffused the empty corridors.

'Dr Aynsley?' Mark's voice echoed into nothing. He turned

82

back into the surgery. His hand closed round the door handle as he re-entered and he felt something sticky on his fingers. He looked at his hand. There was blood on it. And when he looked back to the tape recorder, he could see that there was blood on that, too.

He hurried from the surgery, not knowing what had happened. Aynsley was gone and there was blood on the door and on the tape recorder. The last thing he remembered was lying on the couch listening to Aynsley's voice as the hypnosis had begun. Mark felt cold inside as he hurried down the corridor, sensing that the nightmares were closing in on him. *Soon,* he told himself, *I'll be a gibbering wreck.* Something on the clinically white corridor wall drew his attention. It was a smudge; a smeared hand mark. He moved closer to it, dreading what his mind told him. It was blood.

He ran the remaining few yards to the glass doors which fronted the clinic and which Aynsley had unlocked earlier that morning. They were still open. He blundered through them and out onto the rain-washed pavement.

Fourteen

Joanne was sitting in the living room when she heard Mark coming through the front door. She had woken at four-thirty, aware that her husband was no longer lying beside her; eventually realising that he was not in the bathroom either. Sleep was no longer possible. She had searched the house, finding the note on her bedside table when she finally returned to the bedroom. She looked at her watch as she rose and moved into the hallway. It was six-thirty and still dark outside. Mark was closing the door quietly behind him. It had begun to rain again and his raincoat was streaked and dripping wet.

'Mark? Where have you been? What's wrong?'

Mark started at the sound of her voice and turned to look at her as she moved quickly to him. His face looked ashen, strands of hair lay plastered across his forehead and to Joanne it seemed as if he was unsteady on his feet. Had he been drinking? No . . . there was no tell-tale smell on his breath.

'Walking . . . just walking . . .' His words sounded vacant, far away. She guided him into the living room, wondering whether she should get help. Struggling out of his raincoat, Mark sat heavily in the armchair beside the gas fire as Joanne placed a hand on his forehead.

'You're freezing cold, darling.'

'Yes. I'm sorry if I worried you, Jo. Didn't you find my note . . . ?'

'I found it. What's wrong, Mark? You look awful. You know you're not up to wandering around the streets at this time of the morning.'

'I'm sorry, Jo. Really. I didn't want to disturb you, that's all. I had . . . another dream. I couldn't get back to sleep, so I thought a walk might do me good.'

'And you come back looking like death warmed up. Mark . . . you haven't been back to the station, have you?'

Mark placed an ice-cold hand on Joanne's arm. His eyes seemed glazed. 'No. I haven't been there. Really.'

'I'm going to make some coffee before you freeze to death.' Joanne moved away, leaving Mark staring at the glowing orange grid of the gas fire. Rain whispered at the window.

What if I've killed him and don't realise it? What if he put me into a trance and asked me questions about that day that my subconscious couldn't cope with? What if I put my hands around his neck and squeezed until he was dead? Or beat him to death and dragged him away? Hid his body somewhere, walked back into the surgery like a zombie, lay down and woke up again? That would explain the broken tape recorder. And the blood.

Mark ran his hands through his hair and then over his face. The skin felt like frozen parchment, as if he were touching someone else's face. A corpse's face, perhaps. His fingers were trembling badly.

What the hell am I thinking about? I couldn't kill anyone. I'm not physically capable of killing anyone. If someone punched me, their fist would go straight through this patchwork body of mine. Then what in hell happened to Aynsley? Where did he go to? Oh God, what am I going to do?

Joanne returned from the kitchen. He was still sitting in the same position, staring at the hissing gas fire as if it possessed the answer to some mysterious question. He looked so cold . . . and bloodless.

'Drink this.' Joanne handed him a cup. Absently, Mark took it from her and she watched his knuckles whiten as he gripped it with unnecessary force.

'Thanks, Jo. You'll be bushed by the time you get to work.'

'It doesn't matter. I've no classes today, anyway. Mark, you've got to promise me that if you wake up again like that, you'll wake me up, too. You can't just go walking the streets again.'

'I promise.' Mark lifted the cup to his mouth and Joanne could see for the first time how badly his hands were trembling.

It was in the stones. It walked darkly amidst the stones. It scented me and came for me.

'Was it the same kind of dream again?'

'Yes . . . yes . . . the same. In vivid Technicolor and Cinemascope. Not to mention the full audience participation.'

He's so sad, Daddy. He's been dead so long and he's so lonely.

Mark suddenly sat up straight, almost spilling his coffee. 'Where's Helen? Is she okay?'

'Of course she's okay. She's asleep upstairs. For God's sake, don't scare me like that.'

Mark sat back heavily in his chair, sighing deeply. His hair was dishevelled, he was unshaven, and he looked as if he had just come back from a walk in Hell. For a long time he sat without speaking and, as Joanne sat sipping at her coffee, unable to find anything to say to break the silence, she wondered how long this could go on. How long would she be able to bear the pain of watching him slowly crumble into . . . into what? She froze her thoughts like mental dry ice on dangerous flames. Mark was her husband. She loved him. And he was going though a traumatic recovery period, the horrors of which she could only guess at. By rights, he should be dead. *Oh, my God*, she thought, *what are we going to do?* And her thought seemed to hang in the air like an unspoken but tangible miasma.

When Mark spoke, his voice seemed clearer, less slurred and

85

with a determination that startled her. It was as if he had heard her thoughts.

'I know what I've got to do.'

Fifteen

The fear had returned. The cage was open and it snarled at Mark as he stood in the Central Station facing the platform barrier. And the fear's opponent – the insidious, all but irresistible Impulse – tugged at Mark and tried to drag him towards the gate. It was always there. In his brain, arguing and pulling, raging and tugging. Aynsley was gone and he didn't know what had happened. The broken tape recorder. The blood. Helen's dream. *Oh God, what have I done? Why can't I remember anything?* Mark's fantasy and reality seemed to have merged. Had he really heard his daughter say those things? Perhaps that conversation had been part of his dream. Perhaps it was part of the horror which had stalked him in those stark, silent stones.

He turned and headed for sanctuary again. His brain was too confused. There was too much going on inside his head. His bones ached badly, his leg felt stiff and pained him as he walked. He cursed his ailing mind and body as he entered the cafe, persistent images of dream and reality whirling in his mind like frightened, buffeting birds. He found his usual place and sat down heavily, steam from his coffee cup drifting up into his face. He clasped his hands over his eyes, wanting to burrow up and into his skull, squeezing his brain like a grey sponge, letting the bad thoughts and the tormenting Impulse and fear spurt out over his fingers. He wanted to wring his mind dry until there was nothing left but a comforting, blank emptiness.

He pulled his hands down into his lap, held them there, interlocking and gripping his fingers while a spasm of frustrated rage coursed through him. He squeezed his hands

86

together, strangling the torment; strangling, squeezing . . . and the rictus of confusion was suddenly gone. He was not mad. He was not insane. He was not schizophrenic. Two things he could not explain had tilted the balance in his mind. They *had* happened. They were not dreams. *But I won't think about them now. I won't try to analyse them. Because if I do that, the confusion begins again.*

Mark began to breathe deeply, sucking in lungfuls of the smoky air. A calmness had descended on him. But he knew that the grey, empty plain he had formed in his mind was only a temporary backdrop. That the Impulse to get up and go would return at any instant. And then, inevitably, the fear would follow . . .

He was right. How could it have been otherwise? The Impulse was returning again. It was in him now, talking to him; telling him that it was easy. All he had to do was finish his coffee (there was no hurry), get up and walk out of the cafe. Walk towards the ticket barrier. *You've already got a ticket, haven't you? Of course you have. You always buy one, whenever you come here, because I tell you to. And it doesn't matter which destination. Just give it to the inspector and he'll clip it, give it back to you. Pass through . . .*

No . . . no . . . you must not.

Why?

You must not.

Pass through.

You dare not pass through.

Mark stood up abruptly, spilt coffee splashing over the table in a steaming brown pool. The cup rattled from the table and shattered on the floor. Mark was dimly aware of a voice berating him as he left the cafe.

'. . . can't go breaking cups like that. Bloody lunatic. Coming in here every other day and making a damned nuisance of yourself . . .'

And in the back of Mark's mind, it reminded him of the Ghost Train Man: *Can't go smashing my place up like that. You've got to be made to pay.*

Mark had made up his mind. And he had never known fear so terrible. But he forced himself forward, one leg after the other; the click-click-click of his walking stick beating time like a metronome. The fear knew what was in Mark's heart. It

87

knew his intention and thrashed like a frenzied animal, snapping shreds from the fabric of his soul. It knew that he was giving full rein to the Impulse. He was going to let it take control.

I've got to do it. I've got to go through with it. I'm going insane. I'm going insane and the only way I can save myself is to pass through that fucking ticket barrier.

No. Don't pass through.

I must.

Yes. Pass through and save yourself.

No, no, no, no, no, no . . .

The barrier loomed ahead of Mark like the portal to Hell. The official stood in his small cubicle looking at him as he approached. He was smiling and holding out his hand for Mark's ticket. There was something about that smile. Something that seemed to say: *Roll on up. You can do it, boy. Come on. Let's have your ticket for the sixpenny ride.*

Mark turned his head away mechanically, like an automaton, as he proffered his ticket. He did not want to see the man's face again in case it changed into something else. Something that was the last thing in the world he wanted to see. *Oh God, I'm going to be sick. Hold it. Hold it in. Now, move. Let it take control. Give in to it.*

The inspector handed Mark his ticket and he took it with nerveless fingers. Was that really his hand? Was he really, even now, walking on through the ticket barrier and up the ramp? People were pushing past him as he moved. He was doing it again. Something had taken command of his body, just like in his dreams, and he was walking up the ramp. He was a passenger in his own body. He was walking over the bridge that spanned the King's Cross line now, looking down to the criss-cross rails. The fear was frozen inside him in suspended animation; a knot of curled fear in a glass cage. The Impulse had won. He had let it win. And it was telling him how good everything was going to be now that he had finally seen sense.

Mark heard the crackle of the public address system echoing through the vaulted chambers of the station. It should have been announcing the arrival of the King's Cross train. But it wasn't. It was speaking to Mark.

Welcome back, Mark. You've been away so long. I'm so glad to have you.

The knot of fear twitched, spasmed like a foetus in a womb. And now Mark was moving down the ramp towards the King's Cross platform. The Impulse was right. It had not lied to him. Everything was going to be all right. The aches and pains in his body were gone now that the Impulse had taken over. It was directing his body down to the platform; one leg after the other, click-click-click.

The King's Cross train was coming.

Mark could hear its approach in the rails. His sensitivity had been heightened and he could hear things that no other human being could hear. He knew that no one else could hear the *thrum-thrum-thrum* in the steel railway lines. A hollow, metallic booming like the continued slamming of a distant piledriver. The lines were surging with power as the train came and Mark reached the platform, wondering why no one else could hear it. It reminded him of something as he stared at the lines, the invisible power swelling and rising. It was like . . . like the dream. The dream of the standing stones last night. Of a jutting, angular, dead stone which had suddenly pulsed with life, revealing a network of veins and arteries. It was the same power. The same power that Mark had sensed in the stone was surging in the lines . . .

He had dropped his walking stick. He heard it clatter with a brittle echo on the station platform. But it did not matter. The Impulse was telling him that he would never need it again. And now the other passengers could hear the train coming and were moving closer to the edge of the platform. Mark was moving forward too, just like that time so many months ago. He would board the train, just as he had done before. And then everything would be all right.

The throbbing and booming of the rails was quickening, building to a crescendo, the individual beats of the piledriver merging into a continuous, deafening surge of sound.

Look, said the Impulse. *Look. Here it comes.*

Mark turned to look and felt the imprisoned fear kick inside him again like an unborn baby. The train was hurtling into the station.

He saw the billowing clouds of steam boiling and writhing across the track, and a small voice somewhere at the back of his mind was telling him that steam trains were antiquated relics that no longer ran on main lines; they had been replaced many years ago by high-speed diesel locomotives. But another, stronger voice was commanding him to watch. And as the King's Cross train burst from its shroud of steam, Mark was suddenly eleven years old again, standing in a deserted funfair and watching as the hideous nightmare from a billboard came to life.

The Ghost Train bore down on Mark and he could only stand and watch as the contorted, oil-streaked engine which was also somehow the face of a leering demon thundered out of Hell towards him. Mark could see its eyes, could smell its fetid breath as it hurtled greedily towards him. He could see the cadaver leaning from the driver's cabin in its funeral garb, a peaked driver's cap perched above empty eye sockets. He watched as it tugged hard on the train whistle and heard the engine give an answering shriek in maleficent glee. He could not see the graveyard denizens who rode in the carriages of the nightmare express but he knew that they were there, waiting for him, keeping a seat for him. The lurid green paint which Mark had seen flaking from the billboard all those years ago was now the paint which flaked from the fiercely pulsing, breathing boiler of the mutating monstrosity.

Oh, God, thought Mark. *Must I board this?*

No, Mark. You do not want to board. Move forward to the edge of the platform.

The train had reached the end of the platform and was sliding towards him like a juggernaut. Steam was spewing around it and he could see that its mouth was opening to take him. Black, iron-ridged lips sliding back from glistening, ragged teeth. Orange light from the raging furnace in the depths of the train's maw spilled like luminous saliva across those eager teeth.

Step off the platform, Mark.

The fear inside him had ripped free from its constraints and was born again within him. But it was too late. Too late.

Mark stepped off the platform . . .

The roar of the approaching train filled Mark's head as he pitched forward, the station swinging before his eyes in a drunken arc. There was a pain in his arm; something had hit him there. He was falling. And then Mark felt himself hit the ground hard although there was no pain. He was on his back, looking up at the steel girders and murky skylights of the station roof. He knew that he must be lying across the tracks.

But the sound of the train roared on and on as if it was passing by, and Mark knew that the Impulse had gone. It had fled from him. And he could feel cold, grey dread in the pit of his stomach. People were shouting. There was a hand clamped on his arm like a vice and a blurred face was swimming into view, obscuring the rafters and skylights. A face looming large and white above him. He knew the owner of that face.

It was the stranger who had been watching him in the station. He was saying something to Mark, hissing something into his face. Mark wanted to lash out at that face, make it go away, but he could not move his arms.

'Come on. Get up, you bastard. Get up.'

Mark could not control the nausea; it surged upwards into his mouth, spewing across his shoulder and over the stranger's hand. It clogged in his nose, blinded and choked him. And to Mark, it seemed that the fear within him had finally found a way to get out.

'Christ . . . come on. Get up. It's all right.' And then, louder to someone else: 'He'll be all right. I'm a doctor. No need to worry. He's okay.'

Mark felt himself being dragged to his feet. The station was swinging around and tilting again. For the first time, he could see that he was not on the line at all. He was still on the platform. Crowded passengers filled his field of vision; looks of concern, babbled voices and the sound of the public address system echoing tinnily, distantly angry. Now his arm was around someone's shoulder. His legs felt like rubber. When he tried to walk, he slumped to one side. He felt himself being carried.

Am I dead? Mark asked himself. *Am I really dead?*

When the purple mist returned to seep into his brain and he drifted into unconsciousness, it brought for the first time no dreams of horror or death.

Part Two
Chadderton

Bad Dreamer, what's your name?
Looks like we're riding on the
same train.

Showdown by Jeff Lynne

One

The purple mist held no terror. Somehow its hue seemed less poisonous. It curled and broiled now in tenuous wisps, not like a cauldron, and when Mark held up his hands it parted before his groping fingers like cobwebs. He pulled it apart like a flimsy curtain and was instantly awake.

He was lying on a sofa. Shafts of afternoon light were spilling across his face from the picture windows which occupied half the wall adjacent to him. He could make out the tops of the city skyline just above the lower frame of the windows and struggled up on one elbow to look around. He was in someone's living room or lounge; decorated barely by a bureau, two upholstered chairs and a coffee table. There was a bland, framed landscape on one of the pale blue walls. A door to the left led into a bathroom. He could see a shower curtain and hear water running. No . . . this wasn't someone's lounge. It was a hotel room.

He swung into a sitting position. Someone had taken off his raincoat and jacket. His shirt sleeve had been sponged and it clung wetly to his arm, still bearing the faintly acrid odour of vomit. A single document lay on the coffee table, a soft-backed folder of some kind: *Annual Railway Accident Report – Department of Transport*.

And then, with a feeling of grey nausea in the pit of his stomach, Mark remembered the station. He had given in to the Impulse. In desperation, and despite the fear, he had let it take him through the ticket barrier. He had gone insane and had tried to commit suicide. No . . . no . . . that wasn't right. He had *not* tried to commit suicide. Something had tried to kill him. He knew it with a conviction and clarity of mind that astonished him. The tumult and confusion which had been tormenting him for so long and the doubts and fears about his sanity all seemed somehow a thing of the past. Something cathartic had happened to him on the platform. Something that he could not explain. He had given in to . . . something . . . it had taken control, and it had tried to kill him. But it had not been his subconscious. He had not finally lapsed into schizophrenia. Something *else* had been inside his mind, living there ever since the accident. It had tried to kill him but it had failed and, as a result, had somehow been expelled from his mind. As a result of its failure, the canker had fled. The parasite was gone and Mark's mind felt pure and newborn, strangely cleansed. And . . . something else. There was something else about the clarity with which he could think and see things. Something new and different . . . he could think so much more *clearly*. . .

A figure emerged from the bathroom, standing framed in the doorway, holding a dark jacket and sponging the lapel with a cloth. Mark instantly recognised the slightly paunchy figure, the greying temples which bordered thick, ruffled hair that looked as if it had not seen a comb for some time; the rumpled tie pulled away from the collar. It was the face that had been watching him in the station, that had unnerved him so much when he made his first attempt to cross through the ticket barrier. It was the face that had loomed above him after he had stepped off the platform. Undoubtedly, the owner of that face had pulled him away from death at the last instant. The face of the watching stranger.

'You're awake.' The stranger spoke matter-of-factly, glancing at him only briefly before resuming his work on the crumpled jacket. 'This place stinks of puke.'

'Who . . . ?'

'Now comes the movie cliché: "Who are you? Where am I? What happened? And what am I doing here?" Right? More importantly – is this stain ever going to come off my jacket?' He moved to the picture windows and opened a vent, hanging his jacket over the back of a chair beside the radiator. 'Do you want a drink?'

'Yes.'

'It'll have to be whisky, 'cause that's all I've got. Try to keep it down, will you? I'm paying enough for the room as it is – I don't want to have to pay for the sofa to be cleaned as well.'

'Just who the hell are you?' asked Mark, suddenly angry.

'Don't you recognise me?' The stranger crossed to the small bureau and took out a half-full bottle of Bell's which he placed on the coffee table before vanishing into the bathroom.

'No. Should I?' But the man's face *was* familiar.

'You've got a short memory, Mr Davies. I'm surprised at you. But then again, your memory isn't one of your strong points, is it?'

The stranger re-emerged holding a whisky tumbler and the water glass which he had liberated from its holder above the basin. He sat opposite Mark, pouring two large measures and proffering the whisky glass to Mark. Mark drank quickly, feeling the fiery liquid burning in his gut and wondering how in hell the man knew who he was.

'Why did you try to kill yourself?' The stranger's eyes were penetrating and direct as he sipped at his whisky, leaning forward and cradling the glass in both hands. It was a directness which threatened to throw Mark off balance.

'I asked who you are,' Mark retaliated.

'You are Mark Davies. Thirty years old. Married with one daughter. You were thrown from the King's Cross train by a person or persons unknown on September 25th, last year. You spent eight months in a coma with nearly every bone in your body broken. You made a miraculous recovery but your memory of the incident was wiped clean. No one else on that train saw or heard anything. As a result, the Special Police Team set up to conduct an enquiry chased around in ever decreasing circles before vanishing up their own arses. Why did you try to commit suicide, Mr Davies?'

'Who the hell are you and why have you been watching me?' Mark drained his whisky fiercely, banging down the glass on the coffee table. He fought the urge to get up and leave. For the first time since the accident, it looked as if he might be able to pull together the loose strands of his life . . . of his mind . . .

Something new in my mind . . . so clear . . . I can think so clearly.

'My name's Chadderton, Mr Davies. I've been hanging around in that station for the past six weeks, watching you.'

Chadderton. The newspaper article in Mark's pocket. Detective Inspector Chadderton . . . 'Officer in charge of the investigations'. And then Mark remembered where he had seen him before: in the early days when he was recovering from his coma and life seemed to be a drifting, disconnected limbo between waking and sleeping. Chadderton had spoken to him then; had visited him at the hospital. But he had looked much younger then, more in control . . . *my mind . . . so clear . . . something has happened to him since then . . .* He had never seen Chadderton again after those early days (or months). Only a continuous stream of unfamiliar official faces, some of them uniformed . . . but never Chadderton.

Chadderton had crossed to his jacket and taken out a small black leather wallet. He made to throw it at Mark.

'There's no need. I remember who you are.'

Chadderton returned to his seat, refilling their glasses and handing the tumbler back to Mark.

'Why have you been watching me?'

'You're a fascinating man. I originally came up here to interview you. But I didn't have to seek you out. When I arrived at the Central Station, you were already there. Pacing about like a demented lion in its cage. What is it about the station, Mr Davies? Why do you spend so much time there?'

'How long have you been watching me?' Mark asked again.

'Six weeks.'

'You mean you've had a team of people watching me?'

'No, just me.'

'Wait a minute. You've just been hanging around for six weeks. A detective inspector . . . in a rented hotel room . . . watching me for six weeks. That doesn't hold water.'

'Why did you try to kill yourself?'

'I didn't try to kill myself. I . . . fell.'

'Oh, yeah. Great. You just walked straight up to that platform and stepped off. If I hadn't been watching you, been right behind you and hauled you back, you would be a stain on the tracks by now.'

'You're not in the force any more,' said Mark, instinctively knowing that he was right. *How did I know that? How in God's name did I know that?*

Chadderton sat back in his chair, a wry smile spreading across his face. 'Very perceptive. And you're absolutely right – I'm not a policeman any more. I've been relieved of duty, as they say. I am no longer "officially part of the investigation".' Mark could hear the quotation marks around Chadderton's words. 'But it probably won't surprise you to know that, although the file on Mark Davies is still open, there's bugger all in the way of active investigation going on, seeing as how we've . . . they've . . . been able to come up with less than sweet Fanny Adams since Mr Memory was picked up from the embankment.'

'Hold on! Hold on!' Mark held up his hands in a placatory gesture. 'Let's get this right. You were in charge of my case.

Now you're not. In fact, you're not even a policeman any more. And to all intents and purposes you say the police have given up; have unofficially closed the book on me. Yet you travelled up here from London to interview me anyway. You saw me in the station and decided just to hang around and watch me rather than try to talk to me. Why the hell *were* you watching me? All right, my behavior's been bloody erratic—I admit it—but do you mean to say that it was fascinating enough for you to stand watching me for six weeks?'

'Just as well I did keep an eye on you, isn't it? Bearing in mind what happened . . .'

'Look! I owe you! You saved my life, but I think you should do a little more explaining.'

'Did you try to kill yourself? Is that what you've been hanging around the station for? Is that what you've been trying to pluck up the courage to do?'

'No, I didn't! And no, it's bloody not! Don't talk in circles with me. Either answer my questions or I'm walking out.' Mark gulped at his whisky again, the warmth in his stomach spreading to the rest of his body. He was beginning to feel very tired and his leg was starting to ache badly.

'I'll explain everything to you. Everything. But first, you've got to be totally honest with me, and tell me – did you try to kill yourself and is that why you've been going back to the station day after day?'

Mark felt at an impasse. Chadderton's attitude was offensive and aggressive, but it was intriguing. He had been angrily blunt and direct with him; he had given Chadderton an ultimatum, but he had sidestepped it and Mark felt that Chadderton was used to being obeyed. But he had to find out what was going on – no matter what.

'The honest answer is this: since the accident, I've been recovering not only physically, but mentally. I can't remember what happened to me on that train. But ever since I got out of hospital I've had this compulsion . . . this Impulse . . . to go back to the station, buy a ticket and cross through the ticket barrier again.' *The Impulse has gone. It's been cast out. But it's not dead. It's still alive . . . somewhere . . . not far away . . . but still alive . . . and prowling.* 'At the same time, I've been terrified to cross through. Terrified at what might happen if I do. That's what I've been doing in the station. I've been torn between two impulses. That's why I've been seeing Dr Aynsley – my psychiatrist.' *Aynsley was my psychiatrist . . . no . . . no . . . he IS my psychiatrist. He's not dead.*

Mark sighed and sat back, waiting for Chadderton to fulfil his part of the bargain.

'And when you crossed through the ticket barrier, what happened then?'

'Come on. You said you would explain . . .'

'Listen to me, Davies! This is important. It's very important that you tell me just exactly what happened to you when you walked down onto the platform. I'll tell you absolutely everything that there is to tell, if you'll just say what happened.'

I can tell him. I know I can tell him. He's right, it is important . . .

Angrily, Mark explained, baring his soul to a complete stranger for no other reason than that an inner conviction told him it was right to do so: 'I gave in to the Impulse today. I followed through with it. And when I went through the barrier, it was as if something . . . took possession of my body. I wasn't in control any more. Something else was wearing my skin. I walked down to the platform as the train came in' – *the pounding in the lines . . . the Ghost Train . . . no, I can't tell him that or he really will think I'm crazy* – 'I just didn't have control over my body. Something was talking to me in my head . . . except *talking* isn't the right word . . . and it told me to throw myself under the train. I know it sounds as if I've gone totally loonytunes. For a long time I thought I was a schizo myself. But now I *know* that it wasn't true. I didn't try to kill myself. Something wanted me dead.'

Mark's words had flowed straight from him in a pure emotive surge. He felt breathless, a little drained, and as if he had just prostrated himself across a chopping block. Now he feared that Chadderton would throw him out, having finally received confirmation that he was a raving lunatic.

Chadderton had sat impassively through it all after his initial outburst; the same penetrating thrust in his eyes while Mark spoke. As Mark finished, there was a pause that seemed to hang timelessly in infinity while he waited for Chadderton's re-action; waited for the axe of sanity and reason to fall. *All right, you maniac. Get out before you spew your guts all over me again!*

Chadderton sat back in his chair and turned his eyes up to the ceiling, exhaling air. He looked limp, and when he turned to Mark again, he smiled in a hopelessly careworn sort of way.

'Drink?'

'No . . . no . . . thanks. I've had enough to knock me out, already.'

'Okay.' Chadderton nodded, groaned and rubbed his face roughly with one calloused hand, as if he had just woken up. He leaned forward and poured another drink, Mark still waiting apprehensively for his response. He drank deeply, stood up slowly and moved across to the picture windows looking out across the city.

'Nice place to visit but I wouldn't want to live here. Do you know how many commuters use the King's Cross train between London and Newcastle in a year? Or between London and Edinburgh? No? Neither do I. Must be hundreds of thousands . . .' Chadderton's voice faded as he scanned the city skyline.

The afternoon shadows were beginning to lengthen and Mark could feel a rising irritation at the deliberately oblique way in which the man seemed to approach everything.

'The team that was investigating your high-diving performance,' began Chadderton again, 'wasn't specifically set up for that purpose, Mr Davies. In fact, it had been in existence for just over five years before you hit the embankment and the headlines. You aren't so special, I'm afraid – you're a statistic. You *could* have been special because you're alive. But your memory's gone, so you're no good to us at all.'

'For God's sake, will you just tell me straight!'

Chadderton harrumphed, a laugh with no trace of humor. He moved back across the room and sat down again. For the first time, Mark realised that he had a two days' growth of beard.

'Five years ago, my team was established to examine a number of unexplained deaths . . . murders . . . all related in some way to the King's Cross train. All absolutely motiveless, all involving ordinary people using the train who boarded at one end, disembarked at the other and committed some terrible atrocity . . . or committed suicide. Some of these incidents we were able to link immediately to the fact that the person or persons involved had recently travelled on the King's

Cross train. But as our inquiries led us further afield, we began to look into other incidents which had remained either unexplained or unresolved; cases which had already been dealt with.

'We found that, in a considerable number of instances, people involved in some pretty bizarre incidents had travelled on the King's Cross train within a 24-hour period. In fact, there have been one hundred and fifty identified incidents since the team was set up. And that doesn't take account of the deaths we haven't identified yet. In every single case, they've been ordinary people leading ordinary lives who have suddenly gone out of their minds after riding on that line. For no logical reason at all. One of our boys made the connection with the train journeys by mere coincidence. When we examined it more closely we couldn't believe what we'd stumbled onto.

'The whole pattern is insane – there's no logic to any of it. In '71 a middle-aged businessman clinches a big business deal in Northallerton. He gets on a train to King's Cross, gets off, goes home, shotguns his wife and kids, then sits calmly down on a kitchen seat and methodically gouges out his eyes with an apple corer. Two kids on a camping holiday in '65 wave their folks goodbye at the station. We found the girl dead in Doncaster. She'd been force-fed with a bottle of paraquat. The boy slit his throat in London. We found him lying in rubbish bins just off Piccadilly Circus. Forensic proved that he'd killed the girl. We've identified *one hundred and fifty cases* . . . and we haven't even begun to delve into the whole thing fully yet. I had someone do a perfunctory exercise on incidents prior to 1960 – there's God knows how many similar incidents stretching way way back to 1852. Eighteen-bloody-fifty-two!'

1852 . . . 1852 . . . The date seemed to register in Mark's mind. A memory from school, perhaps? No, it was somehow more significant than that . . .

'Needless to say, the whole damned thing is the country's best kept secret. It's too bloody disturbing, too insane, for the Government to let it be made public. The most incredible thing about it is that the Ministry of Defence just don't want to know.'

'And me? What about me?'

'We believed that you were possibly thrown from the train by someone who was . . .'

102

'Infected?' said Mark, and wondered how the word had sprung so readily to his lips.

'Infected . . . yes, that's an interesting word for it. Something happens to certain people on board that train, on that particular stretch of line. And in five years, we've come up with nothing.'

'What about other railway lines in other parts of the country?'

'It's *only* the King's Cross line. The major line of the entire railway system.'

'What about people who've been . . . involved, in some way? What's happened to those people who've survived?'

'It varies. Some of them have become irrevocably insane. Others recover, but just don't remember anything. You're a case in point. We keep a watching brief on as many as we can, bearing in mind our limited manpower. We're working under cover, Davies, because the top brass think that if it gets out, it will be worse than a loss of confidence in the police force – it might mean a panic.' Chadderton sipped at his whisky and looked as if he had finished talking.

'What do you think it is?' asked Mark quietly.

Chadderton shrugged. 'I don't know. We've been through every possible permutation: mass hysteria; insanity induced by some electro-magnetic, atmospheric, or chemical imbalance. Some kind of unknown disease that infects brain cells, is undetectable by conventional scientific means and has a brief but virulent effect on certain selected individuals. But in the end, we just don't know. All we know for certain is that a person boards a train at any given point on the line – it doesn't seem to matter where – and gets off at his destination, by which time he's dangerously psychopathic.' Chadderton drank again. His capacity for whisky seemed enormous.

'What about biological warfare? Aren't there some forms of nerve gas that induce psychotic behaviour?'

'Yes, there are. But don't think we haven't considered that one, either. I know what you're thinking – what if there's a canister of the stuff gone astray, or been stolen? What if it's lying under a track somewhere with a slow puncture? Or some guy's riding the train, giving everybody a squirt? The point is – this has been going on for some time. It's been going on for over one hundred and thirty years. *One hundred*

103

and thirty years. And they just didn't have nerve gas in 1852.'

'What if there is some kind of communicable mental disease? Has any research been done on that?'

'Continually. But there's still no evidence. That's why it was so important that I find out whether you wanted to kill yourself on that station platform. Perhaps you weren't thrown from that train. Perhaps you were a victim yourself.'

'Yes ... a *natural* disease that perhaps hasn't been identified.'

'What you've told me today could have an important bearing. Tell me again. You said the ... Impulse, was it? ... yeah, the Impulse sort of took you over and you couldn't help yourself. You felt compelled to kill yourself.'

'That's right. It was as if something had been ... trying to get into my mind all along ... and today, I let it in. And when it was in, it just took control.'

'If it is a disease, it's got a peculiar pathology. And for such an apparently virulent disease, it seems to confine itself to passengers on one particular stretch of line. If it's communicable, why hasn't it spread to the rest of the country? Why haven't we had a spate of nationwide mass murder? I've got to be honest with you, Davies. I don't know whether you're a nutter or not. I don't know whether what you've described to me are the symptoms of some killer disease or whether you've just had some kind of breakdown. Perhaps you've been suffering from the disease all along, contaminated by whoever threw you from that train, perhaps not. But I want you to come back with me to London and submit to examinations by experts. They should never have cancelled their watch on you. But they might find something now.'

'You haven't explained why you're not in the force, why you're no longer in charge of this special team.'

A dark cloud appeared to have spread across Chadderton's face. For an instant, he seemed to be reliving some terrible event from his past. 'I was relieved of duty because of something that happened to my wife while I was wrapped up investigating your case ...'

Two

Chadderton had spent all day in the Operations Room reading reports and comparing information on three of the most recent incidents compiled by his Second-in-Command, Hughie Simmonds. He remembered sitting back after another unsuccessful attempt to link the three together, looking around him at the hive of activity and, for an instant, feeling slightly detached. (Perhaps he had been concentrating too hard.) Simmonds was in heated conversation on the telephone; a new red marker indicating the latest incident was being placed on the glass map of Britain which occupied one full wall of the office – a thick red swathe stretching from King's Cross to Edinburgh like some horrible gash across the countryside. All the other team members seemed particularly intense today. Eight were out in the field, the remaining ten pored over paperwork or crouched over computers as the latest information was assimilated.

And then the thought had struck Chadderton forcibly: *All these deaths. All this work, all this investigation, all the paper – and we still don't know a thing. Not a bloody thing.* It was a basic, inescapable truth which depressed and angered him. It depressed him for the obvious reasons, angered him because of the top brass's refusal to admit that the situation was a serious crisis. Then and there, Chadderton made up his mind that he could no longer continue the operation in this form. The government would have to take responsibility. It was time that the Ministry of Defence were directly involved. He would make them do it or he would blow the whole damned gaff wide open. It was the only way. He could not go on. *They* could not go on.

Chadderton's Ford Capri pulled up outside his detached bungalow a little earlier than usual that night. It had just turned six as he climbed out of the car. There was a smell of burning in the air. Someone was burning rubbish in a garden; or someone's barbecue had gone disastrously wrong. The smell was acrid and made him a little nauseous. He felt hollow as he made his way up the garden path, like an empty gourd. He had taken off his jacket and pulled his tie loose from

105

around his neck even before he let himself into the house. He threw his jacket over a chair in the living room, went into the kitchen and took a can of beer from the fridge. He knew that Joyce would not be home for an hour or so yet. She had promised to take the Cortina when she visited her sister. He remembered how puzzled she had been by his insistence that she take the car rather than go by train. He realised how it must have sounded to her.

But you know I don't like driving long distances, Les . . .

I know that, Joyce, love. But I would rather you took the car.

All it's going to take is an hour on the King's Cross train.

I don't want you to use that train! Look . . . I'm sorry, love. But please, for me, will you promise to take the car? I know it sounds crazy but there's a very good reason for it that I can't tell you at the moment. Please?

And then she had smiled that 'I don't know what I'm going to do with you' smile and he had kissed her.

Chadderton moved back into the living room and sat down heavily in a padded armchair, kicking his shoes off and taking a deep gulp of beer. He could still smell that stink of burning even inside the living room. It was a thick, cloying smell. He took another sip of beer and struggled to his feet again, moving into the kitchen to make a sandwich. The garage door at the far side of the kitchen was wide open to the wall. Chadderton walked over and pushed it shut with the heel of his hand, at the same time turning back to the refrigerator. And then he stopped in mid-turn. Something had registered in the corner of his eye. He had seen a flash of blue as the door was swinging shut. He moved quickly back to the door and pulled it open.

Joyce's blue Ford Cortina was still in the garage.

Oh, Jesus . . .

Chadderton burst into the garage, examining the Cortina as if it were just a mirage, not solid reality. The smell of burning was dense in here – thick, smothering and oppressive. Chadderton could see that the sliding door giving access to the back garden had been raised. Thick, oily clouds were billowing across the neatly mown lawn and he could hear the crackling of flames as he blundered across the garage, knocking a watering can from a shelf with an echoing clatter. Something dreadful was whispering in his ear as he came out of the garage and followed the angle of the house which blocked whatever was burning from his line of vision. When he first saw it, he thought:

What the Christ is she burning a sack of rubbish on the lawn for?

And then he saw the can of gas lying beside the burning bundle. In a curiously objective way, his mind was telling him that he had seen something like this before, of course. Something on TV. It was newsreel footage of a priest who had doused himself with petrol somewhere in Asia and had sat cross-legged in the middle of the street and struck a match. And while he burned, he sat unmoving, bolt upright in the center of billowing orange flame and greasy black smoke. Chadderton could see that it looked just like that; the bundle even looked human shaped, cross-legged with hands placed calmly on knees. *God yes*, he thought, *it does look like a human being.* He could see a shred of pink material fluttering at the base of the pyre. It looked just like the fabric of Joyce's favourite dress . . . the dress she had worn that morning when she had waved him off to work . . . and the Cortina was still in the garage.

He was crying out now, a long-drawn-out howl of anguish as he blundered forward, still refusing to believe what his eyes told him. *No, this isn't happening*, he thought. *It's a cruel trick.*

In a dream, he saw himself clawing at a bath mat hanging from the washing line which stretched across the small garden to the shed. He was flapping it around the shoulders of the bundle now, like a shawl, beating and smothering the orange flame. He clawed at the flame with his bare hands as the figure toppled stiffly backwards. His hair was burning, he realised vaguely, his shirt sleeves were shrivelling and disintegrating as he watched himself beating at the fire. But there was no pain. Everything seemed to be taking place from a distance. He was an outside observer watching himself as he thrashed wildly at the burning figure. Suddenly the fire was out and the blackened shape was lost in an enveloping billow of black smoke. Now he watched himself stagger back like a puppet, his shirt blazing. *You're burning*, he told himself. *Move! You're burning* . . . And he forced his body to walk stiff-legged to the

107

small ornamental pool, ordered it to plunge face first into the icy water. Suddenly back inside his body again, he slapped at the shrivelled remains of his shirt and turned to look back at the charred mass in the middle of the lawn. It had broken into two pieces. When he saw the frizzled hand sticking up out of the ashes – the black, clutching hand with a dull metal band on one of the fingers – Chadderton's insides had turned over and out as he vomited onto the neatly cut lawn . . .

*   *   *

'. . . I began to drink. They said my judgement was being impaired by her death . . . by the drink . . .' Mark could see that Chadderton's hands were shaking. 'In a way, I'm just as much a cripple as you are, Davies. But I can't let this thing go. I know that what happened to my wife was more than a coincidence. The bastards tried to make out that she was disturbed to begin with; that maybe my involvement in the investigation had been responsible in part for putting more pressure on her, leading to her final breakdown.'

Mark could see that Chadderton was now trembling with rage. He was clenching and unclenching his fists as he continued: 'Joyce was the sanest, most stable person I've ever known. She knew nothing about the investigation. She had no reason to kill herself, no reason to do what she did . . . It's as if something knew that I was leading the investigation and got to Joyce because it knew it could get to me . . . I've got to find out just what in hell is happening to people on that train. And perhaps you might be able to help me find the answer.'

Mark sipped at his whisky. There was an almost tangible aura of physical and mental pain emanating from Chadderton which he knew only too well. He recognised the agony. 'All right, Chadderton. I'll help you as much as I can.'

'I want you to tell me more. Tell me about everything that's happened to you. Everything that you've felt since the accident.'

'The dreams have been the worst part.'

'Dreams . . .?'

Mark and Chadderton talked of dreams and nightmares.

Three

Philip Gascoyne sat opposite his wife and daughter on the King's Cross train bound for Newcastle. Grace, his wife, was not speaking to him. They had been late that morning getting to the station because of an unforeseen snarl-up of traffic at Marble Arch, which Grace had blamed entirely on Philip and his lack of organisation. What the hell? Philip had said, they had made the train with five minutes to spare, hadn't they? But Grace refused to be placated. It was no way to start a holiday. It had spoilt her whole day. And it was all his fault. *Stupid cow.*

Philip rustled his *Express* angrily and tried to read the political comment. Only two lines of newsprint registered in his brain before his thoughts returned to the previous day at work. And to Tellard, the bastard. Philip had been working as a chartered accountant for years before that poseur had been appointed to share his office. Ever since that day, Tellard had been crawling to the Director on every conceivable occasion. Grasping at every opportunity to put himself in favour, totally committed to back-stabbing anyone at all if it was to his advantage. And yesterday, Philip could cheerfully have smashed his fist right into that smug little face.

So you're off on holiday, old boy? All right for some, eh? Well, I suppose I'll just have to soldier on till you get back. Don't worry about the Hobson Account. I'll take care of it.

The Hobson Account. Philip had taken a special interest in that one and had put a lot of work into it. And God knew what Tellard would do now that he had his hands on it; what slime he would be throwing around; whose ear he would be whispering into; whose good books he would be trying to worm his way into.

God, Andy, I just don't know how he can leave me with all this. Quite apart from the other work to be done, he's just up and buggered off on holiday. He's left me with the Hobson Account too, you know. And that's a real mess, if ever there was one. Suppose I'll just have to pull it all together. Christ, some people . . .

Grace had insisted . . . demanded . . . that they go ahead

109

with their holiday. She didn't give a damn if the Hobson Account was almost at completion stage, you had to have a holiday *sometime*. Couldn't he see how selfish he was being? What about the child, Angelina? She was nine years old and really looking forward to her holiday in Bamburgh. What kind of father would let his daughter down like that? So . . . here they were sitting in the King's Cross train, hurtling towards Newcastle where they could catch a bus to take them on to Bamburgh. For two glorious, rainy weeks looking at the coastline and a bloody castle. Trust Grace to pick on the most miserable time of year possible.

And Tellard would complete the Hobson Account and take the credit for Philip's eight months of hard work.

Philip looked over the top of his newspaper at Angelina. She was sitting next to the window, pressing her face close up against the glass, distorting and pulling her features.

'Angel, don't do that!'

Angelina grudgingly pulled away from the window, mouth pouting, her right cheek rosy from the cold glass. Petulantly, she flipped open a large picture book on her knee and gave it a desultory look. She didn't like riding on trains. It was boring.

'I want some pop,' she said sullenly, without lifting her head.

'In a little while, Angel. When I've finished my paper.'

'I want it *now*!' And the picture book was slammed shut on her lap. 'Mummy says I can have it now, don't you, Mummy?'

'But you've just finished some, five minutes ago,' Philip said through gritted teeth.

Grace had been casting a critical eye over the two outrageously dressed girls sitting across the aisle. They were playing Mah Jong and smoking herbal cigarettes or something. It was disgusting and she thought they ought to be thrown off the train at the next station. At Angelina's words, she turned sharply back to Philip.

'Don't be so selfish, Philip. Get the child something to drink. Can't you see she's thirsty?'

'Yes, Grace.'

Yes, Grace. You bloody cow. I'll just jump up and run to the cafe car, Grace. Then I'll bring it back, Grace, open the carriage door if you want, Grace, and jump out.

'Do you want anything?' When he spoke, he realised that

110

his voice sounded terse and clipped. Grace didn't like it when he got angry. It made her angry too and things had a habit of escalating from there.

'Thank you. A coffee would be nice if you can be bothered,' she said, in a voice that dripped with undisguised sarcasm.

Philip snapped his paper shut, realising, perhaps for the first time since Angelina had been born, how much his daughter resembled his wife. The same nose and eyes, the same tilt of the head, the selfsame pout when she wanted something that Philip couldn't provide instantly from thin air. There seemed to be nothing at all of himself in Angelina. Like mother, like daughter. He climbed from his seat, steadying himself as the train swung on a sharp curve, and checked inside his pocket for his wallet.

'I won't be long.' Grace refused to look at him and Angelina had returned to the carriage window. She was licking it. Philip turned sharply and opened the connecting carriage door behind him, feeling Grace's eyes on his back and sensing her further annoyance that he had booked them onto second-class accommodation for the train ride. *A fine way to start a holiday.* As he passed into the adjoining carriage he let the door slam with unnecessary violence, eliciting a look of surprise from the elderly couple at his left, then headed for the buffet car.

Lurching from seat to seat down the aisle like a drunk, Philip wondered how much Grace really appreciated him. He was a chartered accountant, for Chrissakes! They had a semi-detached villa, two cars, and Angelina was attending a private school. He slaved his guts out day after day to get all that for Grace. It was all right for her sitting in splendid isolation at home; with nothing to worry about but the arrangements for the next coffee morning. For God's sake, he even paid a woman to come in and do the housework.

Oh yes, Grace wouldn't last a day in the kind of environment he had to exist in. Back-stabbing, dog-eat-dog ... wondering and waiting for the next career-minded bastard to knee you in the balls so that he could get his foot on the first rung of that ladder. And you couldn't just sit back and let them do it, either. No way! You had to use the same tactics on them *before* they had a chance to do it to you. It was like a

111

jungle sometimes, full of hidden man-traps concealing long bamboo spikes; and Philip was like an old, wise tiger who knew the game inside out. He had stalked this path many times before and knew every inch of this jungle. And the younger tigers, the newcomers to the jungle, lurked at either side of the path, waiting their chance. Waiting for him to come down lame so that they could take him. And if he played it just right, some of those other tigers would fall into the traps he knew were there. Sometimes, he would even give a little shove. And they'd end up skewered and squealing on those long, savagely pointed poles. He could wait. Even the really clever ones who avoided the traps would occasionally make a mistake. They would poke their noses out of the undergrowth, sniffing for him, and Phil the Tiger would just take their fucking heads off with one swipe of his claw. Just see if he wouldn't. You or me, pal. The law of the business jungle. *Pity you can't make your mates see sense; tell them what they've got coming if they hassle me.* But the young tigers never learned. They just kept coming. Sometimes, the guys in charge of the man-traps would . . . move them around a little . . . put one somewhere concealed, where the day before had been a clearing. So even Phil the Tiger had to watch his step occasionally.

✻   ✻   ✻

Grace watched him go with a feeling she could only admit to as contempt. She remembered how she had envisaged their life together when they had first married and she realised that she had been cheated. There was no other word for it. In six months, she was pregnant with Angelina. And all her hopes of a career at the building society had flown out of the window. She had been type-cast even then. Grace the Housewife. And it was no use Philip going on about part-time jobs – she had no intention of being a part-time anything. Her life had been screwed up because she had married someone who had seemed to fit the bill at the time but who had turned out grade-one useless. She was the one who had to make the decisions; she was the one who kept them afloat while Philip wittered on about the tough time he was having at work.

Tough time? Hah. She knew more about hard times than he could ever guess.

She had been twenty-nine when she married. Thirty when she realised that she was pregnant. They hadn't planned it – but she had still ended up pregnant and, for the life of her, she couldn't imagine any luck worse than that. In the months to follow, she had found herself forced into the role of Mother by Philip, her family and her friends. By everybody. At times, it seemed as if even her own body had betrayed her. It reminded her of a poem she had read at school.

> *Instead of the Cross the Albatross*
> *About my neck was hung.*

The presence which grew and matured inside her was like an unwanted lodger, using her body, tying her to 'home' by invisible but binding chains. A nappy chain. And during those long, long months, she had grown to hate the life inside her. It was Philip's seed. He had put it there. It was his fault. It had been the creation of a new flesh which bound them both together irrevocably. Perhaps in time, had she not become pregnant, she would have realised what a mistake she had made in marrying him. A divorce would have been relatively simple. But that was before the baby was born. Now she was tied to him by Angelina and, oh God, how she hated him for it.

Perhaps one day, when she's grown up . . .

✻   ✻   ✻

Angelina licked at the carriage window, watching as her breath frosted the glass. It was smooth and cool against her cheek and reminded her of that time last Christmas when Julie and Amanda and Ralphie had built the snowman in Amanda's garden. They had been throwing snowballs and she remembered how the snow had felt when she scooped some of it up and compressed it in her small cupped hands. It was *really* cold. Colder even than the ice in the freezer back home; colder than the little blobs of ice in the cube tray which Mummy and Daddy used for their drinks, and which stuck to your fingers when you tried to take them out. It felt really

113

good in her hands; even better when she threw it at Julie and it exploded like white cotton wool into the folded-back hood of Julie's parka.

That was what had started the snowball fight, and soon a disorganised, frenzied pitching of snow had begun at any moving target. Ralphie Goodman was the best thrower of all. He didn't like the girls, he thought they were soft. They couldn't run, they couldn't play football and they were rotten when it came to throwing snowballs. But Ralphie played a lot with the girls all the same. Angelina remembered her Daddy saying once that the Goodman kid would grow up as a *real stud* or a *prancing nancy boy* but he was damned if he knew which. Angelina did not understand what the words meant but she supposed that Daddy thought he should spend more time playing football or something. Angelina was sure that Ralphie liked her better than Julie or Amanda or anybody else in their class. She could tell sometimes by the way he looked at her when the girls were playing netball with Miss Samson in the schoolyard. She was bigger than him by about a foot, but that didn't matter. Mummy was bigger than Daddy and that didn't matter, did it?

Both the same size in bed.

Now why had she thought of that? She didn't even know what it meant.

'It's all the girls onto all the boys!' shouted Amanda, and as the girls squealed with delight, the chaotic flurrying of snow changed quickly to a bombardment of Ralphie.

'Hey, stop it! That's not fair.' Ralphie tried to scoop up snow for more ammunition, leaving himself open to attack. Jerking up his hands to his face as a snowball splattered on his temple, he began to back away as the girls zeroed in on him.

Angelina was panting in excitement, flinging snow in un-compressed, disorganised handfuls, feeling an exuberant thrill pulsing in her that was even nicer than the tingling in her fingers. She had never felt like this before. It was tingly ... yes, tingly, between her legs, and she liked it. Her arms pistoned like miniature windmills, pushing waves of snow at Ralphie's face so that he couldn't see.

'Hey, come on ...'

Almost without realising what she was doing, Angelina had flung herself at Ralphie and they both collapsed into a drift of

114

cushioning snow. She was lying on top of him, pinioning his wriggling body down under her greater weight, thrusting herself down on him and feeling tingly again.

'Get up, Angel. I can't breathe. It's not fair.'

'The girls have won!' shouted Julie.

'Get up. I can't move!'

'You can only get up if you say that you love me.' Squeals of laughter from the other girls.

'No I won't! Get off!'

'Say it or I'll keep you here forever.'

'Get off, you cow!'

Cow: That was a word she had heard many times before, when Daddy and Mummy were fighting late at night and she was supposed to be asleep in bed, but was really sitting on the upstairs landing, her fingers entwined around the banisters and straining to hear every word. She didn't like that word. Seizing a handful of snow, she crushed it down into Ralphie's face, rubbing it in hard – just like she'd seen that clown on telly, pushing a custard pie into the other clown's face. Ralphie made a glugging noise and wriggled all the more. That would teach him. The other girls' squeals of delight built up to a new crescendo, ringing sharply in the crisp winter air. And that made Angelina feel even better.

'Now-say-you-love-me-or-I-won't-never-let-you-up-again.'

Ralphie brought one thigh sharply up and rammed it against Angelina's side, throwing her off balance. As she released her grip on his arms to steady herself, Ralphie pushed hard at her chest. Angelina rolled over into the snow as Ralphie, crusted with white patches that looked like cracked icing from some giant birthday cake, struggled to his feet and wiped his face. Now he was pushing snow into Angelina's face, holding her long blonde hair with the other hand so that she could not squirm away.

Ralphie's blow had hurt her and his rough, gloved hand on her face had grazed her lip. It had really *hurt* her when he used his knee and her lip was stinging now. And she didn't like the way that Julie and Amanda were laughing, because they were laughing at her. She didn't like anybody laughing at her. Not *ever*. Even Ralphie was laughing as he stood back at last and stooped to make a snowball, as did the other girls. Angelina was the new victim as a fresh barrage of snowballs rained down on her.

'Stop it! Stop it!'

'You don't like it when it's done to you, do you?' sneered Ralphie. Angelina covered her head with her arms, feeling the muffled thumping of snow against her elbows. The tingly feeling was gone and she hated them all; how she *hated* that Ralphie Goodman most of all. She hated him more than anything in the whole wide world, and she hated the others for laughing. The bombardment stopped. Ralphie and the two girls were flinging snowballs at each other again. And Angelina knew just what to do. She was going to get even. She would make that Ralphie sorry for what he had done.

She stopped to make a snowball, her fingers clutching at the frozen ground underneath. She dragged them over the earth like a rake until she had hooked a large pebble. Compressing the snow around it, moulding it into the cup of her hands, she stood up again with waves of hate radiating at Ralphie. She took careful aim and threw the snowball at him just as hard as she could. It caught him on the forehead with a loud smacking noise and Ralphie tottered back a couple of steps, snow and ice pattering out of his gloved hands. A blank expression was stamped on his face and then, finally realising what had happened, his hands went to his face. When he looked at them again, the wool of his gloves was dark and sticky. A smudge of blood crept down over his temple. And when Julie began to scream, Ralphie began to scream, too. Scream and scream and scream. And then he turned and began to run furiously back towards home, one hand clasped to his head. He was shouting for his Mummy and Angelina thought: *Yes . . . he should play with the boys more often; he should play more football or something.* And then, she yelled after the howling figure.

'It was Amanda, Ralphie. It was Amanda!'

'I didn't . . .'

'Yes, you did. I saw you. And I'm going to tell on you.'

Amanda was crying now. And it made Angelina feel very good.

※   ※   ※

There was a line at the cafe counter as usual. Philip

116

steadied himself against a carriage window as it slowly inched along, thinking about tigers and man-traps and wondering what Tellard was doing this morning with the Hobson Account.

What a way to start a holiday. He could almost hear Grace's words in his head now. And he remembered last year, when they had holidayed in Tenerife; it had been exactly the same then. A constant round of moaning, complaining and bickering. Nothing was good enough for her. The flight was too bumpy. The hotel was dingy. There were too many people on the beach.

Too many people on the beach? Oh God, I'm sorry, Grace. If I'd known, I would have rung up the authorities; rung up the hotels and told them to cancel all their bookings.

He thought that the holiday might have loosened her up a bit, made her relax. He remembered that night in the hotel when he had bought a bottle of expensive plonk from the hotel bar and had tried to talk her into doing it. She had laughed at him and told him just how pathetic she thought he was. What kind of marriage could you have if there wasn't any sex, anyway? She hadn't let him touch her since Angelina had been conceived. And, after the birth, it had always been completely out of the question. So, it had been a difficult birth. So what? Thousands of other mothers had difficult births and it didn't affect their sex lives afterwards, did it? What kind of husband and wife never slept together? They even had separate beds after the birth, for crying out loud! He was a man like any other man – he needed it. But she shrank back from every approach he made. She couldn't blame him if she found out what he had been doing ever since she had got pregnant and hung that 'No Entry' sign around her waist. He was a man. Even though she might think at times he was less than that. *If you don't think I'm a man, then why not give me a chance to prove it, you cow?* If he didn't get it sometimes, he would burst apart. What with the pressure and frustration at work, he was entitled to blow off a little steam. So what if he paid cash for it? He certainly wasn't going to get it for free – not from Grace.

They couldn't even discuss it.

What she needs is a good fucking. Whether she wants it or not.

The thought sprang into his mind. It was a natural progression from his own thoughts but it seemed to have sprung independent and ready-made into his mind.

A good slapping around is what she deserves for everything she's put you through. Ungrateful bitch. Doesn't she know that she owes everything she's got to you? Yeah . . .

A young man bumped against Philip, trying to pass him.

'There's a line here!' snapped Philip. The young man apologised and stood behind him, and his reaction, the look on his face, made Phil the Tiger feel good. He remembered that day nine years ago when Grace had felt the labour pains. It was nine o'clock in the evening. He was watching *Kojak* and she was sitting on the sofa reading some women's magazine. When she first started complaining, he assumed that it was just the usual moans and groans. She had been like that every day since they found out that she was pregnant. But then he had realised that it was *the time*. He'd packed quickly and got her into the car with a minimum of fuss. Everything had worked out okay. There were no traffic snarl-ups that she could have blamed on him and they arrived at the hospital without incident. They had taken her straight in and Philip followed. They had put a mask on him and he had gone into the delivery room. He could smell that peculiar antiseptic smell that always made him so afraid of hospitals; and when Grace's labour started in earnest, he sat by his wife (just as he had promised he would) holding her hand. She began to squeeze it, as if she was hanging on for grim death and, oh God, it was terrible. He wanted to be somewhere else, anywhere else so long as it was away from that delivery room. He didn't want to stay and watch and listen . . .

It was going to be a difficult birth. There were problems that had not been foreseen and when the nurse said that she thought he had better leave for the time being, Philip felt like getting up and dashing straight out of the room. He had left and he could still hear her cries. They seemed to have set up an echo which reverberated inside his head. He just couldn't bear to be there any more. He had to get away.

Fifteen minutes later he was standing in the bar knocking back brandies when Trudi walked in. She didn't usually tout around pubs; he knew that she was strictly By Appointment Only, so business must have been bad. She made her way to

118

the bar, not seeing him at first, casting a perfunctory glance around for potential customers. Her hair was piled up on her head in a style that had come and gone with the '60s but which might have come back into fashion, and she was wearing that green mini skirt with the gold chain around the waist that always turned him on so much. She had the biggest pair he could ever remember seeing; all the more pronounced by the overly tight sweater she was wearing. When she saw him it was like greeting an old friend.

'Haven't seen you for a couple of weeks, darling. Not being unfaithful to me, I hope,' she said.

Phil immediately began to feel much better. He bought her a brandy and she was nice to him; much nicer than that bitch Grace had ever been.

As his car pulled up outside Trudi's flat and he handed her a ten pound note, they had decided in the hospital that it was going to be a breech birth. Minutes later, in Trudi's flat, Phil was lying on top of her on a rumpled bedstead. Her skirt was pulled roughly up around her waist, the gold chain clink-clink-clinking as he entered her. He pulled up her sweater to expose her breasts as she began to push against his hips, driving him inwards and moaning in perfect pretence: 'Come on, Tiger. Come on . . . show me what you've got . . .'

*   *   *

Grace watched Angelina drawing on the breath-frosted window, writing her name in big, scrawling letters, and thought: *There's more of your father in you than there is of me. It's not surprising, after all. You're his child, not mine.*

Vividly she remembered the pain of bringing Angelina into the world, a pain that Philip had forced her to endure. That day in the delivery room – *delivery room . . . delivery . . . as if I was a parcel to be opened, or something* – was burnt into her mind. She had been to the expectant mothers' classes, she knew just what to do and what to expect. The deep breathing and the pushing. But that still had not stopped her feeling as frightened as hell on the day. Nor had they told her what the pain would be like. She remembered clutching at the oxygen mask, screaming and sobbing because the pain was much greater than she had expected. And Philip sitting there, ineffectual as always.

Why can't you help me? she had almost howled. *It's all your fault, so why can't you do something about the pain?*

Then her vision had blurred: the figures were swimming spectrally, looming above her with distorted hands and faces. But Philip was gone; her pathetic excuse for a husband had deserted her after promising that he would stay for the birth. She might have known that his one show of affection, his big decision to see the birth through with her, was nothing but a bloody sham. It was the least he could have done. In her pain, she realised just how much she hated him. And just how much she hated the small creature inside her.

One of the nurses was saying that there were problems, but that there was nothing to worry about. She would have a lovely, healthy baby very soon.

'Now come on, dear. Deep breaths. That's it . . .' *And the pain had begun again, pain that she could never have believed possible.*

'. . . Come on, Tiger. Come on . . .' *And Philip had let her have it, had really let her have it. He was showing her just what it was all about.* And she was saying: 'Oh yes, yes, I'm sorry . . . I never realised . . .'

. . . And the pain was so great and it was all his fault and, oh my God, I hate you, Philip, I hate the first time I ever set eyes on you, hate the time I let you touch me . . .

'. . . I'll show you, Grace. You like it, Grace, don't you? Don't you . . . ?'

. . . And I hate this . . . hate this . . . parasite you've put inside me. Damn you, Philip, and damn your child, damn you to hell for what you've done to me . . .

. . . Coming . . . coming . . . coming inside the bitch. That's it . . . screw the bitch . . . screw . . .

. . . Damn you to hell . . .

. . . Dying away now . . . going . . . drifting away . . . drifting . . .

. . . Damn you, damn you, damn you, damn you, damn you damn you . . .

'Oh, Mrs Gascoyne! You've got a lovely baby girl . . .'

❉   ❉   ❉

And Something that rode the lines could see that its long waiting had been justified. Could see how good it was . . . a perfect union, built on hate . . . so rare to find . . . how nice was the Tasting . . . and how easily could such empty vessels be filled. The Time was almost upon them . . . almost . . .

*   *   *

Angelina was listening to the sound that the train was making on the railway lines when her Daddy came back with the lemonade. She had been listening for ages, it seemed; listening to its lilting rhythm.

> *Kuh-huh kuh-huh duh-diddle duh-huh.*
> *Kuh-huh kuh-huh duh-diddle duh-huh.*

It was like a nursery rhyme in a foreign language, thought Angelina. There were words in there, she was sure, and if she listened for long enough, perhaps they would become clearer. Perhaps she could hear what they were trying to say.

Daddy had placed the lemonade can on the table in front of her but he had forgotten to bring Mummy's coffee and she was mad. Angelina was too busy listening to the nice train noise to notice the funny look in Daddy's eyes. He was telling Mummy to follow him forward to the next carriage. He had something very important to show her and Mummy was telling him not to be so stupid and to sit down. But Daddy was insisting that she go, and everyone was looking at her now and she was really getting angry because she didn't want to be disturbed. The two girls sitting across the way were smiling and shaking their heads and she could tell that Mummy didn't like that very much, either.

> *Kuh-huh kuh-huh duh-diddle duh-huh*
> *Duh-diddle duh-huh hey diddle diddle*
> *the cat and the fiddle . . .*

Mummy was getting up now and telling Daddy that this had better be *really* important or he was going to be for it. Daddy was telling her that they'd be back in a minute, telling Angelina to drink her pop like a good little girl, but she hadn't really wanted it. She'd just wanted to get him into trouble for

121

being so spiteful. And perhaps she should have been curious about what it was that Daddy thought was so important, but Angelina didn't care. She just wanted to sit and listen to the sound. Because she was sure that there were words in there somewhere; that the train was speaking to her in some strange way, using words that she couldn't understand at the moment, but that she would make out if she listened for long enough. It was trying to tell her something . . . something . . . and it was going to be nice, she knew.

Kuh-huh kuh-huh duh-diddle duh-huh . . .

*   *   *

Grace followed reluctantly behind Philip as he bustled ahead of her, aware of the faces on her back, sensing the sniggers and the snide comments. What on earth was the matter with him? They reached the furthest end of the carriage and Philip was pulling open the door, looking at her and beckoning with an idiot grin on his face. Something was wrong with that grin. She couldn't quite understand why it made her feel uneasy. It was . . . well, glacial.

She stormed past him into the enclosed connecting section of the train which separated the two carriages, hearing the door slide shut behind them. Turning furiously with hands on hips, she saw that he was just standing, still smiling that idiot's smile at her.

'All right, Philip. What the hell's wrong with you?'

Philip smiled that crooked smile again and held a finger up to his lips indicating that he wanted her to be quiet. He looked at the toilet door. It was engaged. Grace could feel anger bubbling up and over.

'Take that stupid smile off your face and tell me what's going on . . .'

The toilet door opened and an elderly man bundled out, looking slightly embarrassed to see them standing there. Grace bit down on the string of abuse she was about to hurl at Philip until the old man passed out of sight into the next carriage. The slight wait served to cool the worst excess of her temper.

'Now what . . . ?'

Philip was still smiling as he seized her roughly by the arm and shoved her into the toilet. The unexpected force took her completely by surprise as she clattered into the small cubicle, hearing him follow behind her, slamming the door and locking it. The noise of the train seemed somehow more accentuated within the close confines of the cubicle. Grace turned furiously, ready to aim a blow at the stupid grin on Philip's face. But he had taken her arms and thrust her backwards against the wall, banging her leg on the toilet seat.

'Philip . . .' she cried out in rage and pain, but his hand was over her mouth and he had pinned her to the wall. She had never realised how strong he was. She could not move and she was very, very frightened as Philip's face pressed closely to hers and she could see his fixed, glittering eyes. *My God*, she thought, *he's gone mad. He's insane!* And now he was pulling at the buttons on her skirt. Her arm flapped out uselessly, trying to stop him, but he slammed her back again, pulling the skirt down, letting it drop around her knees. He began to claw at her slip.

Oh my God, she thought. *He's going to rape me. My own husband's going to rape me!*

Philip was grunting like an animal as he fumbled with his own clothing, and all Grace could see were those staring, glacial eyes as he thrust roughly at her. The pain of the forced entry made her gag against Philip's sweating palm. She tried to bite him, but now he was finally inside, ramming her hard against the toilet wall.

And, as he entered, that which was in him entered also. It was no longer rape. Grace's hands moved up around Philip's neck, braced on his shoulders, and Philip took his hand away from her mouth, because it was all right now. Yes, it was all right. It was a frenzied, torrid coupling, unlike anything they had ever experienced before. It was ten years of pleasure denied. They submitted to it, revelled in it, savoured it greedily. It was a hard, unrefined pleasure, mutually selfish and savage. When they came, they came together like the magazine stories that Grace read so much. And the coming was like the flowering of a dark, violet flower; blossoming and spreading like black fire in their veins and merging their two selves into one flesh. It was a dark tasting of forbidden fruit. A taste of gratification, dark fulfilment and orgiastic pleasure.

123

But it had nothing to do with love.

✻   ✻   ✻

When the straight-backed woman and her loopy husband came back to their seats, the two girls sitting opposite looked up from their Mah Jong game expecting an entertaining family squabble. But when they saw that great big vapid grin on both their faces, it looked like everything was okay, after all. They'd had their 'grown-up' talk out of earshot of the kid and everything was just fine. They were holding hands when they sat down together opposite the kid, which was pretty twee for such a sour-faced middle-aged couple. They were looking at each other now as if they were sharing some great big Secret that no one else in the world could know. Big deal.

✻   ✻   ✻

Philip and Grace were looking at Angelina expectantly as she sat staring out of the window. She was humming in an abstract kind of way. It was a humming that somehow seemed to match the clattering of the rails as the train hurtled on towards Newcastle. It might have seemed to an outside observer that two over-protective parents were waiting with indulgent anticipation while their daughter tried to solve some simple problem of mental arithmetic.

Angelina was smiling now. The mistiness of her expression was clearing and she was sitting forward, still humming. Except that now she knew the melody. Now, she could understand the words. She reached her hands across the table towards her parents and they leaned forward too, each clasping one small white hand. All three of them clasping hands, huddled forward and looking deeply into each other's eyes. Oh and smiling, always smiling. A smile of wolf and wolverines.

Angelina was the fruit of their loins, after all.

Now, they were all one flesh.

124

Four

Aynsley hid in the darkest recess of a dilapidated and abandoned railway carriage which, many years before, had been shunted onto a rusted stretch of line overgrown with weeds and dandelions. The carriage nestled there amid a haphazard jigsaw of railway sidings and tracks in the goods yard. Far away, the distant rumblings in the rails indicated that life continued. But in the isolated yard, there was no movement. No indication of life.

He crouched in a corner amongst the accumulated filth of years, his tailored Savile Row suit torn, one sleeve flapping uselessly. There were ragged marks on his upper cheeks and temples where he had gouged his hands across his face. Blood and rust were caked in his hair. He was sitting in a pool of diesel oil and he could feel its slimy wetness on his thighs. But he knew he could not move . . . dare not move . . . until the Voice in his head told him what to do. And so he had remained for the last fifteen hours, after his headlong and terrified flight had brought him gasping to the goods yard. He had been trying to escape. But he knew now that he could never escape and that he had to do what the Voice said. It was in his head and it had guided him to the goods yard, because this was part of its domain.

He was curled up tightly like a foetus in the corner, knowing that he must remain as still as he could, because that was what he had been told to do. He remembered one day when he was a little boy at school and the class had been particularly noisy. The form teacher had told everyone to be quiet for five minutes just to see how quiet they could be. So they had sat without speaking, listening to the silence. But Aynsley had been better than that today, much better than that. A mouse had scampered across his leg, not knowing that he was there and alive. Now wasn't that *ever* so quiet? He hoped that the Voice would be pleased by that.

Slats of murky light had been shining through the deteriorating panelling of the carriage walls and he had watched as the angle of the beams had slowly shifted. He had watched them creep across the littered floor towards him as the sun rose and moved across the sky. The sun was setting now, he realised, and the light was only three feet from his head. The Voice had told him to hide in the darkness, not to be seen in the light, and not to move. But Aynsley knew that if he stayed there much longer without moving, the nearest thin splinter of light would find him in his hiding place and he would be forced to move. He would be forced to seek out another dark corner. But that would mean disobeying one of the Voice's direct orders and the prospect of the advancing finger of light made him quiver in dreadful apprehension. Sweat crept down his face and across his nose in rivulets. He would have to move. And when the Voice came back, it would know that he had disobeyed. He was moaning now, darting nervous glances around the carriage, looking for some solution to his problem. And suddenly, he had it.

He screwed his eyes tightly shut. In his head, behind his eyes, it was really dark. He could hide in there. He was alone, there was no light and he would not move. There were little pictures in there, too. As he watched, he could see a man and a woman. They were walking on a beach and a little white dog was scampering around their heels. The man was throwing a piece of driftwood and the dog was bulleting across the sand to retrieve it, kicking up little clods of sand. And it seemed to Aynsley, as he looked closer, that the man on the beach looked a little like himself. Except that he looked younger, more self-assured. And he was smiling a big smile and looking at his wife, and she was smiling too.

There were rocks ahead. Big rocks and little rocks, all covered in seaweed, and there were pools with little creatures in them. And now the man and the woman were looking into the pools, looking at the creatures. The woman was poking into one of the pools with the piece of driftwood and saying: *Charles, come and look at this.* The man was walking across and looking into the pool, and the woman was saying: *I've just seen the most peculiar thing. It's slithered under that rock there.* The man was taking the driftwood from her and leaning down across the pool. He was pushing the wood down into the sand at the base of the rock, wedging it underneath, and the woman was laughing and saying: *Careful, darling. You nearly went in that time.* And the man laughed back: *Won't be the first time I've put my foot in it.* He was heav-

126

ing on the rock, turning it up in the water to see what was underneath . . . And the woman was shrinking back in alarm, saying: *Oh, God, Charles, what on earth is that?* The man had dropped the driftwood, a look of disgust on his face, pulling away from the rock as it lolled back into a new position in the water. He was holding back the dog as it barked and yapped at the thing they had uncovered, green ripples of water lapping back at them . . .

Turning over rocks and finding something nasty . . .

. . . nasty . . . crawled out from under a rock . . .

. . . turned over a rock . . .

. . . and he had asked Mark what had happened. And Mark had opened his mind. And it was like turning over a rock in a deep green, slimy pool and finding . . . something that had been hiding in there all the time . . . and he had turned it over and . . . it had come out . . . and . . . *oh, no no no no no no no no . . .*

Aynsley clasped his clenched fists to his eyes to block out the memory. He was whimpering, crushing the remembrance out of his mind. Because if He came back and found him thinking about what had happened, the consequences would be too terrible to contemplate. He forced it back into the deepest part of his brain, could feel his eyes on the knuckles of his fingers. They felt like small, swollen grapes. And when the memory had gone, Aynsley relaxed the pressure and looked at what he had clenched so tightly in his hands. He looked at the spool of recording tape and wondered what the Voice wanted him to do with it. He would destroy the tape if that was what the Voice wanted. He would eat it. Yes, he would eat it and no one would ever know. No one . . .

Something had stirred in the darkness. He was sure of it. He had heard a noise; a scuffling, shifting movement, somewhere close. Aynsley's eyes were wide open and staring as, not daring to move, he darted nervous glances at every corner, every pool of shadow. The shafts of light were only ten inches from his head now. The noise came again and Aynsley realised that it emanated, not from the darkness of the carriage, but from the darkness behind his eyelids. A dark and distant fluttering of wings. Quietly at first, but building, coming closer. It was flying towards him.

The man shrank back farther into the corner, clasping the

spool of tape before him in a prayer-like gesture, and it was like a whirlwind as it came; a terrifying vortex of eyes and claws. He began to scream in his mind: *I haven't moved . . . I've stayed here in the dark, just like you told me to . . . I haven't been seen. And I'll do anything you tell me. The tape, what about the tape?*

It was here now. In the carriage with him. And the man was whimpering and crying and laughing, curling up tightly in the corner of the carriage. It surrounded him. It filled the darkness – *was* the darkness. He could feel its touch in every pore of his skin, a touch of snakes; burning, crawling snakes. And eyes. A thousand disembodied eyes all around him. Eyes that could see right through his skin into his innermost soul; eyes that could see his fear. Aynsley realised suddenly that it was feeding from him. Feeding and growing strong; feeding on his . . .

He waited in terror; waited for it to finish; waited to be told what it wanted him to do, reliving the terror of what he had seen in the clinic earlier that day and of his desperate, hopeless attempt to run away. It was in his mind. How could he ever run away from that? He screwed his eyes shut and waited. The snakes were creeping and slithering behind his eyes, squirming into his brain, feeding there and returning. And then Aynsley had a brief glimpse, deep deep down beneath the snakes, of another picture. It was the young man on the beach again. The young man who looked so much like himself. But this time, the young man was looking straight at him. The picture was gone as suddenly as it had appeared, flashing briefly on the backdrop of his mind. A split-second, single frame from a piece of movie film in his head. It had submerged, been swamped by a sea of twisting, writhing snakes. But in spite of his terror, the face in the picture had registered its plea before vanishing forever.

You can find out. You can discover the truth, the face seemed to have said with eager intensity. *Don't you see? After all these years of searching, you can finally find out the truth. Ask . . . now . . . While you still have time.*

He knew that the face was right. He could find out. All he had to do was ask, because the Voice had all the answers. It knew everything. Still curled up, still frozen like a still-born baby in his terror, Aynsley turned his mind inside-out in one mental effort made easy by the presence of the Voice. Turned it over and out; and then *inwards* . . . to where it was feeding.

128

. . . Like turning over a stone and finding . . .

But he did not have to ask. He could see everything for himself now. And it was turning from where it fed, to where he had intruded, turning to look at him . . .

. . .*Oh, God. It's horrible, horrible* . . .

. . . And Aynsley was tilting forward in his own mind, losing his balance and falling, thrashing wildly and sliding down towards that which flowed up to meet him. He had disobeyed. He had intruded for a second time. And he would have to be punished. But, afterwards, he would be as One with the Voice. And everything would be all right again.

Aynsley knew all of this as it came to him. And as it enveloped him, taking him within its folds of darkness and wrapping him in wings of leather, his reason and sanity were devoured and swallowed by a great, greedy sucking pit.

He was At One with the Voice. He was part of it. It would act through him. And he knew what to do.

Five

Eric Morpeth was not a well man. He should not have been at work today. In fact, he should have gone off sick a month ago – he had been telling everyone that for days. But he had not told them why he felt so bad. He had not told them that he had started seeing things that weren't there. How could he? He didn't want people to think he was going loopy. He was over-tired, under the weather and due for a few days off. But did he get any sympathy? Did he hell.

It had all started, Eric guessed, on the day he had made that old woman move on. She had been asleep on one of the benches, pissed out of her mind, by the look of things, and he had only been doing his job when he had shaken her awake and told her to bugger off. But that was when the trouble had started, and Eric wished to God that he had just left the dirty old bag lying there and had moved on past her. Someone else would have spotted her soon enough and given her her marching orders.

He had heard about the accident just outside the station, of course. Everyone knew about that. He had talked to the driver of the train, Stan Gibbings, about the night it had happened. Stan didn't like to discuss it much, but he had had a few too many pints in the club, and Eric had bought him a whisky to loosen him up a little further.

'I couldn't believe it. It all seemed to happen in slow motion. But I couldn't do a thing about it. Really. Well, I mean, I couldn't, could I? Not travelling at that speed. We were doing about a hundred when I saw her in the lights. I hit the bloody horn until my arm nearly dropped off, but she didn't seem to hear. She was just sort of standing there, like. Right in the middle of the bloody track. Waving her arms about on either side of her, as if she was trying to keep her balance or something. And . . . I'll never forget . . . she was looking down at the tracks as if there was something there that terrified her. She didn't even seem to know that the train was coming . . .'

Eric knew that it was the old woman he had moved on earlier. No one had been able to identify the body, of course. There was no identification in her belongings – or what could be called belongings. Just a bundle of bloody rags. No arms, no legs. They had found one of her arms imbedded in the metalwork of the train; like a tailor's dummy arm, with the fingers sticking out. Just a big stain on the front of the train and a ragged parcel lying in the weeds at the side of the track. A wandering vagrant who had staggered blind drunk onto the lines and had never seen the train coming. But Eric knew who she was, even though he had told no one. Her name was Martha, that much he knew. He had seen her wandering the streets and hanging about the station for years. Now she was dead and Eric knew in his heart of hearts that, somehow, all his troubles had started from then.

He was off duty now. His shift had finished and he was seriously considering not turning up for work the next day. Maybe he just needed a rest. Still in his uniform, he swung his haversack over his shoulder and headed out of the station into the crowded street. He would walk home tonight. Yeah, the fresh air might do him some good. He would go home, Lucy would have his tea ready, he would have a kip in front of the telly for a bit, and then move on down to the pub for a couple of beers. Then he could lie in bed the following morning and get Lucy to telephone in that he'd picked up a bug. Yeah . . .

The day after the train had hit the old woman, Eric had seen his form master from Godley Secondary School sitting on the bench in the middle of the station. He was just sitting there, looking at him, and Eric knew with no trace of doubt whatsoever that it was Mr Jacks. But he also knew that Mr Jacks had died twenty years ago. He remembered, because he had been glad to hear the news. Yet, Jacks was sitting out there, looking at him and grinning the way he used to do at school. And he didn't seem to have aged one bit. Eric had been terrified of Mr Jacks during his entire school life. The man was a sadist, a monster, and he seemed to have taken a particular delight in focusing his attention on Eric.

Morpeth, boy! More work, less talk, laddie!

But I wasn't talking, sir.

And insolence, too. Get the strap, boy. Seems like leather is the only answer for you.

Eric had been standing at the ticket barrier and a crowd of passengers were bustling forward. As he furiously punched tickets, he could still see the silent, straight-backed figure between the jostling bodies. He could still see the same, stiff posture, the same long, bony fingers spread across the knees. And Eric could see that he was mouthing something at him, mouthing it deliberately and meaningfully so that Eric could understand.

Get me the leather, boy.

A train was pulling into Platform Eight and passengers began frantically thrusting tickets at Eric. When the rush subsided and the last of them had clattered onto the platform, he looked back to find that the bench was empty. Jacks had gone.

Eric had seen him, had *thought* he had seen him, on two other occasions. Once, when he had been on his way to Platform Nine, he could have sworn he had seen him standing there on the platform; just standing and waiting as he used to stand in the classroom, with his hands clasped in front of him. A long, cadaverously thin figure with hands that seemed to be grossly out of proportion to his body. The figure was almost in silhouette, a faint wash of grey from the overhead skylight on his features, but Eric was sure that it was him. Eric had looked away purposefully and then back again, expecting the figure to vanish as it had done earlier. But it had not. It still stood watching and waiting as Eric approached.

Eric had turned away from Platform Nine that day; away from the silent shape, knowing that it was grinning at his departing back. And Eric thought that he was going loopy, just as loopy as that other bloke who kept coming to the station day after day, hanging around, looking scared and walking back and forth to the ticket barrier.

The next time that Eric had seen him had been the worst . . . *man*, that had been bad. That was what had finally convinced him that perhaps he was working too hard and needed a rest. He had been in the station again, it was twelve-thirty and time for something to eat. He was heading along Platform Nine towards the ramp which would take him over the main line and into the station itself. Tadger and Davey Robbins would probably be waiting for him there. They would pop across the street to the pub for a pint and a sandwich. He remembered how thirsty he had felt that day.

He was walking close to the platform edge and had seen a really smart tart in a red dress; a real aristocrat. Eric reckoned that he was a pretty good judge of character and he knew, he just *knew*, that she would really go at it hammer and tongs between the sheets. She had that look on her face. Snobbish like, but dying for it. She passed him as he began to whistle 'Who's the Girl Dancing in the Red Dress?'. He turned to watch her departing figure, thinking: *Oh, yeah. I'd like to make you dance, darling.* Still moving, he had turned back to face the way he was going.

And then something had seized him by the ankle, something that felt like a hard, bony claw. Eric had gone full length on the platform, hands still in his pockets, absorbing the full impact on his chest and completely winding himself. He was lying right on the edge of the platform, and had turned his head trackside as he fell to avoid smashing his teeth out on the concrete. Before his eyes a face was rising over the rim of the platform, only inches from his own; a grinning face which he knew only too well.

Lewd thoughts, boy. Get the strap. Seems like leather's the only thing you understand.

Displaying an agility totally out of keeping with his rotund,

132

plump figure, Eric had leapt away from the platform edge and onto his feet as if he had been given an electric shock, startling passersby who had moved forward to help him. Eric turned on them sharply, said something he couldn't remember afterwards, and then looked back to the rim of the platform. The face was gone. And in sudden realisation, Eric knew that no one else on the platform had seen that horrible face or had heard what it had breathed directly into his.

Eric had fled then, without looking back. He gasped in air and clutched at his aching chest as he pounded across the ramp, while passersby watched in astonishment or amusement. And that lunch-time Tadger and Davey Robbins had begun to wonder if Eric Morpeth really was on his way to becoming an alcoholic.

A rest, that's what's needed, thought Eric as he strolled out of the main city center, following the railway embankment. *And exercise, too.* He realised just how much he had let himself go in recent years. He was really out of shape. Perhaps he should get back into training, start up the old five-a-side football again. He had been a nifty player in his day.

Not far to go, he thought. The incline of the bank evened out just above and beyond him where the embankment wall had crumbled away. From there it was a three hundred yard walk to Eric's terraced council house. He thought of former glorious days, speeding down the pitch, punching that bloody ball straight into the back of the net. He remembered vividly the wild exhilaration coursing through him as he turned for a victory run back to his team-mates, knowing what a fantastic goal he had scored and knowing that everyone else thought so, too. It made the victory all the sweeter . . .

Less talk, more work, said a voice from somewhere beyond the crumbling embankment wall. Eric stopped in his tracks, feeling the paralysis of fear spreading instantaneously from the base of his spine to his legs; coursing upwards and through his body like fiery embalming fluid. *It's a taste of leather for you, boy.* A terrifyingly familiar figure was standing on the embankment in the long grass, just beyond the tumbled, overgrown stones.

He's so tall. God almighty, he's so tall, thought Eric. It was as if he was back in the classroom; a small, plump schoolboy quivering before the towering wrath of a vengeful demigod.

133

And as the abominably tall, grinning shape moved through the grass towards him, Eric tried to run but could not. He could only stand, screaming silently in his mind as Mr Jacks leaned down towards him, blotting out the sky and reaching for him with those horribly white, skeletal hands. The grin was twisting now, spreading wider as Jacks moved down on him. It was a parody of a face. A face that had ceased to be human. It was a leering visage of shining, pearly teeth. It was the face of Mr Sardonicus. It was the face of The Joker from the Batman comics that Jacks had confiscated from Eric on his second day at Godley Secondary.

Yes, I'm afraid that it's the leather for you, boy. And that face was next to his, eyes glittering like green marbles, furrowed crow's-feet wrinkling outwards insanely. Eric could smell the cheap tobacco on Jacks' breath: the tobacco that he always stuffed into that Meerschaum pipe of his, stinking the classroom out and giving Eric headaches. He could almost taste it. He could taste something else, too: blood in his mouth where his teeth had clamped in paroxysm on his tongue. He could taste raw fear in the pit of his stomach, fear that spilled out from his guts. The hands were around his neck now, squeezing and squeezing. Eric could feel his eyeballs beginning to pop under the pressure and, unable to resist, felt his senses blurring. He was being carried now, he thought. Half carried, half dragged over the fallen rubble towards the railway embankment. Dimly, he could feel the ragged stones beneath his feet and then a hissing and swishing as he was pulled into the long grass. And all the time, the towering shadow above him blotted out the light. He became aware that he was moaning as he was laid down in the grass, the stalks and stems waving above his line of vision. He had wet his pants. And the towering figure stood above him; long, long legs like stilts stretching up into the sky, all perspective distorted. In its hands it now held a stiff leather strap that was somehow much, much too long and straight, with a savage point at one end. When the terrible leering head swooped down on him from the sky, brandishing that terrible strap, Eric tried to find his voice and give vent to his terror.

The face filled the sky, rushing down to him. And it was black now. Everything was black. There was purple pain at his throat. Purple, boiling pain tearing at his throat. And the terrible pain helped Eric to find the scream which had been building inside him. He screamed and screamed and screamed. But the screaming was always in his mind. And Eric went quietly to his death.

Six

When Aynsley stood up from the corpse, wrenching the pointed iron railing from the ticket collector's throat, he knew that he had pleased his Master.

Come, the Master had said. And he had left the sanctuary of the abandoned railway carriage and followed the fluttering of wings along the track. It was getting dark now and Aynsley had kept to the shadows as he moved, losing all sense of time and not knowing how long he had shambled along by the side of the tracks; the beating of wings always ahead of him and leading him to his destination. When the wings flurried away from the track and up a steep, grassed embankment, Aynsley followed on all fours, crawling like an animal, clutching at the tall grass for support. There was a wall at the top; part of it had fallen down and he could see a small street beyond.

There, said the Master. And Aynsley had torn the rusted metal railing from the embankment fence before returning to the long grass again where he crouched, waiting for his next instruction.

Wait, said the Master. He sat still and silent for a long time. Just as he had waited in the railway carriage. Eventually, the Chosen Food had come.

Aynsley had moved quickly and had not been seen. He had killed the man in the manner that the Master had instructed him. And the Tasting of fear had been good.

Aynsley slumped cross-legged into the long grass beside the body, head cocked to one side like an attentive child as he waited for further instructions. A marionette with its strings cut. He had obeyed as he knew he would always obey. He had

135

been wrong to call Him a 'Voice'. He was, always had been, his Master. And all he wished was to serve.

Good, said the Master, *The Tasting of the little man's fear was good. And now, the Time of Arrival is almost upon them. Three have been chosen. My Catalysts. But first, One Who was Chosen has twice denied Me of the Tasting. He must be tasted.* Aynsley began to nod his head vigorously in understanding and agreement. *Now!* said the Master; this time so loudly that Aynsley could hear the echoing in his head. He pulled himself awkwardly to his feet and looked back down the embankment to the railway lines. There was a flurry of wings in his head again, like a pigeon in a loft. And, as he watched, Aynsley became aware of the power in the railway lines: a throbbing, powerful, living force which he alone could see and feel. The power in the rails would show him where to go. And when the power could go no further, when the lines could go no further, the flapping of leathery wings in his mind would lead him. And when he got to where he was going, the Tasting would be good.

'Davies . . .' muttered Aynsley. He began to descend, his foot catching in a tangle of weeds. He fell the rest of the way, crashing through the grass and tangled roots, rolling into the gravel-filled gully at the side of the track. The steel rail beside him was surging with power. He scrabbled forward on his belly until the rail lay directly before him, only inches from his face. It was alive. Yes, the rails were *alive*. With each pulse, he could see the veins and arteries in the metal and realised that the line itself was an artery of Something Much Greater. He knew what he had to do. He gripped the rail tightly with both hands and felt the power flowing into him.

This way . . . this way . . .

Aynsley gave a stiff, exaggerated nod and then began to laugh. A low, chuckling laugh which began deep down inside and gradually convulsed him. There was no humor in it. The laughter was not human. He climbed to his feet again and began to follow, shambling forward in the deep shadows of the embankment, one foot moving awkwardly after the other.

'Davies . . .'

Seven

Mark had been talking for over an hour.

The sun was beginning to go down, throwing the city sky-line into bas relief as it crept down below the horizon. Clouds of starlings flocked and swarmed in the darkening sky towards the city center, clustering for the night on every available ledge of every available building, their noise almost drowning the traffic sounds of the homeward-bound nine-to-five population.

Chadderton sat and listened, his head on one side, a chubby forefinger placed thoughtfully against his temple. The bottle of whisky on the table beside him was nearly empty but he did not feel the alcohol's effect. It took a lot more than that to get some reaction from him these days. Yes, sir, a lot more. Davies was describing every dream that he had experienced and Chadderton realised that it was as if some inner floodgate had been opened inside him. It all just poured out. And it confirmed what he had always thought about the man sitting opposite him.

Davies was deranged.

He was telling him about another dream now, but the format was the same as all the others: standing stones, prehistoric carved rocks, burial chambers and sacrifices; the product of a sick mind. Davies had clearly lost control and Chadderton was faced with two choices: Davies' mental problems were simply a result of his fall from the train, or – and this was a much more crucial possibility – he was suffering from the same 'disease' that all the other poor bastards travelling on the King's Cross train had contracted. Davies was *alive*. And Chadderton realised that even if he was no longer in charge of operations, someone would still listen to him if he was able to turn up with living evidence. Inwardly, he cursed his own shortsightedness in the Davies affair. Perhaps wrongly, they had assumed that a surviving victim of an attack who had no memory of the incident would be of no further use to them. But he now realised ruefully that Davies should have been given a continuous intensive examination by experts in the months follow-ing his emergence from coma – and screw the lack of resources

137

and manpower. Of course, the media interest and coverage had not helped matters. Even Davies' psychiatrist – who was it? Aynsley, yes that's right, Aynsley – had not been given the full, inside story.

Perhaps Davies had picked up from his intended killer a strain of this . . . 'mental bug' . . . or whatever the hell it was. Perhaps the 'bug' had run its full virulent course while Davies was in coma, leaving him now with only a trace, a non-psychotic trace. Perhaps? Perhaps? Chadderton believed that the best thing to do was to go along with Davies for the moment and try to persuade him to help them; persuade him to go back and submit to examination by specialists. Perhaps *they* would find something . . .

Davies was telling him about another dream, again of standing stones – a horribly graphic dream of a girl with her lips sewn together. And, as he talked, Chadderton remembered how his own horror had happened. He reached down to the table and poured the remainder of the whisky into his glass. He gulped it down in one draught and began absently to caress the scar tissue on his forearm as he listened to Mark's talk of dreams. Davies was describing a dream where he had been transported to a long avenue of standing stones on a remote isle. And something that belonged in a nightmare was chasing him . . . finally catching up with him.

'Oh, God . . .' Mark suddenly stopped. His face looked deathly white.

'What's wrong?'

'When I woke up, I went to the bathroom. That's when I heard my daughter calling out in her sleep. I went in to comfort her and she woke up. She told me that she had seen Robbie, that he had visited her before. She knew that he was dead, knew that he belonged to the Ghost Train Man . . .'

'You mentioned it to her, that's all. You must have told her about your dreams, or maybe she listened to a conversation you had with your wife. Kids can be very impressionable.'

'No!' snapped Mark fiercely, 'that's just the point, don't you see? I never mentioned anything about the dreams to my daughter. Why should I? And I never even told Joanne anything about that particular dream. But Helen was dreaming of Robbie! Jesus Christ, I don't understand how . . .' Davies was running a hand through his hair, and then a sudden realisation

138

hit him. 'If what I've got is some kind of unknown hallucinatory mental disease, I could pass it on, couldn't I? I could be contagious. Perhaps Helen's caught something from me.'

'Take it easy . . .'

'You've got to drive me home, Chadderton. I've got a bad feeling about this.'

'You said that you would do anything you could to help, Davies.'

'I will. But you've got to drive me home now.' He looked at his watch. 'I've been gone all day. Jo will be worried sick about me.'

'I want you to undergo an examination under intensive medical supervision, Davies.'

'Yes, yes. I'll do anything you say. But for God's sake drive me home now.'

'Okay.' Chadderton stood up, draining his glass. 'We'll need to tell your wife all about it, I suppose.' Mark was pulling on his jacket, looking at his watch again. And Chadderton thought about what he had said about being contagious. He had pulled him away from a train, had practically carried him back to his hotel room and had spent all afternoon cooped up with him. If Davies was right, then there was a fair chance that he might have transmitted whatever it was to him. In his heart of hearts, Chadderton couldn't have given a shit. He was dead inside already. 'The sooner we get you into an observation ward the better. Don't worry about your wife and kid. If what you say is true, we'll look after them.'

'We?'

'Okay, Davies. *They.*' Chadderton pointed to Mark's half full whisky glass. 'You want that?' Mark shook his head. Chadderton picked it up and drained it.

'Please. We've got to hurry. I've a . . . feeling . . . that something bad is going to happen. Something terrible. I've got to go home, now.'

Chadderton pulled on his coat and carefully scrutinised Davies as they headed for the door. *All right,* he thought. *I'll take you home. But then we're both heading south, even if I have to hold a fucking gun to your head, Davies.*

139

Eight

Joanne could wait no longer. She flipped through the small note-pad on the telephone table in the hall until she found the number for Aynsley's clinic, picked up the receiver and dialled. Helen was in the living room, sitting on the carpet and watching a video cassette of cartoons that Mark had recorded for her last week. A medley of cartoon noises drifted into the hall as Joanne listened to the ringing tone at the other end. After a few seconds, a young woman with an all-purpose accent answered.

'Can I help you?'

'Hello, my name's Mrs Davies. I was just wondering if my husband has been in to see Dr Aynsley today.'

'Well, Dr Aynsley hasn't turned up today, I'm afraid. But if you like, I can check his appointment sheet.'

'Yes, please.' Joanne waited and worried. She remembered how Mark had been this morning; his disconcerting, faraway look, the deathly white pallor of his face. And she remembered how she had felt. A bad feeling that had crept into her mind increasingly of late: *I don't think I can stand much more of this.* But she had pushed that thought out of her mind again. Mark needed her now more than ever. And she needed him. She remembered Mark saying: *I know what I've got to do.* Within half an hour he had left the house again without saying another word, without giving her any of the assurances that he usually gave. It was almost four-thirty now and Joanne cursed herself for letting him go out again in that state, and for not doing something about his absence earlier.

'Hello, Mrs Davies?'

'Yes.' Frightened now. Her heart thudding loudly in her chest for no reason she could immediately identify.

'No, I'm afraid Mr Davies didn't have an appointment today. Why? Should he have?'

'No . . . I wasn't sure.'

'But I see that he does have an appointment for Wednesday morning at ten. I'm afraid we have no idea what's happened to Dr Aynsley, Mrs Davies. He hasn't phoned in – so I'm not sure whether alternative arrangements can be made yet. Can I ring you back? We're in rather a turmoil today. There was a break-in last night, you see . . .'

'Oh, I'm awfully sorry. Yes of course. If you could ring me, please, I'd be very grateful.'

There was only one other alternative now, Joanne thought as she replaced the receiver. The station. He must have gone back to the station. She walked quickly back into the kitchen, locking the door and window. When she returned to the living room, Helen was kneeling forward only a few inches from the television screen, scrutinising Daffy Duck as a low railway bridge slammed him from the roof of a fast-moving train. His flattened body rattled across the tracks like a spinning ten-penny piece.

'Come on, darling. We're going for a drive.'

'Where are we going?' Eyes still glued to the screen as Daffy straightened himself out again.

'I think we'll go to the railway station.'

'Will Daddy be there?'

'Perhaps.'

'All right.' Helen tottered to her feet, pressed the 'off' switch on the video, just as Daddy had shown her, and pulled the plug from its socket in the skirting board. For some reason she could not understand, Joanne felt emotion choking up into her throat as she watched Helen run into the hall, jump up onto the telephone seat and pull her anorak from the peg on the wall.

'Why is Daddy at the station?' asked Helen five minutes later, her rag doll, Looby-Lu, cradled in one arm as Joanne closed the front door and locked it. 'Has he been away or is he going somewhere?'

Joanne thought: *Both, my love. And we can't do anything to help him.* Then, she answered: 'He's been away and I expect he'll be waiting for us to collect him now.'

The car stood a little way off in the driveway in the shadow of a hedge which stretched the two hundred-foot length of the drive to the road. It was very quiet tonight, but then it was quiet most nights in this neighbourhood. Fields bordered the back of the house and their nearest neighbour, Mrs Frederickson, lived five hundred yards away down the hill and out of sight.

Joanne wondered what she would say if she found Mark sitting on a bench in the Central Station, or huddled over a cup of coffee in the buffet. Kind, sympathetic words? Or harsh ultimatums? She just did not know. *Let's wait and see if he's there first,* she thought. *But what if he isn't there? What if I search and search and can't find him?* It was a possibility that she refused to acknowledge.

'Do you promise to be good, Helen? No bouncing around on the seat or I'll have to strap you in.'

'I'll be good.' Joanne opened the back door of the car and Helen scrambled inside, neatly arranging Looby-Lu on the seat next to her, folding her small rag arms across her lap. Joanne got into the car, squirted water onto the misted windscreen and let the wipers clean if off for a couple of seconds. The engine turned over at once and Joanne drove slowly across the crackling gravel towards the two gateposts at the entrance to the drive. Slowly, because she had once scraped the car door against one of the posts when she had approached too quickly. She remembered breaking the news to Mark, ringing him up at the office that day.

I'm sorry, I've bumped the car.

You've had an accident? Oh God, are you all right, Jo?

Yes, yes. I'm fine. It was just a scrape on the paintwork, that's all.

What happened?

I scraped a gatepost.

Where? In town?

No . . . no . . . it was the gatepost in our driveway.

You mean . . . you haven't even got the car out of the drive?

. . . No . . . she managed to squeeze out, on the verge of hysterical giggles. He was laughing now, roaring with laughter, his voice slightly distanced as he rolled back in his seat, holding the telephone away from him. And now she was laughing too, uncontrollably.

There had been lots of laughter then. But those days seemed far away now. The gateposts loomed up on either side of the car and, since the accident, Joanne was especially wary at this point. *Perhaps,* she thought, *we should get them taken out. Why have gateposts when you haven't even got a gate or . . . ?*

Helen's scream ricocheted in the confines of the car, high and shrill, turning Joanne's nerves into solid ice: 'Mummy, Mummy! *There's a maaaaan . . .*!' And from the corner of her eye, Joanne could see that the hedge was thrashing wildly at the side of the car as if it were alive. There was a flurry of movement and something crashed through the hedge and slammed down onto the hood. The car jerked as Joanne's foot came off the clutch; the engine spasmed, lurched and died. Before Joanne could register what she had seen, the windscreen starred like a giant cobweb as something hard swung against the glass.

'Helen! Get down!' And there was another savage blow, a *thunk* of something solid and the hissing of shattered glass as thousands of glittering fragments showered into the car. Joanne instinctively shielded her eyes, felt glass stinging on her cheeks and hands; Helen was still screaming wordless, bawling cries of sheer terror. Then Joanne saw the man for the first time. In an instant, she had taken in the ravaged, stained face, the matted filth, the wild streaked hair, the ragged jacket and trousers. He was pulling an iron railing back across the bonnet of the car. She could see the insane glittering of his eyes in the half-light as he lurched around the front of the car, making his way towards where she sat, raising the railing in one hand like a spear. The next few seconds seemed to go on forever.

Joanne thrusting the gears into reverse and switching on again. The engine coughing into life as the wild man rounded the front of the car and moved towards her, grasping forwards with his free hand. Her foot lifting from the clutch pedal as the other pumped hard at the accelerator. A flurry of tattered coat sleeve as a blood-streaked arm clutched at her through the gaping aperture where the windscreen had been, seizing the lapel of her coat. The face leering sideways at her through the aperture; the arm drawn back to plunge the iron spear into her body.

The car hurtled backwards up the drive with a screech of tires. Joanne saw the man twist away from the hood, but he was still clutching at the frame of the windshield and she could see his legs trailing in the gravel as the car dragged him backwards. She hammered at his fingers with the heel of her free hand, steering blind with the other, and heard a shivering clang as the iron railing spun away across the drive. Now the man was clutching the metalwork with both hands as the car slewed off the drive into the garden and continued backwards towards the house, with Helen screaming: '*Mummeeeeee* . . .' Then the hands were gone from the car and Joanne could see the ragged body rolling over and over on the grass, smashing into the ornamental fountain and knocking it into the pool. She twisted round, correcting her steering as the car roared towards the front of the house, tugged desperately at the wheel, braked . . . and then the car slammed sideways into the porch. More glass flew through the air; Joanne was jerked to one side as the panelling of the offside door crumpled inwards under the impact. There was another muffled thump as Helen fell between the seats in the back.

Joanne grabbed the keys from the dashboard, kicked open the door and climbed out. The man was still lying on the grass, moving faintly and dazedly. She opened the car's rear door. Helen was sobbing and Joanne lifted her quickly out from between the seats; the Looby-Lu doll fell forgotten onto the pathway. Joanne held Helen to her as if she were only six months old again, cradling her daughter in her arms as she ran round the car to the front door of the house. She could feel her heart pounding, her neck aching badly due to the whiplash effect in the car. She groped at the lock with her keys, glancing backwards over her shoulder to see the man rising groggily to his feet. Stifling a cry, she jammed a key into the lock. But it wasn't the right one; it was the key to the back door – not the front – and the lock would not turn. The man was looking around on the grass; he had retrieved the iron railing and was picking it up as Joanne fumbled for the correct key, found it and rammed it into the lock. When she looked back, the man was shambling across the lawn towards her and gabbling like a maniac, his head bowed and with the railing clenched in his fist. Helen was whimpering, her arms wrapped tightly around Joanne's neck. She began to shout: 'He's coming, Mummy! He's coming . . .'

The door was suddenly open and Joanne was through quicker than thought, slamming it shut behind her and leaning heavily against the wood. Fighting for breath, she twisted the lock and felt a muffled thump on the other side. She tugged her daughter's small reluctant arms from around her neck and lowered her to the floor, focusing her attention on the telephone at the other end of the hall. The door shuddered under a heavy attack from outside. Another blow, and this time Joanne was appalled at the ferocity of the impact; instinctively, she braced herself against the panelling. Helen stood crying in the middle of the hall, not knowing where to go or what to do; wondering why her mother couldn't make the horrible man go away.

A sliver of wood whirled into the hall as the pointed tip of the iron railing burst through the wooden panelling only three inches from Joanne's head. Helen screamed again, holding her hands across her eyes to blot out everything as Joanne lurched away from the door, grabbed her daughter and moved desperately to the telephone. With a splintering crack, the railing pierced the door again, wriggling and twisting as the man pulled it free. An entire length of panelling twitched to the carpet. Terror mounting inside her, Joanne snatched up the telephone and dialled 999 – she could see the man now, a blur of shadowed movement through the long rent in the woodwork as he launched a savage attack on the door.

'Emergency. Which service, please?' said a tinny voice at the other end of the line. The railing stabbed inwards again. Turned, twisted and wrenched an entire square panel from the door.

'Police, please! And hurry . . . Oh, God . . .'

'Connecting you . . .'

The man's hand was scrabbling through the aperture towards the lock, fingers spasming and fumbling for the catch.

'Mummy! He's getting in!' Helen clutched tightly at her legs. Another shivering blow at the door. A voice on the other end of the line. But it was too late now. Too late even to blurt out an address as the door burst inwards. Joanne dropped the telephone, leaving the receiver swaying and dangling on its flex, scooped up her daughter again and bundled her into the kitchen. She slammed the door shut and could hear heavy breathing in the hall as the man entered, the heavy tread of his feet crunching on the fragments of wood that littered the hall carpet.

There's no lock on the kitchen door! Joanne realised, with horror thrilling through every fiber of her being.

She could hear an insane babbling and ranting as the man reached the telephone; a light tinkling as he picked it up, and then a frenzied scrabbling and ripping as he began to tear at the receiver like a wild animal. She could hear the snapping of the cable as it tore loose from the wall; the slam and clatter as it was thrown across the hall.

With one sweep of her arm, Joanne knocked everything from the kitchen table and, in slow motion, watched herself drag the table across the floor to the door; watched as she up-ended it, the legs sticking out into the room. The door handle was already turning as she thrust the table forward and jammed the rim underneath it. She could hear him laughing crazily as he began to throw himself at the door, knowing at the same time that it was only made of flimsy wood, that he could punch his fist right through at any moment. She moved quickly back to the kitchen bench, to the rack of table knives hanging on the wall. She took the thick, brown-handled knife with the sharpest cutting edge and turned back to face the door.

The man was still laughing, only now it was a horrible, low, chuckling noise as he twisted at the door handle and began to push with all his weight against the door. The door was opening, a shriek of protesting wood on floor tiles as the table rasped aside. Joanne moved purposefully, the terror thrust behind her, feeling ice-calm and collected deep inside as she pushed Helen down into a corner, turned the knife over in her hand so that the blade was pointing downwards and then forced herself to move towards the opening door. A claw-like hand was thrusting around the corner of the door, grasping at the wood like a mottled, hungry spider. Joanne saw herself raise the knife high, bring it down hard and sharp on the tattered arm, felt the blade sink deeply. The man shrieked and suddenly the arm was yanking away, dragging the knife backwards with it. Joanne twisted the knife away, felt the tip of the blade snap inside the arm. And the man was screaming and screaming. Quickly she threw her hip at the door, slamming it shut again. She pulled the table back into place, wedged it there and listened, panting in desperation as she held the knife high and waiting. The man was gibbering and crying, retreating from the door. She could hear his footsteps on the littered carpet again, the slight creaking of the ruined front door as he moved outside.

My God, she thought, *he's going away . . . going away . . .*

But Joanne knew that the logic of nightmare demanded that he would not go away, that he had merely retreated for an instant. She looked at the large glass windows, realising that if he should move round into the back garden, there could be no stopping him from getting to them. She could not hear him any more, could only hear her own ragged breathing. Quickly, she moved to her daughter, crouched down low amid the shattered crockery and waited. She resisted her first impulse to push the table aside and fling open the door, to dash up the stairs to the bedroom – and the telephone extension on the bedside table. What if he was still out there, lurking in the hall and waiting for her to open the door? Pressing Helen close to her breast with one hand, keeping the knife raised high in the other, she strained to hear every sound from the back garden. Just one noise was all she needed, one tell-tale sign of movement – his breathing or a footstep – and she would know that he was out there, that she could make a dash for the stairs.

She could hear moaning. A low, desperate moaning from somewhere in the darkening gloom of the back garden. She was sure of it. *Now!* she told herself. *Now!* And they were both moving forward, shambling across the kitchen below the level of the window sill towards the table, Joanne's eyes glued to the large panes for any sign of movement. She was pulling the table edge from under the door handle, wincing as the wood scraped harshly on the floor, and realising that the man must be able to hear the noise. She stood up quickly, pulled the table roughly aside and, heedless now of the noise, tugged the door open. As she turned back to Helen, she could see the dark and rearing shape beyond the kitchen window; stifled a scream as two outthrust arms lunged through the glass towards them in an explosion of glistening shards. She grasped Helen to pull her away, but the impetus of the arms was greater. Clawed fingers tangled in Helen's long blonde hair, jerking her backwards away from Joanne and towards the window sill as sheets of glass cracked, splintered and shattered around them. The man was laughing triumphantly. Helen slammed into the wall, lost her footing but was kept from falling to the floor by the remorseless grip on her hair. The other arm snaked downwards over the shattered sill towards her.

And then Joanne was at her daughter's side, slashing at his arms with the knife, feeling the sharp cutting edge slicing through the ragged sleeves and into the flesh. An arm twitched away and covered his head as she lashed out in frenzy at the black tattered mass which was his face. But the other gnarled fist remained clasped in Helen's hair as the little girl twisted and screamed. Joanne felt the blade slice across the man's forehead,

147

saw him lurch backwards and fall away from the window, dragging Helen upwards towards the jagged fragments of glass jutting from the shattered window sill. Sobbing, she seized a handful of hair close to Helen's scalp, gripped hard to counteract the dragging force of the man's hand and sawed furiously at the rope of hair between her own hand and the man's unbreakable grip. She felt the hair finally part and saw the man's hand vanish over the sill, still clutching a handful of Helen's beautiful hair. Helen was deathly white and silent as Joanne snatched her away and ran out into the hall. *Oh God*, she thought, *she's in shock.*

The man was howling as he clambered over the window sill and into the kitchen.

Joanne stumbled up the staircase, hearing the insane screaming and the crunching of broken glass behind her; she was crying out angrily and bitterly in her mind: *Where are you, Mark? Why aren't you here?* Reaching the landing, she hurtled into the bedroom, swung Helen quickly onto the bed and moved to the wardrobe beside the door. She could hear him coming up the stairs towards them, could hear the heavy, irregular breathing, the muffled tread on the stair carpet. She could feel the invisible *rushing* of air as the man blundered quickly towards the door. And in one slithering motion, she had pulled the wardrobe in front of the door, a small part of her mind recalling, even in the immensity of her terror, that it had taken Mark and herself almost a quarter of an hour to move the wardrobe from one end of the room to another when they were redecorating. She threw her weight against the wardrobe and twisted round to the bedside table and the telephone. The man was throwing himself at the door, howling and moaning in frustration, sounding more animal than human. Joanne saw Helen sit up, get up off the bed and walk calmly round to the other side, saw her pick up the telephone and begin to dial.

'Ask for the police, darling! Tell them our address . . .' But Helen looked up at her from the telephone, tears brimming in her eyes.

'It's broken, Mummy.'

And Joanne realised how stupid she had been. With the downstairs extension destroyed, the cable ripped away from the wall, there could be no chance that the upstairs telephone would be in working order. The connection had been severed.

And now the wardrobe was easing away from the door under the onslaught from the other side. Joanne turned back to her daughter to tell her to hide in one of the cupboards, to get out of sight. She was completely unprepared for the inhuman impact that followed. She was falling away from the wardrobe onto the bed, the wardrobe itself toppling over backwards from the door. The door crashed open on one shattered hinge. *He couldn't be so strong*, thought Joanne. *Nothing could be so strong.* She struggled to her feet as she saw the blur of motion which was the ragged man-thing lunging at her from around the door. She saw the swinging railing and felt the blow on the side of her head, but there was no pain. Everything was disjointed. She realised that she had fallen across the bed again as the ceiling swam into view and she saw the shattered door swaying on its hinge. Her angle of vision tilted crazily again across the room and now she could see the impossibly tall, ragged man standing in the middle of the room, shoulders hunched, head bowed and iron railing dangling from one horribly mangled hand. She could hear his strangled breathing. And then she saw the small blonde figure which stood before him, looking up intensely into his insane face. Joanne heard the childish voice, lonely and forlorn in the suddenly vast bedroom, and could see her daughter's face set in outrage and defiance.

'You hurt my mother.' It was a simple, childlike condemnation carrying with it an impossible, hopeless threat. Joanne was screaming, groping helplessly across the counterpane towards them and feeling the pain bite at her temple. The man was raising the iron railing in a painfully slow arc as Helen stood, her lip trembling, the same condemnation of the monster above her impressed on her features. The man was chuckling as he brought the railing to its fullest height.

It was inevitable, Joanne knew, and she screamed at the awful fate which had brought this thing to her house, screamed a wordless plea and felt the universe swing and tilt as the railing began its descent.

And now everything was exploding into chaos, into a frantic whirl of action. The man was falling away from Helen as something hurtled into the room from the doorway and took him around the waist. She could hear a man shouting, saw the monster whirl round as the form pinioned his flailing arm.

149

They were crashing across the room and the man-thing was lunging and thrashing like a wild beast. But Joanne did not believe what she saw. It was a nightmare and she knew that the worst things always happened in nightmares. It was a cruel joke. Helen lay broken and dead on the carpet. She knew that this could be the only truth before she fainted away into a maelstrom of pain and color.

Nine

'Oh, no . . .' Davies said in a small voice as Chadderton drove up to the gateway of his house. Chadderton could see that there was a Morris Marina bent around the front porch of the building, with smoke billowing from the radiator. Broken glass glinted sharply in the garden. Chadderton seemed to feel a familiar thrill of horror permeating the air as he swung the car savagely into the drive and towards the house. He could feel the same dank chill in his bones that he had felt on the day that his wife had . . .

He could see that the front door appeared to have been hacked apart. Davies was yelling at him to hurry, had opened the car door and jumped out even before Chadderton had braked to a halt. Chadderton was close behind, feeling a dreadful familiarity as Davies vanished through the frame of the front door. Wood splinters and fragments littered the carpet, the kitchen door was open and Chadderton could see that the kitchen window had been broken. Davies bulleted ahead of him to look into the kitchen as Chadderton moved to the living room door.

'Joanne!' Davies' eyes were starting from his head in horror-stricken desperation. And then they both heard the crash and the scream from upstairs. Chadderton reached the stairs before Mark, took them two at a time without realising it and rounded the top of the staircase. He saw the shattered bedroom door and heard a small, tearful voice from inside the room.

Chadderton hurled himself at the doorway. Moving fast, he saw the ragged shape standing in the middle of the floor, towering over the small child, and took in the prone figure of a woman on the bed groping towards the two others. Chadderton kept moving, saw the iron railing in the man's hand raised high to strike and collided with him as he started to turn, grabbing the upheld arm and keeping it there. Chadderton was a heavy man, his bulk carrying the man sideways away from the child and into the far corner of the room. But the man was incredibly strong and Chadderton could feel his grip twisting on the man's arm as the latter whirled simultaneously to wrap his other arm around Chadderton's neck.

Chadderton had a vision of a wild, blood-streaked face; of insane, staring eyes and straggling matted hair as they collided with the bedroom wall. The man was moaning and gibbering and Chadderton realised: *God, he's trying to bite me!* Chadderton slammed him backwards against the wall again, jerking the arm which held the pointed railing away from him and jamming it as hard as he could against the wall. Davies was suddenly at his side and had seized the railing, twisting it with all his strength from the man's grip. As the railing left his hand, life seemed to vanish altogether from the tattered scarecrow. *It's as if somebody's pulled the plug out,* thought Chadderton grimly as the man collapsed against him, sliding down the wall and finally coming to rest on the carpet, eyes closed, breathing heavily and painfully. Chadderton stood back from him and turned to look as Davies strode quickly across the room to his wife and cradled her in his arms. Chadderton moved over to them and saw the blood on the woman's temple.

'I think she's all right,' said Mark. And then Chadderton saw the little girl still standing in the middle of the floor, her concentration centered on the collapsed heap in the far corner of the room beside the window. He saw the look of hate on her face, and watched as she ran round the bed to Davies' outstretched arm. She collapsed weeping into his embrace, huddling close to him. The woman was beginning to stir again as Chadderton moved around the bed to the telephone. He lifted the receiver. It was dead. When he looked back to the threesome on the bed, the woman was awake but dazed and calling Davies' name over and over. Chadderton felt a gnawing at his insides as he watched and listened; saw something there that he knew he had been denied forever and remembered standing at a graveside in the rain one summer morning. He remembered feeling that everything he had lived for was gone. He fought down the old, bad feelings, forced himself away from the family scene and back to the human wreck in the corner.

He crossed to him again, listening to his tortured breathing. There was something strange here. He wasn't sure just what it was yet, but he knew that something very peculiar indeed was staring him in the face. The man was more than just a psychopathic tramp. He took in his battered appearance, the torn clothing, the bloodstained face and wild hair. There was something about him . . . something . . . that didn't scan. Something about the cut of the jacket. Something about the tattered shirt – as if it had been an expensive buy once upon a time. The shoes were caked in mud but with fancy buckles at the side . . .

Davies was suddenly beside him again. Chadderton turned to say something about his wife, who was cradling the child in her arms, but when he saw the look on Davies' face, the words died away.

'Aynsley? . . . Aynsley?'

'What?' asked Chadderton.

'It's Aynsley,' said Mark. 'Dr Aynsley. He's my psychiatrist. I'm sure it's him.' He knelt down, looking closely into the tramp's face. 'My God . . . it *is* him.'

Chadderton started to say: *Christ, you must have some fucking hang-ups if you can do that to your shrink,* and then he remembered. Dr Aynsley. He had met him several times – a hundred years ago it seemed – to discuss the Davies 'accident'.

'It can't be.'

'It's him, I tell you. I thought he was dead.'

'Dead? What do you mean, dead? Davies . . . just what in Christ is going on here?' Chadderton was kneeling now, looking into the agonised face and suddenly realising that it *was* Aynsley, realising that Davies had been neglecting to tell him something very important indeed. The woman was rising from the bed, moving towards them.

'Is he dead?' she asked.

'No, Mrs Davies. He's not dead. But your husband hasn't

152

been telling me everything he knows about this and I think it's about time he did.'

'What's happening, Mark?' said Joanne. 'For God's sake, what's going on? It seems like everything's falling apart.'

Something was horribly wrong in that devastated bedroom. Chadderton could feel it. He could still sense the same tangible miasma in the air that he had felt on the day of his wife's death. Suddenly, it seemed that he was back on that first day of the nightmare; as if he had only just found that horribly familiar smoking ruin on his neatly cut and trimmed lawn; as if he had walked straight out of one nightmare and into another. Chadderton's out-of-body view of himself plunging into an ornamental pool to douse his burning arms had fused seamlessly into this new nightmare of a ragged and dishevelled wild man lying crumpled on the deep-pile bedroom carpet of a detached suburban house on Tyneside. He fought against the feeling; tried to react in the way that he had been trained. The woman was hurt, possibly concussed, and the small white-faced girl sitting on the corner of the bed was unhealthily silent. The front garden looked as if a VC10 had crash-landed and, only moments ago, Chadderton had been struggling with something that only looked like a man. He knew that he had to get the woman and the girl to a doctor; that he should pull down the white knotted cords which hung from the bedroom curtains and tie up the wild man before he took it into his head to go berserk again; that he would have to get to a telephone and call the local police. But in that timeless moment, Chadderton felt locked in his own illogical nightmare and watched as Davies knelt down directly in front of the figure which lay slumped against the bedroom wall, gripping him fiercely by the lapel. Davies' face looked as pale as marble in the semi-darkness and it seemed to Chadderton that the thin pink scar on his forehead and hairline was suffused with blood, standing out in vivid contrast as a thin red slash. Davies was staring intently into the wild man's face as if the answer to a terrifying secret could be found there.

'Aynsley . . .' Davies was shaking him violently. Chadderton tried to intervene, but found that he could not. 'Aynsley! You remember what happened this morning? In the clinic? You remember, don't you?' The human scarecrow stared ahead vapidly, a thin stream of saliva escaping from the corner

153

of its mouth and hanging like a strand of gossamer spider's web from its chin. Davies jerked on Aynsley's lapel again, slamming him back hard against the wall, and Chadderton found that he had raised his own arm in futile protest. His voice seemed harsh and ragged when he spoke.

'Davies . . .'

'Goddammit, Aynsley! What happened this morning? Remember! I phoned you up early this morning. I arranged to meet you at the clinic. You suggested that we try hypnosis again . . . remember? You put me into a trance – you hypnotised me. You can remember that, can't you?'

The scarecrow was looking at Mark as if it had noticed his presence for the first time. But the eyes were uninterested in him. They remained blank and unresponsive.

'You said you would try and find out what happened to me when I boarded that train. You said you would try to take me through that ticket barrier again. Remember! For God's sake remember, Aynsley! What happened to you? *What happened to me?*'

Aynsley was chuckling now. A low, guttural and hollow sound that seemed preternaturally loud. Laughter which was not reflected in his still vapid and empty eyes. 'So you're asking the questions now, doctor?'

Chadderton could see how the woman was reacting to the sound of that voice. He watched as she moved quickly to where her daughter sat on the bed, pressing the small blonde head to her breast and covering the child's ears with both hands as if the sound of the unnatural laughter could be tainted. Davies shook the scarecrow again and the laughter ceased. Chadderton moved towards him, willing himself to take an active part in this nightmare, but feeling something inside which told him that this was a bad dream that somehow could only get much worse for him if he tried to participate in it. Davies was staring at something that the scarecrow was clutching tightly in one blood-encrusted fist. He gripped the fist in both hands and wrenched something from it. The wild man reacted, rocking backwards and forwards where he lay, shaking his head and moaning as Davies stood up. There was an expression on the man's face of naked fear.

'You can't play it!' Aynsley's tattered arm clawed out towards Mark in a futile gesture. As he tried to rise, Chadder-

154

ton moved quickly forward to restrain him, seeing at the same time what it was that Davies had taken from the scarecrow. It was a spool of tape.

'Listen, we've got to get him to a doctor. Your wife and the kid, too.'

'No! Wait!' said Mark fiercely, his gaze still fixed on the human wreckage on the floor. 'Tell me everything, Aynsley . . . or I'll play the tape!'

Aynsley was struggling uselessly to rise. He was making a low, moaning noise as he continued to stare with mounting terror at the tangled tape clenched in Mark's hand. 'I can't . . . tell you anything.' Aynsley's voice was harsh, the words apparently causing him great effort. 'If He finds out I failed Him . . .'

'Who, Aynsley?'

'I can't tell you!'

'Get the tape recorder from my study, Jo. Bring it in here.'

Joanne looked uncertainly at Mark for a second and then at Chadderton with an expression of bewilderment. Chadderton was still in his nightmare and could not react.

'Go on!' Mark's harsh tone shocked her into action. As she left the room he turned his attention back to Aynsley, the psychiatrist's wild and frightened eyes watching in horror as she vanished from sight. The little white-faced girl sitting on the edge of the bed still levelled her accusatory look at him.

'All right. All right . . . but promise me you'll destroy the tape.'

'Tell me!'

'This morning . . .' Aynsley retched, wiped one trembling arm across his mouth and continued. 'I asked you about what happened on that day. The day you fell from the train. You told me what happened . . . you told me . . .' Aynsley's voice choked away. 'I can't tell you! I can't!'

Joanne re-entered the room carrying the small portable tape recorder from Mark's study desk. Taking a silent instruction from Mark's grimly set face, she placed it on the floor and plugged it into a socket in the skirting board beside the door. Aynsley was shuddering now, a long low moan escaping from his lips.

'Tell me, by God. Or I'll play the tape.'

'You crossed through the barrier . . . you got on the train

155

. . . Please don't make me tell you any more! You don't understand. He's gone now. When His purpose is . . . diverted . . . thwarted . . . He has to go back and feed so that He can grow strong again. If you play the tape . . .'

Mark moved quickly to the tape recorder, unravelling and rewinding the tape in his hands, not noticing how Joanne flinched away from him as if he meant to hurt her.

Aynsley began again in slow, measured words, still slurred and quavering: 'I asked you what happened. You were reliving it. I managed to . . . turn a stone in your mind . . . I unlocked your memory. And He was in there . . . waiting in your mind . . . but only a trace of Him . . . not whole.' Aynsley began to laugh again; the same horribly hollow noise. 'It was a man-trap . . . a fail-safe . . . put there to stop anyone finding out . . .'

'What was in my mind, Aynsley? *What?*'

'Please . . .'

'What was it?' Mark was roughly slotting the tape onto the machine, pulling the tape and threading it through to the empty reel.

'Azimuth,' replied Aynsley, the word sounding as if he were choking on mud. 'God help me, it was Azimuth . . . eyes . . . wings . . . He saw me. He came out of you and went into my mind . . . entered through my eyes. I tried to keep Him out . . .' Aynsley began to make futile clawing movements over his eyes, his shredded fingers matching the horizontal scratches stretching from his forehead and down his cheeks. 'But I couldn't . . . Don't you see? That small part of Him which was left in your mind was feeding there. *It was feeding from your mind. Feeding from your fear.*'

'Who is Azimuth?'

'He claimed you once – but you escaped. But He has always been with you since that day. You gave in to Him today. He told me. But this man . . . ' Aynsley pointed at Chadderton. 'This man saved you. Twice He claimed you and twice He was denied. Now He's gone from your mind . . . He has been denied the Tasting of you . . .' Aynsley retched again, and then continued: 'I *had* to kill you, Davies. I had to kill everything that was yours . . . ' His voice had become a choking, desperate plea. 'I *had* to. He wanted me to do it.'

'I was . . . possessed . . . by something?'

156

'No, not possessed. Not really possessed. Not yet. You were . . . haunted.'

Except for the harsh, ragged breathing, Aynsley was silent now, staring wildly at Mark, his glassy eyes imploring him to question no further. The eyes widened, suddenly focusing sharply at the sheer horror of Mark's intention as he leaned downwards to the tape recorder.

'Don't play it back! You'll conjure it up! Don't you see? *It's on the tape* . . . '

Mark punched his finger down onto the 'play' switch. The spools began to turn. The tape slithered through the machine.

Ten

Mark was no longer kneeling on his bedroom floor. His surroundings had vanished completely as if the lights had gone out. He was in an eternal, unfathomable black void of night. And the spangling mist which floated behind his eyes was the mist that always preceded his worst nightmares.

Joanne and Helen were gone. Chadderton was gone. And the thing which had once been Aynsley was also gone. The tape recorder was no longer lying on the carpet before him. But he could hear the sound it was making and a low moan was escaping from his lips as he listened and remembered.

It was the harsh, malefic shriek of a banshee fading from a high, reverberating falsetto to a low and droning bass as the lights went out and the Ghost Train suddenly lurched to a halt in the thick and cloying darkness of a world of living nightmares.

Mark wanted to run. But the black void stretching away beneath him made him sure that if he attempted to move he would pitch forward. Turning head over heels, arms pinwheeling as he fell and fell into unknown depths for ever and ever.

'What happened?' asked a small voice in the darkness. 'What happened, Mark? I think I've cut my head.'

Mark was sitting in the Ghost Train carriage, next to Robbie. As if in a dream, he saw his hand wander to Robbie's head, feeling in the semi-darkness that it was warm and wet. And he could hear himself saying: 'I think there's been a power cut or something . . .' as he followed through with the ritual.

'What are we going to do?' a small, frightened voice asked in the darkness.

'Don't worry. Someone will come in a minute.'

Someone will come in a minute.

This dream was going to be different. The realisation convulsed Mark's stomach in a tight knot of terror and broke the subservient impulse to act out his part in this horrific nightmare. For the first time, he knew that he was free to act. Free to escape the bad dream.

'Come on, Robbie, we've got to get out!' And he was pulling the small figure in the school uniform from the carriage and down onto the darkened track, realising that things were going to be different in this dream because he wasn't a little boy in school uniform any more.

Someone will come in a minute.

Mark was holding Robbie tightly by the sleeve of his jacket. He could see that the interior of the Ghost Train was horribly familiar but still, somehow, different. He began to run down the track, pulling Robbie along behind him. The recesses at either side seemed deeper, the indistinct figures of the papier mâché monsters were set further back in their cavernous darkness. The Ghost Train track itself was broader . . . they were running on gravel . . . the steel lines were thicker and heavier . . . Mark couldn't see the ceiling above . . . no dangling rubber bats from an overhead rail.

And he realised that everything was bigger, that the train lines were more like the railway tracks for a real train. That this track stretched deeper and deeper underground than it was humanly possible to believe.

Somewhere behind them, the distant howling of a train siren echoed forlornly.

The Ghost Train was coming and Mark knew that it was the same train that he had seen on the billboards outside the fairground; it was the same train that only today had shrieked and pounded into Newcastle Central Station, when something had taken control of his body and tried to make him throw himself from the platform. It was coming now and he could feel the power surging in the lines.

Mark kept running, unable to run as fast as his fear wanted, knowing that they had to move faster if they were ever going to escape. Robbie's small form tripped and stumbled along behind him. There was nowhere to run and hide other than the stone recesses at either side of the track, and Mark knew in his heart that side-stepping into one of those would result in the ultimate nightmare. They were *bad* places. Once inside, they might remain there forever as permanent exhibits. All they could do was keep running ahead of the train, hoping that they could reach the end of the line. But Robbie was too slow, he was stumbling again and Mark knew that they did not have much time. The Ghost Train was coming up behind them: a low, ominous rumbling was shaking the catacomb through which they ran. Robbie was too slow. Mark would have to carry him.

Mark stopped and turned back to Robbie, stooping downwards to pick him up. Robbie's arms were already held wide like a child waiting anxiously for its mother to lift it from the cot. Mark flinched back just before their arms embraced; felt his scalp crawling tight and his heart pumping liquid fear instead of blood.

Maggots boiled and writhed in Robbie's empty eye sockets, his jaw sagged and parted as he held up skeletal hands before his face. As Mark stood back in horror, Robbie was looking at those hands, even though he had no eyes – looking at what had happened to him, as if in disbelief. Shreds of decayed school uniform crumbled from his arms. And now Robbie was holding his hands out to Mark again in a horrified plea. He was trying to speak with a mouth that could never speak. Maggots were spilling outwards and Mark knew as he turned to run that Robbie was trying to say, *Help me!* In his mind, Mark was screaming: *I can't help you, Robbie. Oh, God. I can't. Because you're dead.*

Dead, Dead, Dead, DEAD, DEAD!!

The lines were roaring and the stone walls trembling as the nightmare express bore down on Mark. He could not turn back to look but he knew that Robbie was shambling from the line and crawling into his recess at the side. The Ghost Train was right behind him, only seconds away. The train whistle shrieked, momentarily drowning out every other sound of its approach. And the voice in the shrieking was the same voice which had spoken to Mark through the speaker today, when something had tried to kill him.

Welcome back, Mark. I'm sooooooo glad to have you!

The train was rounding a bend. Mark knew without looking because the track was suddenly lit up all round. Dull orange light shone into the ghastly recesses. The denizens of those recesses, he knew, were even now crawling forwards. Crawling to their entrances to watch as the Ghost Train swept forward to run him down.

'Oh, God,' Mark was crying through choked sobs, feeling hot, fetid breath on his back like an opened furnace door and knowing that the train's gaping maw was opening wide to take him. Jagged teeth like broken gravestones. Coiled serpent's tongue lashing and squirming. Hot, grey steam hissing and billowing as it came, the same nightmare passengers leaning from the windows, leaning out and laughing, laughing, laughing . . . And something much worse was on the train, waiting for him.

Mark's legs had lost their strength. The horror was too great. He crashed to the sharp gravel, while the ululating train whistle shrieked directly behind him. As he fell, he knew that there were some things worse than death. The shrieking enveloped him.

And then was gone.

Mark clambered to his feet and looked back down the track. The Ghost Train had vanished. The lines were cold and still. Tenuous wisps of steam swirled and parted and, somewhere, far away, Mark thought that he could hear a train whistle drifting lonely and forlorn as it disappeared into the stygian depths of the tunnel.

Mark knew that this dream was going to be different. Not knowing why the Ghost Train had failed to take him, he searched for a way out; for a way to escape this nightmare once and for all.

What's the matter, kid? Can't you take a joke, then? You gotta start smashing my place up like that just 'cause I put the lights out?

Mark knew the owner of that voice. He had heard those words so many times before that he could not be mistaken. A tall, thin form was stepping from one of the recesses. Feet crunched on gravel, faint light glinted on Brylcreem. And the figure was so tall, so abominably tall. Nothing human could be so tall. It was striding purposefully towards him, covering ground faster than he could believe possible.

You paid to come in, didn't you? You wanted to be scared?

Mark could see that the stone recesses at the side of the railway line were gone. In their place, solid, irregular standing stones jutted upwards like a line of broken teeth. Those damned stones. They meant something. *Something.*

It's only a dream . . . only a bad dream . . . thought Mark as he plunged away down the railway track. The lingering steam from the passage of the Ghost Train seemed to have thickened and closed in all around him in a cloying mantle. There was a smell of ozone in the air. The track ahead seemed to go on forever.

It's only a dream and I'll wake up soon.

But this dream was horribly different and somewhere behind him, the Ghost Train Man was following.

Skiving off from school. Is that what you're doing, eh?

Mark screamed as he had not done since childhood. Impossibly tall, and with arms spread wide across the track to catch him, the Ghost Train Man was suddenly in front of him, swooping forward like a huge, Brylcreemed bat with that horribly out-of-proportion smile and those perfectly even, glinting teeth filling Mark's vision. And now there was a pressure on Mark's throat and he was being held against a rough stone wall; pinioned by a knotted, sinewy forearm as purple mist boiled behind his eyes. It was 1963 and Mark was an eleven-year-old boy lost in the Ghost Train. The Man had caught him.

Anybody ever tell you that you've got a face like a girl, kid?

And Robbie was dead. The Ghost Train Man had caught him and put him in one of those recesses alongside all the other people he had caught alone in his kingdom. The Ghost Train Man had caught Mark and Robbie could never save him this time . . .

*　　*　　*

161

Davies had pressed the switch on the tape recorder and, suddenly, Chadderton's worst fears had been realised. Reality and nightmare had fused into one. The feeling of living a dream had taken over completely. The events in Davies' bedroom had tipped him over. He had slipped over the edge of reality into an all-enveloping blackness. All around him – nothingness. And Chadderton wondered if this was what a nervous breakdown was really like. He was sure that his mind had decided that it couldn't take any more. It had opted out.

But there was no real escape here. No place to hide. Because Chadderton was suddenly standing in bright sunshine on his back lawn. His shirt was open, his tie hanging loose. He knew that he had just arrived home, that his jacket was hanging over the back of a chair and that a fresh can of beer was waiting for him on a side table. He had seen his wife's car parked in the garage when he knew that it should not be there. He had followed that terrible smell of burning out into the back garden.

There was no sign of that frightful burning mound on the lawn. No thick, oily smoke billowing up from a huddled, shapeless mass. Only a scorched circle of blackened, smouldering grass. Chief Inspector Trafford was standing before it and looking at him with a bemused smile on his face. The smell of burning still hung in the air, thick and cloying; stinging the back of Chadderton's throat and threatening to make him retch.

'We're taking you off the enquiry, Les. I think you know why.' Trafford began pacing, casting his eye over Chadderton's garden with patronising approval. 'You've been through a lot. Had a terrible shock.'

Terrible shock. He was saying it just as if he was trying to keep him humored.

It's obviously upset you, I can see. But I'm afraid that the drinking has got a little out of hand, Les. In fact, it's seriously impairing your judgment. Nothing personal, but I'm sure you can see that we're going to have to relieve you of duty. Temporarily, of course. Until you can get your act back together again.' Again, that patronising grin. A fatherly pat on the shoulder. 'Take a rest. That's what you need, Les. How about a holiday? That would be nice, wouldn't it? I know it's been quite a while since you were able to take a real holiday.

Take your good lady wife . . .' Trafford was pointing behind him, into the garage. And Chadderton knew that she was in there somewhere. He knew that she wasn't dead; that she hadn't taken that train. She had changed her mind about the visit and had been drinking coffee with Mrs Colquhoun next door. He stumbled forward towards the garage and for the first time noticed the other smudges on the lawn. The blackened marks were footprints, he realised, as he drew closer to the yawning garage entrance. Charcoaled footprints leading from the circle of blackened grass on the lawn into the dark recesses of the garage. Something was waiting for him there in the dark, standing next to the Cortina. It was moving forward to meet him. Something which couldn't walk properly.

And Chadderton remembered that this was a nightmare. And that nightmares always showed you something bad, something so terribly *bad*, when you were expecting things to get better.

He collapsed to his knees, holding his hands over his face as the dark shape moved out into the sunlight. He did not want to see and, in slow motion, was crushing the palms of his hands over his eyes as something black with five fingers swung jerkily into his line of vision. There was a glint of gold from one of the fingers.

The pressure was gone from his eyes now and Chadderton was no longer on his back garden lawn. He was in a huge, echoing chamber, looking up at a criss-cross of girders overhead. Pigeons were fluttering among them and sunlight was trying to peep in through a huge overhead skylight. He looked around him. He was in Newcastle Central Station. But there were no people about. The station was completely deserted and, as he watched, an old newspaper floated spectrally across the platform away from him. He began to run, not really knowing where. Just away. Away. *Away.* He had still not lost the feeling that something very bad was going to happen. It was as if something wanted him to see what he would rather not see. If only he could get out of the station. Get out and get away. Get away and not see. But now he realised that the exit had been bricked up. Spinning madly in the centre of the station, he looked for another way out but could find none. Somewhere above, he could hear laughing. It echoed mockingly, bouncing from girder to girder, echoing long and loud.

163

Chadderton knew that it was Trafford's laughter.

'You bastard!' Chadderton was screaming hysterically. The sound of his voice seemed to cut through everything like a diamond on glass. It surged upwards and outwards, rebounding into his own head.

Now, the station had undergone an instantaneous alteration. The Victorian superstructure and the high, vaulted arches and girders remained. He was still standing in the center of a chamber of sorts. But it was no longer a station . . . it was a gallery. It reminded him somehow of the Victoria and Albert Museum. There were glass cases positioned around him, containing exhibits and what seemed to be stiff waxen characters in period uniform. But, damn it all, he could still see the station buffet across the way. He could still see the newsagent's shop. There was a glass booth standing right next to it.

Chadderton moved towards one of the boxes and looked in. It was a wax dummy with two heads. Chains dangled from manacled wrists, eyes bulged and protruded. There was a piece of card on the glass: 'See the Two Headed Thing.' Chadderton moved away from it. The horrible glass eyes were disquieting; they seemed to follow him as he passed. The other cases were filled with similarly disturbing specimens. Cheap and tatty exhibits from a twopenny-halfpenny arcade. A second-rate Chamber of Horrors.

He looked for another way out. He remembered that there was a second exit just beyond the buffet and began to move towards it. As he walked, he could see another glass case standing beside the exit itself. The box was turned away at a slight angle so that he could not see the occupant. And as he moved towards it he became aware of a thread of unease somewhere inside him. The horrible inevitability of nightmare seemed so much more tangible now as he drew closer.

Cat and mouse, thought Chadderton. *This is a game of cat and mouse. Something wants me to find that exit. No . . . something has put that last exhibit next to the exit so that I'll see it.* No longer in control, he moved on, the glass case looming larger and larger before him. And, worst of all, he knew that he could not hide his eyes again this time. That he would be made to look into that case and see what was in there.

Chadderton drew level with the glass case, turned and looked inside.

164

It was his wife. He had known all along that it would be her. She had burnt and someone had come along and swept her up and put her in this case with all the other exhibits.

Oh dear God, I must wake up. I must wake up. I MUST WAKE UP.

Joyce's eyes flickered open. She was still alive.

And Trafford was laughing again as Chadderton's screams disturbed the pigeons nestling on the rafters above. Screams that echoed and rebounded as the glass case began to open and his wife reached out towards him, begging for an embrace. Trafford had appeared beside him now, laughing and laughing and laughing. And Chadderton, suddenly in full possession of his body again, lunged forward to take Trafford by the throat. He began squeezing that throat as hard as he could; they collapsed to the floor and Chadderton was lying on top of Trafford, trying to squeeze that damnable laughter out of him. But Trafford continued to laugh. Chadderton was weeping in rage, cursing and uttering throaty abominations.

'I'll kill you, kill you, kill you kill you kill . . .'

And as Chadderton's hands continued to throttle, Trafford continued to laugh.

*   *   *

Joanne had just found Mark's note: 'Couldn't sleep. Don't worry if you wake up and I'm not there. Back soon. Gone for a walk. Love, Mark.'

It was raining heavily outside. November wind was snapping at the window casement. *He shouldn't be out in this,* thought Joanne. She hoped to God that he hadn't decided to go back to the station again. And then she heard the front door shut. She ran to the bedroom door, opened it and saw Mark standing downstairs in the hallway, his coat soaked through and dripping wet. There was a pool of muddy grey water on the mat and Mark was looking up at her, his face white and drawn. Even from here, she could see the livid pink scar across his forehead as if it had been newly made.

No, thought Joanne. *It didn't happen like this last time.* And then she was moving down the stairs towards him.

'Where have you been?'

165

'Walking. Just walking . . .'

'You look like death warmed up.'

Death warmed up. The words seemed to hang heavily in the air as she took his arm and pulled it around her shoulder. He looked as if he were about to collapse there and then on the 'Welcome' mat.

'Get me upstairs to the bedroom, Jo. I've got to get upstairs.' And again, Joanne had that strange thought which seemed to make no sense: *It's not supposed to happen like this. It didn't happen like this last time.*

Mark was a dead weight against her, the wet fabric of his coat dampening her nightdress, making it cling to her side. He was groaning with every step, eyes screwed tightly shut, strands of hair plastered across his tense, white face.

'Get me upstairs, Jo.'

To Joanne, it seemed as if Mark had just been fished out of the canal, he was so wet. And God knew what state he would be in after this. *Get those clothes off, get him dried and into bed and then straight on the telephone to the doctor.* He was in a weak enough condition to begin with. A case of pneumonia was something with which she knew he could never cope.

They moved into the bedroom and Joanne guided him into the chair beside the bed.

And then, strangely, she was in bed and Mark was standing naked in the middle of the room looking at her. She couldn't remember taking off his clothes and towelling him dry as she had intended. But she supposed she must have done. There was an S-shaped scar on Mark's hip – another legacy from his terrible accident. He was looking at her now in unutterable misery.

'Joanne . . .'

She held her arms out to him and he moved to the bed, pulling back the covers and slipping quickly in beside her. His body felt icy cold as she pulled his head tight against her breast; caressing his hair and wanting her love to make everything all right again. He was kissing her roughly now and she was responding to him, wanting the warmth of her body to flow into him and dispel the ice water that seemed to be flowing in his veins. Urgently and desperately, she wanted him to enter her. And when he did, it was like ice again. But everything would be fine. She was going to make everything well and by

166

this one act of lovemaking she would make him whole again.

Mark's face was pressed tightly down into the hollow of her shoulder and neck as he moved inside her, and everything was going to be better . . .

But he was chuckling against her skin in a way that she did not like. A low, guttural, hollow sound that she had heard somewhere a million years ago. There was no warmth in her body now – it had been taken from her in one terrible spasm of fear. She pushed hard at Mark and could see the look of horror on his face as he pulled back, his eyes looking through her and focusing on some frightful inner realisation.

'Oh God, Joanne. What's happening to me?' A hoarse, horrified whisper. And then Mark had lurched away from her and she, in her fear, was crouching against the headboard with the sheets pulled up protectively around her, knowing that something was terribly wrong.

'It's the accident, Jo. It wasn't my fault. I can't help what happened to me. Really, I just want to get better. And you can help me be . . . be . . . ' Mark was struggling for a word and Joanne wanted to tell him that the word was *Whole . . . I want you to be whole.* But she could not tell him.

'Oh, noooooo . . . ' Mark was clutching at his face with one hand as he lay on the bed, propped up on one elbow. 'Everything's . . . everything's . . . going to pieces, Jo. *Going to pieces, Jo* . . . GOING TO PIECES, JO . . . '

Mark pulled his hand away from his face and Jo wanted to scream but could not.

One of Mark's eyes was smeared in a glistening chunk across the palm of his hand. The fingers of his hand were, even now, shrivelling and peeling, corrupted fragments of flesh falling to the bedspread. Mark was looking at his hand and uttering short, hoarse cries of horror. He was clambering from the bed, backing away from her into the center of the room. But his legs were flaking and crumbling and would not support him. He fell heavily to his knees and the impact dislodged his lower jaw which crumbled downwards, falling away from its socket. Mark was using his other hand to try and keep it in place but it was no good because his other hand was liquefying and flowing. His other eye was popping from its socket as Joanne fought to find the scream that had been building up inside her. And when she saw that his penis was missing and could feel the

167

ice-cold deep inside her, the scream finally came to her lips. But the scream could not end the nightmare: Mark was still disintegrating before her, and although he could not speak now, she knew what he was mouthing: *Going to pieces . . . going to pieces . . . going to pieces.*

Eleven

Helen knew something bad was happening when everything vanished.

She had been sitting on the edge of the bed, watching as her Daddy and the Other Man came in and rescued them from the Bad Man. She knew that Daddy would come, it was what happened in every fairy story she had read. 'Here comes the Cavalry', Daddy would say, with comical inevitability, every time they watched a western on TV. And she also knew that something had happened to her when the Bad Man had hit Mummy. She supposed it was what Mummy called 'The Bad Shock' and that the best thing to do was just sit on the edge of the bed and be quiet until her mind told her that it was okay to be normal again. Helen remembered how Tracy Allen had looked that day in the schoolyard when she found out that her sister had been hit by a car. She had gone all white. 'White as parchment,' Helen had heard their PE teacher say later that afternoon. And although she didn't know what parchment was, she guessed that it must be pretty white. Tracy hadn't spoken a word but her eyes were all glassy and one of the other teachers had taken her home for a long rest. When Helen asked her about it, Mummy had told her about 'shock' and how it might take a little while to get better when something really bad like that happened to you. In her own way, Helen understood all of this, even though she had always thought that a 'shock' was something you got from seeing something really nasty – like one of the Doctor Who monsters when they crept up

168

behind you and grabbed you. Helen had always thought that you screamed when you got a shock and that it made your hair go all spiky and your eyes pop out on springs, just like the characters in some of the comics she read. But she could grasp the concept, even though she thought the word was wrong. She understood that she was in shock now and wondered whether the sudden darkness had anything to do with it.

Daddy had pressed the tape recorder switch (she didn't know why, but he seemed to think that it was important) and darkness had suddenly spread from the spools. Just like the purple ink which had spread from Daddy's splayed fountain pen nib onto the desk blotter on that day she had crept into his study when no one was looking. Except that this darkness just grew and grew and grew. It didn't stop in a round, purple spot, as it had done on Daddy's blotter. It had continued to spread and now the room was gone, Daddy and the tape recorder were gone, Mummy was gone, the Other Man was gone.

There was only Helen, sitting on the edge of the bed. And over there, in the same position and splayed out on a purple backdrop, the Bad Man lay crumpled like Helen's Looby-Lu doll. There were long strings fastened to the Bad Man's hands, feet and head. Just like a big puppet. And the strings stretched way up into the purple blackness. The strings were glinting silver in the darkness and, as Helen watched, something far above pulled on one of them and the Bad Man's head moved jerkily around to look at her. Another twitch, and the Bad Man was pulling his legs into a sitting position, clambering clumsily to his feet, wobbling and weaving. And Helen knew now just what the Bad Man was. He was a puppet – only a puppet, and puppets couldn't scare anybody. With that realisation, she also knew that the funny feeling which held her immobile in the real world did not restrict her here. The puppet was dancing now, slowly and clumsily, its mouth a horrible black slot twisted upwards into a grin. It was dancing for her, wanting her to dance as well. If she would only step down from the bed and come closer . . .

Will you, won't you, will you, won't you, will you join the dance? Come closer, little girl, and we'll embrace and dance like you have never danced before. We'll dance for all time. I'll be yours, you'll be mine.

Helen knew that the puppet was horrible. She would not

dance. But it was not the puppet of which she was really afraid. It was whoever pulled the puppet's strings: the Puppet Master. She let her concentrated hatred spill out towards the puppet. It was a hatred of anything that could enjoy frightening people so much. Because, she knew, making people frightened was something that this Puppet Master liked doing best of all. In an instant, the piano wire strings parted and the Bad Man collapsed into a disjointed jumble of twisted limbs.

'Very good, little girl. Very good. The strings are cut. The puppet collapses.'

Helen turned as someone stepped into view beside her, pulling the purple blackness momentarily aside like some plush, velvet curtain. The voice was smooth, purring like a sleek, contented cat, and Helen could see that he was a young man, perhaps younger than Daddy. He was wearing a white shirt and black trousers. There was a pointed party hat on his head, just like the ones that you got out of Christmas crackers, and there were party streamers on his shoulders. His face was white, very white (like parchment, Helen couldn't help thinking), the eyes were very dark and his hair glinted with an oily something. He smiled a lot, but Helen couldn't really make out his face. It was like one of those old photographs of her grandfather that Mummy kept in the attic. Grainy, black and white photographs. And of one in particular, where Grandfather had moved while the picture was being taken and his face had become all smudged. This man's face was like that . . . like a smudged photograph. And no matter how hard Helen looked, it seemed, by a trick of the horrible purple dark/light, that she could never see his face properly.

Helen did not like this man at all. There was something particularly nasty about him. Most of all, she did not like that big, big smile and all those perfectly even, white teeth.

'All the better to eat you with, my dear,' said the man, flashing his vulpine smile as he moved to the puppet, nudging it with the toe of his shoe as if making sure that it was really dead, really only an inanimate object.

'You can hear what I'm thinking!' said Helen incredulously.

'Oh, yes. I know all about you. And what you're made of. Sugar and spice and all things nice.'

'Where are my Mummy and Daddy?' Helen was suddenly defiant and outraged.

'Let us say . . . I have arranged a little diversion for them. A little amusement, *n'est ce pas?*'

Helen knew that the man's last phrase was French. She didn't know what it meant, but she didn't like it. People who spoke French just liked to be clever. She knew, because Sharon Bellford's Mummy had started Linguaphone lessons last year and Sharon kept coming up with these stupid French words just to impress everybody. And Sharon Bellford was a creep of the first order.

'You'd better not hurt them.'

'How can dreams hurt, little one?'

'Am I really dreaming?'

'That would be telling.' The man performed a small pirouette, vanished from sight for an instant behind another swirling purple curtain and reappeared again at Helen's left.

'Who are you?' she asked.

The man appeared to give serious consideration to the matter for a few seconds. When he answered, it was as if he had found the perfect reply: 'I am . . . the Puppet Master . . . the Prince of Dark Dreams. Yes, that's exactly right. All that you see and hear is mine. The Master of this Kingdom. And soon, perhaps, the next?' The man was laughing now and Helen guessed that if he could read minds then he was probably talking like that deliberately because she read a lot of fairy stories and they all had words in them just like that. She was not impressed. And the man's face had suddenly clouded as if he had heard her again.

'Where are my Mummy and Daddy?'

'Tiresome, my little one. Tiresome. But . . . as you wish.'

And in an instant, Helen could see a fairground with a huge, spinning Ferris wheel and closely crowded sideshows. It was night, and she could hear the jumbled babbling noise that thousands of people always made when they were together in one place. All kinds of music drifted up to her from the sideshows as she wheeled above the fairground. She could see the Big Dipper, plunging and veering across the sky on its nightmare trellis framework of steel girders. Daddy and Mummy were sitting in the front seat of the front carriage. The Other Man was sitting in the back, hands clinging tightly to the rail. There were no other passengers. All three of them were sitting, staring blankly ahead as if frozen in time. Mummy's hair was streaming out behind her; there was a red mark on her temple where the Bad Man had hit her. The rollercoaster was plunging downwards into a dip, and Helen could see that there was no track at the bottom leading sharply up to the next crest. There was only a black, gaping hole dug into the earth at the bottom and the track led straight downwards into this. Before she could shout any kind of warning, the carriage went roaring downwards into the hole, the sound of clattering wheels echoing loud and then fading, fading . . . as they vanished underground into uncharted depths. Helen could feel herself floating nearer to the hole. She felt sure that she would follow.

'Where are we going?' she asked.

'Not we. *They.* They're going to a place where their worst bad dreams live.' Again, the purring voice, like a cat playing with mice.

'Stop this. Stop it and take us all back.'

'Little Helen,' said the Man in an admonitory voice, 'they're grown-ups. And grown-ups only care for themselves. They always think they know what's best, even when you know they're wrong. They always win, don't they? They're always telling you what to do. *They* know best – at school and at home. They're always so right. But they're not perfect, Helen. Not by any means. In fact, they're hardly *ever* right. I can tell you that because I *know.* Look at your Daddy! He should be looking after you, shouldn't he? He should be spending much more time with you, shouldn't he? Lots more time with you than he has been – you know you've felt that yourself. You can't lie to me. Because I can see what goes on inside your head.'

'That's not fair. Daddy had an accident. He was away for a long time in hospital getting better. He nearly died.'

'And since he came back, do you really think he loves you as much as he did before the accident?'

'He still loves me. Of course he still loves me. He told me so. And I know. That's a hateful thing to say!'

'But you know you've felt that way, Helen. Grown-ups! They only care for themselves. They've got no time for the important ones. The important little ones like you, Helen. Your Daddy doesn't love you any more. Because I can read minds – you know that – *and I know.*'

Helen could feel tears brimming behind her eyes. She was struggling against submitting to the inner sorrow which the horrible Man seemed to have conjured up inside her. He was saying things that she knew she had thought in the past; things that had never really formed as straight and positive in her mind, because they were nasty, horrible thoughts and too unbearable to keep inside. But the Man had seen. And the Man said that he knew. And if he could read her mind, then surely he could read her Daddy's mind as well.

They were back in the purple place again. The Bad Man still lay collapsed on the ground. The bed was still there and she was still sitting on it. Another swish of the curtain and the Man with the smudged face was standing before her with his arms crossed, looking at her sympathetically, as if he knew the way things were and that Helen had to accept it. She managed to keep the tears back, because crying was no good. It wouldn't help her against the Prince of Dark Dreams.

'Your Daddy doesn't want you, Helen. He's proved that, hasn't he? If he really loved you, he would be here – I wouldn't be able to stop him. But he isn't. He'll stay where I've sent him because he doesn't deserve your love. But I want you, Helen. I have great plans for you. I can give you everything you've ever wanted. You can live with me in this place forever and you can do whatever you wish. So long as you also do my bidding. Grown-ups have no say here. They don't belong. I will love you, Helen. I'll love you to death.'

A little girl had suddenly appeared beside the Man. She was wearing a purplish kind of nightdress that drifted around her like smoke, blending into the background, and Helen wondered if she had been there all along or if the Man had suddenly brought her out of thin air. The Man was standing aside, displaying her to Helen with a sweep of his hand as if she was some kind of special show-thing. The little girl was moving humbly closer, awed by his presence. She was dark-haired, with clear, deep blue eyes and a wisp of a smile. Helen supposed that she was a couple of years older than herself.

'This is someone very like you, Helen,' said the Man. 'Her name is Angelina and she knows what I say is true.' The little girl was looking up at him, as if anxious to state her case. The Man nodded and, for a second, Helen could see only the smile and no other detail of his face at all. *Just as if he had moved before the picture was taken*, Helen thought again. And the Man looked back at her knowingly.

'He's right,' Angelina said, 'everything he says is true. He can see right into your mind. He can see what you fear the most. I was just like you once. And my Daddy didn't love me . . . even my Mummy didn't love me. But now I've given myself to the Prince and he'll keep me for ever and ever. And the grown-up world can't never tell me what's right and wrong again. They can't never tell me what to do. Because anything I want, I can have. Anything *you* want, you can have. There's a time coming soon, Helen, when everything's going to change. The grown-up world is going to be different. And it's people like us that will be in charge.' Helen could see how passionate Angelina was becoming. Her lip was pouting, she was trembling. 'And they're all going to be sorry. *Very sorry.* You can be part of it all, Helen. All you have to do is give your love to him. Isn't it wonderful? And if your Daddy doesn't love you, does he deserve your love?'

Angelina stood back and looked at the Man again. He was nodding. He was pleased and she was so glad that she had said all the right things. The Man was turning back to Helen, holding his hands wide apart as if to say: 'There you are! Out of the mouths of babes, my little one. What more is there to be said?'

Something was wrong. A tiny part of her mind had responded immediately to what the Man had said about her Daddy. Because, no matter how much she disliked the Man, she knew that what he was telling her was partly true. She had felt sometimes as if her Daddy had changed, and that perhaps he had no more time for his daughter. Helen was fighting down that part of her which believed the Man because another part of her mind was telling her to be careful. And the thought suddenly came to her that, just because the Man could read minds, it did not mean that he was bound to tell the truth. He *could* lie about things to get his own way, couldn't he? It was a thought that Helen struggled to keep hidden from the Man; she knew that there was a way to mask her thoughts from him, but she hadn't quite found out what it was yet. The Man had sensed something. The glittering, pearly smile had faded slightly. Anger was beginning to smoulder in the eyes, just before his face shifted and blurred again.

'Helen. You mustn't hide from me like that. I can see. *I know*. And you mustn't hide from me.' Angelina seemed frightened now. She was standing back from the Man and it seemed to Helen that her nightdress was billowing slightly in a small wind. Billowing and curling around the little girl like the shrouds of darkness all around. As Helen watched, it seemed to her that Angelina was no more than a ghost. A flimsy picture from a storybook. A storybook where the wicked witch could become an innocent little girl if she wished. There was a sweetness about Angelina that wasn't right. It was like eating too much chocolate and feeling sick, like Helen had done last Easter when Aunt Emma had given her those Easter eggs. The chocolate was nice but when you had too much and felt sick, the thought of eating more was bad . . . really bad . . . And it seemed that Angelina was like that. *Sickly sweet*, thought Helen. *You're no good. You're wrong*. And Angelina was suddenly gone from sight as if she had never been.

'Helen!' The Man's voice was echoing in her ears, loud and threatening and just like the voice from a bad dream that calls your name through the bedroom doorway and you know . . . you just know, that . . . something . . . something horrible . . . is going to come in.

'You're hiding from me, Helen. You mustn't do that. I want you.'

Helen did not want to look at the Man, because she was frightened that he might become something else – something that she did not want to see. But she hung onto that feeling which she knew was keeping the Man from her deep thoughts, still not understanding it and knowing that, because she could not understand it, the Man was still able to work his way in behind her eyes to see what was there. In that instant, she heard again in her head something that Angelina had just said: *He can see right into your mind. He can see what you fear the most*. And then she remembered something else that she had first felt instinctively about the Man when the Bad Man Puppet was dancing before her: her instinctive hatred for anything that could enjoy frightening people so much.

'Helen . . .' The voice was slow, like a tape running down. Slow and horrible and thick with menace. Helen clung to the feeling which was keeping the Man out of her mind as he

175

floated around the periphery, trying to get in and not liking it when he could not. She could not keep him out for very long, that much she knew. And what would happen when he *did* get inside after she had disobeyed him?

He can see right into your mind. He can see what you fear the most.

It was bedtime and Helen could not sleep again because the wardrobe standing in the corner of the room had two round handles on it, just like a pair of eyes. Those eyes were watching her in the dark and waiting for the moment when she fell asleep so that it could start moving forward, casting off its wardrobe disguise. She was calling to Daddy now. Daddy was always there, laughing and telling her that it was only a wardrobe. He would hang a towel across the door handles, as he always did – making it blind. He would kiss her and put the lights out, telling her that he loved her and that she should go to sleep or she would never get up in the morning for school. And when Helen looked across, the towel would be wrapped firmly around the door handles that looked like eyes and everything would be all right.

But Daddy wasn't here now. He was somewhere else. Somewhere where his dark dreams lay. And there was nobody to put the towel over the door handles.

. . . anything that could enjoy frightening people so much.

'I know who you are!' Helen shouted, her eyes screwed tightly shut, her hands held tightly together on her lap. 'You're what brought my Daddy the bad dreams. You're what's been making him not able to get well. It's you!' And with the knowledge came a flood of that peculiar feeling which kept the Man away. She was not lying in her bed at night with the wardrobe any more. She was in another, lighter, empty place. Somehow, she knew that the Man could never get her here. But she could not stay here for very long and could not keep the Man back unless she could find out what the feeling was that kept him at bay.

There was somebody else here with her now. It was somebody she had seen in her dreams before. She had a vague recollection that she had once told her Daddy all about her dream visitor. It was the little boy who liked to speak to her. The little boy she knew her Daddy had known a long time ago as Robbie. He was standing in the empty grey before her

176

and he was hiding his face because he did not want her to see and be frightened. Robbie was dead and his face wasn't nice.

Robbie was moving closer now, and she felt so sad. Her sadness was welling up in her throat, and she wanted to tell him that she was going to make everything all right for him. She didn't want him to be lonely any more.

'Don't feel sad.' Robbie's voice was muffled, more difficult to hear than before. He was speaking slowly, articulating each word carefully so that she would not miss anything. 'Nothing here is real. Not even me.'

'Of course you're real, you're . . . you were a friend of my Daddy's. You told me so in a dream.'

'Yes. I was a friend of your Daddy's. But I'm not real. I don't exist. Your Daddy's friend was killed in an accident when he was a little boy. I only exist in your Daddy's memory. And that's why I *am*. The Man made me to give your Daddy the bad dreams. Be careful, Helen. You can't resist him for much longer. Just remember . . .' The last word had come out all wrong, but Helen knew what he meant. '. . . re-mem-ber . . . that *nothing* is real. He can use what you're frightened of against you. And he's not a *man* at all, Helen. There is no Man. He only looks like that because he chooses to do so. His name is Azimuth.'

It was a name that Robbie had mentioned before and she had not been able to hear properly. But here in the safe place, she could make it out at last.

'You must get back and warn the others. Tell them what you *feel*. Tell your Daddy what you feel. He has escaped from Azimuth twice and because his mind has been touched by Azimuth, it has left him with a special power of understanding. Tell him what you feel and he'll know what to do.'

'If you're not real, if you're a part of my Daddy's dreams, how can you speak to me like this? How can you be a part of *my* dream? How can you warn me about the Bad . . . about Azimuth . . . if he made you?'

Robbie had turned away from her as if to leave. He made a noise which sounded like a broken sigh and which made her feel even sadder.

'Why aren't you doing what Azimuth tells you?'

'Because,' said Robbie, '. . . because there are some things

177

that are even greater than Azimuth, Helen. What can be created can be used for good as well as bad.'

Helen could feel that the safe place was slipping away. The Man . . . Azimuth . . . was somewhere out there in the blackness, temporarily locked out of her mind by the special feeling which even Robbie knew about.

'What is it that keeps him out, Robbie? Tell me!'

'You know what it is. *Feel it.* You must find out for yourself or it's no good. You know how to stop him, Helen.'

Helen could feel a door handle turning stealthily, could feel the pressure against the special door which was keeping Azimuth out.

'How, Robbie? *How* do I stop him?'

'You know . . . you can feel it . . . use it. Use it, Helen!'

But the safe place had faded as the door handle turned and the door into her secret place swung wide to admit the Big Bad Wolf. Helen was falling and falling into that horrible purple blackness from which she had come.

* * *

Helen was lying in bed again. Daddy had put out the light and everything was purple black. Once again, Helen thought: *He can see what you fear the most.* And she knew then that Daddy had not put the towel across the wardrobe's eyes – she knew that without even looking. She knew that he was somewhere else and could not help her; knew that Azimuth had failed to convince her that she should love him as the other little girl so obviously loved him; and that something very, very bad was going to happen as a result.

Helen refused to look at the wardrobe, clenching her small fists to her eyes as she heard the sound of furniture being moved in the darkness. A hollow, muffled thud as something heavy inched forward towards her.

'I know who you are! You're the Ghost Train Man! You're not even real!'

'No . . . ' said the slow, dragging voice in the corner of Helen's bedroom. 'No . . . but I'm very real to your Daddy. And now that I'm here, I can make myself just as real to you, Helen. As real as real can be. *All for you.*'

Helen dug deep inside for the feeling which she knew would

178

make everything all right. It wasn't as strong nor as tangible as she had felt it before. But it was there somewhere, deep down inside, and it was the only thing that could save her, if she could find it and use it properly. But she was so frightened, and the more frightened she became, the stronger the Ghost Train Man became and the harder it was for her to remember how it felt.

Another heavy, dull thumping on the thick pile of the bedroom carpet, just like the time when Mummy and Daddy had moved the wardrobe from one end of the room to another when they had been decorating. Making the wardrobe 'walk' on its pointed edges, Daddy had called it: thump, thump . . . and *thump*.

Daddy and Mummy and the Other Man were in the place where their worst nightmares lived – the Ghost Train Man had said so. Bad things were happening for them too and, for an instant, Helen's fear for her parents was greater than her own. And the spark of that feeling was the key to the special secret inside. Helen grabbed for it, fanned it like someone would fan the dying embers of a campfire in a forest, hoping that the fire would keep the dark creatures in the deep, dark forest at bay. A flame licked upwards, and Helen knew that the dark shapes behind the trees were shrinking back from the flame into deeper shadow. She embraced it, let it grow – still not understanding it – but letting it grow anyway, feeling how *pure* it was inside her and knowing that if she were a grown-up she could never do it, because it was too complicated for grown-ups.

Now she knew that Azimuth had made all dreams one. That irrefutable fact came to her as she climbed higher and higher inside and let the feeling make the bedroom and its monster freeze and fade. Daddy, Mummy and the Other Man were all in the same dream. And everything was going to turn out bad, everything was so horribly wrong . . .

And Helen could see . . .

. . . Joanne was frozen on the bed, watching as Mark collapsed and shrivelled like a vampire confronted by a crucifix in one of those Hammer films that Mark liked so much. But this wasn't a movie. Mark was crumbling and disintegrating and she wanted to turn away, but she could not. Mark was kneeling in the ruins of his own decay; an arm had fallen away, the fingers still clutching and gripping at the air; the flesh had all but peeled from the now hairless skull like old paint from an outhouse wall. And his face . . . oh God . . . his face. Something gave a reverberating snap deep inside him, like a damp log spitting sparks on an open fire, and Mark's rib cage split apart as his entire body collapsed inwards into a ruined pile. The head tried to turn and look up, but couldn't make it. The vertebrae had disintegrated. The skull rolled away, cracked apart like a month-old eggshell and began to crumble into powder . . .

'. . . So the best thing you can do is just take your punishment, son. I mean, you've got to be made to pay . . .' The purple mist was spangling before his eyes as it always did. Mark could feel himself sliding as the unrelenting pressure squeezed his windpipe closed. Somewhere, he could hear the rustling of clothing . . .

. . . And Chadderton squeezed and squeezed as hard as he could to choke off that hysterical, mocking laughter that issued from Trafford's throat. His wife had burnt to death but, somehow, she was still alive. *Still alive and burning forever.* Trafford had made it happen, had wanted it to happen. And he kept on laughing as if it was the best joke in the world and *Kill you kill you kill you, Trafford. You fucking bastard, I'm going to kill kill kill you* . . .

. . . And the bedroom doorway was opening slowly and Joanne felt herself drawn to it, expecting another nightmare to be standing in the door frame. But it was Helen. She'd had a bad dream and wanted to get into bed with her mother. Joanne knew that when she looked back, the decayed, crumbling remains of her husband would be gone. She was right. There was something much worse there now. It was Dr Aynsley, the Wild Man, and he was crouching feral and naked on the deep pile carpet watching Helen as she walked sleepily into the room, not seeing him. His eyes were glinting, his face smeared with a strange blue paint and his teeth looked too sharp to be human. His face was streaked by matted hair, there were patches of fur on his body. He had an erection. And he looked at Joanne with an expression that said: *She can't see me. You know she can't. And I'm going to finish off the job and really enjoy it.* He was scrabbling forward now as Helen approached. *Oh no no no no* . . .

Joanne could see the iron railing which the Wild Man had used to smash down their front door. It was lying, scarred, solid and heavy by the side of the bed. Suddenly, the paralysis was gone and Joanne was lunging full length across the bed to grab the iron spike. Aynsley was scrabbling across the carpet towards Helen and *why, God, oh why* couldn't Helen see him? Why couldn't she hear her screaming a warning to get out and run away? Why did she just stand, rubbing her eyes and moaning softly at the distant memories of a bad dream? Joanne swung the railing sideways and up as she lunged forward. The bedroom had become an endless stretching plain between herself, Aynsley and Helen. And now she was running towards them as Aynsley, all perspective distorted, reached for her daughter with a hand that suddenly seemed bigger than the room. Joanne raised the railing to its fullest height.

You won't have her! You won't!

The railing started its long descent . . .

. . . Helen could see that all the bad dreams were one. And the good feeling was flowing and blossoming inside her like warm sunshine, chasing the shadows. *Am I too late?* she thought. And now the dark clouds were racing and the sun was pouring through. Helen could feel it. She could understand it in the way that only a seven year-old child could understand it. And, more importantly, she could use it. It did not matter that Daddy was not here to hang the towel over the wardrobe's eyes because, now, she could do it herself. The wardrobe was halfway across the room, its big eyes glowing in the dark just like the Bad Man's eyes, as Helen leaned towards it and draped the towel around them. It was only a wardrobe now. Helen was spreading outwards, following shafts of rich, warm sunlight into the Land of Shadows, and she knew that this would be the hardest part. Something, somewhere, was moaning: low and throaty. And the moan was building, rising in volume and pitch until it became a shrieking, roaring noise filled with pain, anger and frustration. She could not let it do what it wanted to do because what it wanted was *wrong* and she hated anything that could want to frighten people so badly. She knew what she wanted, knew what she needed to do now more than anything else . . .

. . . And the tape spools were suddenly right there before her. Helen seized them from the machine before they could fade away again. She was tearing them, ripping them apart and destroying the evil that was on them.

181

. . . Loud, loud shrieking and pain and falling, falling, falling . . .

The metal railing fell from Joanne's hands, thudding heavily to the carpet as she staggered away; just in time to see the stranger who had grappled with Aynsley roll away from the prostrate form of her husband. And she just had time to think: *He was strangling Mark and I was going to kill him . . .* before the walls of the bedroom began to tilt and sway. Joanne put out a hand to stop the wall from slamming into her, trying to halt its crazy swinging, and then knew that she was lying on the floor and her mind was sinking into unconsciousness. A dreamless, nightmare-free sleep.

Mark felt the pressure go from his throat, spasmed and began to cough in lungfuls of air. The purple mist had gone. The Ghost Train Man had gone. Suddenly, Mark was back in the bedroom, lying on the carpet next to the tape recorder. Chadderton was beside him, struggling to rise to his feet, and Mark thought: *Oh God, is this part of the same nightmare?* But things were different now, he knew that. The dream had ended and somehow he was back in his own home.

Chadderton had seen Trafford's face become Davies' face at the last moment. He had seen what he was doing and had pulled away, believing that he had nearly killed him. All the time he had been strangling Trafford, that horrible, damned laughter had been echoing in his head, driving him on. But the laughter had changed and become a deep and desperate screaming, and Chadderton had thought: *That's stopped your laughing now, hasn't it, Trafford? Now I'm going to kill you and stop your laughing forever.* And then the face had become Davies and everything had changed.

Chadderton tried to roll up and stand, but his legs would not support him. He could hear Davies coughing and gagging next to him, and started to say: 'What the Christ . . .?' but the words would not come just yet. He looked up and saw the little girl standing over the tape recorder. The spools of tape were clenched in her small white hands and Chadderton could see that she had torn them to pieces. There was blood on her fingers but her face looked as blank as when they had burst into the room and saved her from Aynsley.

The screaming in Helen's head had gone now. She knew that she had found that feeling, had used it against Azimuth, and that he . . . it . . . had been chased away. But she also knew that she had not beaten him for good. She had not killed him because he could not be killed. The screaming had stopped and there was a new sound inside her head. It was the horrible little girl. She was giggling and laughing. She knew that, although Helen had stopped Azimuth from getting what he wanted now, there was a greater plan soon to begin that Helen could never stop.

My Catalysts are coming and the Great Tasting will still take place, Helen. Now it was the voice of the Ghost Train Man speaking through the evil Angelina. *Nothing can stop that. And you can't even help your Daddy any more.* Helen knew that Azimuth was right. In the real world she had been in shock. And what she had been through in the Bad Place had sent her even deeper into her own mind. Because only there could she rest and get better. There were so many things that she wanted to tell her Daddy about Azimuth. So much she could tell him that he could use. But she knew now that she could never do that. She was in deep shock. She could not speak, could not warn Daddy about what Azimuth had been planning for so long . . . Azimuth's pain and anger had vanished now. It had been a minor defeat. He could not stay in their minds as he would normally have wished; Helen had prevented this by using the power. But the One who was Chosen and had Denied would never know what that power was, because Helen would have to stay in her Safe Place for a long time until her mind could heal. As Helen pulled the safe, white curtains across her mind, Azimuth was laughing, knowing that the Time of Arrival was imminent and could not be prevented.

Mark stood up, rubbing his bruised larynx, and stumbled across the room to where Joanne lay. Chadderton was on his feet now, bent double with one hand on the counterpane to balance him. Joanne was moaning as Mark picked her up. 'Oh Mark, I had a terrible dream . . .'

Mark looked back into the corner of the room. Aynsley still lay there, unconscious now, like some battered rag doll that had been thrown across the room by a petulant child.

'What the bloody hell is going on?' Chadderton was easing himself up onto the bed, rubbing his forehead. 'I think I must have cracked up.'

Mark helped Joanne to the bed, eased her gently down and

183

looked back to where Helen stood by the tape recorder. The spools of tape were hanging in shredded ribbons, falling to the carpet like discarded party decorations. Mark moved quickly to her, swept her up into his arms, holding her close to him. Instantly, she was asleep and Mark, not knowing yet what had happened, was weeping freely as he realised that, whatever had happened, Helen had saved them all from something worse than madness.

Twelve

The King's Cross-to-Newcastle train was late.

But for once, Grace had not blamed Philip. Thousands of commuters, all on different errands and heading for different destinations, swarmed over the station as they had done for many years. And none of the faceless thousands paid any heed to the thin, dark-haired man with the stooped shoulders and the big, big smile; or to his wife with the bouffant hair-do; or the small daughter with the ringlets, as they stepped down onto Platform Eight with their two suitcases and carrier bag. After all, there was nothing special about them, was there? Faces like any others: three of the faceless thousands. Faceless. And no one suspected anything of the Face which hid behind their masks.

The Gascoynes moved up the stairs which led to the over-track bridge. They were in no particular hurry as the other passengers pushed and jostled past, not noticing that all three wore the same identical smile, shared the same secret and had the same purpose. Grace carried a suitcase. Philip carried a suitcase. Angelina carried the plastic carrier bag. And all the time, as they ascended the stairs, they smiled. Smiled, smiled, smiled.

*   *   *

Eric Morpeth had not turned in for work today and Tadger Wright was not at all pleased. For the past week he had been listening to him moaning on in the pub about how unwell he had been feeling and it had started to get right on Tadger's nerves. If he was going to go off sick, if he fancied a few days in bed and a couple of early afternoons on the beer, then why the hell didn't he just go ahead and do it instead of bending every bugger's ear about how bad he was? Tadger stood at the ticket booth at the foot of the ramp from Platform Nine's bridge, punching tickets. And each time he punched a ticket, he was punching a hole right through that little fucker Eric's eyeball and hoping that he really would catch some sort of bug while he was skiving. Then he would *have* to be on the sick and it would serve him right, an' all.

Tadger had paid no attention to any of the people who had handed him tickets that day, and didn't even see the family with the great big smile that bundled towards him with their suitcases. But when the man pressed the tickets into his hand, Tadger felt something he had only ever felt once before in his life and had hoped he would never feel again.

The first time had been when he was twelve years old and staying with his Aunt Freda in Bermondsey. Aunt Freda was a huge fat woman who, in retrospect, he supposed must have been suffering from elephantiasis. Both he and his widowed mother were staying with her for the week, because Aunt Freda was very, very ill and the doctors had only given her a short time to live. Tadger's mother was out in the back kitchen, filling a coal scuttle, and Tadger had been sitting in a chair next to Aunt Freda as she lay in bed. He did not want to be there. He would rather have been anywhere else but sitting in this dingy bedroom with its stuffy smell and this great whale of a woman lying under a mountain of bedclothes. Aunt Freda had started to make a noise; a low, moaning noise in the back of her throat, and Tadger had called in panic for his mother. But she was filling the scuttle and the sound of coal chunks rattling against metal drowned out his call. Tadger had just begun to rise to his feet when a huge, pudgy white hand snaked out from the bedclothes and fastened on his wrist. The grip was solid but clammy and Tadger had felt something like an electric shock shooting up his arm and down his spinal cord. It was as if a squid's tentacle had suddenly flopped out and caught him. And

185

Tadger had screamed until his mother finally came running to pry him loose from Aunt Freda's dead grasp, finger by stiff finger. Tadger had never forgotten that moment.

And now, Tadger felt the same dull, horrible thrill of horror as those tickets were pushed into his hands. It brought back with startling vividness that memory which had haunted his dreams since childhood. His stomach rolled in one convulsive heave and he looked up directly into the face before him, expecting to see the enormous figure of his long-dead aunt standing before him in all its flabby white immensity. But it was a tallish man with a slight stoop, dark hair and white face, with a knowing grin that seemed to look right inside his soul, to that dull afternoon forty years ago in a dingy bedroom in Bermondsey. Tadger stamped the tickets and thrust them back at the man as if they were contaminated. The man smiled again and moved away. The woman behind him was looking at Tadger, too . . . and the little girl . . . and for an instant Tadger thought: *Christ, they've all got the same face,* before he realised that it wasn't their faces. It was the smile. A horrible white, poisonous smile. Tadger's stomach rolled again. And he began to wonder if Eric's tales of over-work might also apply to him. *Maybe a coupla days rest . . .*

Thirteen

Matt Jackson had been a taxi driver for the past fifteen years. It was a good life. You got to be your own boss (more or less). You could work whatever hours you liked. Late shift, early shift. All day. What the hell? So long as there was enough cash to pay the bills, keep Mavis happy and make for a couple of nights on the booze. In his day, Matt had been a brickie's labourer, had done his National Service and had enjoyed it (which seemed to put him at a distance from every other square basher he had known), and had tried his hand on the trawlers that operated out of North Shields. He had been sacked from the latter when he had beaten the crap out of the skipper when the old bastard queered up the back wages owing to him. Being sacked made no difference to him – he had intended to pack it in anyway. And so to the taxi rank. Point A to point B, pay the man, next customer if-you-please!

It had been a slow morning. It was drizzling lightly and Matt had watched as the thin crust of snow on the pavements dissolved slowly to slush. He had picked up two punters: total score – £4.50. Big deal. There were two taxis in front of him now and Matt wondered how they had been doing this morning. Two hippies climbed into the first cab. If this had been 11.30 at night, and he had been the first taxi in the rank, there was no way he would have picked those two up. The first taxi was pulling away now and Matt recognised the driver as Jack Fisher. He wondered if Jack's wife was still screwing around with that night club owner. The next cab moved up and he followed slowly behind as a young girl climbed into it. The driver was Ernie Bishop and Matt knew that he would be using his best tap-up patter on her for however long it took to get to where she was going. Poor old Ernie. *Just like the old Benny Hill record*, thought Matt. He never got anywhere with the birds. Never would, unless his best friend told him about the old b.o. problem. But then again, Ernie didn't have a best friend, so Matt supposed that he was stuck.

Girls were the worst when it came to bother on the taxis. He'd had more problems with 'hen' night crowds than he had ever had with bachelor nights. He remembered a night two years ago when a really smart bit of stuff had puked on his back seat and then had the bloody cheek to try and run away without paying. Matt didn't have time for drunken bints. He'd chased her, taken her purse, grabbed the three quid that was owing to him and then chucked the purse straight into the canal, leaving the bird in question shrieking and yelling on the canal bank. He knew the type. All fur coat and no knickers. *Never again*, Matt had thought. *No more hen party pick-ups.*

Matt was a big man, had always been big. He knew how to handle himself, and on the occasions when there had been real aggro, there had been one or two sore heads the following morning. But trouble of that kind was rare. Matt had been driving taxis for fifteen years and he could sense trouble straight away. And when you sensed it, well, you just drove on, man . . .

187

The girl in front was just shutting the taxi door when a face appeared at Matt's passenger seat window. A knuckle rapped on the glass.

'Are you free, please?' It was a middle-aged man with a big smile. Behind him, Matt could see what he presumed were his wife and daughter.

'Sure. Hop in! The door's open.'

'We've got some suitcases,' said the man as Matt leaned across and threw open the passenger door lock.

'Okay.' Matt climbed out on his side and moved round to the back; the man took another suitcase from his wife and followed him. The woman and the little girl were climbing into the back seat as Matt took the suitcases from the man and fitted them neatly into the boot.

'I hope they'll fit all right,' said the man, with the same big grin on his face.

'No trouble,' said Matt, moving back to the front and climbing into the driving seat. 'No trouble at all.'

The man climbed into the front passenger seat and slammed the door. He was still smiling when Matt asked: 'Where to?'

'Osborne Road, Jesmond, please,' said the man. Matt picked up the mike from the dash and radioed in his pick-up and destination. He pulled away from the taxi rank.

For the last time.

*   *   *

'You on holiday?' asked Matt after a while.

Some punters liked to talk, others didn't. It didn't usually bother Matt one way or the other, but business had been really slow this morning, and the previous punters hadn't been in the car long enough to say, 'Hello, goodbye'. Matt was sick of the quiet, and besides, he felt like hearing his own voice.

'Holiday? Yes . . . ' said the man, and from the corner of his eye Matt could see that he was turning to look at him, smiling again. Now why couldn't everybody be as friendly as that? All those miserable faces wandering around town like extras from a zombie film. It made a change to see someone who was happy, particularly on a rotten morning like this.

'Yeah? I can always tell. Accent plus suitcase equals business. Accent plus suitcases plus family equals holiday. Staying with friends or family?'

'Both,' came an answer from behind, and Matt looked in the mirror at the woman sitting in the back. She was smiling at him. And Matt could hear the little girl giggling into the back of her hand. No kidding, it made a change to see so many happy, smiling faces. Matt could not see the little girl. She was seated too low on the back seat. The woman looked pale but fairly attractive. There were two hard lines at the side of her mouth and for an instant, Matt thought: *There's a face for frowning, not for smiling.* But she was smiling all the same and it made him feel good as he cruised up from the city center, took a slip road and headed for Jesmond.

'Oh . . . I forgot,' said the man suddenly. 'I need to buy some . . . chocolates. A present, do you see? For the family. Do you think you could pull into that side street there? I think I can see a shop.'

'No problem,' said Matt, swerving from the main road. He could see the sign of a small corner shop. He had never been down this way before but he supposed that it was a sweet shop. The buildings on the other side of the street were in the process of being demolished. A silent bulldozer stood in a pile of rubble. There were no workmen to be seen. *Probably on one of their half-hour tea breaks while the country goes down the frigging drain*, thought Matt. The car was rounding the corner now and Matt could see that the man had been right about it being a shop. But the place was derelict and looked as if it had been so for some time. Matt began to turn, to tell the man that there was another shop on the main road just a little way up and that it was on their way to Jesmond anyway, when something small seemed to bounce up over the back of the seat behind him. Two small arms were suddenly wrapped around his neck, squeezing tightly, and Matt started to yell: 'What the hell . . .?' but the woman was lunging forward too and something had gone snap inside Matt's head. Just before he blacked out altogether, he had a crazy, distorted view of the man sitting next to him, still smiling his big smile.

'No problem,' said the man as Matt's world slipped into darkness.

189

Fourteen

Chadderton wanted a drink more than he had ever needed one in his life.

'I was right . . . you're a carrier, Davies. It's some kind of mental disease. And you've given it to me, you bastard!' Something had broken the spell of nightmare and Chadderton felt able to move now, able to participate.

For a while, Mark was unable to answer; clutching his daughter close to him, tears streaming down his face. He kept his face away from Chadderton who sounded as if he had just come out of a hangover. Joanne was moving now, saying sleepily: 'Oh God, what *was* it, Mark? Am I going mad?'

'You're wrong,' Mark said to Chadderton, his voice sounding choked and preternaturally loud in the bedroom. 'You know you're wrong. You're just too frightened to admit it. It's not a mental bug, or whatever you say . . . it's . . . ' And Mark groped for the words to sum up what it was that had invaded their minds, knowing that somehow they had been saved from it; knowing that even though it had touched their minds and wanted to stay (*wanted to stay, just as it's stayed with me for all these months*), it had been expelled by something Helen had done. Knowing that it had claimed him three times and that three times he had denied it. And that it was . . . was . . .

'It's evil,' said Aynsley.

The wild, ragged man was speaking in a cultured Oxbridge voice which Mark recognized of old. 'Its name is Azimuth and it's as old as time. And it's evil.'

'It was a bad dream,' said Joanne in a small voice. 'It was all just a bad dream.'

'I told you not to play the tape.' Aynsley's voice sounded ridiculously normal; like a cultured English don trapped inside a huge, broken and dishevelled ventriloquist's dummy. The wild glinting of his eyes had faded to a dull, unhealthy glaze. It was bizarre. 'Azimuth was on the tape. When you played it of your own free will you conjured it up.'

'Fuck *you*!' Chadderton suddenly exploded, the abrupt burst of anger dizzying him so that he had to grope his way back to the bed. 'Where do you keep the booze, Davies?'

And Joanne, needing desperately to put everything in perspective, seized upon this simple request to bring her back to the ordinary world. A world where maniacs didn't destroy your car, hack their way through your front door, into your house and into your worst dreams. 'It's downstairs. I'll get it.'

Mark did not like the way she was reacting now. 'Your head, Jo . . . ' he began.

'It's all right. Really, it's all right. I'll be back in a minute.'

Back in a minute, thought Mark. *I'll just get the meat out of the freezer. I've got one hundred and one things to do today, Mark. Try to keep Helen out of the kitchen. You know what she's like.*

She was gone now, moving through the shattered door frame as if she had a slight hangover. Just like two wedding anniversaries ago when they had got stoned on her home-made wine. Bitterly, Mark remembered that he had missed their last anniversary. He had been lying comatose in a hospital bed and she had been here with Helen, praying for him. *And something evil had been riding the lines.* Mark laid Helen gently down on the bed next to Chadderton. She was sleeping soundly as if nothing had happened at all.

'It's a bug, that's what it is. We've all caught it, now,' Chadderton breathed angrily.

'It got into my mind, Mark,' said Aynsley. 'I'm sorry. It got into my mind and I had to do what it told me.'

'Where is it now? Where has it gone?' Mark heard himself say.

'It's been cast out again. But it's stronger now than it's ever been. You've got to do something now while there's still time. It's been trapped on the line, feeding on the line for a long time, Mark. Feeding and growing strong. It could never venture very far from the rails before but it's getting stronger every day. Soon, it won't be trapped on the line any more. It'll be free to move where it wishes. But it's still a prisoner, Mark. You've still got time . . . ' Aynsley retched, a convulsion that seemed to shake his entire frame. 'It used me. It got inside me. It got inside the tape. That's how it came here. It's a prisoner of the lines. But the time is coming soon when it'll have fed and grown strong enough to escape . . . '

'For Christ's sake, let's get out of here,' said Chadderton, still leaning heavily on the bed, running one hand through his ruffled hair. 'We've got to get this nutter to a hospital. Your wife and kid need help, too. Just give me a minute to pull myself together, that's all.'

Aynsley convulsed again, his breath catching and spuming with a sibilant, rattling sound as if his insides were likely to bubble upwards and outwards through his mouth at any second. His eyes started from their sockets. 'Please . . . ' And now he was holding out his hand to Mark in desperation. 'Take my hand, Mark. Take it and you'll know.'

Mark could feel an old familiar feeling creeping around the base of his spine, curling around his nervous system and snapping at his soul. It was a familiar fear. And it was saying: *What if whatever he's talking about is still in him? What if he wants to touch me so that it can get back into me again?*

Aynsley retched again, spittle spraying onto the carpet. He looked up at Mark and seemed to see what was going on in the latter's mind.

'It's gone, Mark. It's not in me any more. I'm no more use to it. *It's used me up.* Take my hand, damn you! There isn't much time left. Don't you see? Azimuth used me, burned me up inside so that it could make all your nightmares.'

Chadderton was slowly standing up, finally orientating himself and pushing all of this lunacy back into the dream world where it belonged. Reality had taken over again. 'We're going to the police,' he said in a manner that brooked no disagreement.

'No, don't listen to him, Mark! You've got to trust me and take my hand. He's too frightened to believe. I *saw* all your bad dreams. I saw your wife burning in that glass case. I saw you killing Mark, thinking that it was Trafford. That's what Azimuth wanted!'

'Shut up, shut up, SHUT UP, YOU CRAZY BASTARD!' Chadderton refused to look at him, refused to let reality blur at the edges again. The man was a dangerous homicidal maniac; the fact that he knew what only Chadderton had seen in his hallucination did not fit in with the equation. It was not real. The only thing that was real was . . . was . . .

Mark moved quickly across the room to Aynsley and Chadderton saw the look on his face: as if regardless of the consequences he had made a decision to grasp a poisonous snake lying on the floor. Aynsley's claw-like hand was clutch-

192

ing upwards at Mark as he reached for it, and something inside Chadderton, something which had as yet refused to submit to rationality, made him lunge forward to prevent the contact being made. But it was too late. Mark had taken the outstretched claw with both of his hands an instant before Chadderton's hand closed on Mark's shoulder.

Two years before, Chadderton had been changing a bulb in his living room, standing on a chair and twisting at the small glass globe which refused to part from its socket; cursing and swearing at it while his wife looked on, laughing helplessly. Her laughter was choked off when his finger had completed a circuit and the resultant shock had sent him sprawling to the carpet. What he felt now was the closest comparison he could make. As he touched Mark, a dull, buzzing, *dragging* feeling shot along his arm. As if something had seized every nerve ending in his arm and given a short, hard tug. Chadderton pulled back quickly, gasping. Mark was kneeling down beside Aynsley and they were looking at each other; just staring at each other as serious as hell. Chadderton moved back to the bed, while the two men continued to stare into each other's eyes. And in Chadderton's spinning thoughts, he could hear himself thinking: *No. Not ready yet. Do not pass Go. Do not collect £200. What the hell . . . am I cracking up? Have I really gone over the top?*

Joanne entered the room again, a bottle of Bell's whisky dangling from one hand. Vacantly she brushed a strand of renegade hair from her forehead, appearing not to see Mark and Aynsley. She moved to the bed and cradled Helen as Chadderton seized the bottle from her. He unscrewed the cap, dropped it to the carpet and swallowed a mouthful of whisky, still watching as Mark and Aynsley stared and stared. Davies' face was deathly white, concentrating hard on something. Even from where he sat, Chadderton could see the beads of moisture on the man's brow. Aynsley's eyes were dull and vacant, far away. Chadderton could sense that Joanne, sitting beside him, had finally seen them and was leaning forward in alarm. Without realising why, and to his consternation, he realised that he had gripped her arm and was preventing her from rising. The little girl was mumbling in her sleep. To Chadderton, it seemed that she was calling for her father. The woman turned to her daughter again but Chadderton retained

193

his grip on her arm while he took another swig from the whisky bottle. He thought: *I'm waiting for something. Waiting until something has been completed.* And again, he had the feeling that reality, *his* reality, had temporarily blurred around the edges. He began the task of ignoring these insane, instinctive urges and feelings, to pull himself out of the nightmare and back into the real world. And while Chadderton struggled, Mark and Aynsley continued to stare at each other in silent communication. Next to him, he could hear that the woman was crying. Soft, bitter tears. He drank again.

And waited.

Fifteen

When Matt finally awoke, it took him a long while to realise where he was and what had happened. It was dark. He appeared to have been crammed into a tight space and he could not move his arms or legs. Then he became aware that he was in a car. He could hear the engine, feel the movement below him. For an instant, there was a spear of light before him and he could see a cross-section of rubbery lines; a stamped-out cigarette butt. Then he realised where he was: in the back seat of his own taxi. He recognised the rubber mat on the floor, which had taken him so long to hose down when that smart bint had puked all over it last year. He was pushed down under the back seat of his own taxi and could not remember how the hell he had got there. Something was wrong. He could see a woman's leg in front of him. He tried to move. In the next instant, something sharp was being thrust savagely against his neck. He tried to make an outraged protest, but the sharp point pressed even harder. He knew that it had drawn blood. Matt had only known terror like this once before. During his National Service days, he had been swinging across a gully on a length of rope as part of an assault course. The rope had tangled around his legs and he had swung back and forth over the gully, convinced that

194

he was going to fall; that he was going to die. He had the same feeling now as the sharp tip gouged his throat. He ceased to struggle and kept perfectly still. The pressure at his throat eased a little. From somewhere above him, he could hear the little girl giggling and, suddenly, he remembered his pick-up at the Central Station. He remembered the smiling man and his smiling wife. The little girl who giggled in the back seat. And he remembered taking the turning off to stop at the shop for the man. It was the last thing that he remembered. Matt clenched and unclenched his fists, felt the fabric of whatever it was that they had tied him up with, suddenly realising that it was the length of washing line that he always kept in the boot to tie luggage onto the roof-rack. He supposed that the woman or the man must have hit him with something, for he could feel a dull aching on the back of his head and something dried and crusted on his neck, which he knew could only be dried blood.

The car went over a bump in the road, the impact knocking the wind from Matt's lungs. He wondered how long they had been travelling, and the sudden metallic click from the dashboard told him that the man had not turned off the clock. A crackling from the radio, and Matt recognised Sylvia's voice from the office.

'Matt? Where the hell are you?' Silence. And then: 'Matt! You know you've got a pick-up at 2.30. Please confirm that your Jesmond pick-up is completed.' Another pause and Matt could just imagine Sylvia sitting at the switchboard, chewing gum, reading *Woman's Own* and getting more heated as he failed to answer. He had a pick-up at 2.30. It must be pretty near to that time now. He had made the Central Station pick-up at 11.00am. Christ! They had been driving for hours. He had been out for all that time. Where the hell were they taking him? Matt tried to squirm round so that he could get a better view. Instantly, the sharp point was pressing hard against his throat. He stopped moving. He had gained an inch, could see the top of the driving seat and could just make out the still, implacable head of the man as the radio crackled into life again: 'Matt! You're going to be in trouble if you don't answer.' A sudden mumbling of voices in the office, and Matt could just overhear Sylvia saying to someone: 'I don't think he's in the car. I think he's just parked it somewhere and buggered off.' And then, he could hear a male voice (he didn't know whose)

195

mumbling something: '. . . like him . . . pub.' Matt wanted to scream at her: *You stupid bint! I'm not at the pub, I haven't buggered off! I'm in the car with three bloody loonies! And I've been kidnapped or something!* But the sharp point against his throat prevented him from making any sound. Another click, and he realised that the man had switched the radio off.

The car was swinging round now, turning off the main highway. As the center of gravity shifted, Matt felf himself sliding further down toward the floor. The pressure on his throat began to ease again. He had a sudden glimpse of a Texaco gas pump in the top left hand corner of the wind-screen and realised that they were pulling in somewhere for gas. Suddenly oblivious to his danger, he began to struggle upwards. A small, slender hand knotted in his thick, black curly hair, yanking him backwards; and the point was at his throat again, only harder and with a brutality that meant business. *Christ!* thought Matt. *She's going to kill me!* He could hear the little girl giggling again. A bead of blood trickled down his neck as he heard the driver's door open and the man get out. Matt listened, his heartbeat thudding desperately in his chest as the man moved to the gas pump. He heard the clunking rattle as the man unhooked the hose. A scrabbling at the gas tank as the hose was fitted. *Self service,* thought Matt desperately. *Oh, God, it's self service and no one's going to see me.* He could hear the gas surging into the tank. After a while, there was another clunk as the hose was pulled away and returned to its bracket. Silence. Matt could imagine the man walking over to the office. In his mind's eye, he saw the man enter, stand in the line. He could see the fat, balding assistant behind the counter flashing a smile at the man as he looked out into the forecourt and saw the taxi sitting there; saw the woman and her daughter sitting composed in the back seat, unaware that they were keeping a big, ex-National Service man stuffed down between them with a knife at his throat.

'How's business?' Matt could imagine the Fat Man saying.

'Not so bad,' replied the Man with the Smile.

'Haven't left your meter running, have you?'

'Some chance. That bitch has been watching the clock ever since I picked her up. Expect the kid'll have chocolate all over the back seat by now.'

The Man with the Smile was paying for his gas and the Fat

Man was smiling as he handed over the change, wishing him a nice day. And now the Man with the Smile was coming back. Matt heard the car door open, heard the Man climb into the car. Seconds later, the engine was gunning into life and the car pulled out of the station and onto the highway again, heading for its unknown destination. For the first time in his life, Matt fainted.

Sixteen

Mark pulled away from Aynsley with a force that made Chadderton unconsciously tighten his grip on Joanne's arm. The dark strands of sweat-soaked hair plastered across his forehead made him look like some pearl diver who had been underwater for too long and had suddenly surfaced, gasping for air. He took a step back, arms still held out towards Aynsley. Joanne called his name softly and bitterly, as if he were suddenly lost to her. Aynsley's claw-like hand remained outstretched and Chadderton could see that his eyes had rolled up into his head, the whites glinting dull in the now faded daylight: pinpoints of light in a tattered, ragged mass.

'Standing stones,' said Mark in a hoarse, choked voice which Chadderton barely recognised.

'Now you know all I can give you,' said Aynsley slowly and gutturally. The hand flopped to the carpet and there was an expression on Aynsley's face which could have been a token smile or a hideous grimace. 'All used up . . . all used up . . .'

Mark backed to the bed and sat down beside Joanne, heavily enough to make a gout of whisky slosh from the neck of the bottle across Chadderton's legs. He was still looking at the broken rag doll on the floor as he pulled Joanne close to him. Her arms went round his neck, face buried into his chest. Chadderton released the woman, looked back at Aynsley and in that instant knew that *something* was going to happen. The nerves in the arm which had touched Mark were aching with a

197

dull, nagging pain. He could feel something wrong in the air and for a second, the horrified thought came to him that reality was about to slip away yet again. Next to him, he became aware that Davies had sensed the same thing and was holding his wife even more tightly.

Aynsley's face was still contorted in a fixed smile or grimace, lips drawn back from yellowed teeth, skin wrinkled and cracked like the visage of some huge Capo Di Monte figurine. In the darkness, Chadderton could see that his head was sagging slightly. And now, there was some kind of movement around his chest. The ragged shirt front was moving . . . no, not moving. It was smoke. Thin wisps of oily black smoke were drifting around his torso, from his shirt, from inside his jacket. Dirty, black tendrils of smoke, shifting and twisting upwards like small black serpents. A smell of ozone seemed to hang heavily in the air. Chadderton became aware that a dark, bluish light was beginning to suffuse the room. It made him think of the time he had lain blind drunk in a second-rate hotel in Leeds. The blue neon hotel sign was just below his bedroom window and lit up the darkness of his room with a cold, blue, blood-less light. The same unhealthy blue light was now spreading through the room, creeping along the walls and throwing sharp angular shadows up the bedroom walls and over the furniture. Three faces shone deathly blue in the reflected hue, like corpses three days in the water. Now, Chadderton realised that the light was coming from Aynsley. And it was somehow a *dark* light. Aynsley lay in the same position, a phosphorescent blue surrounding him, like ice on fire, issuing *from* him as dark snakes curled from his shirt front, casting a brighter flicker of light across the psychiatrist's ghastly, frozen features. The flame burst and flared, smoke billowed thick and black and, in seconds, Aynsley's body was burning.

'Oh no . . . not again,' moaned Joanne, giving voice to the inner horror which had suddenly revived in all three of them. Blue flames crackled and spread. In seconds, all sight of Aynsley's body was consumed by flame. Held frozen in horror, they watched the burning man-shape in the corner of the room. Too horrified to react, they could not see that the flames which crackled and swirled around Aynsley were not spreading to the rest of the room; that although the flames were licking at the bedroom window curtains, the fabric of the curtains did not ignite. The burning mass was crumbling now, the sagging ball of flame which had once been a head was caving in, falling away. The body was disintegrating and shrivelling. In another instant, the flames were gone. The thick black smoke was disappearing. Fading into nothingness and leaving no trace. A pile of charcoaled ashes smouldered in the corner and a yellow substance trickled greasily on the wall where Aynsley had been propped, crackling in the heat. A single, blackened shoe poked incongruously from the ruined mass which had once been a man.

Chadderton felt the spell break. They were all back to reality. The nightmare had ended. The grisly remains on the carpet were the only proof of what they had been through. Chadderton found his feet, moved quickly to the light switch beside the bedroom door and flicked it on. Light would chase the shadows away forever. He turned back as the room lit up; the smouldering pile still lay in the corner, specks of soot dancing in the air.

And despite himself, Chadderton realised that the nightmare had not ended. Something inside told him that the real nightmare, the nightmare to end all nightmares, had not yet even begun.

*   *   *

It was dark when Matt awoke. They were travelling over rough ground, jolting and bumping. His mouth felt baked dry and salty, and he realised that the woman's hand was still clenched in his hair. It was not a dream. He groaned aloud and felt the grip tighten as the car swung round a tight curve and began bouncing over even rougher terrain. There were no streetlights to brighten the interior of the car as they moved. From the dashboard, Matt heard a metallic click. The meter was still on. *That's some fare they're gonna have to pay*, a small, frightened voice tried to joke in the back of his mind.

'Look . . . ' he said, the words croaking in the back of his parched throat, '. . . look . . . if it's the money you want, just take it. There's not much but you're welcome to it. There's a wallet in my jerkin pocket, 'bout twenty quid. You don't need me for anything.' The little girl began to giggle. The man and

199

woman remained silent. 'What is this? Kidnapping?' Again the giggling; again the silence. 'You've got to be kidding, mister. Kidnapping? Me? I'm just a taxi driver scratching around for a living. I'm worth nothing, zero . . . Nobody's going to pay anything to get me back . . . nobody I know's *got* anything. So come on, mister. Just let me out. You can have the car . . .'

Suddenly the car had stopped. The woman's grip twisted, making Matt cry out in pain, and then forced his head downwards again. Boiling rage, heedless of the consequences, began to take over inside him. He started to struggle upwards, but at the same moment he sensed that the man in the driving seat was leaning over towards him. There was a sharp blow on the side of his head and the interior of the car was suddenly lit up by a cloud of sparks. In a dream, Matt heard the car door open and felt cool night air blowing on his face as he was dragged out. The ground swung up to meet him and he noticed in a curiously detached way that it consisted of churned-up mud and grass. He was being carried now. Someone had his legs, someone else was struggling with his head and shoulders. The moon see-sawed crazily across the sky and then everything went black again.

*   *   *

Philip and Grace had studied the map very carefully on the train. Emble Cottage was two miles out of Bamburgh, easily reached and with good access to the town but remote enough to give them all the privacy they needed for a nice break in the country. The long drive from Newcastle had been made in silence. There was no need for words. Everything had already been said. They had been told everything. They were one. And, smiling all the time, they had finally arrived in Bamburgh, taking the route into rougher country to find Emble Cottage nestling in trees at the summit of a rise overlooking the surrounding countryside.

Still smiling, Philip carried the bulky form of the taxi driver to the front door of the cottage. He groped for the key in his pocket, found it and opened the door. The lights were working. Just as the brochure had said: everything in readiness for their arrival. Angelina ran in ahead of them, clapping her hands and spinning a little dance in the center of the room. It was

200

perfect. Just perfect. Low oak beams supported the ceiling. And all this . . . this . . . olde worlde furniture. Angelina turned back to look as her Mummy and Daddy dragged the big fat man into the center of the room and left him on the floor. He was beginning to moan as Daddy ran quickly to the car for their suitcases. Mummy was hunting for the central heating controls; had found the thermostat and was turning it on.

The fat man was burbling baby words. Daddy came back to the cottage and shut the front door on the cold night outside. Angelina ran to him and he embraced her. Excitedly, she looked up into his eyes, expectation written all over her small face. And now Daddy was nodding indulgently, meaning that it was time. They could do it now. Angelina ran into the kitchen to see that Mummy was already preparing things. She ran to help her. Mummy had found the kitchen drawer where all the cooking utensils were kept and was rummaging through it. Between them, they selected two bread knives, a cleaver from the rack above the sink, an old steak knife with a broken tip but a sharp cutting edge, and a skewer. Grace found the most important thing of all in her handbag.

A needle and a reel of nylon thread.

They moved back into the front room. Smiling, always smiling. Daddy had taken off his coat and was standing over the taxi man who was waking up. That was good.

Azimuth was speaking to them again. They could hear all the words. He was hungry. He needed to feast on the fat man's fear. And then he would tell them their part in the Arrival.

Not a snack this time, thought Angelina. But a long, slow meal.

Matt finally woke up.

The horror began.

It took him two days to die.

Seventeen

Mark, Chadderton and Joanne exchanged no words as they drove to the General Hospital that night. Joanne had started humming; a small, childlike lullaby as she cradled her daughter in the back seat of the car. Helen had slept through the nightmare of the burning, was still sleeping as they arrived at the hospital, and was admitted for shock. Chadderton did all the talking. There had been an accident. Mother and daughter had been in a car smash while returning from a shopping trip. Mother had hit her head on the windshield, daughter had been severely shaken up. Joanne had insisted that she was all right as she was given treatment for the cut on her head, and then had collapsed as her daughter was taken away. Joanne was admitted, too. Also suffering from shock. Chadderton had flashed his ID, the Nurse-on-Duty had failed to notice that it was no longer valid, and the necessary forms had been filled in.

Silently, Mark and Chadderton walked back to the car. In the car park, Mark suddenly broke down, one hand covering his face, his shoulders convulsing as sobbing racked his body. Tears flowed freely between his fingers. He had not cried that way since he had been a child. Chadderton moved on to the car, lighting a cigarette with fingers that shook badly, allowing Mark the privacy of a grief that was more like relief.

The drive back to Mark's house was also made in silence. Black and blue shadows chased across their faces. It began to rain and liquid light and shade joined the chase as they moved on through the night. When they finally took the turning into the driveway, the wreck of Mark's car was hidden in the larger shadow of the house, crouching against the porch. The moon sparkled on the garden pool and Chadderton could just see the rim of the ornamental fountain jutting from the dark water. A tyre track gouged its way across the garden into the shadow. Chadderton parked his car in the drive. As they both moved towards the house, the shattered door frame creaked slightly in the evening air. Chadderton turned to the wrecked car, leaned in and braced himself against the window frame to push. Mark came forward to help but Chadderton shook his head: 'You're in no fit state. See what you can do with the door.' They were the first words that had passed between them in over two hours.

As Mark went into the house, Chadderton heaved against the car, using his anger and feeling the crunch of tires on broken glass as it moved. Minutes later, the car was in the driveway. Mark had found a piece of panelling in the cellar and had just finished nailing it to the shattered door when Chadderton entered. Without a word, they both mounted the stairs to the bedroom. Mark flicked the light switch. The smell of ozone was still strong. Together, they stared at the pile of ashes in the corner of the room; both knowing that it would not have vanished, that the pile would still be there. Evidence of the nightmare.

'Why didn't the room catch fire?' asked Chadderton quietly, almost to himself. 'Why couldn't we move?'

Mark tried to say: *I don't know. Why did any of it happen?* But the words would not come.

'It's time to talk,' said Chadderton.

'Yes.'

'What happened between you and Aynsley?'

'Not here. Downstairs.'

In the living room, everything seemed more real. There were no shattered doorways, no broken glass, no pile of ashes that had once been a human being. Mark began to speak as soon as he had put on the gas fire and sat heavily on the sofa. He explained what had happened at the surgery: the dream, the hypnosis, Aynsley's disappearance.

'The tape? What the hell happened with the tape?' asked Chadderton.

'Aynsley told us,' Mark replied. 'Something evil attacked me on that train. It got into my mind and hid there like a parasite, feeding on my fear. When Aynsley unlocked that secret and made me remember, it came out of me and invaded his mind.'

Chadderton was looking down as he listened, clenching and unclenching his hands.

'The tape was playing while all this happened,' Mark continued, 'so the evil was taped as well. It had possessed Aynsley but we got rid of it somehow when we came back for Helen and Joanne. God help us, I summoned it up again by playing the tape. That's how it got into our minds.'

203

'Then it's still in our minds, hiding in there as it did with you.'

'No . . . Something happened. Helen was involved somehow. Something she was able to do got it out of our minds altogether and chased it back to where it came from. Listen, Chadderton – when you saved me from throwing myself in front of that train, the evil was in me then. But it was . . . ' Mark hunted for a different phrase to express himself from the one that immediately sprang to mind, but could not find it. '. . . It was cast out of me by your actions. It was temporarily beaten. It had to get away, feed and grow strong enough to try again. And when that happened I could feel that something had also happened inside my mind. It's been in there, Chadderton,' Mark continued, rapping on his forehead with his knuckles, 'and because it's been in there, it has inadvertently opened something up. I don't know what it is but it's like a new *awareness*. I can understand how this thing behaves without knowing exactly what it *is* yet. Aynsley tried to help me. But his mind was really too far gone. I know that it's a force . . . a very old . . . very evil force. It's probably been "alive", if you can call it that, since the beginning of creation. Aynsley called it Azimuth. It feeds on fear, Chadderton. It feeds on our greatest fears and under the right circumstances it can conjure them up. Somehow, it lives and travels on the King's Cross train. And it's . . . growing . . . towards something.'

'I don't understand. You say that the Evil's on the line – then it's in you, it's in Aynsley and it's on the tape at the same time.'

'It exists on the line. You heard Aynsley. It's somehow trapped on the line and it's been travelling there for years. It left a *trace* of itself in me, a *trace* in Aynsley, a *trace* on the tape. It has put a trace of itself into everyone who's ever travelled on the line and committed one of those atrocities afterwards. Can't you see it? Someone gets on a train at King's Cross. The Evil is also somehow on that train, on that line. It chooses him as its . . . its . . . food. It works its way into the person's mind, feeding on his everyday fears and doubts. But it has to make those fears greater, has to build them up so that it can feed well. It continues to feed, and the fear grows stronger and stronger. Hours later, the person gets off the train at his station in a dangerously psychotic condition. And by that time, a trace of the Evil is able to leave the train with him. But only for a short time, because the Evil is still tied to the line . . . and while the sphere of influence exists in the mind of its victim, the person causes more fear, death and horror. And the Evil can feast again before it's forced to withdraw its trace and return to the railway line.'

'You say "the line". There isn't a specific carriage or train, then?'

'No. It's the line itself.'

'All right. So the line is . . . possessed or something. There's something very old – ancient – and evil. It's not human and it feeds on people's fear like some kind of vampire. It can conjure up a person's worst fear in that person's own mind. Just like it did to us, earlier.'

'Right. When Aynsley touched my hand, he was somehow able to convey all of this to me before he burned. Somehow, his act has heightened my own awareness and instinct about Azimuth.'

'But how the hell did it get on the line in the first place? The King's Cross to Edinburgh line was operative from the 1850s. That's over one hundred and thirty years ago. How did it get on the line? Why is it trapped there? And if it's as old as you say it is, where did this thing exist prior to that? Why can it only exist on that one stretch of railway line – why can't it spread and travel to the other railway networks?'

'I don't know yet. Something's blocking me off. I only have instincts in general about it. My mind's still closed on certain things. I still don't know what happened to me on the train; still don't know what threw me off. Aynsley may have found out, but he wasn't able to pass it on to me.'

'What did you mean about standing stones?'

'What?'

'When you broke contact with Aynsley – or whatever it was you were doing – you said, "Standing stones".'

'Did I? God . . . yes. Aynsley told me something – but nothing specific enough to help.'

'I don't think we can ignore their significance in your dreams either, Davies.'

Mark remembered fleeing down the Ghost Train track with Robbie and seeing the standing stones on either side of the line like silent gravestones. He opened his mouth to tell Chadderton about that last deadly fantasy, but then noticed how the other's gaze was suddenly being directed towards the rows of books above Mark's stereo unit.

'You've got quite a few volumes up there.'

'Yes. I've done a lot of reading since the accident. That's all I've been really capable of.'

'Bet you've got a book up there on prehistoric remains,' said Chadderton.

Mark felt his heart lurch for a reason he could not explain. 'Yes . . .' he said slowly, 'there's a book on them there somewhere. I had it before the accident . . .' *Before* the accident . . . *now why did I say that?* he thought.

'Ever looked at it recently? Ever tried to tie up some of those dreams that you were telling me about? See if any of the places you dreamed about really exist?'

Mark suddenly felt a small knot of fear in his stomach, the impulse to tell Chadderton that he was being a fool. The standing stone dreams were all part of the fantasy that the Evil had conjured up in his head. There was no relevance. And then he knew he was wrong. The standing stones, the burial chambers and the carved stones *were* relevant. He had always thought so; had been thoroughly convinced in his last nightmare that they were somehow very important. It was the fear of discovering the Evil's secret that prevented him from recognising the fact; the fear of what the consequences of the discovery would bring.

'I've never looked in the book. It would have been like giving my nightmares some kind of credence, substantiating all the fears that I was trying to hide. I think you'd better get the book now, Chadderton.' Mark was suddenly beginning to feel a little sick. 'It's on the third shelf.'

Chadderton crossed to the shelves, rummaged around and finally found the volume he was after. Seconds later, he had the book spread open on the coffee table in front of Mark.

'Before we start,' said Chadderton, and Mark could see that his hands were shaking badly as he turned the pages, 'I've got to tell you that I can't make myself believe everything you've told me. I just can't do it. But there's something about what's happened to us, something about what you've told me, that I can't ignore. I've seen things that I can never explain and I don't want to believe them. But I've seen them and I know I'm not mad – so I know I've got to believe them. But something inside me is fighting it all the way. I'm following the logic of what you've said and of what Aynsley was babbling before he . . .' Chadderton suddenly could not find the words to describe what had happened. 'I think I might know the relevance of these things. But before I say any more, I want you to go through this book with me and tell me every time you think you recognise any of the sites. Okay?'

He turned to the first page. Instantly, Mark saw a familiar grouping of ancient, weatherbeaten stones from a familiar nightmare.

Meanwhile, two miles outside Bamburgh, in an isolated cottage, the Catalysts were in commune with their Master.

*   *   *

An hour later, Mark finally sat back from the three-inch thick volume. The spasm of fear which had first curled in his stomach at Chadderton's mention of standing stones had stayed with him as he crouched over the book. Now that he was sitting back, the weariness of the last two days was settling on him like a dark mantle. His shirt was soaked in sweat, clinging to his back.

Chadderton had pulled down an RAC road-map from the bookshelf and spread out a map of England on the coffee table beside the book. And every time Mark had recognised a grouping of stones or an ancient burial mound from one of his nightmares, Chadderton marked its position on the map with a large cross. Chadderton had scribbled down the name of each site as Mark recognised it and, with each identification, the memory of the nightmares had flooded back to Mark with a startling intensity. The map was covered in crosses.

Chadderton gazed at the map for a long time. He was clenching and unclenching his fingers again. Mark closed his eyes, fighting back the weariness, afraid to sleep in case his nightmares should return, despite his new-found inner conviction that when the . . . thing . . . had left his mind, so had his bad dreams. He closed his eyes, feeling the strain pounding on the nerves behind them, and heard Chadderton scribbling something. When he looked over to him, the other man was sitting back in his chair, taking the volume with him and pulling the map roughly across the arm of the chair.

'What are you thinking . . .?' began Mark, but Chadderton silenced him with an impatient gesture. Mark's eyes were closing again. Despite himself, sleep was going to win. His body needed to recover. The last thing he saw before unconsciousness overtook him was Chadderton hunched over his book, his eyes far away; lost in the depths of some undeniable, inescapable conclusion.

Mark's sleep was deep and dreamless.

Eighteen

When Mark awoke, sunlight was streaming in through the curtains. His sleep had been untroubled and somehow 'cleaner' than he could remember since the accident and his final drifting back from coma into the land of the living. For the first time for months, he felt refreshed. There had been no purple mist, no scenes of horror, no desolate moors and jutting crags of ancient stone.

Chadderton was still in the armchair opposite Mark. He was asleep, the RAC map spread across the chair like some giant party streamer. His stubble was beginning to thicken into a beard. The thick, ruffled hair was more dishevelled than ever. It seemed to Mark that he had known the man for a long, long time – not merely twenty-four hours. He moved, sat upright and groaned at the stiffness in his limbs; the familiar nagging pain of a body that had once been so badly broken and had so miraculously recovered. He wondered if his 'miraculous' recovery had been due in some way to the malignant parasite which had been hiding in his mind, realising that perhaps he would never really know. Chadderton was in a deep slumber and Mark supposed that he would stay that way for some time. The book on prehistoric sites was open on the coffee table but, even upside down, he could see that Chadderton had been scribbling in it, underlining passages. A single sheet of paper from the bureau lay across the pages. Mark leaned across and picked it up. The names of the sites which he had identified were scrawled on it, some of them with a scribbled page number, obviously related to the book. Mark read the list, pulled the book round to face him and turned to the page numbers which Chadderton had indicated:

1   *The Merry Maidens* (Boleigh). It is claimed that the stones are still charged with enough 'ancient power' to give some people a shock when they lean against them. The stone crosses erected nearby may have been put there to negate the pagan influence of the site.

Mark felt a chill creeping round the nape of his neck. With startling clarity, he saw a network of living, pulsing veins in a slab of cold rock; saw himself in a dream standing in a stone circle while robed figures dragged a young girl to the sacrificial altar, her lips sewn cruelly together. He tried to shrug off the feeling and, almost submitting to his previous temptation to resist finding out the the truth, found himself about to put the book down. Angrily, he forced himself to look back at Chadderton's scribbled list.

2   *Chysauster*. An Iron Age village. Thought to have been a prehistoric 'university'. Possibly inhabited by astronomers and geomancers. Considered by some that the underground chamber was possibly a storage chamber for some form of accumulated cosmic energy.

3   *Boscawen-Un Stone Circle*. Regarded by many as the most important megalithic power center in Cornwall. The stones lie between Catchall and St Buryans in a perfectly unbroken circle. There is a multiplicity of astronomical orientations.

4   *The Fogou* (Carn Euny – near Sancreed). Another Iron Age village with a semi-underground structure set into a trench . . . a deep trench, leading into a round chamber used for many different purposes. Although its original function is still a mystery, it remains one of the most remarkable prehistoric monuments in the country.

Mark knew the purpose of the trench and the round chamber; not wanting to read further, he continued anyway.

5   *Bowerman's Nose.*
6   *The Nine Maidens.*
7   *The Hell Stone.* A chambered long barrow on the crown

of a hill near Portesham. It was a druid site and a place of divination where blood sacrifices were made.

8 *Stonehenge*. Britain's most famous circle of standing stones. It lies on an east-west ley line with Glastonbury Abbey and Canterbury Cathedral, running all the way into the Welsh mountains with numerous earthworks marking its route.

9 *Stanton Drew*.

10 *Silbury Hill*.

11 *West Kennet Long Barrow*.

12 *The Rollright Stones*. Seventy-six stones situated between Oxford and Stratford-upon-Avon. Legend tells of a conquering king and his army who were turned to stone by a witch on the hill overlooking Long Compton. At certain times, the stones are said to go down the hill at midnight to drink from the spring and kill anyone they may meet in their path. Some say that on one night each year, the king and his warriors congregate at a feast under the hill to celebrate the day when they will resume their flesh and blood roles and march again to conquer England. Detailed dowsing of the stones has found that they are transmitting energy between themselves; also, that the flow has two exit points and traverses the countryside above ground in straight lines – called 'overgrounds' . . . The site is unguarded and there have been reports that black magic rites are believed to be performed there. In 1975, police were called in on Midsummer's Eve to a disturbance on the site and found the body of a puppy, believed to have been used as a sacrifice . . . Diameter of the stone circle is thirty-five yards – the same as Stonehenge.

13 *Heydon Ditch*. Associated with legends of specters, this is an ancient earthwork rampart about five feet high which runs for several miles. Archaeologists' excavations have revealed burial pits containing decapitated skeletons.

14 *Royston Caves*. A bell-shaped chamber hewn through chalky soil which was discovered by workmen enlarging the crossroads over two hundred and fifty years ago. Only fragments of bone and cloth have been found so far. Although more recent mystical carvings were found inside, it is believed by some that the cave dates back to prehistoric times and was used for magical underground ceremonies.

15 *Arbor Low*. A stone circle with double-entrance enclosure. Five miles south of Bakewell. The site is an earth circle with a large cairn built over the bank to the south. Inside this is a ring of stones, now completely flattened.

16 *The Giants' Hills* (Skendlebury). Long mounds with megalithic burial chambers. Evidence of sacrifices, as corpses

were found lying together on beds of chalk within great timber enclosures which had then been covered over.

Mark struggled to continue reading, remembering the wild Blue Man and his hideously transformed servants; the barbarous acts of torture which he was forced to witness; the feeling of being buried alive.

17 *The Twelve Apostles/The Hanging Stones/The Death's Head Stone/The Panorama Stone.* Perched high above Ilkley are bizarre patterns recorded on the Hanging Stones. Clusters of similarly marked stones on the neighbouring hilltops of Baildon and Snowden Moors. Groups of carvings can be found on dozens of the flat rock outcrops on the edge of the moor.

18 *The Devil's Arrows.* Three large megaliths considered to be 'mark-stones', indicating a ley line or an intersection point between lines. Strange fluting sounds have been reported from these stones.

19 *The Rudston Monolith.* The tallest standing stone in Britain at 25 feet and weighing 40 tons. Situated just west of Bridlington in the grounds of Rudston Church, it has been dated back to 1600 BC and is assumed to have already marked some ritual pagan site before the Norman church was built around it, presumably to assert Christian authority over the stone, which is still said to have substantial mystical significance.

20 *Danby Rigg.* Complex ring cairn on the North Yorkshire moors. Its rubble bank is worn down and only one of its four stones remains. Excavators found two urns at its center, upside down and containing cremated bone and charcoal.

21 *Roughtinglinn and Duddo* (Northumberland). The former is six miles north of Wooler. Carved cup-and-ring marks can be found on an extensive area of undulating sandstone. The markings have been likened to others throughout the country. Five stone monoliths can be found at Duddo.

22 *Arthur's Seat.* This is a huge conical hill in Edinburgh which is considered to be an important geomantic point crossed by four ley lines.

23 *The Callanish Stones.* The village of Callanish lies on the West Coast of Lewis, fifteen miles from Stornoway. The circle and alignments are situated on a low promontory of land at the head of Loch Roag. Until fairly recently, certain families in Lewis were held in secret esteem as 'belonging to the stones', although the reasons are unknown. It is said that local people still congregate secretly at the Callanish Stones on May Day and

Midsummer morning. On such occasions, it was believed that 'something', perhaps a deity, came to the stones and walked down the avenue, heralded by the call of a cuckoo . . .

The book which Mark held in his hands had suddenly become loathsome, dangerous to touch. Again, he saw himself in a nightmare, fleeing down a line of jutting stones from something incredibly hideous which was right behind him.

He had lied to Chadderton. He had bought the book only four months ago, deciding that he was going to kill the bad dreams once and for all; would prove to himself that no matter how real they seemed, they were only dreams . . . only nightmares. He had intended to look through the book quietly, when Joanne and Helen were asleep; flip over the pages one by one and look at the photographs until the book was finished and his nightmares had been exorcised forever. But he had never opened it. He had put it on the third shelf, where it had remained until the previous night. He realised that secretly he had felt that his mind might tilt over the edge into insanity if he had recognised, no matter how obscurely, any of the stones pictured in the book.

Mark steadied his trembling fingers and turned to a large, full-colour photograph of the Callanish Stones which, by some cruel twist of fate, mirrored his exact remembrance of those terrible stones from his dream. If it had been possible to photograph a dream, this would have been the picture. There was no room for doubt.

Two pages of the volume had been turned over at the corners. Mark turned to the first and saw that Chadderton had underlined a section in pencil. He read:

> Standing stones may not be merely the oldest monuments in the world but perhaps the most remarkable. Antiquarians and prehistorians have been baffled by the thousands of stones, single monoliths and rough stone circles which are scattered apparently at random throughout the British Isles. Occult theorists dismiss orthodox archaeology and suggest that the stones follow lines of energy and power meandering across the landscape in certain patterns. Early man was aware of this power and harnessed it by erecting places of worship at highly charged points along the path. There are reports of individuals receiving shocks when they touch these once holy stones, but the mono-

liths are apparently only charged with power at certain times. These 'ley lines', then, represent invisible tracks on which some power may once have flowed and could be seen as the veins of a life force which formed around the globe as the earth cooled. Perhaps the rocks themselves are capable of being 'charged' with vibration. Alfred Watkins, author of *The Old Straight Track*, published in 1925, first propounded the 'ley line' theory. Riding across the hills near Brewardine in Herefordshire, he pulled up his horse to look across the landscape and became aware at that moment of a network of lines standing out like glowing wires all over the surface of the country; lines which intersected at the sites of churches, old stones, prehistoric burial chambers and other spots of traditional sanctity . . .

. . . The term for the ancient art of divining centers of energy on the earth's surface and the alignments which link them, is 'geomancy': a prehistoric tradition of spiritual land management through magical divination; 'spiritual engineering'. It was used in ancient times to find the correct sitings for places of worship and their geometrical relationship with burial places, wells, beacons and astronomical observations. Religious sites were positioned upon these lines of energy, especially at intersections where the flow crosses . . .

. . . The complex image of the dragon motif in legend and mythology has been regarded as colourfully allegorical, but there is a body of belief that the symbol may refer to the earth current charted by these ley lines. Indeed, the 'Dragon Current' of Feng Shui, an ancient Chinese geomantic system in the siting of tombs and other buildings, specifically avoided the occurrence of straight lines in the countryside because of the belief that baleful influences travelled along such routes . . .

. . . It has been suggested that crimes of violence and suicides occur more frequently on ley lines because of the electromagnetic field which affects the brain. As an interesting aside, sitings of 'elemental' spirits on ley lines and poltergeist activity where ley lines intersect are said to be frequent. Representing the dark side of Nature, elementals take many forms and are believed to be disembodied non-human forces deriving their existence from earth 'currents' and appearing to humans in many varied guises, based on the viewers' own subconscious thought patterns . . .

. . . Who were the druids? Very little is known about them. Druidism would appear to have been a basic form of sun and nature worship, practised by all the Celts. Relying on oral traditions, it left no written records. Arriving in Britain some 1,500 years after the building of Stonehenge, Julius Caesar

213

wrote: 'They have discussions concerning the stars and their movements, the size of the universe and the earth, the order of nature, the strength and power of the immortal gods, and hand down their learning to young men . . . The druid priesthood is taught to repeat a great number of verses by heart, and often spends twenty years on this preoccupation; for it is deemed unlawful to commit their statutes to writing for two reasons: to hide their mysteries from the knowledge of the vulgar, and to exercise the memory of their scholars.' Strabo added: 'On account of their evil sacrifices the Romans endeavoured to destroy all the superstitions of the druids, but in vain.'

. . . Some occultists suggest that the druid culture and religious practices were founded on a much older religion which contained the secrets of Stonehenge, a structure which the druids merely venerated as a symbol of forgotten knowledge. Many believe that they inherited a system of Bronze Age religion, magic and astronomy, guarding ancient secrets in a desperate nationalistic resistance against the Roman invaders . . .

※   ※   ※

'Well?' Chadderton's voice startled Mark from his reading. The passages that Chadderton had underlined in the book had turned his insides to ice. The book felt frozen to his hands, as if he could not drop it even if he wanted to. Chadderton was sitting with his chin cradled wearily in the cup of one palm, elbow on the chair rest.

'Well,' echoed Mark, his voice sounding dry and rusty.

'What does your new-found instinct tell you about all that?'

'It tells me that a lot of it is true,' said Mark. His voice sounded far away, as if someone else was talking and he was listening. 'A network of megalithic standing stones and burial chambers stretching across the British countryside to serve some kind of purpose. All linked somehow. Some of it they've got wrong . . .' *Is this really me?* thought Mark, '. . . the druids did inherit a special knowledge from another ancient race, they knew just what they were doing when they . . . when they . . .'

'When they what?' snapped Chadderton, now leaning forward intently.

'When they . . .' and the spell was somehow broken. 'It's gone. The feeling's gone.' The book suddenly slipped from

214

Mark's lap and thudded to the floor. He made an effort to pick it up, felt pain stabbing through his back. Chadderton moved across quickly and retrieved it. He was looking at Mark in the same way that he had looked at him yesterday in his hotel room, with an expression that seemed to indicate that he was humoring a lunatic. Chadderton's look, the feeling of *knowing*, the fact that Joanne and Helen were in hospital, the pile of ashes on the carpet upstairs, the dreams. All of these things suddenly converged on Mark in a furious rage.

'Don't you look at me like that, you bastard! You know what you've seen. You've been through your own private hell. You saw what happened upstairs. You experienced the same kind of thing that we all did. So don't let's go back to playing the game of: "Should-I-believe-him-or-should-I-ring-the-booby-hatch" . . .'

Mark's outburst seemed to register with Chadderton. The expression changed, softened, as he sat back in the chair with the book.

'You've read everything I underlined in the book?'

Again, angrily: 'Yeah. Just about.'

'All right . . . all right . . . I spent all night poring over this book and there were times when I felt like getting that whisky bottle from upstairs and starting on a bender that I would never come out of. Drink myself to death. But I stuck with it – followed through with the logic of it. And now I think I've got an answer. I want you to listen to me, bear with me. By the time I'm finished, you may feel like ringing the booby-hatch yourself. On the other hand, that special "feeling" you've got just might agree with me.

'Your book says some people believe that thousands of years ago . . . in the Bronze Age, I think it says . . . or maybe even earlier than that, people were able to tune in on special lines of power running through the earth. They erected holy places and standing stones at key points along the flow – a whole pattern of them across the country. A long, laborious task. The book says that it was all started by early man; that the druids inherited the knowledge and kept it going. But nobody knows what the power is, how it could be harnessed if it ever existed, and what purpose it was supposed to serve. Okay. Now, bear with me. I'm just kind of summing up in my own mind, from what I've read. Whatever purpose these "ley" lines were supposed to

215

serve, the whole scheme of things was screwed up by the Romans when they invaded. You might say that the druids ended up relegated to variety hall status. And when the Christian conversion was established, they knocked down all kinds of stuff, built churches over the sites, uprooted standing stones.

'Let's suppose that over thousands of years, these stones and sacred burial places have been built along the lines of force for a very special, single purpose. In the book it hints that the idea was to achieve some kind of perfect "pattern" across the country. But what if the purpose wasn't meant to be beneficial to mankind? What if all these inter-connecting "ley" lines, all those harnessed lines of power, were being drawn up for . . . for an *evil* purpose? Now, this Azimuth thing, you say it's evil . . . a very old, very ancient evil force. What if the purpose was to summon Azimuth? To summon him by completing a mystical pattern right across the countryside?

'There's no mention of this Azimuth thing in the book,' he continued, 'but if it's an ancient, evil power . . . as you say . . . then the chances are that it was some kind of god. Or, as the book says . . . a very powerful "elemental" force. I think the entire system, built over thousands of years, was like a mystical circuit. Once it was completed, they could summon up their god and bring him here to Earth. But the work wasn't completed. The Romans and the Christians saw to that. And when all of those standing stones were knocked down or pulled up, the "circuits" which had been established so far were disconnected. But if the circuit wasn't completed, how come this thing is here with us now? Right? How did it get here? Why is it riding the King's Cross line? I think you've probably already guessed what I'm going to say next . . .'

Mark nodded, and his instinct told him that everything Chadderton was saying was true.

'There was a big railway boom in the nineteenth century,' Chadderton continued. 'All kinds of main lines being built all over the country. The King's Cross to Edinburgh line was first established in 1852. And I think the engineers who laid that line unknowingly completed some special part of that "ley circuit". Somewhere along the way, a crucial inter-connection of standing stones, burial sites, ley lines and megalithic monuments was made with the railway line itself.'

Chadderton spread the RAC map out across the coffee table again and motioned to Mark to move closer.

'I marked out all the sites that you say you dreamed about and tried connecting them up myself to see if they made any sense. At first, they didn't. Until I looked through the appendix of the book and saw this . . .'

He flicked through to the back of the book and handed it back to Mark once more, tapping a photograph emphatically. Mark looked at the photograph and saw instantly that yet another detail of his terrible nightmares existed in reality.

He saw an ornate grille of iron bars set into a wall. And beyond those bars lay a simple block of limestone, two feet square.

'Is that the stone crossed by iron bars you kept dreaming about?'

Mark nodded weakly and read the text below the photograph.

> The London Stone. An interesting relic which can be found on the north side of Cannon Street, opposite Cannon Street station, and situated in a niche behind ornamental iron bars set into the wall of the Overseas Chinese Banking Corporation. According to one tale, Brutus, the semi-mythological founder of London, laid the stone as an altar and ordained that so long as it remained inviolate, London would be safe. Although regarded by some archaeologists as the 'milestone' from which the Romans measured distances along their network of roads, it is believed by others to have an older, more occult significance. It has been moved three times in the last 250 years.

'There's more,' said Chadderton, retrieving the book. 'You told me that sometimes you dreamed of being buried alive and then finding yourself floating up through a station platform in King's Cross. Well, listen to this . . . "Boadicea, the pagan warrior queen, fought her last battle against the Romans at Battle Bridge in 61 AD. Her army was slaughtered and she killed herself with poison given to her by her Chief Druid, Sywedydd. No burial remains have been found. But some say that her body, priests, entourage and potent mystical symbols lie buried beneath Platform 10 of King's Cross Station, the site of the climactic battle." '

'King's Cross station is built on a mystical site?'

'Why not? It says in the book that London was a powerful

magical "centre" and that there are probably a great many undiscovered ancient sites which have simply been built over. They dug up a temple not far from St Paul's Cathedral not so long ago. It says that Westminster is built on the site of a druidical circle. Here's something else . . . In the appendix relating to Arthur's Seat in Edinburgh it says that, in 1836, two kids searching for rabbit burrows discovered seventeen four-inch coffins containing miniature wooden figures in different costumes, which had apparently been buried there in a cave at various intervals over many years.'

The stone. The platform. The coffins.

'So . . .' continued Chadderton, scribbling furiously on the RAC map, 'we mark the London Stone here and King's Cross here. Arthur's Seat is already marked. We have to assume that the sites you've dreamt about have a special significance, okay? Even though there are hundreds of these standing stones and whatnot on the west coast which must still all be part of the overall pattern. Thank God, the Bristol railway line isn't affected. Now watch . . .'

Beginning at the southernmost site marked on the map, Chadderton drew a rough connecting line between each site, moving north. Moments later, he had completed a zig-zag pattern the length of the country.

'Notice anything interesting?'

'Yes. Apart from the southernmost and northernmost sites, the King's Cross line traverses and intersects with the pattern you've just drawn.'

Chadderton's eyes had lit up as he started to speak faster, more urgently: 'So, by accident, a certain part of the overall circuit was completed by the King's Cross line. But I suppose that originally these lines were constructed with some kind of . . . magic, or invocation, or special ritual . . . whatever . . . The railway line itself was a sheer fluke. It brought Azimuth here. It summoned him, or *it*, up from wherever the hell it was. But it couldn't get through completely. Remember what you told me about your feeling that this power was "a prisoner of the stones"? Aynsley said it, too. Well, that's exactly what it is. Azimuth was summoned, but it's trapped on that particular stretch of railway line and it can't get off. Invisible but real, riding that line for the past one hundred and thirty years. And it's been feeding from people who've travelled on that train . . .'

'Feeding on fear.' Mark took over from Chadderton, feeling the impulse, feeling the truth like a new heartbeat inside him. 'It's been feeding on fear, just like I told you before. And getting stronger all the time. In my dreams, I saw those people being killed, people with their lips sewn together. Chadderton, their lips were sewn together because those maniacs didn't want them to scream. They didn't want them to give voice to their fear by screaming. Because all the time, it was their *fear of death* that Azimuth was feeding on, not the death itself, not the actual spilling of blood. It's feeding all the time, Chadderton. When it's well fed and strong it's been able to venture off the track for short periods. Very soon, it's not going to be held on the line any more . . .'

Mark's head was beginning to spin. Mentally, he realised that he must pull away. He was keyed in to something that could burn out his mind. It was too dangerous to submit to these impulses for too long. But there was something very, very important in the back of his mind that he had to grasp now. His vision began to blur, there was an aching throb behind his eyes and the room began to tilt crazily. Dimly, he was aware that Chadderton was rising from his seat, that he had grabbed his arm and was shouting: 'Davies! Come on, Davies! Pull out of it . . .'

And then Mark was back. His eyes felt as if they were pulsing. Chadderton was looming over him.

'We're too late, Chadderton. Azimuth has put itself into three people who were travelling on that train. They've got off, they're free to go wherever they want. It's using them as catalysts for some terrible plan it's got in mind. I can't touch whatever it's going to do. *But it's almost free of the line!* And it's got three people in its possession, they'll do whatever it wants. It's going to use them in some way to free it from the line completely.'

'How long have we got?'

Mark thought of Joanne and Helen lying in hospital beds; thought of that tall, ragged madman looming over his daughter with a metal railing held high. He thought of the secret, unknown horror which had claimed him on the King's Cross train.

'Days,' said Mark.

219

Nineteen

The dull, heavy feeling in the pit of Chadderton's stomach, which he had felt on that first evening at Davies' house, had never left him. It had negated any real craving he might have for alcohol. He was quite unaware that this was the first time in five months that he had gone for forty-eight hours without getting slewed out of his mind.

He and Mark were travelling along the motorway in Chadderton's car. It was 3.15 in the afternoon, Chadderton was driving and he gripped the steering wheel in front of him tightly to prevent the trembling he could feel in his fingers. He believed that it was fear making him do this; hadn't thought that it also might have something to do with withdrawal symptoms. It was both. Mark sat next to him, staring silently out of the window. They had not spoken for over two hours, ever since they had been back to the hospital. Chadderton had sat in the car while Mark went in to see his wife and daughter. Helen was still asleep – the doctors had carefully avoided words like 'comatose' – and Joanne was recovering well. Whatever words had been exchanged between Davies and his wife, he had not mentioned them to Chadderton on his return. Davies' face looked white and bloodless, the skin drawn tightly across his face. Chadderton wondered just how much he could be relied on.

It was beginning to rain again. Twenty minutes later, Chadderton turned off the main highway and into a side road. Mark looked at him, puzzled.

'This isn't the way to . . . ' he began.

Before he could finish, Chadderton had pulled up sharply on a grass verge at the side of the road, away from passing traffic. They were in the middle of nowhere, only a couple of trees at the top of the embankment breaking the monotony of a dull, grey sky. Chadderton kicked open the driver's door, clambered out and slammed it behind him with such force that the entire car rocked. Mark struggled out too, feeling his legs' reluctance to do their job, feeling sharp pain in his hip as he braced himself with the walking stick and looked over the top of the car at Chadderton who was pacing back and forth, growling under his breath.

'What the hell . . . ?' Mark began again.

'This is crazy!' yelled Chadderton at the top of his voice. 'Absolutely bloody crazy! Magic and possession! In-bloody-visible demons riding across the countryside in bloody railway trains . . . ' He continued to pace back and forth between the car and the embankment, his voice shaking with rage. An articulated truck passed by, momentarily drowning his words. Mark watched in puzzlement as Chadderton snarled something unheard in his direction, waved a clenched fist. The truck passed on and his voice became audible again: '. . . must have some hang-ups if you can even send your own bloody psychiatrist out of his frigging mind! The whole damned thing is bloody mad! Trafford . . . Trafford, I wish you could see me now! I wish you could see what's going on here . . . '

Chadderton sighed heavily, his shoulders slumping as his head dropped and he stared at the ground. He began to take deep breaths.

'Chadderton . . . ' Mark began; and was silenced as, without raising his head, Chadderton held out a hand towards him in a gesture that demanded silence. He sighed deeply again, as if expelling something bad from his guts. And then, suddenly, he was moving back towards the car.

'Okay. I'm all right now.'

Mark's look of incomprehension slowly dissolved. He began to laugh, slowly at first, but building inside him, at the utterly bizarre sight he had just witnessed. And even as he laughed, he knew that his wife and daughter were in hospital, his own life was in ruins, the prospect of a world-shaking horror was imminent. He knew all these things and yet he laughed. He was still laughing as the car pulled away from the embankment and back to the main road.

Twenty

The evening mid-week services at St Christopher's were never particularly well attended. And although Parish Mass on Sunday was occasionally a different matter, Father Daniels always

221

felt saddened that such a large, beautiful church should stand empty so often. There were perhaps fifteen people present that evening. Old Mrs Cavendish, who had seven sons and three daughters, all of them living away from home and none of then in contact with her. Her living room was a silent gallery of frozen, faded photographs of children grown into uncaring adulthood. Mr Phillips and his wife – both so quiet that he had never been able to find out what kind of people they really were.

It was almost sunset and large shafts of golden light were spearing downwards through the stained-glass windows. Light was shining directly into his eyes as Father Daniels began the service. Consequently, it was some time before he first noticed the two men sitting at the back of the church, silent and unmoving. He continued, noticing that they did not sing after he announced the hymn numbers. During prayer, they did not kneel like the other parishioners. They did not recite the Creed. And when the time came for Communion and the parishioners moved forward to the altar rail, the two silent men remained in their seats. Father Daniels realised that they were disturbing his concentration, that he was allowing them to let his thoughts wander. It wasn't fair to the other parishioners. He put the two mysterious figures out of his mind and steadfastly continued.

The angled shafts of sunlight had crept further across the church walls by the time the service had ended. As Father Daniels processed with his two altar boys down the aisle and into the vestry, he deliberately did not examine the two men as he passed them. In the vestry itself, he listened to the parishioners' final hymn as he removed his robes and resumed an earlier conversation with Johnny Fallup about the outrageous interest charge on the hire purchase instalments on his new motorcycle. But at the back of his mind, he still wondered about the two silent men in the back seats.

The time for private prayer after the final hymn always passed quickly and Father Daniels, now clad in his sombre black cassock, moved out of the vestry to talk to the parishioners individually before they left. His suspicions about the men were confirmed. They remained sitting, facing front. He knew that they were waiting for everyone to leave. That they were waiting to talk to him.

Mrs Cavendish was, as always, full of praise for her sons and daughters and told him a family tale that he had heard many times before. Smiling, he listened and felt sad. Mr and Mrs Phillips thanked him quietly and left. He decided that he must pay a social call on them in the next week or so and find out what they were *really* like.

'Well, gentlemen,' said the priest, as his last parishioner vanished through the doors of the church into the gathering night, 'I'm Father Daniels. How can I help you?' He turned to face them as they rose from the back seats and came towards him.

'My name's Mark Davies,' said the tall, thin man with the walking stick. There were dark circles under his eyes, as if he had been sleeping badly. Father Daniels could see a livid scar on his forehead, just below the hairline. 'This is Insp . . . This is Les Chadderton.'

The other man was perhaps Father Daniels' age. He had stone-grey hair and did not seem to have shaved for a couple of days. His words were tight and clipped when he spoke: 'We need to talk to you, Father. Is there somewhere we can go?'

Father Daniels looked at his watch. It was late and he and his wife had been invited to dinner at the home of a close friend. Tonight was one of his relatively free nights and he had promised Sheila faithfully that he would meet her there promptly.

'There's a nice warm fire in the vestry,' he said. 'We can go in there, if you like.'

'Thank you,' said the tall, thin man called Davies as they moved through the connecting door at the side of the font. The church was echoing and lofty. It reminded Mark of the Central Station.

*   *   *

A wind had begun to gust outside. Mark and Chadderton slumped into the two seats proffered by Father Daniels. Mark tried to suppress a groan as he sat. It had been cold in the church and his joints had seized up again after sitting for an hour in the same position. Father Daniels could not help but

223

think that they had the look of two guilty men about to make confession.

The room was fairly spacious. An ancient bookcase standing against one wall housed numerous theological volumes. A large gas fire hissed angrily as its grille began to glow orange. Father Daniels plugged a battered kettle into a socket above a small bench, took three cups from a nearby cupboard and arranged them by a teapot before sitting down heavily in an upholstered armchair that looked as if it had been there for a hundred years.

'This is all very mysterious, Mr Davies. What can I do for you?'

The wind moaned softly beyond the wide windows above the bookcase. A flurry of crisp brown leaves rattled across the glass and was gone.

'I don't quite know how to begin,' said Mark, looking across at Chadderton. The priest noticed how the man called Chadderton kept his head down and stared at the carpet, his hands clenching and unclenching.

'Try,' said Father Daniels.

'Do you believe in evil?'

Father Daniels sat back, looking reflectively from Mark to Chadderton, elbows resting on the heavily padded arms of the chair and holding his hands before him in a kind of cat's cradle of fingers. After a while, he said: 'That's not a bad try, young man. And quite a question to ask a priest, I might add. Is there a purpose behind your question or are you both here simply for a moral debate?'

'There's a purpose, Father,' said Mark.

'I'm a priest. Of course I believe in evil. Are you Anglo-Catholic?'

'No,' said Mark; and then quickly: 'I'm not talking in abstract forms. By "evil" I mean an outside, independently active, *intelligent* force.'

'My answer again is "yes". But it's not quite as simple as that, as I'm sure you must really appreciate. You say you aren't Anglo-Catholic. Are you a Christian?'

'Yes,' said Mark, 'I believe I am.'

Father Daniels looked across at Chadderton.

'No . . .' he replied to the unasked question. 'Listen, Davies. Rather than get into a debate on good and evil and little pink fairies, I think we'd better just tell him everything that's happened.' Chadderton fumbled in his inside pocket, produced his police identification card and handed it to the priest. 'I'm an ex-police Inspector. I haven't been . . . operational . . . as they say, for about two months. You may well have read something in the newspapers about Mark Davies . . .'

'Mark Davies . . .' said Father Daniels as he rose creakily to his feet and crossed to the small bench. 'Davies . . . yes . . . wait a minute . . . something to do with a train accident, I think.'

'That's right,' said Mark. 'There was a large-scale investigation after I was thrown from the King's Cross train. Inspector Chadderton was in charge of it. I was in a coma . . .'

'That's right!' exclaimed Father Daniels as memory of the incident flooded back. 'A coma. What a terrible thing to happen to you, my boy.'

The panes of glass in the window were rattling now as the wind increased in force. Its moaning was louder and harsher as Father Daniels leaned over the bookcase to pull the curtains closed.

'But, you're recovered now, of course. You look . . . very well,' he lied as he dragged the right-hand curtain across.

And then all hell was let loose in the vestry.

In that instant, the windows exploded into the room in a whirlwind of glass and shattered wooden frame. The curtains billowed monstrously like huge wings as Father Daniels was flung across the room like a rag doll. Mark's hand instinctively flew to his face as glass shards sprayed him. Chadderton tipped from his seat to the floor. And all around was the shrieking, banshee howling of the great wind which had preceded the explosion. Books flew through the air, ripped pages flapped and fluttered angrily in the maelstrom. Father Daniels lay on the carpet, mouth working soundlessly in the raging, howling wind that plucked his voice away.

Something Else had come into the vestry.

Mark knew it immediately and instinctively. He had shared an unknown, hideously intimate fourteen months with it. Host and parasite. An almost symbiotic, nightmare existence. His mind could *smell* it. It was a touch of crawling snakes. It was the face of the gorgon seen reflected in a mirror. And it was here again. *Now.*

225

'*God in heaven, help me!*' Mark found himself shouting as the dark wings of night flapped about him. Sight, sound and sensibility buffeted and whirled. He clawed across the vestry, lashing out with his walking stick at the raging wind that tore at his body. His feet connected with something soft on the floor. He groped downwards, felt an arm and saw Chadderton's face for a brief instant before it was obscured by his flapping raincoat. Something screamed and snapped at Mark's face like a wild, invisible animal as he seized Chadderton's collar and heaved him into a sitting position. Chadderton pulled loose, stumbled to his feet and began clawing and snatching at the air around his head as if he were being attacked by a swarm of hornets. There was the sound of screaming again and Mark lunged around to the right where he knew Father Daniels lay. There was a loud, hollow clunking noise behind him, followed by a cry of pain; the kettle had whirled through the air and collided with Chadderton's leg, scalding him. Mark stumbled across the priest, groped downwards again and began to pull him to his feet. Father Daniels' face pressed closely to his own, and Mark knew that the priest was seeing his own worst nightmare. Mark tried to lift him, slapping his face, trying to make him not see. Chadderton was suddenly beside them, resisting the whispering in his head, seizing the priest's arm and pulling it roughly over his shoulder. Gripping part of the priest's robe, Mark lunged through the whirlwind, pulling them both after him like blind men. Over the raging of the wind, he could hear Chadderton yelling: '*Where? Where?*' And, instinctively again, Mark knew where. The door between the church and the vestry loomed large and solid in front of them and, for an instant, Mark feared that Azimuth had locked it. He tugged at the handle and gave vent to a hoarse, deep cry when it would not open. Somewhere behind the storm, he could hear something that Chadderton had said to him earlier that morning: *Some of the sites were destroyed, standing stones pulled down. Churches were built on some of the sites . . .*

Oh God, is this church built on a ley line?

Chadderton was beside him again, the priest sagging semi-conscious from his shoulder. With his free hand, he grasped the handle and wrenched hard. The door was not locked. The force of the whirlwind had been keeping it shut. Grudgingly, it pulled open.

226

In the next instant, the three men fell through the vestry door and into the church itself. The cold, unyielding marble floor slammed Mark's breath from his body. He felt sharp agony in his knees as the priest fell across his legs. Mark dragged himself away from the door frame, hand still clenched in the priest's robe, trying as hard as he could to drag him as far away from the vestry as possible. Here in the church, there was no wind, only cool, clear air. Mark twisted round to look back at the vestry door which stood wide against the wall. Beyond the threshold, the howling, shrieking wind continued to devastate the room. A snowstorm of paper whirled maniacally. The bookcase tipped forward and shattered on the floor. The curtain rail snapped and the curtains danced wildly in the air.

Azimuth raged invisibly on the threshold between the vestry and the church. But Mark knew now that it could not pass through into the church itself. And, as it raged, he looked quickly at Chadderton. He lay sprawled on the cold floor, his face buried in his hands. He had seen Hell before and he did not want to see it again. Father Daniels gazed openmouthed at the doorway, a look of absolute horror frozen on his face. Mark tugged at the priest's arm, tried to tell him not to look, but his words were lost in the tumult.

And then, the wind was gone, sucked away and vanishing into the night through the ragged gap of the window frame. Pages from torn books fluttered through the door and whispered into the church. Mark felt Father Daniels go limp as he slumped backwards into a faint.

※　　※　　※

Raging and tearing, that which had been fed so well by its Catalysts in their remote seclusion, fled shrieking maleficently in dissipation down dark corridors of night. For a brief instant, it had known a freedom from the lines that it had never experienced before. In secrecy it had lived and fed. Growing stronger upon the Chosen Food which had never dreamt of its existence. Until now. Two Who Should be Tasted had gone to the holy man with the intention of moving against it. With the pulse of food strong within it, drunk on the glut of power which had freed it to act, Azimuth had moved against them.

Unwisely, it now knew. It had not been strong enough to taste them. But the Time of Arrival was imminent. Even now, the Catalysts were returning from their place of communion, summoned to join it on the lines where their final purpose would be enacted and it would be free forever. Two men and one priest. What could they do to resist? The Tasting would be good. And the one called Mark Davies – He Who had Thrice Denied—would be tasted and savored for all enternity.

Soon . . . Soon . . .

❖   ❖   ❖

'What was it?' asked Father Daniels at last. His voice sounded stretched thin; wavering and lost in the echoing, empty church. He sat in the back pew where Chadderton had propped him, his robe disarrayed, thin white hair dishevelled and straggling forwards over his forehead.

'I . . . we . . . think it's some kind of demon,' said Mark quietly. 'Something called Azimuth. Does that name mean anything, Father? Does it have any religious significance?'

'I don't know . . .' said the priest as if he could never know anything again. He was looking down into his lap, knotting his fingers in the same cat's cradle. He gave vent to something between a sigh and a sob. Mark turned back to where Chadderton stood framed in the vestry doorway. He was looking back into the vestry, reluctant to pass through, as if something was hiding amid the shattered ruins of furniture and torn paper. Leaning heavily on his walking stick, Mark limped over to him.

'It's all right, now,' he said. 'It's gone.'

Chadderton looked at him anxiously, as if seeking confirmation that his words were true. Then he stepped into the vestry, shoes crunching on broken wood and glass.

'It's getting stronger, isn't it?' he said.

'Yes,' said Mark. 'In a very short time, there'll be no stopping it.'

'Where has it gone?'

'Back to the lines. Back to feed. I don't think it was strong enough to take us of its own accord yet.'

A light footstep sounded behind them. And in that instant, both men had a vision of something from Hell circling around

228

behind them, trapping them in the close confines of the ruined vestry. They whirled round in alarm, Mark almost losing his balance and tumbling to the floor. Chadderton grabbed his elbow and steadied him as they saw Father Daniels leaning against the door frame, sucking in deep lungfuls of air.

Chadderton moved forward to meet him, but the priest held up a hand to restrain him.

'I'm all right, thank you. I just needed time.'

Mark tried to shrug off a feeling that time had stood still, that the three of them were frozen in some kind of still-life portrait: Chadderton standing hunched, hands clenched; the priest sagging in the door frame; Mark leaning on his walking stick.

'You said it was a demon,' said Father Daniels.

'Azimuth,' repeated Mark. 'It knew we were coming here to try and enlist your help. It knew and it tried to stop us.'

'I felt . . .' The priest struggled to find a word to describe it, clasping his arms around his body as if he had been frozen inside. '. . . *something*. It was evil. And so . . . powerful.'

'Next time it comes, it'll kill us,' said Mark quietly.

'But it's not as clever as it thinks it is,' said Chadderton. 'If it hadn't come here, hadn't tried to stop us, we could have spent hours trying to convince Father Daniels that it really does exist. After all, like you said, all it needs is time. Days. After we'd failed to convince you, Father, you could have dismissed us as a couple of raving lunatics. And that would have been that. But by showing its hand, it's done our work for us.'

'How can I help you?' asked Father Daniels. To Mark, it seemed that the priest was somehow distanced from them by his experience. There was a faraway look in his eyes that reminded him of the look in the eyes of his own wife and daughter when he left them in the hospital. When Mark spoke again, his voice was slow, measured and deliberate so that the priest could understand and digest everything he was saying.

'We have to perform an exorcism, Father. We have to exorcise one of the trains on the King's Cross railway line. It doesn't matter which train – any one will do, so long as it's moving. And it doesn't matter which carriage. Azimuth exists on the King's Cross line itself, feeding on and corrupting its passengers. An exorcism of the line is the only thing that can stop it before it grows strong enough to free itself.'

Father Daniels looked blankly at Mark for a long time,

uncomprehending. After a while, Mark wondered whether he had heard anything he had said.

'Trains?' he said at last, 'I'm afraid I don't . . . trains?'

Chadderton rushed to the priest's side as he convulsed, bent double in the doorway, retching onto the littered floor as the delayed reaction of shock set in. Chadderton helped him across the vestry as Mark pulled a splintered chair upright between them and helped him into it.

'Why did . . . why did you come to *my* church? Why St Christopher's?'

'He's the patron saint of travellers,' said Mark quietly.

'Oh, no. No . . . ' Father Daniels seemed to reply too eagerly. 'Not any more. He is no longer officially a saint, I'm afraid. There's no longer a feast day or a place in the Eucharistical calendar, do you see? This church has only retained its name because . . . '

'Father!' said Mark sharply. 'It doesn't matter. Any church would do, so long as it's a Christian church.'

'I'm sorry . . . I feel so . . . so *terrible*.' The priest wiped a trembling hand across his mouth. '*What was it?*' His eyes had suddenly lost their blank sheen as the horror of what had happened came fully home to him. Mark could see a familiar terror lurking there behind his eyes. 'What in God's name was it?' He was gripping both their arms now, his eyes seeking some rational explanation.

'It can make you see things that aren't there, Father,' said Mark. 'The things you fear the most. By creating fear, it's creating food for itself. This . . . thing, called Azimuth, feeds on fear.'

'It can get into your mind,' continued Chadderton. 'It's happened to both of us. When it attacked us here, it tried to make me see again, but I resisted it. If we'd stayed in this vestry I wouldn't have been able to keep it out much longer. What about you, Davies? Did you see anything?'

'It's tried to take me three times and failed, as I told you. Somehow, for reasons I don't yet understand, I seem to have become immune. It couldn't get into my mind. But as I said, it's getting stronger. When it's free, no one will be able to resist it – not even me. Father . . . did it make you see anything? Because if it did, you must understand that what you saw wasn't real. Only an illusion.'

The priest continued to stare at them, clinging to them all the tighter.

'Did you, Father? *Did you?*'

Father Daniels screwed his eyes shut and strengthened his grip so that Mark could feel his flesh pinching. 'I saw . . . nothing . . . Nothing!' But to Mark, it sounded as if the priest was trying to deny something that he *had* seen.

'I want you to listen to everything we have to say,' said Chadderton. 'Davies will begin and I'll fill in the story where appropriate.'

The priest was nodding his head vigorously, breathing deeply as Mark began: 'It started for me fourteen months ago, with the accident . . . '

Chadderton saw the terror lurking behind the priest's eyes, just as Mark had done, and he understood how Father Daniels felt. He remembered how calm and composed the priest had been when they had first spoken to him in the church. It seemed that a different man was sitting in front of them now and Chadderton supposed that he himself had also changed in a radical way in the space of a single day. Reality and nightmare had hung in the balance and Chadderton had forced the scales down; had forced himself to accept the existence of something that defied sanity. Only by accepting the nightmare could he fight it. A hatred of this thing . . . this Azimuth . . . was building inside him. It was a *pure* hatred, somehow.

He watched the priest as Davies continued with his story and saw the mark of fear etched on his face. To Chadderton, it seemed that the priest had seen the very devil himself.

Twenty-one

The windshield wipers swept hissing zig-zag swathes of rain from Philip's vision as the car sped down the highway en route to Newcastle. Behind them lay a deserted holiday cottage which had been booked for two solid weeks of seclusion. The scenes of horror in three of the cottage's rooms would remain undiscovered for the duration of their holiday period. And by the time they were discovered – it wouldn't matter. Because by that time, the Arrival would have been completed. And nothing mattered after that.

The Tasting had been good and they knew that it had pleased their Master. His anger had been placated after the little girl had prevented the Tasting of Three. But now, One Who had Thrice Denied had sensed their presence and had laid plans to move against them. The Master had told them this during their commune and they had sensed by His terrifying anger that He had been unsuccessful in taking the Two again. But none of this really mattered. They knew what was planned against them. And the Catalysts knew what they had to do. Three faces bearing three spectral smiles nodded in unison.

And the car sped on towards Newcastle.

*   *   *

Father Daniels' hand was trembling as he replaced the telephone receiver. He rose creakily from the telephone seat in the hallway and moved into the vicarage's lounge. His wife was at a bridge party with friends that evening and was not due back for a couple of hours. He was glad that she was not there to see him now. It had been two days since the incident at the church and he knew Sheila had sensed that something was very wrong. His story that vandals had wrecked the church vestry had sounded pathetically weak. She had tried to get him to explain, but he had brushed aside her enquiries with an uncharacteristic brusqueness which had betrayed his inner turmoil.

His hands were still trembling as he opened the drinks cabinet and unstoppered a crystal decanter. It was only sherry for visitors; that was all they ever kept in the house. But for the first time, Father Daniels wished that they had something stronger as he poured out a drink, liquid splashing over the rim of the glass and onto the silver tray. He had seen. Oh, God in heaven, he had *seen* . . .

The Bishop had given approval for the exorcism after two days of deliberation. He had spoken to all three of them, and Father Daniels had hoped beyond hope that he would decide against it. It was too insane to contemplate. Even if he agreed to a secret exorcism, then surely there were priests better qualified than himself to carry out such things. Surely the Bishop could not take the view that, because he had experienced this thing himself, then he should be the one to see it through? But the decision had been made. And he had to obey.

Father Daniels was a man with a social conscience who prided himself on his modern outlook. He recognised the real evils in the world: murder, famine, hatred and greed. By comparison, the evil which he encountered in his own quiet parish was slight indeed. The sins he absolved in confession were usually deeds or thoughts which, whilst requiring God's forgiveness, were perhaps not major matters in the overall pattern of life; arising more often than not from social pressures such as unemployment, divorce or . . . many others.

As a child, the belief in a mediaeval, mythical Hell had been imposed upon him in all its terror. The demonic, hideous terrors depicted in Gustav Doré's paintings were to him a real depiction of what awaited the unrepentant sinner. The depiction of the Devil as a horned, leering monstrosity with forked tail and pitchfork had struck fear and horror into his soul and had been the subject of many a childhood nightmare. One such painting had disturbed him particularly and, even now, when as an adult and a priest he had resolved such childhood terrors by an understanding of the symbolism which Hell clearly represented, the face in the painting would suddenly surface during his sleeping hours. Real evil was perpetrated by man upon man. No one believed in the reality of a Hell any more. It was symbolic.

Father Daniels gulped another mouthful of sherry at the memory of what he had seen standing in the doorway of the vestry. He sat down heavily, reaching for the decanter again, realising that the entire foundation of his priesthood had been upturned. The glass stopper rattled to the floor from his nerveless fingers.

The one, great, unreasoning fear of his life had been realised. The child had known more than the man.

There was a Hell.

Faced with a real Evil for ths first time in his life, Father Daniels felt fear as he had never known it before. How could he possibly vanquish what he had seen? He drank again.

'Why you, Mark? Can't you see that you've suffered enough? We all have. What possible good will it do if you go with them?'

'I've got to go. I'm the only one who knows what it really is; how it thinks. They need me.'

'*We* need you.'

'Joanne, if it isn't stopped, God knows what will happen to us – or what will happen to every living creature on this planet. Don't you understand? Once it's free, really free of the lines, there'll be no way in the world that anything will stop it. It could mean . . . the end of everything. You felt it yourself – you could see what it's capable of. I'm the only one who *knows* Azimuth.'

'But it *knows* you too, Mark. It tried to stop you. And if it's getting stronger all the time as you say, then what's going to happen next time?'

'It's a risk we have to take. The only alternative I have is to stay here and wait for the world to end.'

'Why you, Mark? Why you?'

'I don't know, Jo. I really don't know. But I have to go.'

'If you go, I know that you'll never . . .'

'Of course I'll come back. But if I don't go with them, they'll be walking into its . . . its lair . . . completely blind.'

'Chadderton knows all about it!'

'Yes, he knows. But he can't sense what its motives are. I can.'

'What shall we do if we lose you?'

'You're not going to lose me. If anyone's able to cope with Azimuth, I am. It's taken part of our lives, Jo. And I'm probably the only person in the world capable of dealing with it. Apart from Father Daniels . . . and I'm sure that even he doesn't realise yet what he's up against. Azimuth can't control me any more. It's had its chance and failed.'

'For God's sake, be careful.'

'For your sake, I will.'

'Come back to us, Mark. I lost you once before and I couldn't stand it. Don't be lost again.'

'I love you, Joanne.'

Part Three
The Ghost
Train

Here comes Old Hell in Harness.
    Joe Walter, *Royston Coachman* (1850)

One

It was three o'clock by the time they arrived at the station, purposely avoiding the rush hour.

As they walked through the main entrance, a luggage trolley rattled and clattered past, sending loud, crashing echoes bouncing among the criss-cross girders overhead. Mark could feel fear in his guts as he surveyed the obsessively familiar sights of the newsagent's shop, the benches, the overhead clock, the fluttering pigeons, the cafe, the endless stream of people moving quickly on unknown business. But it was a different kind of fear from the terror he had experienced before. This time he knew that his fear was not feeding some hideous parasite hiding in his mind.

As they moved towards the ticket line, he foud himself examining the people walking past, both passengers and railway employees. Could Azimuth be hiding in their minds? Did that porter bustling past have a small, hidden part of the Thing in his mind, eating away at his brain? Was that young man carrying suitcases to the barrier totally possessed by Azimuth?

'Are you thinking what I'm thinking?' asked Chadderton.

Mark nodded. 'I'm wondering where Azimuth's three special people are.'

'Any more of those "feelings"?'

'Nothing yet. But it's here. And I know it's waiting.'

'Keep your eyes open. If they're around here, they're almost certainly watching out for us. And if they know what we're up to they may try to stop us boarding the train.'

Father Daniels was now at the head of the line. He placed his large, battered briefcase on the ground, something clinking inside. He leaned forward almost confidentially to talk to the ticket clerk and, for some reason that Mark could not explain, he suddenly felt very, very sad for the priest. Father Daniels' words were whispered, so that Mark could not overhear, but the clerk's puzzled reaction was plain enough.

'An entire first-class compartment booked yesterday? I don't think that's right. You have to book well in advance to secure something like that . . .'

Father Daniels tried to speak up, his voice quavering. 'No,

237

I'm sorry, I think you'll find that's right. And the booking is quite specific, an entire first-class compartment on one of the ordinary King's Cross trains. Not a 125. They don't have separate compartments, you see . . . and we . . . *need* a compartment . . . to ourselves . . .' The priest's words dissolved into the handkerchief with which he now nervously wiped his lips.

'This is extremely irregular,' began the ticket clerk, leaning forward and trying to take advantage of Father Daniels' hesitation.

'Look!' said Chadderton, pushing forward to the counter. 'Never mind all of that. Just check for six tickets in the name of Father Daniels. You'll find they're there.'

The ticket clerk fired a glance at Chadderton which was meant to wither. Chadderton returned the glare and, conceding defeat, the clerk moved off into the recesses of the office to look for the tickets. Mark wondered what Chadderton must have been like in the force. He supposed that he had been one hell of a policeman, someone you could not afford to cross on any account. Mark could not think of anyone he would rather have with him at this moment. He continued to scan the station, his eyes eventually drifting to the ticket barrier which had been the focus of his fear for so long. He wondered whether he would be able to pass through again, secretly hoping that he would fail and that he would have to return to Joanne and Helen.

The clerk returned with a wad of tickets in his hand. Sulkily, he clipped them and pushed them over the counter, muttering something about people in high places pulling strings at the expense and inconvenience of the normal paying customer. Mark wondered whether the clerk had any idea what might be pulling his own strings in the not so distant future, if their attempt should not succeed. Father Daniels took the tickets and picked up his bag. With Chadderton close by his side, they turned to join Mark. For all the world it looked as if Chadderton was playing the part of an undercover policeman, guarding the priest and – more importantly – what he had in his bag. Chadderton shot Mark a glance.

'Nothing,' replied Mark in answer to the unspoken question.

The three men walked purposefully across the station towards the ticket barrier.

Mark remembered that walk well. He knew exactly where the 'no-man's-land' boundary began; knew every square inch of the run-up to the barrier. When they crossed the line and he felt no overwhelming panic, no impulse to turn and run, he was surprised. The last time he had passed through, something else had been in charge of his body. Something that wanted him dead. Now he was passing through of his own volition. A strange exhilaration momentarily overcame the fear. Father Daniels handed three tickets to the inspector, who clipped them methodically and handed them back. They passed through.

Mark felt a hand close on his arm. Chadderton was standing next to him.

'How do you feel?'

Was that genuine compassion on his face? On *Chadderton's* face? 'I'm okay,' said Mark, suddenly moved by emotion. 'But we're really in its domain now. God knows what's ahead of us.'

'We'll do all right.'

They crossed the bridge spanning the line, carefully studying everyone around them before starting down the ramp towards Platform Nine. The public address system announced that the King's Cross train was on time and would be arriving in fifteen minutes. Mark remembered how he had seen that train the last time he had been on Platform Nine. He remembered the billowing steam, the locomotive that was more animal than machine. He remembered the ragged, ghoulish passengers from a childhood nightmare; the cadaverous train driver flapping and beckoning from a yawning window. He shuddered. Chadderton looked anxiously at him and Mark knew that he was wondering again whether he had 'felt' anything.

'Someone just stepped on my grave, that's all.'

They reached Platform Nine.

There were about thirty or forty people on the platform, Chadderton calculated. A gaggle of schoolchildren clustered around what he supposed were two teachers. Their brightly colored luggage, smothered in stickers, was stacked neatly in trolleys. Businessmen, families, a few students with rucksacks. He wondered if Azimuth's chosen three were here and what was going through their minds at this very moment if they

239

were. *Their minds,* he thought. *Perhaps they don't have minds any more. Maybe they're just walking puppets: embodied versions of the nightmare.*

Father Daniels sat wearily on a bench. He had hardly spoken a word since they had picked him up from the vicarage. He had simply listened to everything that was said. He neither declined nor assented to any view. And Chadderton could not blame him. Perhaps he thought that he was living a dream, just as Chadderton himself had thought not so long ago.

Mark stood behind the bench, leaning on his walking stick and keeping an eye on the people round about. Chadderton's initial dislike and disdain of the man had gone. He himself had been through hell once, had been attacked in his own mind twice, and that alone was enough to send anyone screaming to the madhouse. He had come to terms with that, but he realised now that Davies had been living through a particularly hideous kind of hell for almost fifteen months. His life had been practically destroyed. He had been living ever since the accident with that frightful thing inside his brain. And he had been fighting it all the way. That took more courage, more tenacity, than Chadderton could ever admit to possessing himself.

The public address system echoed tinnily again: 'The Edinburgh to King's Cross train will be arriving at Platform Nine in two minutes.'

Mark remembered the sound of that loudspeaker as he had last heard it. He realised that the voice of Azimuth had been speaking, but that he alone had been the one to hear it. Father Daniels got up from his seat, clutching the briefcase. Close together, they moved forward, with Mark covering the rear and Chadderton watching the people in front as they milled towards the platform's edge.

Two porters were approaching from offices set back from the ramp which led up to the bridge. Chadderton spotted them immediately. Instantly, he had a vision of two of Azimuth's puppets moving forward to force them over the platform as a third crept up from the other direction. The porters came towards them, apparently engaged in harmless conversation. Chadderton hissed Mark's name and pointed.

'Is it them?'

Mark saw the two porters. 'I don't know. There should be a third.'

Chadderton looked anxiously around for signs of another uniformed figure. Mark gripped his walking stick like a sword as the porters drew nearer. Chadderton shuffled backwards, pushing the priest back from the platform towards the bench, keeping his gaze fixed on the porters. Somewhere, someone said: 'Here comes the train!'

Mark could not immediately bring himself to look back up the tracks. He did not want to see that thing from a forgotten billboard again. There was no sign of a third porter.

'Here it comes!'

The displacement of air told Mark that the King's Cross express was hurtling in towards the platform. He turned stiffly to look, forcing himself to see, half expecting that the monstrous Ghost Train would be thundering in towards him again. But there was no Ghost Train. Only the King's Cross train, as it finally rumbled into Platform Nine.

The two porters passed them by, oblivious of their presence. Chadderton guided Father Daniels away to one side, towards the train and away from the porters. Mark moved up behind. Now there was a rush of passengers towards the train as it finally came to a halt.

And then everything happened very fast.

Chadderton yelled, 'Look out!' and Mark saw someone lunging through the crowd towards Father Daniels. Chadderton spun the priest round and away from the thrusting figure. Someone screamed. A woman's face, wild and contorted with rage, suddenly jerked into Mark's vision as he tried to reach Chadderton. She had appeared from nowhere, clutching at his face with sharp, red fingernails. Mark knew that she was trying to blind him. He had time to see a gout of saliva spew from between champing teeth before his arm went up to protect his eyes. A hand raked his head, tangling in his hair. And then Mark struck out with his walking stick, feeling it jam under the woman's ribs. She shrieked and fell. More people were screaming and Mark looked up to see that the man who had tried to attack Father Daniels was lying on the platform, struggling to regain his feet. A young girl, little more than Helen's age, was clinging to Chadderton's arm. She was shrieking like an animal, burying her teeth in the exposed flesh of his arm as he tried to shake her free. Chadderton punched at the small head and tugged her by the hair. One of the teachers pushed forward

241

and tried to restrain him, shouting hysterically, 'She's only a child. Stop it! She's only a child!'

But now Mark knew instinctively that the little girl was more than just a child; he pushed forward, bringing the walking stick down heavily across the small demon's back. The girl cartwheeled to the platform. A porter suddenly leaped past Mark, obviously intending to restrain Chadderton. For an instant, Father Daniels obscured the form of the man lying on the platform as he clutched the briefcase close to his chest. But Mark could see the glint of metal in the man's hand and shouted a warning to Chadderton. The latter tried to pull the priest out of the way as the man thrust upwards, but the porter had closed with Chadderton and gripped his arms.

'Look out!'

A passenger saw the knife and screamed, and the scream alerted Father Daniels to his danger – Mark was too far away and could do nothing. Instinctively, the priest slapped out with one hand. The blade connected with his palm, slicing flesh, but was diverted from his heart. Displaying an agility that Mark thought he could never possess, the priest swung the briefcase round in an arc. Mark heard the heavy thud as it connected with the man's head and he went sprawling to the platform for the second time. Chadderton had pushed the porter away and seized Father Daniels, dragging him towards the train with Mark following close behind. Pulling open a carriage door, he bundled the priest inside and turned back. Mark saw alarm register on his face.

'For Christ's sake, Davies! Watch out!'

Mark just had time to turn and see that the woman who had attacked him previously had recovered the knife from the platform and was swooping towards him with the weapon held blade downwards. The rage on her face was not human and Mark knew that he was trapped. A porter suddenly appeared between them, fumbling towards her. There was another scream and Mark saw the porter crumple forwards over the woman as the knife plunged into his chest. The little girl was shrieking. Mark clambered aboard the train and Chadderton slammed the door viciously shut.

* * *

242

We've failed! We've failed! Philip screamed inside his head as the solid concrete of the platform slammed the breath from his body. They had been told that the priest must not board the train. And they had failed Him. Terror mounted in Philip at the prospect of the wrath of their Master. He turned in time to see Grace pull the knife free from the porter's body. The people around them had fled in confusion and passengers were now beginning to look curiously out of their compartment windows at the commotion. Other passengers further down the platform had seen nothing of the incident and continued to board the train, unheeding.

Get up, said the Voice in Philip's head. He began to whimper. *There is no failure. The priest has fear! It is good. Now you have a greater task to perform. Board the train.* And Philip, grateful that his Master had decided not to take vengeance, struggled to his feet, grabbed what had been his daughter and hauled her upright. Grace was beside him now and they were running down the platform to the rear of the train, leaving the crumpled body of the porter bleeding on the platform. A small group of people were congregating around the body. A young man turned him over and saw the blood.

'Somebody get a doctor, for God's sake.'

Philip, Grace and Angelina clawed their way aboard the train.

✻   ✻   ✻

Tadger Wright pushed through the small group of people around his mate's body. Everything had happened so fast, there had hardly been time to react. One second, he and Archie Elphick were walking along the platform, talking about the darts match in the Lamb and Thistle. The next, people were screaming and fighting as the train came in. Before Tadger could move, Archie had sprinted forward into the crowd and was struggling with some fellow Tadger had never seen before. Archie was always a fast mover; he kept himself in good shape – not like that little waster Eric Morpeth with his big-mouthed tales of escapades on the football pitch when he was a kid. Three blokes, one of them a priest, seemed to have dived on board the train as quickly as they could to get away from the bother. As the crowd pulled away from the aggro, Tadger just had time to see a man, a woman and a little girl legging it down the platform. Now, there was something terribly familiar about them. Then he saw Archie lying in his own blood, and the bloodstained knife beside him.

'Oh God, Archie. No.' Tadger pushed aside the young man who was bending over Archie.

And then Tadger saw something that he could not explain.

Practically all the train doors were wide open as passengers streamed aboard. Normally, he and Archie would have gone along the platform to shut all those doors when everyone had finally boarded the train. But now, as he watched, the train doors from the bridge end of the platform to the rear of the train suddenly began to slam shut one after the other with a reverberating series of crashes that echoed through the station. It reminded Tadger of a row of dominoes standing on end. At a given command, someone had pushed the first domino and started a swift chain of collapse. People were still boarding at some of the doors as they swung savagely shut, and Tadger saw one old lady go full length on the platform. Her daughter was already on the train and Tadger heard her cry out and try to get back onto the platform to help her mother. But the door was stuck fast.

Tadger stood up and began to run the full length of the train, giving loud, wordless cries. He flung himself at one of the doors and wrenched at the handle. The door would not budge. Surprised faces watched him as he continued to run down the platform towards the locomotive. Even now, the train was beginning to move slowly out of the station and Tadger could hear the cries of outrage from passengers on the platform who had not been able to board.

'Hey, what's going on here?'

'My wife's on that train . . . '

'What in bloody hell is that driver playing at?'

'I've got an appointment. This train can't pull out until I'm aboard.'

The train was picking up speed and Tadger began to yell at the top of his voice as he ran. But there was nothing he could do.

Two

Chadderton bustled ahead down the train corridor with Father Daniels behind and Mark bringing up the rear. The passengers had reacted in stunned silence when they had tumbled aboard, and Chadderton had decided to move on down the train as quickly as possible in search of their compartment. Mark heard a middle-aged man say: 'Some stupid idiot slammed the door shut and the train began to move before that young man's fiancée could get on. It's absolutely disgraceful!'

'Chadderton!' hissed Mark as they continued on their way. 'Where do you think they've gone?'

'They're bound to be on the train,' he replied without turning. They arrived at their first-class compartment. Chadderton slid the door wide and pushed Father Daniels inside. Mark slipped in stiffly, his leg aching again. Then Chadderton followed, slamming the door shut and staying close to the windows to watch for signs of anyone approaching down the corridor.

'They tried to kill me,' said Father Daniels incredulously. 'Did you see? That man tried to stab me.' The priest was staring at the palm of his left hand. Mark saw that it was bleeding badly. Blood glistened darkly on his cassock. Mark moved forward, pulling a handkerchief from his pocket. Father Daniels sat quietly, looking at his hand in disbelief as Mark wound the cloth tightly around the wound.

'How bad is it?' asked Chadderton, his concentration still fixed on the train corridor.

'It's not good. I don't think it's an artery. But it's still not good.'

'Why did they do this?' asked the priest.

'They're possessed, Father. By Azimuth.'

The train was sliding past Platform Nine when Mark suddenly felt something happening in his mind. Waves of vertigo began to spill over him. He sat back heavily in his seat, gulping in air. For a second, he thought that he might pass out. He fought back, willing himself to remain conscious. Chadderton had seen him and came over to him quickly.

'What's wrong? You getting one of those feelings?'

245

'No . . . ' said Mark weakly, 'this is something else.'

'Put your head between your knees,' Chadderton urged him and began to force him down.

'No . . . no,' replied Mark, waving him off. 'I'll be all right.'

Chadderton could see that he had gone chalk white. There were beads of perspiration on his brow. The scar on his hairline showed livid again in exactly the same way it had done that night back in the house. He was trembling.

'Oh, God . . . ' he began to mumble into his clenched fist. 'Oh, dear, dear God.'

'What's wrong?' Chadderton snapped. 'Come on, Davies! What's wrong?'

Mark looked hopelessly up at Chadderton.

'I can remember. I know what happened to me on this train. Oh, my God. *I can remember.*'

'What happened?' Chadderton heard himself ask.

'I wasn't thrown from the train at all, Chadderton. No one threw me from the train. *I jumped.*'

*　　*　　*

Joe had been working as second man on locomotives for six months, serving his time before he could become a qualified driver, and he had been on the King's Cross run with George before. All the way down from Edinburgh, they had chatted about the forthcoming football match at St James's Park. George was good company on long runs like this, and he was a damned good driver. But Joe could not understand why George had moved the train out nine minutes before it was scheduled to leave. He had studied the working timetables back at the depot at the same time as George; he had double-checked them again. And both of them knew just exactly when their train was supposed to leave Newcastle Central Station. They had even talked about it on their way down. There would be an eleven-minute wait before they started off again. And yet, George had set off again within a couple of minutes of arrival, without saying a word.

'What's up then, George?' asked Joe. 'You know fine well we're too bloody early.'

'Light's on green.'

'Yeah, I can see that. But the published time's 15.33. We're supposed to stick to that, otherwise it's going to send all the other traffic to cock.'

'Light's on green,' said George again faintly, as if he was in a dream.

The guard's van communicator sounded. George ignored it. It sounded again and Joe waited for him to say something. But George continued to stare ahead, a vacant sort of look on his face. Joe picked up the receiver. Charlie Watts was on the other end.

'What the bloody hell's going on, George? You pulled off when people were still getting on, for Christ's sake! People were still getting on!'

Joe looked across at George, unable to say anything.

Three

Wednesday 25th September, 8.00 am

Mark leafed through his reports as the Metro train flashed on towards the Central Station, wishing that he had had more time to study them. His attendance at the meeting in Doncaster had been a last-minute affair. George Anderson had originally been scheduled for the committee but had phoned in sick three days earlier. As second-in-charge, Mark had found himself pressed into service.

When the Metro finally pulled into the Central Station and passengers spilled out onto the platform, bustling ahead and up the escalators, Mark deliberately strolled casually behind. He had lots of time to spare before his train was due. His seat was booked first class, so he knew that there would be no rush and struggle to find a suitable seat where he could sit comfortably and study his papers as the train journeyed on to Doncaster, down the King's Cross line.

As usual, the station was a hive of activity. Thoughts of departmental priorities and the best way to present his reports were still occupying Mark's thoughts as he bought a newspaper and headed for the station buffet. After a cup of coffee, he made his way back towards the ticket barrier. He handed over his ticket. An inspector punched it and handed it back, and Mark, his thoughts still on the reports, passed casually through and over the ramp bridging the King's Cross line. There were fewer passengers on Platform Nine than he had anticipated: a gaggle of football fans with brightly colored scarves and holdalls containing, no doubt, a beer simply that would last them to wherever they were going. Families going on or re-turning from holiday. A few students. At the bottom end of the platform, a group of old age pensioners, obviously on a day's outing – probably York, to visit the Minster – and enjoying every minute of it, come rain or shine. The rush and bustle of the Metro passengers had obviously been mostly local commuters to the city center.

The King's Cross train rushed into Platform Nine five minutes later, like some huge juggernaut. Curiously, Mark found himself thinking of Moby Dick, the great white whale, as the sleek, blank locomotive cabin slid past him with its slit-glass eyes fixed ahead on its ultimate destination. The train itself was like an enormous, incredibly fast and powerful animal. *'Thar she blows!'* thought Mark humorously as the train finally halted and he began walking along the platform towards the first-class compartments. Carriage 'C' was rela-tively deserted when he finally clambered aboard. After a short walk along the corridor, he found his compartment. It was empty. Grateful for this chance of seclusion and an oppor-tunity to spread himself out a little, he took off his coat, laid his briefcase on the seat next to him and in five minutes was once again totally engrossed in his papers, pausing only to watch as the train eventually pulled out of the station and across the River Tyne. He never failed to enjoy the view of the river as the train passed over. He wondered how many other passengers had looked down to the Quayside and wondered about the old buildings that still existed there. Bessie Surtees House, the Cooperage. And how many people had gazed up wondering about the trains? He thought of the Newcastle Quayside prints on his living room wall at home. Warehouses and businesses had now taken the place of what had once been a teeming huddle of tumbledown houses and cobbled streets filled with pedlars and ragged kids. He returned to his work as the train crossed the river into Gateshead and headed south.

Mark had no idea that he had fallen asleep. He jerked awake, knowing that he had emerged from a particularly unpleasant dream which he could not remember. In panic, he thought that he had slept past his stop, but a quick glance at his watch assured him that there was still some time to go before they arrived at his destination.

'What the hell . . . ?' He rubbed his face, puzzled. He remembered being absorbed in his notes, but couldn't remember nodding off. He hadn't even been tired. His sleep the previous night had been untroubled and refreshing. 'I must be getting old,' he thought, taking a mint from his pocket and popping it into his mouth to get rid of the sour taste. He felt curiously unsettled, and realised that it must have been his dream. He tried hard to remember, but all that remained was a series of fleeting images: a deep, sepulchral voice speaking obscene words in darkness; something to do with crawling snakes; and the feeling that he had been trying to resist what the words were telling him. He seemed to have clawed himself awake just as he had done in earlier days, when he suffered from those terrible dreams as a kid. Mark thought of the Ghost Train Man, and then put remembrance firmly to the back of his mind.

He stood up and stretched, groaning aloud. He moved to the carriage window and looked out. Warehouses and factories flashed past; barren stretches of British Rail land smothered in weeds and rusted outbuildings. He had no real idea where they were. He moved back to his seat, tidied his papers and slipped them into his briefcase, wondering if he should make his way down to the buffet car and get a cup of coffee before the next stop. He tucked his briefcase on the rack above him; the last thing he wanted was for some yob to stroll in while he was gone and pinch his papers. Perversely, he prided himself that if that did happen, he would now quite relish the opportunity to get up in the committee room and speak without any *aide-memoire*. It should come as second nature to him to deliver a spectacular presentation and have his own department's recommendations accepted. Mark harrumphed at his own lack of modesty and stepped out into the corridor. He slid the door shut and turned away.

And then slammed himself backwards against the door in alarm, even before he had grasped what he saw before him.

249

The train corridor was clogged and smothered for as far as he could see in a cloying white, silken substance. Walls, ceiling and floor had almost been obliterated by a thick mantle of spiralling whiteness which stretched from Mark's compartment door and away down the corridor towards the rear of the train. He looked along the corridor in the other direction, towards the front of the train. It remained unchanged. Everything up there looked normal enough. He moved backwards, away from the tangled white shrouds, looking into the compartment next to him to see if there was anyone there with whom he could confirm this strange sight. It was empty. Mark's first thought was that a fire extinguisher had somehow been triggered and had produced the effect. Maybe by one of the football fans, tanked up on cans of lager. But surely the noise would have woken him? The smothering whiteness also reminded him of something else. And the likeness conjured up a childhood dread of Mark's that he had somehow never quite got over. It looked like a web. Just like the spider's webs that were spun between the cracks on a dilapidated garden wall. A whorling spiral of web, stretching way back into a fissure. He remembered once poking a twig into one such crack, knowing that there was a spider in there somewhere. And when the ugly brute had finally been coaxed out, he remembered how frightened and nauseous he had felt. And now, this mass of web-like stuff brought back his childhood fear of spiders.

For a second, he thought of pulling the communication handle. After all, there might have been some kind of accident. It was impossible to see down the corridor beyond the whiteness. Anything could have happened. In the center of it all, where the corridor should have led, was only a smothering blackness. *Just like the blackness in a spider's web, hiding that horrible eight-eyed face, waiting for a fly . . . Stop it!* thought Mark. But the train was still moving. There was no sign of a fire. Even so, all this stuff everywhere . . .

He slid back into the compartment, trying to avoid looking into the white mass as he moved. He crossed to the emergency handle, reached up and pulled it.

Nothing happened.

He pulled again, and again. But the train continued to move. The handle had no effect.

The bloody thing must be broken, thought Mark. *Well*

done, British Rail! You've got a useless communication handle, and if the whole compartment was on fire, I couldn't do anything about it!

He stepped back into the corridor, keeping to the corridor walls and window where the white stuff was not compacted too tightly. Silk-like fronds swayed gently in the rattling motion of the train. He began to walk back down the corridor, passing the empty compartment in favor of the next compartment along, which might contain a fellow passenger.

. . . Just like the time you poked the twig into the hole and that eight-legged horror came out to look at you. And you knew, you just knew, that if it was big enough it would have no hesitation in eating you as well. Because it was small, it had to eat flies . . . But if it was big . . . as big as a man . . . why, then it would much prefer . . . Shut up! Mark told himself firmly. *Shut up and stop making such a child of yourself.*

He reached the compartment, caught a glimpse of someone inside in a flowing white dress, and slid open the door.

'Excuse me, but I wonder if I might . . . '

And then he realised that what he had glimpsed was not a dress at all. Something that had once been human sat in the seat next to the window: a shrivelled corpse, swathed from head to foot like a mummy in a smothering tangle of web. The cocoon had been webbed firmly downwards into the seat and Mark could see, before he staggered away from the doorway retching, that part of the sunken face was just visible through its abominable shroud. The life juices had been sucked out of the body leaving a brittle, empty husk. And even though the face was less than human now, he could still see there the expression of shock and agony of someone who had first been paralysed and then eaten alive.

Eaten alive.

He twisted round to look at the vortex of web. Both the child and the adult within him knew it now for what it was. He began to pull himself backwards along the corridor wall, hand over hand, watching the tangle of whiteness for any sign of movement. Just as he had watched all those years ago, when he was a small boy. He shouted, in a cracked voice: '*Someone . . . help!*' And as he shouted, the sound of his voice seemed to twitch the white mass. Somewhere, deep in the blackness, something was moving. A frenzied scrabble of movement.

251

Something blacker than black. Now, it was frozen and immobile; still hidden in the center of the tunnelled web. Watching. Again, a nightmarishly fast, twitching movement.

Mark turned to run, to get away, as something behind him burst out of the web and scrabbled down the corridor after him. Mark heard the dry scrape of clawed, spiny legs on the floor; a sibilant hissing and gobbling made by something that had come straight from Hell. He screamed. In that instant, he saw himself being caught in an embrace that defied the worst dreams of anyone who had ever known nightmare. He would be insane before those slavering fangs sank deeply into his body, pumping paralysing venom. He would be able to do nothing but watch as it ate him alive, sucking the fluids from his body.

He saw the emergency door at the end of the corridor. There could be no choice. An angry, insane rattling sounded from right behind him as he felt something sharp and covered in coarse fur scrape his neck. *There could be no choice.*

He flung himself at the door, pulled the handle and hurtled out into space. He had a glimpse of a telegraph pole looming towards him, saw the railway lines streaking past and then blue, cloudless sky. A roaring, whirling sound filled his head.

And then, only blackness.

Four

Dimly, George was aware that young Joe was talking to him, asking him what was going on. Another voice was reassuring Joe, telling him that everything was okay. He had been a driver for thirty-five years and he knew exactly what he was doing. Curiously, George realised that the voice talking to Joe was his own. Joe was saying something about the guard being on the blower, playing blue bloody murder with him. The guard had said that George had pulled away from the station when people were still getting on. Again, something that was using George's

252

voice was telling Joe that Charlie Watts couldn't tell his arse from his elbow. George tried to say: *What's the matter with me?* But he didn't have a voice any more. His own voice belonged to something else. He knew fine well that they had moved off too early. It was unheard of; he had flagrantly ignored everything he had ever learned. Why in God's name had he done it? Why couldn't he speak to young Joe? Why did he remain seated at the driving panel, staring ahead at the track stretching out before him while that other voice (which was also somehow his voice) continued to placate his second man? What on earth could have possessed him to pull away from the station like that?

❖   ❖   ❖

Philip, Grace and Angelina sat in the second carriage from the rear of the train. No one in the second-class section had seen or heard the commotion on the platform. Curious faces had looked up from newspapers and magazines as they had bundled on board, Philip carrying Angelina.

'Had to run,' said Philip by way of explanation. 'Thought we were going to miss the train.' He smiled a blank smile. Grace laughed and tossed a loose strand of hair out of her eyes.

'You're all right,' said an elderly gentleman with horn-rimmed spectacles, beaming up at them. 'The train's not due to pull out of here for ten minutes . . .' Someone had slammed the carriage door shut with unnecessary force, cutting the old man off in mid-sentence. And then the train was beginning to move away. The old man gaped in incredulity as the Gascoynes found a seat behind him. Angelina stifled her snivelling at last. The train slid out of the station past shocked and angry faces. The old man craned his neck to look out of the window, now joined by his wife, exchanging puzzled glances with the middle-aged couple who sat opposite them.

Grace had been hiding her hand under her coat. Checking to make sure that no one was watching, she took a box of paper handkerchieves from her handbag with her free hand, plucking out a handful and wiping her other hand. The dark, blood-red paper was discarded on the floor.

Soon . . .

253

Philip, Grace and Angelina smiled again. A tear glinted in Philip's eye and he thanked the Master for His love and mercy.

*   *   *

Mark's trembling had ceased. The horror of his recalled experience was vivid in his mind. But he felt a completeness now that he had not experienced since the 'accident'. The missing part of his shattered jigsaw was in place. Now he knew what had happened; his presence on the train at last, together with the new *power* which had formed in his brain because of Azimuth's use of his mind, had finally unlocked the last secret of his nightmare.

Chadderton listened in silence as Mark talked. Father Daniels looked at him as if he had gone insane, as if Mark was now something of which to be afraid. Blood dripped from his fingertips to the carriage floor.

'It made me see things that weren't there. I know that now. While I slept, it got into my mind, got into my dreams and dredged up that childhood fear.'

'Jesus Christ,' said Chadderton. 'And all the other poor sods who've been riding this train . . .'

'Azimuth conjured up a pretty drastic kind of fantasy for me. That's unusual, I think. I've a feeling that most of the other people he's fed from didn't go through the same kind of horror. He worked on their phobias and neuroses over a period of time – say a couple of hours, as they travelled on the train. But he plumbed right into my brain while I was asleep and had all that ready for me when I woke up.' Mark gave a sharp, cynical laugh before continuing: 'He must have been hungrier than usual . . . It would have caught me, Chadderton. It *would* have eaten me alive . . . at least in my mind's eye I would have been eaten alive. It wanted to taste my fear and revel in my horror. By the time I'd got off that train, I would have been completely insane. Then it would have acted through me.'

'And like you said before,' continued Chadderton, 'when we were talking about this whole thing being some kind of disease: you lay in a coma for eight months with this Azimuth thing still in your mind. In that state, you weren't any use to it. You couldn't do what it wanted. So it pulled out – it wasn't

254

strong enough to stay with you. It had to return to the line, just as it's done with all its other victims.'

'It left a psychic trace in me. That's why I had the dreams; that's why I saw things that weren't there. And the trace that it left in me was compelling me to board the train again so that it could have another go at me. A small trace feeding from my nightmares all that time.'

'It's horrible,' said Father Daniels.

Chadderton moved quickly back to the sliding door. 'You said that those three . . .'

'Catalysts,' said Mark. 'That's what Azimuth calls them.'

'Catalysts . . yeah . . . You say they're going to do something to get Azimuth off the line altogether and set it free?'

'Yes, they're going to do something. But we've got to begin that exorcism before they do whatever it is they've been told to do. They tried to kill Father Daniels, so it's obvious that they're a little frightened of what we'll be able to do ourselves.'

Father Daniels stood up slowly from his seat.

'Then I had better begin,' he said.

Chadderton stood aside from the door as the priest bent to open his briefcase. Mark watched as he took out a small, silver flask and a Bible with a gold-embroidered cross on its cover. Laying them on one of the seats, the priest next took out two silver candlesticks and a small bowl. The candlesticks were placed on the floor at either side of the sliding door with the small bowl and Bible on the floor between them. Father Daniels knelt creakily in front of them and lit the candles, the flames wavering in the motion of the train. For a short while, he remained there in private prayer and then poured a small quantity of water from the silver flask into the bowl.

'I exorcise thee, O creature of salt. I exorcise thee, O creature of the lines.'

The priest turned slightly to Mark and motioned that he should come closer. Mark moved across and knelt beside him, feeling familiar pain creeping around his spine. 'For your protection,' said Father Daniels and, wetting his thumb in the Holy Water from the bowl, he made the sign of the cross on Mark's forehead. Mark moved away again as the procedure was repeated with Chadderton.

As Chadderton stood back, the priest leaned forward and, dipping his fingers in the bowl, rose to his feet again and began splashing the water down the main seal of the sliding door. Mark could feel that something was stirring uneasily.

'God, the Son of God, who by death destroyeth death, grant that by the power entrusted to thy unworthy servant, the tormented lines which traverse this land and all who travel within reach of their seductions may be delivered from all evil spirits, all vain imaginings, projections and phantasms; and all deceits of the evil one . . .'

Something, somewhere close, seemed to groan as the priest continued. Mark looked at Chadderton to see if he had heard or felt it. He was continuing to watch Father Daniels without a trace of the doubt or bitterness which he had displayed three days ago, even in the face of his own nightmare. But he seemed to have heard nothing as Father Daniels continued with the exorcism.

Mark hoped that Father Daniels could finish sealing them in their compartment before Azimuth made his move.

Five

Now. The Beginning of the End. The Time of Arrival. Now . . .

Angelina slipped past her mother and father when the Master spoke (at least they *had* been her mother and father once upon a time) and stepped out into the aisle between the seats. Philip was smiling, Grace was smiling and Angelina was more excited than she could ever remember being in her life. She ignored the pain in her back where the One Who Should be Tasted had hit her with his walking stick. The pain was trivial; it meant nothing compared to the great thing they were about to do. Angelina realised that she was about to do the greatest thing she had ever done in her life. It was the greatest thing all three of them had ever done in their lives. She turned to look at the middle-aged couple who smiled indulgently at her.

They are to be the first, she thought, and turned to see Philip and Grace nodding at her in expectation.

Angelina crossed to them and held out a hand in a childlike gesture of trust. The middle-aged lady smiled broadly, made a cooing noise and took her small hand. The man smiled too. And then Angelina began walking down the aisle, touching shoulders and arms, stroking hands. And smiling, smiling, smiling her little girl's smile. She could feel the power in her fingertips as she touched. It was just like being in the schoolyard when they were choosing kids to make up a team. All the kids would stand up against the wall and Angelina would go along, touching the ones she wanted to be on her side. She was *always* the captain, always the leader. And she made sure that she got her way. None of the other kids dared cross her. If they did, she would make sure that they suffered for it.

And now, as Angelina moved down the carriage and crossed into the next, she continued to touch hands with people, lightly stroking the knees of smiling adults as she passed. One lady patted her affectionately on the head as she passed. And that was all right, too. Walking and touching, choosing and disregarding, Angelina continued on her way down the length of the train.

Eeny Meeny Miny Mo . . . Eeny Meeny Miny Mo . . .

The first-class carriages were different. They were all sealed off, unlike the open-plan second-class compartments. In those, she had to stop and knock. Then, when someone opened the door and asked her what was wrong or whether she was lost, Angelina would touch his arm, look past him into the compartment and say: 'I just wanted to see what it was like in the first-class part.' The grown-ups would smile indulgently or cluck in impatience before shutting the door. And then Angelina would move down to the next compartment. She had touched. And that was all that mattered. When a rather nervous looking young woman opened the sliding door and looked down at her, Angelina apologised and moved off without touching her. 'There is much to be tasted there,' she said in a small voice as she continued on her way.

*　　*　　*

257

Father Daniels had sealed the door and window frames. He turned back to his seat, picked up the Bible and crossed to his briefcase once again.

'There's someone coming,' said Chadderton from his vantage point at the door.

'It's a little kid . . . no . . . it's *the* little kid.'

'Get away from the window!' Mark hissed urgently. Chadderton pulled back as the little girl reached the window and looked in.

'Jesus Christ!' he exclaimed.

Father Daniels stood back until he was pressed against the glass window on the other side of the compartment, gripping his hands tightly so that his wound throbbed and leaked blood onto the floor. The candles on the floor guttered sharply and blew out.

The face which looked in on them was of something long dead. Mark had seen something like it in a familiar nightmare not so long ago. The empty eye-sockets, the writhing worms and straggling hair.

'*Let me in,*' said a small, childlike voice through a mouth that had no tongue. '*Please let me in.*' The corpse moved to the sliding door, pressed close against the glass and leered at them. A skeletal hand came into view, reaching for the handle. Chadderton uttered a cry of disgust and began to move forward. The wound on his arm where the girl had bitten him was throbbing painfully. Mark's hand suddenly flashed out and closed on his wrist.

'No! Don't go over there! Father Daniels has sealed the door. It can't get in!'

'*Let me in!*' said the death's-head face in a voice filled with childlike petulance and threat that was somehow the most obscene thing Mark had ever heard. '*Let me in or you'll be sorry.*'

'I command you in the name of God to be gone!' Father Daniels, eyes staring, had suddenly thrust forward with the Bible and held it towards the abomination on the other side of the glass. A hideous, contorted and mocking laugh echoed in the corridor outside.

And then the figure was gone.

Father Daniels sat down heavily next to Mark.

'It's begun, then,' said Chadderton.

'Yes,' said Mark, 'and we may not have much time.'
Father Daniels struggled to his feet, relit the candles and continued quickly with the exorcism.

*   *   *

Angelina had known exactly which carriage the Bad Men were in; she had been told. And she knew that the Master had given them all a lesson for trying to stop Him. He had given them a really bad fright. She giggled as she continued on down the train. Touching, brushing. And when she had gone as far as she could, she turned and hurried back the way she had come. When she passed the carriage where the Bad Men were, she ducked down low so that they could not see her. She could hear the priest saying things that she knew her Master did not like, and she hated them for it. Hurrying on, she finally came to the carriage where Grace and Philip sat waiting for her expectantly. She hurried to them, squeezed in past Grace's legs and resumed her seat. Breathless, she sat back and began humming the noise that the train was making on the rails beneath them. *Kuh-huh kuh-huh duh-diddle duh-huh.* She watched, smiling, as Grace took the second knife out from under her coat. It was one they had found on the kitchen rack in their holiday cottage.

'Now?' asked Angelina.

'Now,' said Philip.

Angelina bared her throat, head hunched back on small shoulders, as Grace leaned over and drew the blade savagely across. A gout of red spilled forwards across the table in front of them. Quickly, Grace handed the knife to Philip. Philip stood up and moved to the middle-aged couple sitting opposite. The man was reading the paper, the woman looking absently out of the window. She turned to look at him as he drew level, and saw the little girl lolling forward as her life blood gushed over her mother's lap. She made a small sound and began to scream.

Philip stabbed the blooded knife down hard, pinning the woman's hand to the table top. Her scream snapped off. Her husband reacted first in amazed horror and then lunged at Philip in fear and outrage. But now, his wife had thrust him back into his seat and he just had time to see the insane glittering of her eyes before she plucked the knife from her hand and drove it into his chest with all her strength.

Philip stood and watched as the chain reaction spread instantaneously down the length of the train. He watched as the One Who had been Chosen turned on the others. He watched as father killed son, mother killed daughter, friend killed friend, wife killed husband. He listened to the sounds of Hell echoing and shrieking down the train. He saw blood spilt as it had never been spilt before. He heard terror as never before; could almost feel the fear like a living, thrashing wild thing.

A young girl tried to push past him, screaming a man's name. Philip took the knife from the hands of the woman before him, the knife which she had now used to kill herself, and finished everything for the girl.

He moved back to his own table as a carriage window shattered somewhere; accepted his wife's embrace and returned her smile. He drove the knife in hard under Grace's ribs. Smiling, she slumped from her seat into the aisle. Philip watched her, smiling indulgently all the time. Reversing the knife as his wife's death spasms began to subside, he plunged it into his stomach and twisted. He bent over and fell to his knees beside Grace as the blood ran freely between his fingers.

'Phil the Tiger,' he said aloud, blood spilling over his bottom lip as he finally fell forward over the body of his wife. Sounds of pain, terror and death filled his ears. Philip thought of the Great Thing he had done as mists closed over his vision.

And Azimuth feasted as it had never feasted before.

Six

'Why the hell did I pull out of the station when there were still people getting on?' exclaimed George suddenly. Whatever had been stopping him from saying it before, whatever it was that had been using his voice, had suddenly gone.

'George, have you gone completely out of you frigging skull? I've been sitting here trying to get some bloody sense out of you ever since we left! That's what *I* want to know, damn it!'

'I just pulled out . . . we were way ahead of time . . . we weren't due to leave for another nine minutes . . .'

'George,' Joe was speaking to him in a deadly calm voice now. 'I think you'd better let me take over. I know that you're the driver but I don't think you're well. Do you hear me, George? I don't think . . .'

Joe's voice cut off. Every gauge and dial on the driver's panel had suddenly gone mad. The blue alarm light above them began to flash.

'Christ!' exclaimed George.

'What is it?'

'I don't know! It's . . . everything.'

George slammed on the driver's brake valve. Simultaneous braking would take place throughout the train and grind them eventually to a halt. But nothing happened. The train did not slow down.

'Dear God!' said Joe. 'It's picking up speed!'

George stabbed at the engine STOP button. Nothing. He twisted at the power control handle; found it loose and useless, became aware that he was muttering, 'Christ, Christ . . .' over and over again as his foot stabbed down on the DSD foot pedal which should cut off the power and apply the brakes.

'Nothing's working!' he shouted to Joe.

'What do you mean, nothing's working? That's impossible!'

The master fault lights on the driving panel flashed red, yellow, blue, red, yellow, blue. Joe grabbed at the warning horn lever. The horn remained silent as the train sped on, flashing through the station at Durham and leaving potential passengers gaping on the platform.

'Get back into the bird cage and see what the hell's going on!' shouted George. Joe bundled to his feet, yanked open the cabin door behind them and wormed his way through into the cramped confines of the engine room behind the cab. It was a tight squeeze into the small corridor which lay alongside the main generator. Even above the noise in the engine room, he could still hear George yelling: 'It's impossible for this to happen! It *can't* happen!' He took down a bardic lamp, switched it on and began to scan the gauges. Every single fault light in the engine room was showing, and Joe knew that it was impossible for this to happen. And yet, they were. The gauges showed power failure, even though the locomotive was thundering onwards at an ever increasing speed. High water temperature, faults in the traction motor blowers, the lube oil pressure too low; the fuel gauge did not make any sense at all, the coolant was too low. The whole thing was a massive contradiction. Safety devices which should automatically have 'tripped' were not operating. The engine should have shut down. But it had not.

'What the hell is going on here?' said Joe aloud as he moved on.

The water header tank gauge recording the level of coolant to the engine showed an impossible reading. Again, automatic shutdown should have occurred. To Joe, it seemed that every single gauge in the engine room was deliberately registering what it should not register. He made his way down the cramped corridor past the release valves and compressors to the boiler room door, shadows chasing shadows as he passed with the bardic lamp held before him. Was that something moving back there? No, just shadows cast by the bardic. He went through into the boiler room and stood beside the Stones Steam Generator, a long coiled tube with a brick firepot. The fuel pump, water pump and combustion air fan also registered impossible readings. The Servo Control Unit which controlled the fuel supply to the burner was fully automatic, as was the steam pressure control acting on the water by-pass regulator. Being fully automatic, it was fully failsafe. With its present reading, the engine should have shut down immediately. But the engine had not shut down. Safety devices operating throughout the electrical supply itself had just not 'tripped'. The hot contacts valves were wide open. And Joe knew then that the engine *could not* still be operating. But it was. The motor overload relay was not working. The steam temperature limit control was well above normal. The safety device had not stopped the motor. Joe tried the reset button to no effect and felt panic starting to swell within him. He had never felt claustrophobic in here before, but all he wanted to do now was get out as fast as he could. What he was seeing was impossible. As George had said: it *could not* be happening.

It's like the whole damned thing's alive or something,

thought Joe as he plunged through the boiler room and down the engine room corridor. He felt something drip onto his hand as he moved and instinctively pulled away. In the light of the bardic, he could see that there was a green, slimy substance on it. He looked up. The roof of the locomotive was running with the stuff. From nowhere, the thought sprang into Joe's mind, with an ever-increasing impetus of horror and fear, that he was about to be swallowed alive by something.

'I'm going to die! I'M GOING TO DIE!' he shrieked as he plunged forward.

A shadow moved ahead of him, beside the generator. Joe pulled up sharply, thinking that George had left his place at the panel and followed him into the bird cage. He held up his lamp and had begun to blurt out that everything had gone totally out of control when the light from the lamp spilled across what stood before him. Words froze in his mouth. He felt the scream inside him, but could not give voice to it. When the shape moved towards him, he knew that it was real, that it was alive. The lamp fell from his grasp and shattered on the engine room floor. He clawed his way back towards the boiler room, sobbing as he went, the noise of the generator drowning out every other sound. And then, something seized him by the ankle. He fell heavily against the boiler room door, felt something else snake around his arm, dragging him down to the floor. In amazement and horror, he screamed hoarsely as another length of wiring from the generator itself tore free and wriggled towards him. He tried to back away, kicking at the wiring.

'It's alive!' Joe heard himself scream. 'The fucking train's *alive!*' More wiring wriggled and squirmed free and he knew that a greater horror, somewhere in the darkness, was moving slowly yet inexorably towards him. There was a loud crackling noise above him and a shower of sparks cascaded around his shoulders. He lashed out and tried to rise to his feet. What he had seen back in the bird cage must surely be almost on top of him. 'OH GOD!' A cable squirmed around his leg like a living thing, tightening and squeezing. Above him, the cable which had broken free hung live and spitting sparks. Another wire wrapped around his throat and slammed his head back against the generator's cage. Joe screamed in a high, shrilling falsetto as that which had followed him moved into view in the boiler

263

room doorway. He tried to pull away but the torn, living wiring of the locomotive itself held him secure and fast.

Joe's mind had gone long before the live cable snaked down towards him and 2,550 volts coursed through his body.

✻   ✻   ✻

'Where are you, Joe?' George shouted at the top of his voice, knowing that it could not carry all the way back into the bird cage. Again he slammed at the automatic brake valve, twisted at the power control handle. 'I need you back here, Joe. We're gonna have to try hand signals. That's all we can do . . . '

Something was making scratching noises from behind the nose cone door. George looked down at the small door below the driver's panel. There was nothing in there. Nothing at all. But something was making a noise.

'Joe!' yelled George again. No reply.

And again, the scratching noise. A bump. Something *was* in there, thought George. Perhaps something had broken loose and was rattling around. The door began to shake, almost impatiently. George leaned down and opened the door.

It was his last action.

✻   ✻   ✻

Father Daniels paused only for an instant in his prayer as the sounds of carnage reached their ears. He continued, eyes screwed tightly shut to aid his concentration.

Mark and Chadderton said nothing as the struggling, shrieking bodies fell and stumbled past the door. For an instant, a young man's face was pressed close to the glass before being dragged away. There was nothing they could do to help him. Mark covered his eyes but could not block out the screaming. Father Daniels raised his voice above the noise while Chadderton continued to stare at the sliding door, expecting it to be flung open at any second to admit a horde of blood-crazed maniacs; and not quite believing it when the priest's seal appeared to be working effectively. Chadderton watched in disbelief as a grandmother attacked a young child. A soldier struggled with two football fans, keeping his girlfriend behind him, pressed hard against the glass of the carriage door. The girl

264

screamed at Chadderton: 'For God's sake, open the door! Let us in! Everybody's gone mad! They're trying to kill us!' Chadderton began to move forward.

'No!' shouted Mark. 'You can't open the door! How do you know which ones are infected? You can't . . . '

'We can't just let them die!' said Chadderton, and pulled the door wide open. Father Daniels staggered back, trying to carry on with his prayer as the young girl fell into the carriage. Instantly, a dozen clawing arms groped and clutched inwards as Chadderton tried to shut the door. The young soldier, his tunic ripped from collar to waistband, pushed himself in backwards. Hands tangled in his hair, tried to scratch at his eyes.

'Chadderton, you fool!' And now Mark was helping Chadderton, dragging at the soldier's body and trying to pull the door shut after him. Chadderton heaved and the soldier stumbled into the carriage. Mark slammed the door viciously shut, trapping a hand, hearing bone snap. A young woman's face pressed close against the glass inches from Mark's own, hurling obscenities at him. Father Daniels moved quickly to the door again and sprinkled more of the Holy Water round its edge.

The girl lay sobbing on the carriage floor. Chadderton helped her to her feet and lowered her into one of the seats; the soldier recovered and moved breathlessly over to join her. She flung her arms around him and began to cry bitter tears as he attempted to comfort her. Father Daniels completed the seal and recommenced the exorcism. Chadderton sat beside Mark and, above the sounds of death echoing down the train's corridors, hissed into his ear: 'Is this really going to do any good? You've seen what's going on out there . . . '

Mark looked out into the corridor again. It appeared empty, but he knew that the floor was littered with bodies. The screams of pain and terror seemed to be moving further away now. A bloody handprint streaked the glass of the compartment door.

'Yes,' said Mark simply. 'And, Chadderton . . . it's all we *can* do.'

Chadderton turned to the couple: 'You all right?'

'What's happened?' said the soldier, bewildered. 'What's happened to everybody? They're tearing each other to bits out there.' He was about twenty-five years old, thought Mark. The flashes on his tunic showed that he was a corporal. 'I've never seen anything like it.' A ragged scratch stretching from his temple down his cheek showed where a well-manicured fingernail had tried to reach his eyes. His tangled blond hair had been stained by someone else's blood. The girl continued to sob. She was perhaps nineteen or twenty with long dark hair. Her blouse had been ripped across the shoulder. Mark could see a bruise beginning to swell under her eye. 'Everybody just turned on everybody else,' went on the soldier. 'One minute I was sitting quietly with Anne here, and the next thing this geezer sitting opposite gets me around the throat!'

He looked up at Father Daniels in puzzlement, started to say something more and then stopped in mid-sentence as the priest began to sway unsteadily. Chadderton saw it immediately, heard the priest's voice begin to waver and then leaped to his feet as Father Daniels keeled over and fell heavily to the floor. Mark helped Chadderton to lift him and lay him across a seat.

'He's lost too much blood,' said Mark, looking at the red rag around his hand which had once been a white handkerchief. The priest's face was deathly white, his breathing harsh and ragged. 'We've got to wake him up, Chadderton. We've got to make him carry on or we can't stop Azimuth.'

Chadderton began to shake the priest. Father Daniels groaned, but did not waken.

'Father Daniels! Wake up!'

Mark placed a restraining hand on Chadderton's arm. 'Listen,' he said.

Chadderton listened. And heard nothing. The cries of terror and pain, the desperate pleas for help, the insane raving and shrieking, the sounds of death and dying: all were gone. All they could hear was the clatter of the wheels on the rails, the staccato rhythm of the train as it hurtled onwards.

'They're all dead,' said Mark flatly.

'I want to go home!' cried the young girl into her boyfriend's shoulder. It was the cry of a lost, frightened and bewildered little girl. 'Take me away from here, Tony! I just want to go home.' The soldier pulled her face closer against his chest and looked from the crumpled priest to the two men who crouched over him. He was dreaming, he was sure of it. Any time now he

266

was going to wake up in the barracks, with the prospect of a week's leave ahead of him. This was all just a bad dream. He would wake up soon.

'Everybody?' asked Chadderton.

'Yes,' said Mark. 'Everyone on this train apart from us is either dead or almost dead.'

'Then who's driving the train?'

The train horn howled exultantly as the King's Cross express, its speed increasing with every mile, hurtled onwards to its destination.

* * *

Liberated and strong, it flowed in bloodstained walls and corridors. It revelled in the pounding of the wheels on the tracks. It gloried in the freedom of speed and in the anticipation of its ultimate Arrival. It became the generator, became the carriages, became the locomotive. It took substance in steel and plastic and steam; flowed in circuitry that had now become the veins of a living entity. It flowed and grew stronger, felt the one small sealed part of itself that contained living food and passed on, knowing that the holy man was of no further use to them and that they would be tasted soon. It tasted fear like never before and used it to fuel itself, to drive itself onward ever faster. It sensed the Great Tasting that was to come and was well pleased.

It became the train.

Seven

'What was that?'

Jimmy Blackshaw sat bolt upright, staring at the control panel, and hastily put his mug of tea on the bench beside him. Standing on the other side of the signal box, Angus Walsh was sipping at his own tea and staring out of the window at nothing in particular. He turned to see Jimmy scanning the control panel intently.

'Whassamarra?'

'The lines just switched by themselves.'

'You been putting whisky in your tea again?'

'Straight up, Angus! The King's Cross line just switched itself over.' Jimmy began to make adjustments, fingers dancing rapidly over the control panel as Angus came to join him. 'I knew it. They moved! And I can't switch the bloody things back!'

'What the hell are you talking about, Jimmy?'

'The panel's just gone crazy. I can't do anything with it. Nothing's responding!'

'That can't happen.'

'I *know* that, but . . . Jesus!' Jimmy leaped back from the panel and out of his seat, colliding with Angus and spilling his tea. 'Sweet Jesus! It's red hot!' Jimmy was staring at his hands and Angus could see that they had been burnt.

'What the bloody hell . . . ?' Angus leaned over and touched the control panel with one finger, quickly snatching it back at the fierce heat. 'Get on the telephone, Jimmy! Quick!'

As Jimmy blundered over to the telephone, Angus pulled his scarf from the coat rack and quickly wrapped it round his hands before returning to the panel. He began stabbing at the control buttons. The panel would not respond.

'The phone's not working!' shouted Jimmy in a voice near to panic.

'Oh, Christ. We'd better get out there with emergency lights . . . '

'There's a train coming, Angus.'

'*What?*'

'I can see it. It's a train.'

'But we're not scheduled . . . '

'It's a train, Angus. I'm telling you, it's a train!'

Angus felt the heat scorching through the scarf and pulled sharply away from the panel. 'The line's fixed. There's no way we can change it. There's some kind of overload, Jimmy. We're going to have to get out of here before it blows.'

'There's something . . . wrong . . . with the train,' said Jimmy, his voice getting smaller and smaller. 'Oh God, Angus . . . look . . . it's moving too fast . . . there's something . . . it looks like . . . like it's got a . . . '

'For Christ's sake, Jimmy! Get out there and try to stop it!' Angus had thrown himself desperately back at the panel, his body lathered in an instant sweat. 'Jimmy! Go on!' Angus twisted round to see that Jimmy was turning from the window. His face was as white as a sheet. He was trembling and looked as if he might throw up at any second. Angus could not see the train from his position, but now he could hear it.

And then the signal box began to vibrate.

A roaring sound filled their ears. Every piece of equipment, every fixture and every window pane began to rattle violently. The cabinet by the door crashed over to the floor, the light bulb began to swing crazily.

'Jimmy! Help me!'

But Jimmy was shaking his head, refusing to accept what he had seen and what was now happening. He backed away into the corner of the signal box, hands on ears, sliding down the wall into a foetal position.

'Jimmy . . . Jimmy . . . JIIIMMMYYY!'

Angus' cries had turned suddenly from desperation to mortal pain. Sparks flew from the control panel. A crackling, sizzling sound emanated from the equipment and Angus' body, welded by his fingertips to the panel, writhed and jerked insanely as an unknown power surged through him. His eyes started from his head; his jaws champed together soundlessly. His hair was burning.

Jimmy began to shriek Angus' name over and over, but the roaring sound swallowed his voice. His last sight was the implosion of the signal box windows as the train, which was also somehow much more than a train, screamed past them. A deadly shrapnel of glass shards found Jimmy as he crouched whimpering in the corner.

*　　*　　*

'This is the BBC News. Reports have been received today from a number of sources concerning a curious natural phenomenon at a number of prehistoric sites throughout the country. Experts have surmised that the unusual atmospheric and weather conditions, in conjunction with a mixture of mineral deposits, have resulted in the curious light display which can be seen on such sites as Stonehenge, the Rollright Stones and the Devil's Arrows. Standing stones and burial chambers alike have been observed to be producing a glowing effect which has resulted in an excited response from both the scientific world and believers in the 'ley line' theory postulated by Alfred Watkins in 1925.

'Claims by anti-nuclear groups that the effect has been created by the dumping of radioactive waste have been strongly denied by the Government. A spokesman this afternoon reported that the effect was "harmless but fascinating". More on this later . . .

' . . . and we're just receiving news that the Cannon Street area of London has been sealed off this evening following the discovery of what is presumed to be a terrorist device at the Overseas Bank of China. Apparently planted in the ornamental grille which houses the London Stone, the device was discovered by an office worker who had noticed glowing light and heard a vibrating noise. Bomb disposal experts have been called in . . . '

Eight

Mark sensed movement.

Something was happening. There was a dark *fluttering* deep in his mind and a ringing sound in his ears. And his new-found insight shrilled a warning. A revulsion swept over him which he struggled to subdue before it overwhelmed him. He could feel, smell, touch and taste the madness of Azimuth. He could feel its unclean presence. The sensations were too strong, too overpowering; he could not sort them out and make use of them yet. By effort of will, he separated and dissipated the signals he was receiving, feeling like some strange kind of mental radio operator twiddling dials until he could find the right channel.

And then, he sensed that it was watching them.

'It's here . . . '

The young girl, Anne, had ceased sobbing and was clinging tightly to Tony. Chadderton scanned the carriage for any sign of movement and crept to the sliding door, keeping low. 'There's nothing out there,' he said.

'No, but it knows exactly where we are. And it's watching.'

Mark had an image of some maleficent, well-fed cat toying with a mouse that it did not want to eat yet – not just yet.

Anne was sitting back from her boyfriend now. There was a note of barely restrained hysteria in her voice when she spoke. 'What are you talking about? Who *are* you people? Who are they, Tony? Did they make all this happen . . . ?' And then the girl shrieked loud enough to make Chadderton leap defensively to his feet. The noise of her scream momentarily drowned out Mark's signals. He felt his heart lurch, broadcasting a spasm of fear that he *knew* was being received elsewhere. The girl was pointing at the outside window.

'Oh God, Tony. There was a face at the window. It was looking at me.'

The soldier comforted her again. 'Don't be silly. There's no one out there. It's impossible for anything to look in from an outside window.'

'I saw it! It was horrible . . . horrible . . . Get me away from here, Tony. I want to get off this train. Please, make it stop.'

Again, Mark felt a shrill of warning.

'Chadderton . . . something's going to happen. I can feel it. It's moving.'

'Listen, you two,' said Chadderton urgently. 'I don't want you to question anything I tell you. I know it sounds absolutely crazy, but what you've just been through yourselves is crazy, too. There's something on this train. Something that's not human. It's what made everyone kill each other. It got into their minds and made them do it . . . '

'What the fuck are you on about, man . . . ?'

'Shut up and listen! This thing can make you see things that aren't there, things that aren't real. Remember that! It can make you see things that aren't there. If anything starts to happen, try to resist it . . . ' The soldier was looking at Chadderton as if he had become one of the dangerous lunatics who had just attacked them.

'All right, man. Take it easy. It's all right . . . ' And Chadderton knew that the soldier was trying to humour him.

Savagely, he snapped: 'Listen to what I say! Something's going to happen.'

'Look, there!' said the girl, suddenly pointing into the corner of the carriage beside the window. Mark followed her pointing finger and saw a patch of daylight shining beside the seat, between the wall and the floor of the compartment. He could feel flesh crawling tightly at the nape of his neck as danger signals pulsed in his mind. Chadderton had seen it too and now, as they watched, the patch of daylight began to spread, growing wider and longer.

The floor of the carriage was dissolving before their eyes. Now, they could see the ground flashing past beneath them. Mark stood up, moved away from the widening hole and helped Chadderton to pull Father Daniels towards the sliding door. The soldier pulled his girlfriend to her feet, pushing her behind him and backing away as the floor continued to melt away, moving ever nearer to them. They could see one of the rails now: a quicksilver, flashing movement.

'It's not real!' said Mark as they backed off. 'It's using our fear. It wants us out of the compartment. It wants us to open the door and break the seal so that it can really get to us.'

'If we stay in here we're going to be killed!' said the soldier, and tried to push past Mark. His hand closed round the handle of the sliding door. Chadderton, still supporting Father Daniels, punched downwards and broke his grip.

'We're sealed in here,' said Mark. 'So it can't hurt us. It can only make us see things. Chadderton, take hold of my hand! You – Tony – take my other hand. And keep holding on tight to your girlfriend. Azimuth has been strong in the past in that it always operated in secrecy. Until now, no one knew that it existed.' The gaping hole in the floor spread rapidly towards them. Half of the carriage floor had gone. 'But *we* know. Therefore we can resist. If we try hard enough, we can will its influence away!'

'What the hell are you talking about? We've got to get out!' said the soldier again.

'It's not real! Just tell yourself that!' Mark seized the soldier's hand.

'How do you know?!'

'Trust me!'

'But if we stay in here, we'll fall!'

'If you step out into that corridor you're as good as dead!'

'Oh, God!' The soldier screwed his eyes shut, pressed his

girlfriend tightly to him.

Mark could hear the girl saying: 'It's not real! It's not real!' Chadderton's grip on his hand was almost breaking his fingers. Mark plunged deep into the place in his own mind that knew Azimuth and dug deeper than he had permitted himself to go in the past. Between clenched teeth, he began to mutter.

'It's not real. I deny you. It's not real.'

Chadderton and the girl were chanting with him now: 'It's not real! It's not real! It's not real!' And Mark felt anger inside him rising and building like a flood. Anger at the obscene thing that had claimed so many lives; anger at what had been done to his own wife and daughter. Aynsley burning. Chadderton's wife burning. The dreams. The fear. The deaths. Building and sweeping, gathering momentum, Mark was gathering power. And then it burst out of him.

'God damn you! IT'S NOT REAL!'

The carriage seemed to lurch, the girl screamed and Mark looked down. The floor had returned to normal. As if in defiance, Mark moved swiftly across it. Bringing his feet down heavily and still with the anger inside, he began banging his walking stick on the floor, swearing and cursing in rage, damning Azimuth to hell. The soldier was muttering: 'This can't be happening.' Chadderton laid the priest back on one of the seats. The carriage lurched again and Mark steadied himself against a wall, feeling something there in the very fabric itself. Maleficent anger, hostility and . . . evil. Mark withdrew his hand. It reminded him of a dream when he had felt life in one of the standing stones and had seen a network of veins and arteries in the dark, rugged stone. There was an undead life in these walls.

'Oh God, Chadderton,' said Mark, suddenly knowing; 'Azimuth has *become* the train.'

And then Mark heard the voice in his head.

You have found strength, Sensitive.

It was the sound of death and disease. It was all the horror and abomination ever visited upon mankind, encapsulated in the form of a single voice. It was an unclean, undead filth; an absolute anathema to any living creature. The essence of an unbelievably hostile, rapacious and malefic intent. It was the touch of crawling vermin. All of this communicated instantly to Mark.

273

He spasmed, choked and fell to his knees, the walking stick rattling away across the floor. He clutched at his head to rip the presence of the voice from his mind, and then Chadderton was shaking him by the shoulders, pulling him into one of the seats and holding him there forcibly as he struggled.

'It's speaking to me, Chadderton.' Mark clutched at his temples. 'Oh God, it's horrible.'

'Fight it, Mark! Fight it!'

And suddenly, Mark knew that he did not have to fight it. His mind was closed to its influence. It could not make him do anything he did not wish. But it could speak to him, could communicate with him. And that voice, when it came again, swamped him in nausea.

Fight me? How?

Mark fought down his revulsion. 'It's all right, Chadderton. It can't get into my mind. It can never get back of its own accord.'

Thrice Denied. No sweeter Food than thee.

'It's talking, but I can't shut it off!'

'Mark, listen to me! Let it talk . . . let it talk . . . we might find a way to stop it.'

So speaks the Man Who Sought but Could Not Find! Yes, let me talk, Sensitive. So long have you hungered to know. So long have I hungered to have you. We will talk. But first . . . You must come to Me.

Mark felt vomit rise, could taste its burning sourness at the back of his throat. He swallowed hard. 'It wants me to go to it.'

'But you can't!' hissed Chadderton.

Mark channelled his mind, squeezed the slowly developing power and knew that he had momentarily blocked any transmission back to Azimuth. He knew that in a matter of seconds, Azimuth would break down his defence. 'We can't just stay in here. The only alternative I have is to stay here with you and wait until this train, or whatever the train has become, arrives at King's Cross. Don't you see? King's Cross is the end of the line. Once Azimuth gets there, he'll hurtle off these tracks and be free forever.'

'Go to Azimuth?' said Chadderton. 'Where?'

Instinctively, Mark knew where. 'Up front, in the locomotive.'

'But what can you do, Mark? You're the only one who

understands this thing. If it kills you, what then?'

'I don't think it wants to kill me. In some sort of way, I've become special to it. It wants me, yes . . . in a way I don't understand. But it can't manipulate me and it can't use me. God in heaven, I don't know what it wants me for. And I don't want to go. Frankly, I'm scared shitless . . .'

'I don't know . . .'

'It's the only thing I can do. As you said, I might find out something that we can use against it. Some way we can stop it.'

Chadderton tried to speak again. No words would come. And Mark realised that, for the first time, Chadderton had called him by his first name. It was a trivial, insubstantial thing in the face of the horror they were facing; but somehow, to Mark, it seemed important. He stood up.

'As soon as I step out into the corridor, use the flask and seal the door again. We can't afford to take any chances. When it sees me coming, I don't think that it'll move against you.'

'Mark, you know that you're walking straight into hell, don't you?'

'I know it.'

And then Mark pulled open the carriage door and stepped through. Chadderton slid the door quickly shut, hastily pouring Holy Water down the seal, watching as the liquid runnelled and splashed onto the floor before looking back at the soldier and his girlfriend, knowing that they both believed, as had Father Daniels and himself, that everything was unreal; that they were living a terrible dream that would soon dissipate when they awoke.

When Chadderton turned back to look, Mark had gone.

*   *   *

'Will passengers please move back from the platform,' echoed the speaker at Darlington station. 'The train arriving at Platform One will not be stopping at this station. I repeat: the next train arriving at Platform One will not stop. Passengers are requested to move well back from the platform.'

The waiting travellers on Platform One had never seen so many porters on one platform before. A line of uniformed figures moved people back from the platform edge as the

275

speaker repeated the same message over and over again. The voice was distinctly strained, and the unease of the porters was communicating itself to the passengers.

'Move back, please.'

'Why? What's wrong?'

'The train isn't stopping, that's all. It's safer if you get back.'

'Safer? What the hell's going on? What's wrong with the train?'

And then the wind came.

A cold wind carrying the memories of a thousand winters and the prospect of one great Winter to come. It ruffled the clothes, bit through fabric and chilled the flesh. Slightly at first, but growing stronger, like the onrush of air preceding the approach of an underground train, except that this wind lacked all warmth. Growing and growing. Harsh. Colder than death.

'Move back from the platform, please! Move back!'

The wind had suddenly become a gale, blasting into the station with the force of nightmare. Porters' caps were whipped into the air. Luggage toppled. A woman sprawled full length on the platform, followed by another. And another.

The shrieking of the wind was matched by the shrieking of human voices on the platform as the passengers began to panic and rush for the ticket barriers. But the sucking wind would not be denied.

The first passenger to roll over the platform edge was a young executive. His briefcase burst open, releasing a flurry of papers dancing wildly in the air. A middle-aged woman followed, arms flapping uselessly. And then another . . . and another . . .

Those passengers who had reached the ticket barriers clung to railings and placards as the sucking wind tore at their bodies. Fingers were pried loose, bodies tumbled backwards through the air and over the platform edge.

And then the Ghost Train screamed through the station, horn howling exultantly.

* * *

Mark stepped over the first body, trying not to look at the shattered head, and began to move down the corridor. More

276

bodies lay ahead of him, twisted and broken. The compartment next to their own was wrecked. A woman and two men lay on the floor; a young boy across one of the seats. The window had been broken by the passage of another body and a fierce wind ruffled the boy's hair as the train sped on. The floor felt wet and slippery underfoot but Mark did not have to look down to know that it was blood. The train lurched; he put out a hand to steady himself and felt something wet and warm. Hastily, he pulled his hand away. But it was not blood. Giving a grunt of disgust, Mark wiped a slimy, viscous green fluid from his hand against the rim of an opened sliding door.

A ticket inspector lay like a broken doll in front of him, face contorted. Mark stepped over him, looking at the walls and ceiling of the corridor and seeing the same viscous green stuff trickling downwards. Slime was flowing everywhere; oozing and congealing.

He reached the end of the corridor, ignoring the scenes of horror in the first-class compartments. He thought of Joanne and Helen safely in hospital and fingered the small silver crucifix around his neck that Helen had given him long ago, in another life. He turned at the end of the corridor, and shrank back as he saw that the partition joining the carriages was a tangle of impenetrable web. A familiar horror threatened to swamp him. He clutched tightly at the crucifix and willed the web to vanish. Suddenly, it was no longer there and Mark could hear a low, hideous chuckling in the recesses of his mind.

'Damn you!'

Mark passed through into the next carriage. It was a second-class, open-plan compartment. But it looked like a slaughter-house. Mark fought down his nausea, forced himself to press on, refusing to look at the grotesque, huddled mass of bodies.

'Ma-maaaaaaa!' something screeched under his foot. Mark leaped back in alarm. Glassy eyes stared sightlessly up at him from the floor. It was a broken doll.

Mark kept moving. There was more of the slime in here. It was beginning to run across the windows, dripping from overhead. He knew what was happening. Even now, he could see veins and arteries mutating from the woodwork and metal like a tangle of green creepers. And the farther he pressed on, the more pronounced was the change. As if the mutation had begun from the locomotive and crept back along the train.

277

He knew when he had reached the first carriage. Standing in the doorway, it seemed as if he was about to enter the innards of some abominable creature's gut: a pulsating, green mass of viscera. Bodies littered what had been the carriage floor and Mark knew that, in time, they would be absorbed into the very fabric of the thing itself. Only slight vestiges of the carriage remained; a patch of daylight where part of a window had not yet been absorbed and covered; irregular humped shapes of tangled green which had once been seats. An incongruous suitcase jutted from an all but mutated overhead rack. And everwhere, the pulsing, throbbing movement of some terrible life.

Mark stood back against a partition wall, holding his hand over his mouth. In his mind he remembered Joanne saying: *Why you, Mark? Why you?* And, for an instant, he thought of flinging open the partition door and chancing fate by throwing himself into space for the second time. He was shaking; a low, horrified moan escaped involuntarily from his lips. He could not control his fear. And he knew that Azimuth must know that.

How can you stop feeling fear? he thought. And then he knew that there was no way in the world to avoid it, in the face of what he was doing. Again, he was aware of the laughter that was not laughter, echoing somewhere. And with the laughter, with the knowledge that Azimuth was enjoying his fear, came more of the rage that had vanquished it before. Mark realised that it was the most effective way to combat it. He slammed his fist hard against the wall, felt the pain bite into him. He punched hard again, felt something crack in his finger and then let the pain fuel the rage.

'Damn you to hell, damn you, *DAMN YOU* . . . !'

He blundered ahead into the first carriage, ignored the bodies as he trampled them underfoot, gripped the green tangle that was Azimuth's muscle, sinew and artery to steady him as he moved. He felt the dripping, stinking stuff on his head and shoulders but still he plunged on. And then he reached the front of the carriage. He knew that the locomotive could not normally be reached through a passenger carriage; but also knew, well before he saw it, that the mutating carriage would have formed a link to the locomotive solely for his benefit, enabling him to pass through. Ahead lay a pulsating, living corridor forming a bridge to the engine. Mark moved on, saw

278

that the generator had become something that was part-machine, part-animal. It still functioned, powering the train as it thundered onwards, exuding red steam that stank like a charnel house. Tubing, wiring, conduits and gauges mingled and formed with muscle, sinew and gristle.

Ahead of him, he saw the incongruously unchanged cabin door. The door leading into the driver's cabin itself. Inside that cabin, he knew, was the very essence of Azimuth. Forcing himself forward, denying his fear the opportunity to overtake him and send him screaming back the way he had come, he saw himself reach out for the door handle. It felt hot, but he gripped it tightly all the same. Beyond the door lay the creator of Mark's worst nightmares. Before he could give himself time to dwell on that prospect, he tugged at the handle and flung the door wide. Instantly, he smelt the familiar pungent smell of ozone.

He stepped inside.

A figure which had been seated at the driver's panel stood up and turned to face him as he entered. Mark saw the jet-black, Brylcreemed hair, the malevolent idiot's grin that was somehow much too wide. The glittering green marbles of eyes, fixed on him like a snake. The figure wore the same shirt, the same dress-ring. There was a small trickle of blood on his neck, running down fron his greased hair, where Robbie had struck him with the railing.

'Hello, Mark,' said the Ghost Train Man.

Nine

'This is the Director of Operations speaking.'

'This is Jackson from Eastern Region. I'm afraid that we have a severe problem here, sir.'

'Yes, I've heard a preliminary report. A runaway train.'

'I'm afraid that it could be considerably worse than that. We also have an inexplicable and massive communications failure. The train passed through Darlington a short while ago. Seven-

279

teen people have been killed. They fell onto the line.'

'Killed? Oh my God . . . They *fell* onto the line?'

'I'm still awaiting full details, sir. We've lost contact with Darlington.'

'This is terrible . . . terrible . . . How in God's name did the train get to Darlington? I understood that it was to be diverted.'

'That's my point, sir. We're not able to divert the train. The King's Cross lines appear to be fixed and we just can't change them.'

'That's ridiculous, Jackson. What on earth do you take me for?'

'I'm sorry, sir. But if you check with the people at your end you'll find that the same thing has happened. We just cannot change the line. All traffic has been stopped here; we narrowly avoided a derailment at Darlington.'

'I just can't believe this! Are you seriously telling me that . . . Wait . . . Have you had any crews out to change the line manually?'

'Yes, sir. Three men are dead. Electrocuted.' Silence, then: 'Can you hear me, sir?'

'Yes . . .'

'They tried to divert the line manually. They were killed instantly.'

'But the King's Cross line . . .'

'. . . isn't electrified. No, sir.'

'Signal box reports?'

'We can't get through to any north of York. Hell, we can't get through to *anybody* north of York now. But we have received divisional reports that a number of boxes on the King's Cross route appear to have been destroyed.'

'Christ, what's going on . . . ? What about the train itself? Do we know what has happened on board?'

'We've no way of knowing, sir. All communications are dead. I've sent observation crews up ahead to intercept the train as it passes. But none of them have reported back.'

Silence.

'Sir?'

'We have to get the army and the police involved, Jackson. An emergency plan. I'll arrange for King's Cross to be evacuated at once. I suggest that you suspend all operations and do

280

the same at York. We can't have any more deaths.'

'We're in the process of doing that already, sir, but there's something else you should know.'

'Yes?'

'The train will be here in York in about twelve minutes. We may not have time to evacuate the station completely.'

'Twelve minutes? That's ridiculous. The train only passed through Darlington at . . .'

'Yes I know, sir. *But we've estimated that the train is travelling at 200 miles per hour.*'

'But no train . . .'

'No, sir. No train can travel that fast.'

*   *   *

At the very last, Mark had known that it could only be him.

'What in God's name *are* you?' he said, leaning back heavily against the cabin door, trying to keep as much space as possible between them.

'You know who I am. I am the Ghost Train Man.'

'I know that you're trying to use my fear against me, Azimuth. I know that you don't really look like that. You've been in my mind, dug into my childhood nightmares and taken on that guise because you think it will frighten me.'

'Ahhh. Very, very clever, Sensitive.' The words hissed like water on live coals. 'But then, if I were to show you what I really am, you would go mad. All men have fear and I can find it. I am the Ultimate Fear that lives in all men.'

'What are you?' Mark asked again in disgust.

'I am the rails, the generator, the locomotive . . . At last, I have flesh.'

Beyond the Man, Mark could see through the front windscreen as they hurtled onwards, impossibly fast.

'You said you wanted to talk to me.'

'Ah, yes. To talk. I will taste of all men when I arrive. The Man Who Sought but Could not Find will be tasted soon – just as I tasted his woman. The soldier and his woman are inconsequential, the holy man, too. But you . . . ah, you . . .' The Ghost Train Man was pointing at Mark with one long, bone-white finger. 'You will not be like the others.'

281

'Why do you want me?'

'All upon whom I have set my hand, I have tasted. None have denied. But you . . . you have thrice denied me. Now I cannot take your mind. None has ever done this before. All have been tasted. You are . . . *dear to me* . . . and you can give me so much. Here! Look back . . .' And suddenly, the Ghost Train Man had swung his arm and the cabin was gone.

They were standing in an empty nothingness, a limbo, the abode of the demon. Mark clamped down his own mental defences, knew that if he clung tightly to his self-will, no harm could befall him.

'See! See here!' cried the Ghost Train Man.

Mark saw a church, saw a group of children kneeling before the altar rail. He saw a priest – a bishop – in full regalia, passing along the line of children, blessing them. He looked closer and saw himself as a child. Sitting not far behind him was his mother, weeping into a handkerchief and wishing that her husband, Mark's father, was here to see. The bishop placed his hand on the little boy's head, and Mark remembered how he had felt then. It was his Confirmation. And despite the light-heartedness and unconcern that Mark feigned when he was playing with his friends in the schoolyard, he felt strongly that this was the right thing to do. The other kids would joke about it all, and dismiss it offhandedly. Mark would joke about it too, because all the others did so. But, secretly, he felt it deeply. And now, in this nowhere place with the Ghost Train Man, he realised that he still felt it, even though he had not been to a church service since Helen had been baptised. Indeed, he had not even been inside a church again until he had gone with Chadderton to speak to Father Daniels.

'See?' said the Ghost Train Man with indulgent glee. 'And now . . . see!'

Mark was twelve years old. He was sitting in a classroom, talking to Father Wilson who had been dead now for fourteen years. Mark was telling him that he wanted to be a priest. And Father Wilson was asking him why.

'I just think I should be, Father.'

'Now you know that's no answer. Why the sudden decision, my boy?'

After a moment's hesitation, Mark said shyly: 'Well, the other kids sort of went through with the Confirmation, you

282

know . . . like . . . it was something that you just *do*. It didn't really mean anything.'

'And it meant more to you, is that what you're saying?'

'Well . . . yeah. I felt strongly about it, Father. So I think perhaps that I should be a priest or something.'

Father Wilson slapped him on the back and laughed. 'You're a good boy, Mark. You feel things more deeply than the others. You're sincere. And there's absolutely nothing wrong with that. But you've got your boyhood ahead of you yet. You've got a lot of living to do. Let it rest for a few years and then, if you still feel the same way, we can talk about it again . . .'

The image had gone. Mark and the Ghost Train Man stood facing each other against a backdrop of nothingness.

'That doesn't make me special,' said Mark.

'Ah, but yes . . . it does. There is much to savour here, Thrice Denied! You offered yourself to the Other. You gave freely. And that offer still has its mark in your blood. It is always a part of you.'

'What do you want?'

'Renounce your offer before me. Bow down and worship me. Acknowledge me as All and I will make you Man Supreme among Men. I will embody and walk within you. I will be of your mind but I will not taste you. All things will be yours when this vessel arrives.'

'Walk within me? But you're doing that in the train. You're turning this train into your own flesh. You haven't any need for my body.'

The Ghost Train Man laughed, eyes sparkling in unholy glee.

'Yes, this vessel will be my own flesh. But I have need of disciples, Sensitive. My chosen, through whom I may embody and feed, with all mankind to feed upon. First will come the Great Tasting. Then will come a gathering of those who remain. We shall breed them, Sensitive. Breed them for the Tasting as your own kind breed cattle. And of my chosen, you shall be supreme! All can I give you!'

Mark felt his mind tilt as it was assailed by visions of what Azimuth promised. Images of gratification in every form jumbled for space in his brain. He saw himself as a king with the remnants of a shattered mankind subservient to him. He alone would choose the sacrifices to Azimuth. Power and glory for ever and ever. A supreme being with mastery over all. He saw cities being toppled and rebuilt at his command, saw in that brief instant every imaginable form of pleasure . . . and pulled back, slamming down his defences before he could be irrevocably lost in his own mind.

'Bow down and worship Me. Renounce your offer and acknowledge Me as All.'

'No! You want me to . . . renounce . . . because your possession of me would be all the sweeter. I renounce *you*!'

'Do not spurn me, Sensitive! I sensed your promise when first I made to taste you. For too long a time have I been trapped within these lines. Riding these rails, feeding and tasting of pitiful creatures' fear. Such as you are rare to taste. I have a claim on you. You are mine. And the promise you made to the Other must become a promise to Me. I waited for you to return. But you resisted. And your resistance was sweet.'

Again, the hissing, sibilant sound of water and fire. 'Do not spurn Me, Sensitive. You should be overjoyed that I have wanted you.'

'Go back to Hell where you belong!' shouted Mark.

The Ghost Train Man's face was flowing and changing as anger consumed him. Contorting and spreading like a wax mask in a flame. Mark could feel waves of hate radiating at him. Deep inside, fear was scratching and struggling to be free and Mark knew that this of all things would work to Azimuth's advantage. He fought back, thought of Joanne and Helen, fuelled his anger. He thought of the months of lost life; of this hideous parasite feeding from his mind. He thought of all the other men, women and children who had been consumed by this monstrosity. And, as he fought, Azimuth's rage grew stronger. Mark knew that now, free will or not, Azimuth meant to destroy him. The blurred face before him was shifting and changing. Mark fought down his own fear and horror as the eight jewelled eyes of a spider appeared on the darkening visage. A sibilant voice was hissing at him: *You would have died without Me. And now, I may not have you, I may not embody within you, Sensitive. But here . . . in my domain, in time, I can destroy your mind.*

Mark felt his resolve slipping. He turned away from what the Ghost Train Man was becoming. He screamed his anger and rage and knew that he was going to lose.

And then, he grasped at his shirt, found the small silver crucifix and gripped it tightly. In that instant, he saw Helen in a hospital bed, still in shock, knowing that she had not moved for over three days. But, as grief for his daughter flooded his soul, he could see that she was sitting up in bed. Her eyes were clearing.

'Daddy . . .'

A nurse was hurrying across the ward towards her, was trying to restrain her, trying to make her lie down again. Helen's eyes were flashing and angry.

'The Bad Man!'

'There's no bad man, dear. Now come on, try to sleep. Just lie down and relax!'

Mark could see that Helen was looking upwards straight at him, as if he was floating near the ward ceiling. Instinctively, he knew that his daughter possessed a special inner power that could help him, but that she was not strong enough now to save him from Azimuth.

'The Bad Man!'

Mark felt his last defence crumbling when he saw the small shadowed shape walking noiselessly down the ward towards Helen's bed. He knew that the nurse could not see the new-comer as he finally drew level on the other side of Helen's bed. One arm was held upwards across his face, shielding it from sight. The other was held out across the bed to Helen, and Mark realised that the small figure was almost transparent; he could see the bed right through him. Helen's hand moved across the counterpane and grasped that of the little boy. She looked up at her father with an increased intensity as Azimuth finally crawled through Mark's defence.

'No!' shouted Helen and Mark felt something powerful beyond words flowing from her. He felt it blast into and through him, cleansing his cobwebbed mind. He felt Azimuth retreat from the attack. He felt it wither and retreat, spewing hate and malice. The screaming echoed louder and louder, then began to diminish.

Helen lay back in bed, closed her eyes and slept again.

Robbie was gone.

Mark felt all sensibility leave him. He pitched forward into a blank, safe place and knew nothing.

✻   ✻   ✻

The speaker at York station repeated its message over and over again.

'Passengers are requested to leave the station immediately. Please follow police instructions and leave the station by the nearest exit.'

It had been a much more difficult task to evacuate the station than had been anticipated, even with police supervision. Two trains, unaffected by the sudden and inexplicable fixing of the King's Cross line and unaware of the danger, had arrived at other platforms, disgorging a flood of passengers. Keeping order was almost impossible as the milling crowds were hastily directed towards the exits. Something was very, very wrong. The speaker continued to repeat its message. The sense of unease began to grow; there was a feeling that *something* was coming.

Then came the pounding sound in the rails and the approach of a great wind.

The atmosphere had changed. An instinctive rising tide of panic began to manifest itself in the bustling passengers. The entreaties of the speaker and the shouted police commands to evacuate the station in an orderly manner fell on deaf ears. The panic swelled and suddenly there was a chaotic rush for the ticket barriers. The station echoed to frenzied screams as the terrified crowd swarmed at the barriers in a desperate attempt to get away from the station. Passengers who fell to the platform were crushed underfoot. Police struggled desperately to control the crowd, their own instinctive fear at the unknown approaching horror suddenly overcoming their sense of duty as they joined the fearful stampede.

A great roaring filled the station. The superstructure began to vibrate. Windows and overhead skylights suddenly exploded, showering the crowd with deadly shards of glass.

When the mutated King's Cross train rounded a bend and screamed towards the platform, the first passengers to see it were insane even before it exploded into the station.

Ten

'No. Let me stay dead. You promised . . .'
You cannot dwell within Me until you have completed your bargain.
'I did everything that you told me, Master. Everything.'
No, not everything. Four of the Chosen Food still live. I must taste them.
'Oh, Master. I'm so tired. Please let me die.'
No, I will give you strength. When the four are tasted, then you may join Me.

Death's abyss gave way to swirling patterns of light as new life began to focus and merge. Swimming upwards from the depths of a dark, dark lake towards the speckling of light on the surface. Higher and higher; faster and faster. And now, exploding upwards into the light. Breathing.

Phil the Tiger pulled himself up from the floor. He looked at what had been his wife and child, looked at the carnage around him and was well pleased. Grinning, his face streaked with blood, he looked down to where the knife still protruded from his stomach. He pulled it out slowly, marvelling at it. There was a five-inch gaping wound there; an intestine glinted blue-white in the aperture. But Phil was not dead. Dark fire surged in his veins, and he let it flow, let it blossom and spread. The essence that was Philip Gascoyne mingled with another essence, of Azimuth. And then, eyes glittering, the Undead Catalyst pulled itself stiffly to its feet, swaying from side to side, the gory knife fixed in its fist. It laughed. And the laugh was not human. It looked at the knife in its hand, examining it thoughtfully, and then laughed again before dropping it to the bloody floor.

It shambled down the carriage towards the rear of the train, paying no heed to the broken bodies that lay sprawled and contorted in its path. It trod on broken limbs and scattered luggage as it flopped and clawed its way stiffly past the buffet car and into the guard's van.

The guard lay awkwardly in his small office compartment, a radio receiver clenched in his fist, the radio wire wrapped tightly around his neck. His face was blue, eyes starting from his head. But the Catalyst ignored him as it moved to the glass case housing the fire axe. At the second leaden kick, the glass shattered and the Catalyst pulled the axe free. For a second, the Catalyst swayed from side to side, the axe swinging loosely in its grasp. Then it left the guard's van, clutching the axe firmly. It laughed again.

It stumbled back in the direction of the first-class carriages.

✻   ✻   ✻

'This is Flight Two-Niner-Seven to Flight Control. Over.'

'This is Flight Control. Go ahead, Two-Niner-Seven.'

'What the hell is going on down there? The entire country-side is just a massive criss-cross of light beams. Somebody playing dot-to-dot down there? Over.'

'We're aware of the situation, Two-Niner-Seven. Proceed on a circular course and await further instructions. Over.'

'Where the hell are the landing lights, Flight Control? We can't make out anything in this crazy zig-zag. Over.'

'Continue on a circular course, Two-Niner-Seven. We've got a crew out marking our own lights with beacons and flares. Over.'

'Flight Control, we . . .'

'Didn't catch that last one, Two-Niner-Seven. Over.'

'We've got a systems failure here, Flight Control! Stand by. Over.'

Silence.

'Flight Control, this is Two-Niner-Seven! We've got a massive systems failure here. It's crazy. None of my instruments are making any sense. I'm going to have to put her down now.'

'Two-Niner-Seven! The flares and beacons are being placed at . . .'

'Flight Control, we don't have time. We're coming in. Over and out.'

Three minutes later, Flight 297, with its one hundred and thirty passengers and twelve crew, hit a housing estate.

✻   ✻   ✻

'Developments, Brigadier?'

'We've sent up two helicopters for an infra-red scan of the train and received only one brief report before communications broke down again. There was a rather panicky, garbled message about the actual appearance of the train but we couldn't make any sense of it. However, it would appear that everyone on the train is dead.'

'My God! And the helicopters?'

'Both crashed. Systems failure. We've sent men out to the line to observe as the train passes. But we're not getting anything back. We're experiencing the same kind of communications breakdown. No one has come back to report. Have you heard anything further from Jackson at Eastern Region in York?'

'Nothing.'

'We have to assume that the helicopter report is accurate and that there is no one left alive on that train. And if we assume that the thing is going to increase its speed at the present rate, it will hit King's Cross like a bomb. I'm therefore authorising a controlled derailment. Since we can't touch those bloody railway tracks, I'm sending out a squad to blow up a stretch of line outside Doncaster. That seems to be the only way we're going to stop the damned thing.'

*   *   *

Chadderton watched as the soldier finished applying the tourniquet to the priest's arm. They had sat him up in his seat so that the blood would not flow so freely.

'Here,' said the soldier, 'hold his arm up like this.'

Chadderton took the priest's arm and the soldier went back to his girlfriend.

'What's going to happen, mister?' said the girl, her voice trembling; little-girl fear and helplessness still registering on her face.

'I don't know,' replied Chadderton, feeling weaker and more helpless than he had ever done in his life. There had been no alternative to allowing Mark to leave the compartment and go to the foul thing that was driving the train. But Chadderton still felt bad. Mark was walking straight into hell. And there could be no guarantee, despite his new-found 'instinct', that he would ever come back again. Helpless, Chadderton sat looking at the priest. They had tried repeatedly, since Mark left, to get him to recover. He remembered what Mark had said about Father Daniels being the only person who could stop Azimuth; about the exorcism being the only thing that could halt it. He remembered the look of fear on the priest's face when they had been attacked in the church vestry and, for an instant, he wondered if Father Daniels' fear reflected a lack of faith in his own ability to vanquish what he had seen. He wondered whether an exorcism would ever stop Azimuth in its tracks; or whether the priest's own fear had militated against them from the very beginning. He thought of the abomination that had been in his own mind, revelling in his hate and horror. He thought of his wife; of a neatly trimmed, well-kept back lawn and a car that was in the garage when it should not have been there . . .

Chadderton pushed the remembrance to the back of his mind; concentrated hard on the hand which gripped the priest's arm. It was the same hand that had yanked Mark back from certain death; it was the hand that had stopped Aynsley from killing Mark's daughter. And, Chadderton could now see, it was a hand that was not, for the first time since his wife's death, trembling in an alcoholic palsy.

Out of the corner of his eye he saw a flash of movement from down the corridor, strained forward to look and saw a familiar figure staggering towards them.

It was Mark.

He looked dazed, as if he had received a shock that had tilted the balance of his mind. He was blundering against the sides of the corridor as he came. And for some reason he was carrying a fire axe in his hands.

Chadderton called to the soldier: 'Here, take his arm. Mark's coming back!'

And, as the soldier came to the priest's side and took the wounded hand, Chadderton rose quickly and moved to the sliding door to break the seal and admit that which returned.

*　　*　　*

Safe within the blank greyness which kept Azimuth at bay,

Mark drifted amid memories of his life before the accident which had crippled him. With astonishing clarity, he relived a playground incident when he was seven years old, that he had previously forgotten. He relived his marriage to Joanne; Helen's birth; his first day at school; the face of a young girl crying in the street as she rushed past him to some unknown destination. On the latter occasion, three years ago, he had been on his way to work and had kept on walking because it had nothing to do with him. But the face of that young girl had haunted him ever since, and if he could have turned back the clock and offered help, he would unhesitatingly have done so.

It was nice here. There were no problems, nothing to worry about. If he wished, everything that had happened since the accident could be erased from his mind. The accident itself could be made never to have happened. Existence in this safe, calm and peaceful place would be eternal. A constant wandering back and forth down the corridors of memory; each opened door revealing a new secret, a new memory that had been hidden for many years.

A small voice was whispering at the back of Mark's mind. He could not hear what it was saying, it was too far away. But the tone of the voice was urgent, almost frantic, and Mark decided to ignore it, intent only on exploring his own mind, never to return. But the voice followed him; refused to be placated, refused to go away. Mark did not want to hear what it was saying because he knew that it would want him to leave this place and return to . . . to . . . what? The present did not belong here and he did not want to know about it. The voice was becoming louder as it drew nearer and Mark tried to run away from it. But it was catching up with him and at last he knew that he could not really ignore what it had to say. The words were becoming clearer now and he recognised that the voice was his own. He could hear what it was trying to tell him.

Now he could see himself lying crumpled on the floor of a cobwebbed driving cabin. He could see the King's Cross train screaming down the line. The Ghost Train Man had gone, but the unspeakable miasma which permeated the cabin told Mark that Azimuth was still present. Invisible, unseen, but still there. He could feel the power which Azimuth was drawing from the railway lines beneath, was instantly aware of the fantastic network of power lines that radiated across the face

291

of the countryside. Waves of power, hideous strength and growth surged from the driving cabin down the entire length of the train. And the proximity of power created new changes in Mark's own mind. He knew that he could use his mind as he had never done before. In a strange way, he was the parasite now, feeding from the power which exuded from Azimuth. But it was a power that he could not tap directly, for keying into it would mean an acceptance and acknowledgement of Azimuth that Mark could never permit. Huddled on the cabin floor, he drew strength from the unholy force in the same way that the traveller takes warmth from a raging bonfire. He had a fleeting image of himself in the past as some kind of blood donor, his veins tapped by the vampiric Azimuth. Now, the transfusion had been temporarily reversed and Mark, the former host, was drawing strength from Azimuth, the ultimate parasite, as power flowed into his veins.

And then Mark saw Phil the Tiger stalking down a blood-streaked corridor clutching a fire axe in his hands. With a wave of revulsion, he realised that the essence of Azimuth had dragged the Catalyst back from the grave and was embodied in him. He could feel its anticipation of another horror to come, knew that Azimuth had fed on two hundred and thirty-four human beings but still gloried in the opportunity to feed on four more. An *après-déjeuner*, as the Ghost Train Man would say. And then Mark saw Chadderton, the soldier and the girl, and knew that Azimuth had tricked Chadderton into seeing something else. He saw Chadderton's hand on the sliding door . . .

Chadderton! No! Don't let it in! It's not me! It's not me!

He saw Chadderton shrink back from the door, his hands flying to his ears as if he had suddenly been subjected to a high-pitched, piercing noise. Mark knew that he had heard.

Chadderton moved quickly back to the sliding door as the soldier came to join him. Instantly, Mark knew that he was seeing through Chadderton's eyes and that he could now see who was really moving down that corridor towards them.

A savage, ululating scream drowned Mark's senses. He felt a surge of inhuman hate being directed at him, concentrating on him with an intensity that was meant to destroy him. He fled back to the safety of his own mind, feeling the hate close behind him like some huge, black tidal wave threatening to

292

engulf everything. The safe place seemed too far away now. Behind him, the denizens of a million nightmares hungered for his soul and he could feel his own power waning. The warning to Chadderton had cost him too much; he had gone too far. An immense roaring filled Mark's mind. He could feel the crest of the huge black wave tipping down on him from above.

And then, at the last moment, he plunged through into greyness. Somewhere, a thousand miles away, the tidal wave was crashing against an impregnable bulwark with the ferocity of death, fear and insanity. Now Mark knew what he must do. He could see that there was another way to stop Azimuth.

In the safe, grey place in his own mind, he did something that he had not done since he was a child. He prayed.

*   *   *

Chadderton recognised him immediately. He was the man who had attacked them on the station platform and who had wounded Father Daniels. But he also knew that the man who lurched towards them was no longer alive. Chadderton had seen many dead men during his years in the police force, and the dishevelled, blood-stained wreck which drew closer was most certainly a dead man. It looked, he realised, just like the thing that Dr Aynsley had become. His head was still ringing from the voice which had suddenly punched its warning into his brain. Somehow he knew instinctively that it was Mark's voice, that it could not be a delusion created by Azimuth. The voice had impressed itself into his consciousness, leaving an identification more irrefutable than police-photographed fingerprints.

Chadderton shrank back from the door as the thing on the other side drew level. He felt the soldier shudder involuntarily as it looked in on them, weaving from side to side.

'It's got no eyes! Where's its eyes?'

'It's all right. The door's sealed. It can't get in.'

Behind them, Chadderton could hear the young girl whimpering. Her face was buried in her hands; she refused to look at what stood beyond the door.

And then the thing laughed. Until that moment, Chadderton had thought he had seen and heard all that hell had to offer.

But that laugh was somehow the most hideous and inhuman thing he had ever heard. With a feeling of dread in the pit of his stomach, he realised that it was laughing at what he had just said. In that instant, he knew that the thing was somehow going to break the seal and get to them.

Phil the Tiger raised the fire axe back as far as the cramped corridor would allow and swung it sideways at the sliding door.

'Look out!' yelled Chadderton.

The top of the glass panel in the door shattered inwards, sending slivers of jagged glass slicing across the compartment. The soldier instinctively moved to protect his girlfriend. Chadderton flung up an arm to shield his face, frantically looked around for something with which they could defend themselves as the rest of the glass panel exploded and the axe bit deeply into the wood, sending a splintering crack chasing down to the floor. Incredibly, the seal was holding. The thing was laughing again now, blood and saliva spilling over its bottom lip. Once more the axe struck, and Chadderton knew that although Azimuth could not break the seal directly, it could focus its power on this undead thing to destroy the entire doorframe around the seal.

Chadderton clawed at Father Daniels' briefcase, tried to find something there that he could use, and found nothing. The axe bit into the sliding door panel again, and stuck. Suddenly, the soldier had leaped forward from the seats and seized the axe just above the blade, wrenching at it in an effort to wrest it from the thing's grasp. Chadderton moved quickly to help him but a ragged arm suddenly flashed through the aperture and hurled the soldier to the floor. The girl screamed. Chadderton's hand closed around a sliver of wood lying on the compartment floor. Lunging forward as the thing wrenched the axe free from the wood, he stabbed through the aperture and felt the wooden shard plunge solidly into the thick flesh of the thing's thigh. The sliver snapped, and Chadderton tried desperately to side-step as the axe swung through the air towards him. The blade missed his head by a fraction of an inch, but the haft of the axe caught him full on the side of the face, the blow slamming him hard against the compartment wall. Chadderton felt himself sliding to the floor, tried to fight the inertia which threatened to engulf him. The sounds of the girl's screaming and the axe thudding and cracking into the wood seemed far away. Something heavy crashed to the floor, and Chadderton knew that the sliding door had finally collapsed under the onslaught and that the thing was through into the compartment.

In a hideous nightmare, he saw the ragged man-shape throw the soldier across the compartment, saw the dull glint of light on the fire axe as the Catalyst swung it high and knew that he could never get to his feet before that axe came down again. The thing laughed.

'No! No! No . . .'

Chadderton watched as the axe blade cut a swathe through the air towards Father Daniels' head. It was as if the scene were being played in slow motion. He heard the girl's scream echoing long and shrill, watched as the axe swept through its downward arc and knew that there was nothing he could do.

A gout of blood sprayed the compartment.

Uttering a hoarse, horrified noise deep in his throat, the soldier flung himself at the Catalyst.

Chadderton struggled to his feet, fighting to regain his senses, and saw the soldier grappling with the Catalyst against the compartment wall. It had pinned him there by the axe haft and was crushing him. The soldier's hands were cupped under the thing's chin, pushing its head away from his throat. Chadderton remembered how Dr Aynsley had tried to tear out his throat in Mark's house and, not wanting to look at what was left of Father Daniels, not wanting to admit that their last hope of defeating Azimuth was gone, he threw himself at the thing. He hooked his arm around its neck, feeling the flesh deathly cold against him. It was like trying to move a statue. The soldier was making high-pitched gasping noises, and the girl was clawing and tearing frantically at the thing's face. Suddenly, the Catalyst shifted position and jabbed the axe haft backwards into Chadderton's midriff. Chadderton crumpled to the floor again, hugging the crippling pain in his stomach. The soldier slid downwards across Father Daniels, a small trickle of blood seeping from the corner of his mouth. Chadderton heard the girl scream as the thing seized her, but could not get to his feet. He heard the ripping of material as it began to tear the clothes from her body, heard that inhuman laughter again and knew what the Catalyst intended. Chadderton tried to move again, retched and felt himself sliding into unconsciousness . . .

Eleven

'I renounce my faith . . .'

Mark had returned. He was lying crumpled on the floor of the driving cabin again. He could see what was happening in the compartment. He could see the broken seal; the body of Father Daniels; the two men lying on the floor. He could see that Azimuth had channelled itself into the Catalyst for a mild diversion, not content in the knowledge that soon the Ghost Train would reach its destination and all Earth would be subject to its unleashed, evil influence. Mark could see what it wanted to do with the girl. As he spoke, his hand dropped away from the silver crucifix hanging around his neck.

Instantly, the converging, invisibly pulsing lines of power in the driving cabin surged with vitality. The air crackled, a blue light suffused the cabin . . . a light that was somehow *dark*. It blossomed and spread, until the details of the driving cabin began to grow thinner and vanish. A great roaring filled Mark's ears, as of some terrible wind. And then he knew that the very essence of Azimuth had returned to the driving cabin. The evil touch of wings and eyes was with him once again. It had heard him and returned rejoicing.

Thrice Denied! Of your own free will you speak! And so shall it be! I will embody within you. I will be of you. And you will be mine.

Mark gave himself willingly.

It entered through his eyes as he knew it would. It slithered into him like a seething, wriggling mass of abominable voracious snakes. It plunged deeply and greedily into his mind; a hideous, rapacious invader. It had lied to him. It *would* feed from him. It would consume him. And now he could not stop it because he had given himself willingly. He had offered up the virgin territory of his mind and now that Azimuth had been admitted, it would greedily devour. But Mark had known that this would happen.

Mark was thirty years old. He had been twenty-nine when the accident had happened. Now, as Azimuth swarmed into his mind, he retreated before it down the halls of memory to the time when he was twenty-eight, happily married with a

296

promising career, a wife whom he loved deeply and a beautiful daughter. And as Mark retreated, he took with him the central core of his mind, the very *essence* of his being. Azimuth came after him, consuming and digesting two years of Mark's life, anxious to claim everything of Mark as it ravaged onwards. It was drawing power from its feasting, becoming stronger and faster. Mark leaped backwards in time, taking his individuality with him down through the years.

Twenty-five, twenty-four, twenty-three, twenty-two . . .

And Azimuth followed greedily, tasting and raping everything that Mark had ever experienced, everything he had ever loved or hated. Everything good was pillaged and distorted to make food; everything bad was expanded and savoured for the Tasting.

. . . Fifteen, fourteen, thirteen, twelve, eleven . . .

It claimed and tasted everything, defiling Mark completely. And still Mark pressed backwards, keeping himself from it as it advanced.

. . . Six, five, four, three, two, one . . .

It swallowed and engulfed, tasted and orgasmed as its possession neared completion. Barely ahead of this thing from Hell, Mark was a newborn child. His lifetime of experience belonged to Azimuth. But still he pressed backwards in time . . . back . . . back to the time of his birth.

And beyond.

As a foetus in his own mother's womb, Mark carried and retained his essence and individuality. Unborn and *without sin,* he lay sheltered and protected from the ravages of that which possessed his born self. It was a place that the Evil could not enter. Moreover, he knew, it was a place that Azimuth had disregarded. Exultant in what it believed to be its complete possession, Azimuth turned aside and withdrew. Within the womb, for the first and last time in the history of mankind, an unborn child shed tears for the sacrifice of its own life to come.

Twelve

Chadderton grasped for the rim of the seat behind him, steadied himself and began to rise. The Catalyst stood motionless beside the ragged gap which had been the sliding door. It held the girl with one arm. Sobbing, with one sleeve of her blouse hanging like a rag from the thing's other clenched fist, she seemed to have given in to whatever fate lay in store for her. Beside him, Chadderton became aware of movement as the soldier began to recover consciousness. Chadderton stood up and saw that the thing's jaw was hanging slack and loose. Blood and saliva dripped to the floor. For the first time, he noticed the blue-white glint of an exposed intestine in the thing's stomach. Now he realised that, somehow, the motivating force behind the Catalyst had been temporarily withdrawn. Standing like a zombie, the thing that had been Phil the Tiger was awaiting its next instruction.

Still intensely wary of the Catalyst, Chadderton moved to the soldier and helped him to his feet, never for one moment taking his gaze from the thing's face.

'Anne . . .' croaked the soldier, wincing at the pain of two broken ribs. Instantly, the thing tightened its grip, a deep frown settling on its features.

'Noooo . . .' When it spoke, it sounded like something that had never been human. The girl ceased struggling and the Catalyst stood waiting for its Master to return. And then, slowly and with a hideous unhealthiness, a smile began to spread across the thing's features.

'Get the girl!' shouted Chadderton, lunging forward shoulder first and taking the thing full on. The soldier dragged the girl away as Chadderton and the Catalyst hurtled out into the corridor in a frenzied scrabbling of arms and legs, colliding with the corridor wall. Chadderton felt the thing's grip around his throat; knew that the hideous power which had enabled it to smash the door and which they could never have beaten in the compartment, was somehow dissipated. But it was still more than strong enough to rip his head from his shoulders.

The thing slammed him hard against the corridor window. Chadderton felt himself being lifted clear from the floor as he

298

lashed out at its head. It slammed him backwards again, holding him aloft by the throat. He could feel his windpipe being squeezed shut; could hear the window glass cracking behind him under the pressure. He tried to brace himself against the window and push forwards, taking the thing off balance. But the Catalyst quickly compensated, dashing him backwards again. The window shattered. Chadderton felt a terrific suction sweep the glass away. A biting cold wind dragged at his body.

This is how I'm going to die! he thought. There was a kind of poetic justice about it. And then, he was being pulled into the corridor again. The soldier had grabbed the thing from behind and had succeeded in swinging it round. Diverted for an instant, it turned on the soldier, flinging Chadderton aside into the compartment like a rag doll. A howling, buffeting wind whipped at them as the Catalyst slammed the soldier to the ground.

In the compartment, Chadderton struggled to his feet. The girl had fainted. He clambered towards the corridor and saw the axe lying amid the splintered ruins of the sliding door. The Catalyst and the soldier were beyond Chadderton's line of vision as he stooped and grabbed it from the floor. A heavy, thumping sound was coming from the corridor as he emerged.

Suppressing an involuntary cry of rage and nausea, he saw that the soldier was dead. The thing had knocked him to the floor and was stamping viciously and methodically on what was left of his head. The thing was chuckling now as it turned to face Chadderton, the soldier's body still jerking on the corridor floor, fingers clenching and unclenching. Rage swelled within Chadderton. Raising the axe high above his head, feeling it clunk against the carriage roof as the Catalyst advanced towards him, he brought it down with all his force. Quickly, the thing's arm flashed up to meet the blade and took the full force of the blow, diverting the weapon from its head. But the impetus of the blow swung the thing's arm downwards, trapping its hand between the blade and the ragged sill of the broken window. The axe bit deeply through the thing's wrist and embedded itself into the sill. The Catalyst's severed hand twitched to the floor.

Savagely Chadderton tugged the axe free and drew back. The Catalyst held up the ragged stump before its face. To

Chadderton, it seemed that the thing was wondering at this new development. But it showed no pain and there was no blood. It was, after all, dead. It smiled. And continued to advance on Chadderton.

Chadderton backed away down the corridor as it came, keeping the axe thrust threateningly outwards. He stepped on a body lying on the corridor floor behind him. He wavered and almost fell. Quickly regaining his balance, he continued to retreat as the undead thing lurched after him. And, as it came, a single thought screamed in Chadderton's head:

How can you kill something that's already dead?!

* * *

'Director of Operations? This is Brigadier Anderson. I'm giving orders that everyone is to pull out of King's Cross at once. The same goes for your own control staff. I want you all cleared out of there immediately.'

'What about the derailment at Doncaster?'

'Four separate charges were laid and detonated. The lines were untouched.'

'*What?*'

'Yes, I know it's impossible. But the railway lines were unmarked. We damaged the embankment but the lines are intact. We're moving down towards you to try again. I don't know what we're faced with here, but the train is on its way and I want everyone out of King's Cross . . .'

'Brigadier! Hold the line! I'm getting a report that . . . there's some kind of disturbance in the station down here . . . What? . . . Brigadier, something's happening down here on Platform 10 . . .'

'Put the Commander in Charge back on the line. I want everyone out of that place . . .'

'The platform is *glowing*, Brigadier. Oh my God, I don't believe what I'm seeing . . .'

Silence.

'Put my man on!'

'I don't believe it . . . it's glowing brighter . . . the platform is starting to break up . . . *My God, it's splitting open . . . It's . . . Oh my God . . .*

300

Silence.
The Ghost Train was on its way.

*   *   *

Azimuth had tasted and was gone.

Mark emerged from hiding, knowing that his mind had been tasted and defiled. Travelling back up the ruined corridors of his memory, he could see the complete extent of Azimuth's pillage. His mind had been raped.

Now Mark was once again in the driving cab, once again aware of the power that surged there. It had claimed and tasted everything that it had found in Mark's mind. *But he had hidden himself from it.* Now, Azimuth had returned to the train, believing that it had completely absorbed Mark's individuality. It presumed that his mind had been totally eaten and that only the physically living but empty shell of his body remained. It would return later and fill that shell with its own unholy force, reanimating it as its Chief Disciple.

Now Azimuth flowed and surged within the walls, transferring its full essence into the thing which thundered on white-hot rails towards King's Cross Station. It had withdrawn from the Catalyst and Mark knew that he had bought Chadderton some time.

The Time of Arrival was imminent; Mark was aware that Azimuth must concentrate on that above all things. Four times denied, Mark knew that it would never sense that he had escaped it. His consciousness, his will, were apart from Azimuth now. Here in the driving cabin, he knew that as Azimuth powered the train on towards Arrival it would pay no heed to the crumpled form which lay on the floor. Mark knew that he had only one chance for humanity. If he missed that chance, no hope would be left. Power surged and flowed above and around him. Opening his ravaged mind once more, he tentatively and hesitantly probed for the key.

*   *   *

Chadderton raised the axe for another blow as the Catalyst

301

continued to advance on him. Back down the corridor, a series of panic-stricken, high-pitched screams reached his ears. The Catalyst turned to look back and Chadderton swung the axe hard. But the undead thing had anticipated the attack. The ragged stump of its forearm lashed out and diverted the blow, the other hand seized his face and dashed him hard against the corridor wall. The axe clattered to the floor. Chadderton clutched at the grip on his face, somehow managed to tear himself free and lurched away. The screams ricocheted down the corridor as he struggled to regain his balance, expecting to feel the thing upon him at any second, expecting to feel that final blow of the axe. When he looked again, the Catalyst was lurching back along the corridor towards their compartment. Standing in the ragged gap of the doorway, Chadderton could see the soldier's girlfriend looking down at his mutilated body. Her hands were pressed tightly to her chest as she screamed, unaware that the undead thing was making its way back to her, dragging the axe behind it. It could have killed him, but it had not. Obviously, thought Chadderton, it intended to finish what it had started with the girl.

'Get away from there!'

As Chadderton began to run after the Catalyst he saw the girl look up, still screaming and seemingly frozen in the shattered doorway.

How can I stop it?

He was almost upon the Catalyst again when a thought sprang into his mind, apparently from nowhere. It came in a way that made Chadderton think that the idea had been planted in his brain from somewhere else. It seemed like a suggestion from far away and, for an instant, Chadderton thought he recognised a trace of Mark's presence in his mind.

'Get Father Daniels' flask from the compartment! The silver flask on the seat beside him!' shouted Chadderton.

The girl seemed unable to hear him as the undead Catalyst staggered towards her. She had stopped screaming now, but her gaze was still fixed on the thing as it drew nearer, like a small nervous rabbit entranced by a snake.

'Damn it! If you want to live, get that flask! Move!'

And then the girl vanished into the compartment. An instant later, she reappeared with the flask. The silver flask which contained Holy Water.

'Throw the water at it! Throw it!'

The girl was fumbling with the stopper and it seemed to Chadderton that she might drop it. In seconds, the Catalyst would be on her. Chadderton tensed himself for a forward leap at the thing if she should fail to do it in time. The stopper rattled to the floor and, in the next instant, the girl had stepped forward, her face stark and white as she jerked the flask at the shambling marionette. A jet of water ribboned through empty space and splashed across the thing's head and shoulders. And still it came on. The girl was sobbing; she jerked the flask again and water cascaded over the Catalyst's chest. The thing began to raise the axe with its one good hand and Chadderton tensed to leap at its arm. But now the axe was clattering to the floor and the Catalyst had stopped. It began to open its arms away from its chest, looking down to where the water had landed. A low, moaning noise was beginning to issue from its throat.

'Get back into the compartment!' yelled Chadderton as a sudden premonition swept over him. Thin wisps of smoke were beginning to curl upwards from the thing's shoulders and head, dancing in the wind which whipped through the shattered corridor window. Now the smoke was thickening and billowing, and the low moan was building and bubbling in the thing's throat. The Catalyst clutched at its chest as smoke began to envelop its form. The corridor was filled with the stench of burning and the thing began to shriek in fear and pain.

'Master . . . Master! MASTER!'

With a sound like the sudden flap of a canvas sail, the Catalyst's upper torso and head burst into thick, oily orange flame. The blast hit Chadderton, singeing his hair and eyebrows as he leaped back, shielding his face with one hand. Shrieking filled the corridor; the blazing marionette whirled and began to blunder in his direction. As the thing clutched at the corridor wall, flames transferred to the gristle and tissue which Chadderton saw for the first time was growing there. It hurtled towards him, arms outstretched and groping. Chadderton flung himself backwards from the fiery embrace, crashed to the floor and felt the undead fireball pass over him. He was burning again, just like that faraway time in that neatly-trimmed back garden. His jacket was burning and he forced himself to roll over and over. The screaming was receding now and he

303

squirmed round to see the burning figure lurching away from him down the corridor in the direction of the locomotive. Everywhere it touched, hungry flame leaped and licked at the corridor walls. Chadderton felt something flap over him and looked up to see that the girl had reappeared from the compartment and had thrown her overcoat across his burning jacket. She did it mechanically. Chadderton could see that she was in shock; it reminded him of the look on Mark's little girl's face not so long ago. He knew that the Catalyst was screaming its way back to its master, spreading fire as it went. Even now, flames were beginning to take hold of the corridor. The green creeper-like tissue, which hung thickly at the far end of the carriage, was burning and sizzling fiercely. Chadderton took the girl's arm and pulled himself to his feet.

The Ghost Train was burning. There was only one way to go. Chadderton turned towards the rear of the train, dragging the girl after him.

Thirteen

Azimuth was stronger than it had ever been. It surged onwards and ahead to its ultimate freedom, glorying that its imprisonment on the lines would soon be over forever.

Mark continued to probe secretly, keeping his existence apart from Azimuth, knowing that one mental slip on his part would be the end of everything. He saw the lines of force across the countryside, saw how they interconnected with the King's Cross line; finally understood how the 'connection' had accidentally been made. He advanced down the King's Cross line itself, towards London. Following the surging, pounding lines of force, he moved ahead of the Ghost Train, testing and probing.

And then, he found what he was looking for: another line under construction which branched off from the main line a hundred miles ahead; a stretch of local line which extended three-quarters of a mile but which had not yet been completed. A railway line leading *nowhere.*

He felt danger and fled back to meet the train. But Azimuth was still unaware of his presence. He saw that the soldier was dead; saw the Catalyst advancing on the terrified young girl while Chadderton hovered behind it, unsure of what to do next. Mark decided to risk it, planted the thought in Chadderton's mind, and then realised that he had made a mistake. Instantly, Azimuth had sensed him. Forces stronger than himself converged on him yet again, more dangerous and powerful than they had ever been before. It began to hunt, puzzled that it should have scented him when it knew that he no longer existed. Mark fought to hide, realising that he had found the way to defeat Azimuth, only to let it slip away from him because of his concern for two human beings.

Waiting to be discovered, he suddenly felt agonising pain shoot throught the fibre of Azimuth's being. Azimuth turned aside from its search and brought its concentration to bear on the source of the pain, believing that this was where the unseen presence was to be found. The pain grew greater. Azimuth shrieked, the depth of its agony sending more spasms into Mark's consciousness. Something was burning. And, as Azimuth turned aside, Mark seized his opportunity and plunged into the power source which permeated the atmosphere, knowing at the same time that he was laying himself wide open to discovery and attack. In an instant, it was done.

Mark flowed ahead down the line, took control of the points, and switched. He felt the points move, felt the rails shift and lock. Using Azimuth's own power, he fused the points so that they could not be altered. The Ghost Train had been diverted onto the line under construction. It had been diverted onto a line with no ending: a one-way ticket to the limbo from which Azimuth had been summoned.

Now, Azimuth had found him. A shock wave hit Mark full on. Azimuth tried to flow into his mind and destroy him but found only the ruins of his memories, the pillaged temple of his thoughts. It searched the ruins like a scavenger hunting for a refugee. It scented him and gave chase. But Mark was long gone to his place of safety. Howling and screaming in rage, fear and pain, Azimuth returned to the line and attacked the change which Mark had brought about. But the change had been made with its own power. The alteration in Azimuth's line of force was immutable.

The spasm of rage and pain which Azimuth now vented on the railway lines, stretching hundreds of miles back to Edinburgh, contorted and withered them like living tissue. Screeching and protesting, the lines buckled and curled upwards and sideways, like steel snakes in a fire.

Mark doubled back and returned to his body in the driving cab. Azimuth surged and flowed through the fabric of the train, too concerned now to notice his presence as it tried with all of its strength to reverse what Mark had brought about. Energy crackled and flared in the driving cabin as Mark clambered slowly and painfully to his feet. He had forgotten the constant, gnawing pain in his bones. There was a great roaring sound behind him; some kind of commotion. Something was clawing blindly down the train towards the locomotive. Something that screamed and thrashed and spread fire. Fire.

Fire.

The danger signal registered with Mark seconds before the driving cab door burst inwards to admit the flames of Hell itself. He curled tightly down on the floor as a blazing fireball exploded into the cabin.

'MASTER!'

The screaming belonged to some abominable demon-child that was in dying agony and which shrieked for help from its inhuman master. Mark felt his hair burning as he flung himself out into the living corridor which formed the bridge to the rest of the train. The bridge itself was burning furiously. The generator still pounded maniacally as flames licked around it. Frantically, Mark scrambled away from the cabin, feeling the searing blast on his back as the cabin erupted into flame. The force of it hurled him forward, pitching him down the corridor and into the mutated carriage ahead. He knew that the thing which had burst into the cabin had been the Catalyst. Now, its frenzied screams were drowned by a harsher, louder and more inhuman bellowing.

Thick green steam curled and billowed in the carriage. The overhanging green cartilage and muscle hissed and spluttered, exuding a stinking odor. Flames leaped and danced sporadically. It reminded Mark of trying to burn a pile of wet leaves. Ahead of him, the next carriage was a raging mass of flame.

There could be no way out.

Mark turned to the carriage window beside him. Could it be done?

Of course it can't be done.

They do it on TV.

But that's not real.

Two SAS men once did it for a bet.

But they were killed.

I can't stay here!

The wind will rip you off the roof. There'll be nothing to hang onto. Your body can't take it.

Fuck it!

Mark tore a suitcase free from the overgrown mass that had once been a seat and swung it at the all but absorbed window. The glass shattered instantly, tattered green creepers whipping out through the ragged gap. Mark could feel the suction on his body. He plunged through the smoke to the window frame and braced one foot on the window's rim, reaching upwards and over into the blackness above him. A spurt of flame belched from the driving cabin as he forced himself through the aperture. The wind screamed and tore at his body.

❊   ❊   ❊

Chadderton dragged the girl after him down the train, the fire axe firmly clasped in his other hand. For a little while, she had wanted to return for the soldier's body, but he had been able to convince her that by now the carriage they had been in was a fireball. Smoke curled and billowed around them as they pressed on, and Chadderton knew that the fire was creeping slowly but insidiously along the length of the train towards them. Somewhere above the roar and crackle he could hear another sound: a distant howling that could have been the wind but which he knew was more than that. As they stumbled into the guard's van, he could feel the occasional shuddering which seemed to shake the train as if it were a living creature in agony.

Chadderton did not know what had happened to Mark when he made his way to the front to meet Azimuth, but he knew that he had at least been alive up to the moment when he had put the idea of the Holy Water into his head. But he had heard and felt nothing since then and he could only believe that Mark was dead.

He pushed the girl ahead of him into the guard's van and turned to examine the dividing section which separated the van from the preceding carriage. It was a thick, all-enclosing casement of heavy duty rubber. He looked down at the floor, shielding his eyes against the smoke. He could not see how the van was linked to the carriage. He began tearing at the floor, trying to lift the metal plating to see if it housed the link. He had no way of knowing that all carriages were vacuum-sealed, that the guard's van could not be separated manually from the rest of the train.

Chadderton knew that they could not jump from the train. Not at this speed. At standard speed, the fall would almost certainly be fatal. But now, at the fantastic speed that this train was travelling, there could be no hope whatsoever. For a second, he thought that perhaps he should throw the girl from the train anyway and then follow her. After all, they would be better off dead than living in a world where Azimuth was free to feed from the human race. He crammed the thought down, refused to give it further consideration and continued to tear at the metal plating. He pushed the girl back as smoke swirled spectrally around them, and attacked the plating with the axe. In his heart, he knew it was hopeless.

※　　※　　※

Groping blindly through fast-swirling smoke and poisonous fumes, Mark clawed hand over hand. Physically, he knew that he could never make it. He called on the new-found power which still inhabited his ravaged mind to fuse mind and body, thought and action together. His mind told his body that it would not allow him to fail. It commanded his hands to find a grip where there was no grip. It forced his body to resist the raging whirlwind that threatened to scoop him from the train like an autumn leaf. It told the pain to dissipate. *Pain, pain, go away. Come again another day.* The child within him threatened to upset the delicate balance, but his mind adjusted and commanded full attention. His left hand groped upwards and

308

found a ridge of metal about one inch deep. Exultant, he heaved himself upwards. Hand over hand, one foot at a time, looking for every rivet, every indentation in the metal, ignoring the fear within him that tried to tell him he could not possibly succeed. Inch by inch, slowly and positively. Mind over matter.

Mind over matter . . . Come on . . . another inch . . . now, your left foot . . .

And suddenly, Mark was on the roof of the train, smoke swirling and streaming past him as the King's Cross express pounded onwards. He began crawling back along the train, over the carriage roofs, feeling the hot metal underneath him as the fire raged and spread. Slowly, slowly. He steadied himself against an air vent, screened his mouth with one hand as clouds of foul-smelling smoke from the vent engulfed him. He crawled slowly around it and rested on the other side, gulping in several lungfuls of clean air before continuing.

Instinctively, he knew that Chadderton was in the guard's van. He began to crawl again.

*　　*　　*

Chadderton flung the axe to the floor. He had dented and gouged the metal, but there was no way he was going to be able to break the housing and unlink the guard's van from the rest of the train. They were going to have to take their chance by jumping after all.

Something exploded further down the carriage and Chadderton looked up to see that the buffet car was beginning to burn. Soon, the fire would reach them. He moved to the guard's office, disregarding the stiff, blue-faced corpse on the floor, and wrenched the fire extinguisher from its clasp on the wall. Savagely, he struck the operating device against the wall. Jets of white liquid spurted outwards. He aimed the nozzle at the partition dividing the van from the carriage, soaked the rubber, coated the partition with a thick layer of foam. When the extinguisher ran dry, he stood back and hurled it through the nearby window.

'What are you doing?'

'We've got to buy ourselves a little time. The foam might

309

hold back the flames, but the biggest danger to us right now is the smoke. If we break all the windows in here, the place won't fill up with it and at least we won't suffocate.'

Perhaps suffocation isn't such a bad idea, he thought. *It's probably a better idea than throwing yourself off the train.*

He retrieved the axe and began breaking the windows. Smoke billowed past them, sucked out through the jagged gaps. The sound of rushing air and the clatter of wheels on the tracks drowned out any further conversation. The buffet car was blazing when Chadderton looked back.

God in heaven, what are we going to do?

Les . . .

Mark?

Yes . . .

Where are you, for Chrissakes?

Above you. On the carriage roof, I'm nearly with you. But I'll need help . . .

The voice in Chadderton's head faded momentarily. He felt himself panic. He had believed Mark dead. Now, more than anything else, he didn't want to be alone to face death.

Mark? You still there? Without realising it, Chadderton was not speaking aloud. Instinctively, he was *thinking* back. The fact that he had not used his voice had not registered with him.

I've stopped him, Les. I've stopped Azimuth. I've sent him back to where he came from . . .

Without asking questions, Chadderton believed Mark immediately. It had something to do with the way the other man was speaking in his mind.

Keep moving, Mark. Don't stop!

I'm here.

Chadderton looked up at the heavy duty divider which separated the van from the last carriage, seized the axe once more and began hacking at the rubber. Something else exploded in the buffet car. Flame blossomed angrily. Chadderton attacked the rubber as if it were alive, saw the tangled green stuff that rippled and intertwined in it and realised that it *was* alive. The axe swung until his arms and shoulders felt as if they were coming apart. He had succeeded in tearing a hole in the rubber above him. He discarded the axe, reached up and ripped the rubber apart with his bare hands. In the suction of the train's passage, a huge chunk tore up and away from sight,

310

leaving a gap three feet wide.

'Mark!' Chadderton was shouting now, the girl looking at him as if he had suddenly gone insane. And then, she stifled a scream as a head appeared in the gap. It was Mark.

The train shuddered again and something up at the front screeched and ripped away. Mark clutched at the rim of the gap, his hair dancing madly in the wind. Chadderton steadied himself against a wall and grabbed for the axe again.

Get back from the gap, Mark. I'm going to widen it.

Mark was shaking his head now. Chadderton watched as he took in several deep breaths. It looked as if he was gathering his strength.

It'll take too long, Les. We don't have the time. Leave it . . . I think . . . I think I can find the strength to do it myself now . . .

What do you mean, do it yourself? Look, just shut up and move back. You aren't going to be able to stay up there much longer.

I can do it!

Chadderton took an involuntary step back as the rubber casing at the side of the dividing section began to peel back with a groaning, cracking sound. For a second, he thought that the train was about to disintegrate around them. Then he saw the look on Mark's face and knew what was happening. Even from where he stood, he could see the familiar scar standing out vividly against the pale white skin. Smoke flashed and streaked around him as the rubber peeled back and ripped away. Chadderton held the girl to him as the final section cracked apart and was whisked away from the train. He leaned forward, reaching up towards Mark, feeling an idiot grin spreading across his face.

All right, you clever bastard. Come on down.

No, not yet. Stand back.

Chadderton retreated into the guard's van with the girl as Mark hunched himself forward on his elbows to look down at the metal housing concealing the link between the van and the carriage on which he lay. For five long seconds, nothing happened. Then the metal began to buckle. Groaning and screeching, the plating began to twist. Chadderton moved the girl further back. And then the casing ripped apart, metal plates clattered aside and spilled away from the train. Beneath, red steam rose from the ragged hole. Chadderton could see the white-hot lines beneath as the train thundered onwards. Mark was smiling now and Chadderton jumped forward, holding out his hand. Mark reached down to take it. They were going to make it.

And then, when their fingers were inches apart, the smile of relief on Mark's face suddenly clouded. Chadderton could stretch no further. He strained forwards, not understanding why Mark was holding back. Their fingertips were almost touching.

Reach down, Mark. I can't get any closer.

Oh, my God, Les. Oh, my God.

What is it? Come on, man! Take my hand!

Mark's smile had turned into a mask of tragedy. Even from where he stood, Chadderton could see that tears were coursing down his face.

Tell Joanne that I love her, Les. Tell Helen, too.

What in God's name are you talking about, Mark? Take my hand!

Mark was slowly withdrawing his hand. Chadderton tried to lunge out and grab him. It was no good. They were too far apart.

Mark! WHAT ARE YOU DOING?

I can't, Les. Don't you see? . . . It's still in me!

At the last moment, just before their hands touched, Mark realised what had happened. He had damned Azimuth back to Hell. There could surely have been no escape . . . but, yes, Azimuth had found one way to escape. Fusing his mind and body to pull himself out of that burning carriage and over the rooftops, Mark had let slip a vital defence. Now, he realised that Azimuth had seized its last opportunity. As Mark had crawled back, something else had crawled back to safety with him. It had found a place in his mind: a tiny, ruined place that he had overlooked. He had saved it; was in the process of saving it. It had left the driving cabin, knowing that it was on its way to limbo. Ever the parasite, it had almost found a way to be free. If Mark touched Chadderton's hand, it would transfer immediately to him. And be saved.

It's still in me!

No! Mark . . .

Mark pulled back his hand completely. Now, angrily, he

312

refocused his gaze on the link between the carriages.

No, Mark! No!

With an explosive clang the metal link flew apart in its housing. Slowly, gradually, the gap between the carriages began to widen.

Speechless, Chadderton watched as the train pulled away. And in that moment, he *felt* something screeching and tearing itself out of Mark's mind. Something which fled from him towards the front of the train again in a desperate bid to save itself. Mark slumped on the roof of the carriage, the smile returning to his face. Smoke billowed around the ragged gap below him as the train moved rapidly away and the guard's van began to slacken speed. Mark was fumbling in his shirt now and fading daylight sparked on something that hung around his neck. The dying rays of the sun seemed to imbue it with a magnificent luster, as if the light were coming from within. He was holding it tightly to his chest. And he was still smiling. In that instant, Chadderton knew that Azimuth had been beaten.

The train suddenly veered to the left and began to scream down a branch line that Chadderton knew was not part of the main line.

'Do something!' yelled Chadderton. 'Save yourself! You can do it!'

But his words were borne away on rushing wind. There was a two hundred yard gap beween them now as the Ghost Train thundered on ahead in its billowing shroud of flame and smoke. The guard's van suddenly juddered violently. Chadderton grabbed the girl, steadied himself against the wall and watched as the van continued on down the main line, knowing that Mark had switched the points once the train had passed onto the branch line. The van trundled at an ever-slowing pace down the King's Cross line and Chadderton and the girl watched as the Ghost Train screamed from sight behind a screen of trees. They listened as Something howled its anguish to the uncaring sky. They watched the train's invisible progress by the trail of smoke, the glitter of flame through the dense tree cover.

And then, a grinding, shrieking, tearing sound. A roaring series of explosions like the mammoth bellowing of some great beast. A great glare of flame against the horizon. A twisting cloud of flaming debris. A carriage suddenly rearing above the

313

tree-line before vanishing from sight. Another explosion, igniting nearby trees. On and on and on. The shrieking of rending metal. And now, another shrieking, not meant to be heard by human ears. A shrieking that echoed long and loud and then began to fade away into the distance. Moving off, further and further away into the night sky . . .

Chadderton felt bitter tears coming, fought them, would not allow them to surface. The explosions seemed to go on forever. With the girl beside him, he watched as the train blew itself savagely apart, mushrooms of orange flame lighting up the countryside. For the first time, he became aware of what seemed to be a criss-cross of searchlights both behind and ahead of the railway track. One by one they were going out.

'You poor bastard,' he murmured at last, still staring at the blazing wreck as the first sounds of the railway police and army trucks drew near to the stationary guard's van.

And then he realised that his pity was misplaced. Mark had faced his own worst fears and had beaten them. How many men could say that? And, in that realisation, Chadderton could feel a sense of triumph within him. For an instant, it seemed that the thought had been put there by someone else . . .